PRAISE FOR *SAVAGE JUSTICE* BY RON HANDBERG

"Handberg delivers the goods in his first suspense novel. . . . Powerfully realistic: *Savage Justice* will be popular with Scott Turow fans."

—*Library Journal*

"Riveting. . . . Shocking revelations set up a race to the climax and a final retribution that most readers will cheer, as Handberg wraps up his gripping story."

—*Publishers Weekly*

"*Savage Justice* captures the taste and the heat and the pressure of a journalistic hunt; it's a complex story of depravity and power that won't let you go. One of the best first novels I have ever read."

—John Sandford, author of *Silent Prey*

By Ron Handberg

SAVAGE JUSTICE
CRY VENGEANCE

Available from HarperPaperbacks

CRY VENGEANCE

A NOVEL

Ron Handberg

HarperPaperbacks
A Division of HarperCollinsPublishers

HarperPaperbacks *A Division of* HarperCollins*Publishers*
10 East 53rd Street, New York, N.Y. 10022

Copyright © 1993 by Ron Handberg
All rights reserved. No part of this book may be used or reproduced in any manner whatsoever without written permission of the publisher, except in the case of brief quotations embodied in critical articles and reviews. For information address Carol Publishing Group, 600 Madison Avenue, New York, N.Y. 10022

A hardcover edition of this book was published in 1993 by Birch Lane Press / Carol Publishing Group.

First HarperPaperbacks printing: June 1995

Printed in the United States of America

HarperPaperbacks and colophon are trademarks of HarperCollins*Publishers*

10 9 8 7 6 5 4 3 2 1

To Deborah, Greg, and Melinda,
whose lives have given my life joy
and meaning

ACKNOWLEDGMENTS

Many people were important to the completion of this book, but none more important than my wife, Carol, who never faltered in her spirited and loving support, and our children, to whom the book is dedicated. My thanks also go to Nancy Mate, Jack Caravela, and Carol Ellingson, who provided early and continuing encouragement and criticism, and to other friends who willingly gave of their time and experience: Reid and Cindy Johnson, Debbie Olson, Quent and Bee Neufeld, Sharon Hendry, Dennis Armstrong, Trish Van Pilsum, Jerilyn Miller Lowe, and Anne Birch. Finally, my grateful appreciation to my editors, Gail Kinn and Hillel Black, for their skill and patience in helping to shape the final work.

CRY
VENGEANCE

ONE

Jessica had never seen a body before. Not a murdered body, anyway. Oh, sure, on television. But never like this, twenty feet away and getting closer. Not that she could see the actual body. Just the bag, slung on a kind of cart, bumping up the steep path from the river flats below.

She could detect the outline of the corpse inside the wet, sagging canvas. She could tell where the arms and legs lay and saw the feet sticking up. And the head. Was that the point of his nose?

Echoes of the thunder from the passing storm still rumbled to the east, sounding like a kettle drum amid the dancing streaks of lightning. All that remained now of the slashing rain and hail was a fine mist that seemed to hang in midair, enveloping them, sparkling like ballroom glitter in the floodlights.

Jessica felt the sharp elbow of the policeman dig into her ribs, pushing her back, almost into the lens of the camera. She heard the photographer behind her grunt and fight to keep his balance in the oozy muck left by the storm and trampling feet.

"Move back, sweety," the cop grumbled. "This is no god-damned fashion show. Keep your distance."

"Sorry," she whispered, unheard, into the night air.

Straps around the bag kept the body tight on top of the gurney despite the sheer incline and the slippery roots and rocks that made the path almost impassable. The men at the front and back of the litter were breathing heavily, their faces dripping more from their sweat than the mist. They paused ten feet from the crest of the hill, inhaling deeply, hooding their eyes to escape the glare of the camera lights.

"We can't see where the hell we're going," the one in front shouted. "Give us a break with those lights, okay?"

"Screw 'em," Bill Kendrick, the photographer, muttered. "You can't shoot in the dark. Keep the light right on them, Jess."

She did as she was told, pointing the portable light with one hand while holding the shotgun microphone with the other. The other television people did the same, prompting a string of low curses from the men with the cart.

Two policemen finally inched their way down the hill, grasping tree branches for support, helping to pull the body-on-wheels the final few feet to the top and over a small railing that guarded the precipice. Kendrick and the other photographers pushed past the police line, fighting one another for position to get a shot of the bag of flesh being loaded into the medical examiner's wagon.

Jessica was caught in the crush, buffeted by the pushing and shoving bodies, trying to stay on her feet, her own small frame dwarfed by those around her.

"Keep the light high, Jess!" Kendrick shouted.

"I'm trying," she gasped, but it was fruitless.

Kendrick glanced down at her, surprised she was still by his side, fighting her way through the pack. Gutsy, he thought. Her face was spattered with mud, her short brown hair a wet and tangled web. The yellow rain slicker, three sizes too large, hung on her like a tent.

Hardly the same young woman who only hours before

would have stopped almost any man in his tracks, he thought.

"You okay?" he yelled.

She looked up, grimacing. "I guess so, but these guys are animals."

Kendrick laughed as the gurney was loaded into the wagon and the confusion began to ebb. "Welcome to the big city, Jess."

The rain had also washed away any footprints or other human signs in the sand along the riverbank. Even the heavy imprint of the body had disappeared. The police flashlights could be seen for a hundred yards in either direction, their beams moving up and down the beach and the hillside like so many fireflies in the mist, searching for any clues that the rain or the river—or the killers—had not carried away.

The water lapped quietly against the decaying driftwood and other flotsam that years of the river's slow, almost invisible flow had brought from who knows where upriver and pushed against the littered shore. It was a watery, ever-moving garbage slick. A plastic milk carton bobbed in the current a few feet out, a onetime fishing buoy now wedged between two moss-covered boulders, temporarily delayed on its voyage to the Gulf.

"So what have we got?" Matt Meecham asked.

"Driver's license says he was Edward Hill," the young detective replied. "White. Five-eleven, a hundred and sixty pounds. Born in '57. Makes him thirty-six. Lived in south Minneapolis. On Pikely."

Meecham stood back, hoping the Clorets had doused the booze on his breath. He could feel his sweat trickling beneath his arms and rolling down the back of his neck and the crevice of his ass.

"And?"

"It wasn't pretty, Captain," the detective said. "He was bareassed naked, half in, half out of the river. Cut up pretty bad and missing what we'd both consider a vital part of our anatomy."

"No shit," Meecham said, reflexively touching himself in the darkness.

"We found his billfold at the top of the hill, thrown into some bushes. But no clothes, no weapon, nothing else."

They were standing near the river's edge, and Meecham could feel the water seep through the soles of his shoes, soaking his socks, creeping between his toes. He lifted one foot, then the other, tugging against the suction of the sand.

"Damn," he muttered.

Meecham had been quietly sipping his vodka tonic in the back booth of Barney's when a uniformed squad had come in search of him. He wasn't surprised that they knew where to find him; he spent more time at Barney's than he did at the Homicide office.

"Beeper not working, Captain?" they'd asked.

"On the fritz," he'd answered, slurring the word—*frittschh*—knowing they didn't believe it but not giving a shit. Rank meant some privileges, right? Besides, he was only three years from retirement and had long since abandoned any hope of climbing higher on the police ladder.

That was an hour ago. He had reluctantly followed the uniforms out of the bar, trading the air-conditioned solitude of Barney's for the steamy, bug-infested riverbank.

"Know anything else about him?" Meecham asked.

"Still checking," the detective replied. "The computer's down again."

"What about here?" Meecham asked, turning his head aside, scanning the darkness, hiding a belch.

"Scratches on the body make it look like he was dragged down the hill and killed here. The rain took care of any visible blood. Sand samples are on the way to the lab."

A squadron of mosquitoes buzzed around their heads, darting into their ears and around their eyes, touching down wherever they found bare skin. "Fuckin' things," Meecham muttered, flailing blindly in the night air. "How'd we find him?"

"Some kid walking along the beach with his fishing pole.

He was heading home to get out of the rain when he spotted the body. Scared the hell out of him."

"Who's going to notify the next of kin?" Meecham asked.

"Brinkman. She just got here. Says she'll take the preacher along."

"Tell them to spare the gory details. Nobody needs to know those now."

"What now?" Jessica asked as she and Kendrick watched the taillights of the medical examiner's wagon disappear down the darkened street. "Should we stick around for a while?"

"Nah, I don't think so," he said. "The cops will never let us down on the flats tonight. They'll be pokin' around down there for hours, and it's too damn dark to shoot anything, anyway. The assignment desk may want to get somebody out here in the morning."

Jessica still held the microphone in one hand and the light in the other, forcing her to blink away the mixture of mist and perspiration that dripped from her forehead into her eyes. She felt wet all over.

"You sure the cops won't say anything now?" she pressed.

"If they do, it'll be bullshit. They don't know anything yet. Trust me, Jess."

She knew better than to argue. Kendrick was a veteran of the news staff, one of its best photographers; he had probably seen his first murder before Jessica took her first steps. Street-smart and newswise, with more sources than many of the station's best-paid reporters—street vendors, cabbies, whores, and assorted other hustlers who had come to know and trust him.

Kendrick was in his fifties, built like a fireplug with bow-legs. He liked to talk with a growl and front a perpetual scowl, but he was known around the newsroom as gentle and easygoing, especially with new reporters he was assigned to break in. Reporters like Jessica Mitchell.

He must feel like a baby-sitter, she thought. Rocking the

cradle of a kid who doesn't know what she's doing, who must seem like the rawest rookie just out of journalism school. He wouldn't be that far off, and she couldn't help but wonder what he'd tell the people back at the station.

Theirs had been the closest news car to the scene when the first call had come over the police radio an hour before: a DOA on the riverbank just below the University of Minnesota campus. They'd been on their way back from covering a protest rally downtown when the station dispatcher had diverted them to the murder scene.

"Five to one it's some kid who flunked his physics final and couldn't face his rich-bitch parents," Kendrick had groused as they stood on the hill in the midst of the storm. "He probably took a dive off the Hennepin Avenue bridge."

But word had quickly spread from the river below that it was no suicide. Whoever was down there had met a most untimely and gruesome end, and *not* at his own hands. The police had been tightlipped. Except for one, who had stuck his finger down his throat and feigned a gag. Jessica and Kendrick had gotten the message.

So they had waited—along with crews from the other TV stations and the newspapers. Waited for the parade of cops, and finally, for the medical examiner's cart, to make their way down and back up the greasy path.

Waited in the thunder and lightning and hail and rain for what turned out to be thirty seconds of video of a body in a bag.

But she would never forget it.

"Stand by in the studio! Twenty seconds to air."

Jessica stood in the shadows beyond the cameras, watching with rapt attention as the floor director counted down to the opening of the news. The excitement of that final "Three . . . two . . . one . . ." never faded for her; news flowed through her veins as surely as did the red and white blood cells. Despite what she had endured that night, she could think of no place she would rather be.

She managed to dry off quickly while Kendrick edited the murder tape. Then she sat at her computer and tried to match her words to his pictures, finishing her script ten minutes before the newscast began.

"Now, live from the Channel Seven newsroom, this is NightWatch . . . with Alex Collier and Barbara Miller . . . Charlie Nichols with weather . . . and Scotty Hansen on sports."

The floor director's arm flashed down, and the red light above Camera 2 blinked on.

"Good evening everyone," Collier began, "a major summer storm rumbled through the Twin Cities tonight, leaving an inch of rain and pea-sized hail in its wake . . ."

That was the wondrous thing about television news, Jessica decided as she watched quietly from the wings. The reason she found it so electric, so *exhilarating*. There was no retreat, no backing up and starting over again. Once that red light came on, you forged ahead, ready or not. You couldn't stretch deadlines or hold the presses. Not on live television. When the clock struck six or ten, you went on the air. Period. No excuses, no pleas of "Gimme another minute."

"The storm knocked down trees and power lines in many areas." Barbara Miller, Collier's coanchor, was reading now. "It interrupted activities all around the Cities, including the annual 'Take Back the Night' rally and march in downtown Minneapolis."

The screen was filled with pictures of the rally before the storm hit: a sea of women and a sprinkling of men spread across the sloping grass of the park, sitting on blankets or lawn chairs or perched atop picnic tables and park benches.

The crowd surrounded a large platform, covered by a red-and-white tarpaulin, with large audio speakers at each end. Handmade signs bobbed in the air: No More Violence, No More Rape; Let Us Live in Peace, Not Fear; and Yes Means Yes, No Means No.

Barbara's narration continued. "A crowd of several thousand was in Loring Park to hear speaker after speaker call for action to make the streets of the Twin Cities once again safe for women. Safe from increasing rape and violence."

A young woman dressed in cutoffs and a T-shirt emblazoned with the words STOP RAPE then appeared on the screen. Barbara's narration identified her as Sarah Andrews, one of the organizers of the event:

"Some woman is raped in this country every five minutes," Sarah said into the camera. "Every five minutes of every day of every week of every month of every year. Think about it! We have to get the rapists off of our streets and out of our homes. We want to make this community safe for everyone."

Jessica had conducted the interview with Sarah at the rally before being detoured to the murder scene. Watching her now on the screen, she again marveled at the woman's composure and confidence on camera. It was clear she knew that only a few seconds of whatever she said would actually be used on the air, and she intended to make the most of it. Someone I should remember, Jessica thought.

"You don't stop rape and violence with indifference," Sarah's interview continued. "You stop it with outrage and with action. That's what this rally is all about."

The videotape showed the rally end and the march begin but then evaporate as the demonstrators were pelted by rain and hail.

"The march through the downtown streets was cut short by the storm," Barbara continued, "and, at last report, only a few of the demonstrators actually reached the end of the route."

Jessica knew her murder story would be coming soon. Right after the commercial break, she'd been told. A murder, even if they didn't know much about it, always got a big play on the newscast.

"Have to spill a little blood early," Dick Lyons, the ten o'-clock news producer, had said slyly. "Keeps them interested through the dull stuff."

So she waited for the commercials to end. Waited and

again wondered about the guy in the bag. Was he young? Old? Have a family? Do they know yet? She tried to picture a face, tried to hear a voice or a laugh. To give him an identity, a life before death. But she saw only the drooping bag.

TWO

Gladys Hill had been caught in the storm, too. Walking home from the neighborhood supermarket. Pulling a small wagon loaded with four bags of groceries, watching as they teetered and almost toppled each time the wagon crossed a crack in the sidewalk.

Gladys knew where most of the cracks were by now. She had made the same trip, twice a week, for four years—ever since Herbert had died, leaving her a widow and without transportation. She adjusted to life without Herbert, but she did miss the car on grocery-shopping days. Gladys never did learn how to drive and thought it was too late to do so now.

By the time she had reached her front door, both she and her cargo of groceries were drenched. She hoped her son, Edward, would be home—to help carry in the bags. But he wasn't there. The door was locked, and the house was dark. She struggled inside, trying to keep the soaked sacks from splitting apart in her arms.

There was a note from Edward on the kitchen counter. "Had to meet someone. Won't be back till late, so don't wait up. Eddie."

Gladys quickly put the groceries away, then hurried to make sure all of the windows were shut against the rain. It didn't take long; the house was small, only four rooms downstairs—not counting the bathroom—and Edward's bedroom upstairs.

She and Herbert had bought the house shortly after Eddie was born in 1957 and had done little to it since. Herbert hadn't been much of a handyman, and it was always a stretch to meet the monthly bills, let alone improve or expand the house or buy something larger or nicer.

So they had stayed on, passing the years quietly, tending to the small yard and a tiny vegetable garden in the back. Herbert had his raspberries, and Gladys had her tomatoes and zucchinis. The best in the block, she'd been proud to say.

Edward, a shy and introspective boy, was a good athlete but a poor student, a child who seldom laughed and who seemed to have few friends. But he was all they had, and they had come to cherish him despite his strange and distant disposition. He had been their only relief from the tedium of middle age and middle class.

Then, a year before Herbert died, Edward had his first brush with the law. They were stunned and baffled by his arrest and repulsed by the charges. Life changed for all of them, immediately and irrevocably. They had been unable to mask their shame and anguish, and Edward had turned further inward, becoming even more of a stranger.

Tonight, by the time the rain eased, Gladys had changed into nightgown and robe and was sitting in Herbert's favorite chair, glancing at the newspaper, watching the television news flash by.

At the station, the commercial break ended, and Alex Collier began reading the next story. Jessica's story.

"Minneapolis police say they have no leads in the murder of a still-unidentified man whose body was found on the Mississippi River flats near the university earlier this evening. . . ."

Jessica leaned forward, listening intently, reciting her words silently as Collier read them into the camera. She knew them by heart, memorizing them without trying. She had always had almost total recall, a near-photographic memory. Even as a kid she could recite Shelley's poetry after one reading, and she still knew the dates of practically every war ever waged, of every peace treaty ever signed.

From her earliest years, growing up in the small town of Madelia, Jessica had had a desperate desire to *know things*, pestering her parents and teachers with questions, never accepting quick or easy answers. Maybe that unflagging curiosity is what led her to journalism.

"The police are still at the scene investigating," Collier reported, "and so far they have not revealed how the man died or how long the body may have been there. . . ."

The pictures were there, Jessica thought, but by the time they got to the television screen it all seemed so distant . . . so impersonal . . . so antiseptic. You didn't feel the mist on your face or the muck on your feet. You didn't hear the creaking wheels of the cart or see the feet sticking up. It was as though she were viewing it all over again through some kind of prism that distilled the horror from it, made it fit for family viewing.

"An autopsy will be conducted in the morning," Collier concluded, "and police are expected to reveal more details of the murder at that time."

The story was over almost before it began. A blink of the television eye. Another night, another murder. No different from other nights, other murders. Except to Jessica. She was hooked. She had been there. The sight of the corpse held her captive, and she found herself unable—and unwilling—to break free from it.

Gladys watched the news with impatience and without much interest. It always seemed the same: protests, murders, and politicians, night after night. She was eager to see the weather forecast and then go to bed. She never stayed up for the sports. Herbert always did, and that had been all right with her. It meant that on most nights she could get to sleep before his foghorn snores began shaking the walls.

She was still waiting for the weather report to begin when the doorbell rang. Edward forgot his key again, Gladys thought. But then she remembered the note. It said he'd be late. She tightened the belt of her robe and walked to the door. She had left the light on for Edward and saw two people standing beneath it. One was a woman in uniform; the other, a man in a cleric's collar.

Her knees weakened, just as they had when Herbert's boss showed up at the front door. She had known then that something was terribly wrong, and she knew it now. Edward? An accident? Another arrest?

She leaned her head against the door, breathed deeply, and then pulled it open.

"Yes?"

"Mrs. Herbert Hill?" said the woman in uniform.

"Yes. What's wrong? What's happened?"

"May we come in, please?" said the man in the collar.

Gladys stared at them, then slowly stepped back, allowing the door to swing fully open. She watched their eyes; the eyes always told the story. Herbert's boss wouldn't look at her. Neither would these two.

She backed up beneath the archway dividing the small entry and the living room, clutching her robe to her body as the two visitors, crowded together, shifted uncomfortably inside the door.

"Is it Edward?" she asked, her voice as weak as her knees. "Has something happened? Is he all right?"

"Maybe you'd better sit down, Mrs. Hill." The collar was speaking again. "I'm afraid we have bad news."

They introduced themselves: a Lt. Freda Brinkman and Pastor Thorgard or Thorson. Gladys couldn't recall the exact name, but she did remember the words "police chaplain."

"Your husband home?" the lieutenant asked, peering past her.

Gladys shook her head. "He's dead and gone. Four years now."

She later vaguely remembered leading them into the living room and sitting down in Herbert's chair. Waiting, hearing only the muted sound of the television set across the room. Never feeling more alone or more frightened.

"Mrs. Hill . . ." The chaplain knelt beside her, searching for words, while the lady lieutenant, Brinkman, remained standing and aloof, staring down.

"Mrs. Hill." The chaplain again. "I'm terribly sorry to tell you that a young man identified as your son was found dead tonight. Murdered. Near the university."

The pictures she had just seen, almost ignored, on the TV news flashed before her eyes again. Police in the rain. Reporters. Something being shoved into the back of a wagon. Her son? Eddie? My God, don't let it be.

"I don't understand," she stammered, the tears coming faster now. "How? Who would have—"

"We don't know anything yet," the lieutenant said impatiently. "We want you to get dressed and come with us . . . to see the body, to make a positive identification."

Gladys remained huddled in the chair, clutching the robe to her body, sobbing. The lieutenant leaned down. "Mrs. Hill, we don't have a lot of time."

"Easy does it," the chaplain said with a cautioning glance at Brinkman. "Give her a moment."

He extended his hand, and with great effort Gladys struggled to rise. "Is there anyone you can call?" he asked. "Friends? Family? Someone who could come with you?"

"No, there's no one," she whispered. "It was just Eddie and me. No other family, and . . . I wouldn't want to . . . bother my friends. Not for this. They wouldn't understand."

Gladys remembered changing from her robe to a dress, then only the overwhelming weight of sadness that seemed to crush her small body. And the cleric's comforting voice, his hand beneath her arm, guiding her out the door. Supporting her. She did remember shutting off the outside light as they left. The light she had left on for Edward.

THREE

Sarah Andrews sat cross-legged on the living-room floor, pointing the remote control at the TV like a pistol, zapping from station to station, trying to catch the coverage of the "Take Back the Night" rally and march on each channel. It was impossible. All of the stations played the story at about the same place in their newscasts, leaving her with only snippets of each report.

"Hey, Kim," Sarah shouted as she finally saw her own face pop up on the television.

"I'm watching in here" came the reply from the bedroom down the hall.

"You got Channel Seven on?"

"Yes, Sarah, relax. I see you."

Sarah's face, tightly framed, filled the screen. Her dark eyes seemed to leap out, flashing with the same anger as her words. "We have to get the rapists off of our streets and out of our homes. . . ."

Sarah studied her image carefully. Not bad, she thought. Good eye contact. Steady. Confident. Obviously no stranger to the television camera.

"Lucky you did the interview before the storm," Kim said, walking into the living room. "You look like a drowned rat now."

"Shhh, listen."

". . . you stop it with outrage and with action. That's what this rally is all about."

Her picture disappeared as the scenes of the ill-fated march began. Even now Sarah could feel the sting of the rain and the tiny hailstones against her skin, still shuddered at the lightning that had crackled overhead, the flashes reflected frighteningly on the glass walls of the office buildings.

She and Kim were among the few who had walked to the end, defying the storm, holding their protest sign high like a shield, chanting the familiar slogans until their throats were raw. They came home a half hour before, soaked to the skin. Kim had already showered and now sat wrapped in a warm robe, her head encased in a turban towel. Sarah was still in her damp T-shirt and cutoffs, shivering from the chill.

"You're going to get pneumonia," Kim warned.

"It'd be worth it for the kind of coverage we got. Pretty good, huh, even with the storm?"

Kim shrugged. "I'm just glad it's over," she said.

Sarah gave her a sharp glance. "You okay?"

"Just tired, that's all. And I honestly wonder what good it does."

"What do you mean?" Sarah demanded.

"How many years have you been doing this, Sarah? And what difference has it made? More women are getting raped and beaten and killed every day, and no one seems to really care. A few minutes on television isn't going to change that."

"Thousands of women screaming about it may."

"It didn't help me."

Sarah looked at her sympathetically. "No, but it could help someone else."

She had met Kim Hawkins a year before while volunteering at a local rape crisis center. Kim had wandered in one night—alone, distraught, still traumatized, almost immobilized, a week after being raped. She had been living in a hotel since the attack, unwilling, unable, to return to her apartment. She had talked to no one except the police.

Until she met Sarah.

Kim told her she had a job but no place to live, that she could never live alone again. Could the crisis center help? she asked. Was there a shelter? Someone like herself looking for a roommate? Someone who would understand what she had been through?

It had taken Sarah only a moment to decide. Kim was so pathetically in need, and Sarah had the room. She had been living alone since her boyfriend had moved out months before. We'll give it a few months, she told her. Until you're back on your feet and can find something else.

A year later, they were still together. An unlikely pair, even they had to admit. While both were in their early thirties, Sarah was blessed with model-like beauty and a self-assured stridency. Kim was on the plain side of pretty, shy, soft-spoken, staying in the shadows.

Sarah was a lawyer, a prosecutor in the county attorney's office, responsible for trying many of the crimes against women in the city. She was also an activist, a spokesperson for the women's movement who had become a favorite source for the media. A good "talking head" who was often sought out for interviews.

"It's easy," Sarah once told Kim. "Say something in thirty seconds that seems to make sense and has a little color to it and they'll use it every time. You can play 'em like a fiddle if you know the tune."

Kim was content to leave the public posturing to Sarah. She worked at a routine job in a brokerage office, a good employee who made few waves and attracted little notice. Even before the rape she had been a woman who had stayed to herself, with few friends, dating only now and then. Since the rape she had become even more withdrawn, emerging from her shell only when pulled along by Sarah. Like tonight.

For Kim, Sarah provided a safe haven, a refuge where she

had found protection and comfort, where she could slowly work to rebuild a tranquil life ripped apart by a demon in the darkness.

For Sarah the relationship was more complicated, one she still struggled to understand. Perhaps it was that Kim satisfied the unfulfilled motherhood in her, for in many ways she was like a child—dependent, in constant need of her reassuring presence and encouragement. A child afraid of the dark. Afraid of life.

Kim was also a friend and companion, an alter ego, the flip side of Sarah's assertive self. Calm, quiet, always there, ready to help, willing to listen, never threatening to compete on her own jealously guarded turf. As Sarah watched Kim now, without her makeup and in the dim glow of the picture tube, she could see the thin lines spreading from her eyes. Crow's-feet—twenty years early.

"Think I'll go to bed," Kim said, slowly standing, hugging the robe to her body.

"Already? The news isn't over yet. It's early."

"For you, maybe. But I'm exhausted."

Sarah knew from hearing Kim's wandering nighttime footsteps that she hadn't slept much in the past few weeks. But then again, she hadn't slept well in a year. Since . . .

"Good night, Kim," she said. "Try to get some rest."

The only response was the sound of her slippers retreating down the hall. Sarah turned back to the TV in time to see the story of the gurney coming up the hill in the rain. She quickly turned up the volume.

Jessica's eyes were fastened on the clock on the studio wall, studying the precise but jerky movement of the red second hand toward twelve. It was in perfect sync with the outstretched fingers of the floor director, counting down the final ten seconds of the newscast. Finger by finger.

On cue, one of the technicians touched a button on the computerized control panel, dimming the studio lights, leaving the anchors in silhouette against the twinkling, superimposed skyline of the cities behind them. Another button rolled the credits, and a third triggered the audiocassette of the closing music.

"Clear in the studio!" the floor director shouted once the screen finally faded to black. He had already yanked off his headset, heading for the door and the bar down the block.

Jessica had hardly moved for the entire half hour, staying in the background, hugging the wall, out of the way, unnoticed as the newscast sped by. Her eyes were never still, moving from person to person, watching them perform their functions with practiced ease. So professional, she thought, so confident. So different from the people at the tiny station she had just left, where practically everybody was a beginner—just like her.

She still marveled at the size of the studio. Its two-story-high ceiling was a cobweb of steel beams and girders supporting tons of air-conditioning equipment and hundreds of lights of every size and description. The studio alone was bigger than the entire station in Duluth.

"C'mon, Jess. Lights out." It was Dick Lyons, the producer, standing patiently in the shadows by the studio door. "Time to go home."

"Coming," she replied, embarrassed to be found alone, feeling like a stagestruck child who'd just watched the same Broadway play for the tenth time. Who couldn't bring herself to leave the theater despite the darkened stage and the absence of the actors.

"Thanks for the help on the murder story," Lyons said as they walked back toward the newsroom. "Must have been miserable out there in the storm."

Jessica shivered again. "I got soaked, but I also got educated. It was a mob scene, Dick, people running all over each other trying to get pictures. It was never like that in Duluth."

"I'll bet," Lyons said with a small smile.

"But it was more than that," she said hesitantly. "No one seemed to care that a dead guy was lying on that cart. It could

have been a rock or a piece of driftwood. I was amazed . . . but
. . . I never got a chance to cover a murder in Duluth. We
didn't have many up there."

Lyons laughed. "Well, get used to it, because we have
plenty of them down here. Seems like somebody's getting
killed every other day. Most of them are druggies or some guy
caught screwing around with somebody else's wife or girlfriend."

Lyons was in his early forties, Jessica guessed, although
his flaming red hair and face filled with freckles made him
look younger. His nose and the tips of his ears were peeling
from too much sun, and there was a squint to his eyes—from
too many hours of staring at a newsroom computer screen.

"You think they'd let me do a follow-up tomorrow?" she
asked tentatively.

"Depends on what else is happening, Jess. Leave a note for
Laurie. It can't hurt to ask."

Laurie Sanders was the assignment editor, responsible for
deciding who would cover what on any given day. Jessica
didn't know her well, but then again, she didn't know anyone
at the station very well yet.

"I'll do that," Jessica said. "It's probably nothing, but . . .
that body, I just can't get it out of my mind." Then she paused.
"Kind of morbid, huh?"

Lyons smiled. "Join the crowd. You have to be a little sick
to be in this business. I learned that years ago, the first day I
walked into a newsroom. They'd set up a pool on when the
pope would kick off. I was really offended. But, shit, I won
fifty bucks."

The newsroom was almost as deserted as the studio by the
time Jessica reached her tiny cubicle, tucked away in a corner, just a few steps from the assignment desk. It was a space
reserved for the newest reporter on the staff: smaller, more
cramped than the other desks, and more open to the searching
eyes of the assignment editor, who was always looking for a

free body to attend some news conference that no one else wanted to cover.

But Jessica was grateful to be here, determined to prove herself. She knew she was lucky; two years in Duluth had seemed like a lifetime, but many young reporters like herself spent far longer than that, in cities smaller than Duluth, before getting an opportunity to move to a market and station like this.

"Ready to go, Jess? I'll walk you to the ramp." Bill Kendrick was standing a few feet away, smiling, still carrying his camera and light bag.

"In a second, Bill, thanks. I have to write a quick note to Laurie first."

She switched on her computer and quickly brought up the assignment-desk message file: "Laurie: I covered the murder on the river flats tonight and would like to follow up on it tomorrow, if that's okay. Don't worry, no overtime. I'll call you early. Thanks. Jessica."

Jessica said little as she and Kendrick walked toward the parking ramp. The humid haze hanging around the street-lights looked like hordes of gnats and from a distance reminded her of the fog that rolled into Duluth off Lake Superior. But that fog was cool and damp; this mist-filled air felt suffocating. She knew she would find little relief in her tiny, un-air-conditioned apartment.

"You have to get home right away, Bill?" she asked as they neared the ramp.

Kendrick glanced at her. "I really should, Jess. It's hot and it's late. What'd you have in mind?"

"I thought maybe we could stop at the cop shop to see if there's anything new on the murder."

He hesitated, already anticipating the cool shower at home, already tasting the cold can of Coors sitting in the refrigerator.

"Give it a rest, Jess. Wait until tomorrow. They're probably not even back from the river yet."

"Maybe so," she said as they reached her car in the ramp,

"but I think I'll stop by, anyway. I've never even seen the place."

"They won't say anything," Kendrick warned. "It's not like the old days when the street cops would tell you anything you wanted to know. It's a lot tighter now."

When he saw she had not changed her mind, he gave her a quick smile and headed for his own car. Jessica followed him out of the ramp, then turned away toward city hall.

To Kim, it seemed like hours had gone by since the TV had gone off, since Sarah had showered and gone to bed. But he knew far less time had passed.

The rally had only rekindled the horrible memories, and the images from it ricocheted in her mind: the strident signs, the fiery chants, the choked, sobbing words of women like herself, rape victims whose lives, whose very beings, had been forever altered by the brutal violence done to their bodies.

Kim's body had long since healed, but the rest of her remained an open, bleeding wound. She lay staring at the ceiling. Her pillow was a rumpled hump beneath her head, and the single sheet was now a pile at the end of the bed. The hum of the window air conditioner was her only companion.

Kim had tried reading, but she couldn't focus on the pages; the words might as easily have been in French or Spanish. She had finally put the book aside and turned off the bedside lamp.

She tried closing her eyes but found the floating specks of color and the darting comets of light behind her eyelids more unsettling than staring, wide-eyed, into the darkness of the room.

Please let me forget, she pleaded. To precisely whom she wasn't sure. To God? A god who was deaf, then. Please let me put it behind me. Why won't you let me sleep? Like sleep, the answers never came.

She listened to the sounds of the night: the padding of feet in the apartment above, the beep of a car horn on the street below, a phlegmy cough from next door. She was ever alert, ready to jump at the first strange sound. It was not enough. Kim could not escape the memories, the threatening shadows of her own mind.

FOUR

Gladys Hill sat with the police chaplain in the backseat of the squad car, a steel screen separating them from the lieutenant behind the wheel in front. The vinyl seat was cracked and covered with a damp film from the humidity. The stench of stale cigar smoke and the faint odor of vomit choked her.

She reached to roll down the window, but there was no handle. She covered her nose with the back of her hand and tried to breathe through her mouth, swallowing hard.

No one had said anything since leaving the house, although Gladys thought she heard the woman in front humming. *Humming?* At a time like this? Even the chaplain seemed at a loss for words.

The squawking of the police radio filled the void, and she found herself staring, transfixed, into the blinding lights of the oncoming cars. A never-ending string of blazing darts, reflected and intensified by the wet pavement and by her tears. Fiery streaks rushing into her head and through it like an unending tunnel. Her eyes ached, but she could not make herself look away.

"Do you have your own pastor or priest I could call?" the chaplain finally asked. "You're going to need some support . . . some help . . . through this. And I'm not sure how long I'll be able to stay with you."

Gladys was startled by the voice. "What? Pardon me, I'm sorry . . ."

"Are you sure there isn't someone I could call? Your own pastor or priest, maybe?"

"No. No. We don't have a church," she whispered. "Not since Eddie was in Sunday school. We just kind of drifted away. Herbert said the preachers made him squirm. He didn't want one to bury him, but we found one, anyway. The neighbor's minister."

Listen to me babble, she thought. Like some senile old lady.

"There'll be arrangements to be made . . . papers to sign . . ." the chaplain continued. "Someone should be with you. . . ."

They were off the freeway. The blinding string of lights was broken. The streets were darker, softened by the rain. Gladys could hear the low whine of the tires on the wet pavement.

"I'll manage . . . somehow," she replied, her voice as soft as the hiss of the tires. "I always have."

The squad car slowed and pulled to the curb. Gladys could see the downtown office buildings rising in the near distance and the lighted sign outside the Metrodome (Twins vs. Toronto, Tonight) blinking a couple of blocks away, but she did not recognize the building that now stared back at her in the darkness.

"This is the morgue," Lieutenant Brinkman said through the screen. "This won't take long, and then we'll stop by our offices for a few minutes."

Gladys was unable to speak, almost unable to breathe. Her throat was constricted, her mouth dry. She tried to swallow and almost choked again. She put her hand to her throat, rubbing it, feeling the sagging skin and the beat of her pulse. Racing. Her whole body felt limp, drained.

My God, can I do this? Can I look at him now? Do I have the strength? Please, God, give me the strength.

Then the car door opened, and the moist night air enveloped her. She could breathe again.

Once inside the building, Gladys was led down a long, dimly lit hallway, with closed doors on either side. Everything was gray: gray tiles on the floor, gray paint on the walls and doors. Even the air seemed a smoky gray. The only sounds were the hollow clicks of their heels on the tiles and the faraway chatter of a radio.

The corridor ended at a set of metal double doors that swung open into a large room with blinding bright lights. Much cooler than the hallway, the room was lined by metal lockers with stainless-steel doors. Like the refrigerators in restaurants, reflecting the glare of the lights.

They paused just inside the doors. "I know this will be difficult," the chaplain said. "And nothing we can do . . . or say . . . will make it easier. If you feel ill or faint, please tell us so we can assist you."

A doctor whose name she didn't know led them across the room, toward the row of lockers. Two other people working in the room looked up and quietly watched the procession.

The doctor opened one of the locker doors and slowly pulled out a litter draped in white. The chaplain moved closer to Gladys, putting a hand beneath her elbow.

"Are you ready?" the doctor asked, his eyes fixed on hers, his fingers touching the top of the white sheet. Gladys nodded but then looked away, feeling her knees weaken again.

The sheet was folded back. Gladys closed her eyes, held them tight, willing this nightmare over, willing herself to wake up, to hear the sound of Eddie's key in the door. To hear his footsteps across the floor.

"Mrs. Hill? Please. It must be done." The doctor's voice was gentle but impatient.

Her eyelids opened, and she stared down at her son. His eyes were closed, his skin was a pasty white, lips slightly apart, the edge of his teeth barely showing. Grimacing? In pain? She saw with amazing clarity. Every pore in his skin, every darkened whisker. Had he shaved tonight? The tiny hairs in his nostrils. The small scar on his cheekbone. When he fell off the trike on his fourth birthday. It was like yesterday.

Gladys felt their eyes on her. She nodded and turned away, stumbling toward the door, shaking off the supporting hands, knowing she had to get out, to get away. She heard their voices behind her but saw only a bright white blur through the tears.

Still clammy, her clothes clinging from the rain and humidity, Jessica sat in a small waiting room outside the Homicide offices, ignored by the parade of uniformed and plainclothes policemen who went in and out of closed office doors.

She felt like a lost child who had been brought to the police station, handed a lollipop, then told to sit quietly in a corner until her parents picked her up.

Kendrick was right: No one talked to her. She asked twice to see the head of Homicide but got only mumbled responses and occasional wolfish glances from the cops passing by.

After almost an hour, as she stood, ready to leave, a big man in blue suspenders walked out of his office, the stub of a dead cigar clamped between his teeth. He spotted her immediately.

"You looking for me?" he asked gruffly. "I'm Meecham, Matt Meecham. I run this little outfit here, although no one seems to pay me much mind."

The cigar never left his mouth, although it shifted to one side when he spoke. Flecks of tobacco stuck to his lips, and traces of ash clung to his suspenders. His tie dangled beneath his collar, and a loose shirttail hung out over one hip.

She took a step toward him, holding out her hand. "I'm Jessica Mitchell. A new reporter at Channel Seven."

"And a mighty pretty one at that," Meecham boomed, finally taking the cigar from his mouth and grasping her hand.

"They get younger all the time, don't they?" he said to no one in particular.

Meecham tried to relight the cigar. A No Smoking sign hung on the wall in front of him. "So what brings you here this time of night?" he asked after blowing out the third match.

"I wondered if there's anything more . . . anything new . . . on the murder out on the river flats," she said. "I was there tonight and thought I'd try to do a quick follow-up."

"No kidding? A TV reporter doing a follow-up? I thought you left that to the newspaper guys."

Jessica said, "I need to know who the guy was and how he died. One of the cops out there indicated it wasn't pretty."

"Did he, now?" Meecham asked wryly. "Since you're new in town, you probably don't know the rules. We can't say anything, not anymore. That's up to the chiefs. They don't trust us peons to talk to you media types. It can get us into a lot of trouble."

"So I've heard, Captain, but maybe you can give me a break." She quickly glanced around and moved closer, speaking softly, enticingly. "I'm not looking for everything you've got, just the basics."

Meecham guffawed. "You are a pup, aren't you?"

She blushed but held her ground, challenging him.

He leaned toward her, his voice a hoarse whisper. "You didn't hear this from me, okay? Let's just say the guy didn't drown, all right? He was already dead when he took his little swim, but I can't . . ."

Meecham's voice trailed off as his eyes moved from Jessica to the door. She turned to look as Gladys Hill and her two escorts walked into the Homicide waiting room. They had just come from the morgue.

"Later," Meecham said as he turned to greet them.

"This is Mrs. Hill, Captain," Lieutenant Brinkman said, giving Jessica a curious glance as she passed by.

Jessica watched as the old woman moved slowly across the room, appearing dazed. Eyes straight ahead but unseeing. Shuffling feet, stumbling walk.

Meecham led the group into his office and closed the door behind them.

What did the woman cop call her? Mrs. Hill? Poor old lady. I wonder if she's the dead guy's mother?

Jessica debated whether to wait for the meeting to end, hoping to talk to the woman. But she knew that was unlikely and would probably just irritate Meecham. Go home, Jessica, she told herself. Tomorrow's another day.

Behind the closed door, Gladys was seated in a straight-backed chair, facing the big man with the blue suspenders. Lieutenant Brinkman sat next to her, and the chaplain leaned against the wall near the door.

"Mrs. Hill, I realize tonight's been difficult for you," Meecham said, "but we need to know as much about your son as we can. Who his friends were . . . if he had any enemies that you know of . . . anyone who might want to do him harm."

She closed her eyes. The fatigue and emptiness were overwhelming her.

"Mrs. Hill?"

"I don't know of any enemies," she said. "Or of many friends, either. He stayed mostly to himself, and I seldom knew where he was . . . or who he was with."

Brinkman leaned into her. She spoke without Meecham's compassion. "He did live with you, didn't he?"

"Yes . . . yes, he did. But only because he couldn't afford to live anywhere else. He'd lost his job again and had no money to speak of. Just the unemployment check and the few dollars I could spare from Herbert's pension check. He came and went pretty much as he pleased."

Brinkman pressed on. "Then you don't know where he was tonight?"

Gladys shook her head. "I found a note at home . . . saying he was going to meet someone, that he'd be late."

"He didn't say who? *Think*, Mrs. Hill."

She looked up, eyes welling. "I told you I don't know. Don't you believe me?"

"Of course we do," Meecham said, glowering at Brinkman.

"He kept telling me to leave him alone," Gladys said, "to let him live his life. So I did."

Meecham asked, "Was he ever into drugs? Ever have any trouble with the law?"

Gladys hesitated. Surely they knew. Surely they had records. Why were they asking her? The policewoman moved her chair closer, and Meecham leaned forward on the desk. Should she say anything? Why not? He's dead now. What could it hurt?

"No drugs," she whispered finally. "But, yes, he was arrested twice. He was innocent. I know my son. He could never have done the things you said he did. He was never found guilty, but you wouldn't leave him alone."

"We?" Meecham asked. "You mean the police?"

"Yes. You kept hounding him. That's why he couldn't keep a job. He was in and out of jail. It made him bitter . . . a different person."

"In and out of jail for what?" Brinkman demanded.

Gladys looked away, wiped at the tears. Remembering Eddie's plaintive voice on the phone, from jail, pleading for help. "Come get me, Ma. They've done it again. I can't stand it here. I need you, Ma!"

"For sexual assault," she said, rising from her chair, defiant now, no longer whispering. "But they were wrong. Look at your records. He was let go both times. No convictions, just arrests. Mistakes. But he was never the same again."

At that point, the chaplain stepped forward. "Mrs. Hill seems very tired, and I have to get going. Could I take her home now? It's on my way."

Meecham stood up. "Of course. I'm sorry we've kept you this long, Mrs. Hill. But we're going to need all of the information we can get if we're going to find out who . . . who did this to your son."

Gladys prepared to follow the chaplain out of the office.

"One more thing," Meecham said. "Could we stop by your house in the morning and look over Edward's belongings? That may give us a start. We'll call first."

He watched as she nodded uncertainly.

"And . . . Mrs. Hill, I truly am sorry about your son."

His eyes told her he really was.

FIVE

im Hawkins emerged from the apartment building still nibbling one of the Pop-Tarts she had just plucked from the kitchen toaster. She was running late and knew that she would have to forgo the cup of coffee she normally picked up at the Tom Thumb store on her way to the bus stop.

She wore a loose-fitting blouse, a light cotton skirt, and no nylons, but she could still feel the heat closing in around her. Like I'm walking in a heated bubble, she thought, relieved that she had remembered to throw a small stick of deodorant into her purse.

Sarah had left the apartment earlier to prepare for the highly publicized trial of a suburban schoolteacher accused of molesting three of his young female students.

"I'm going to roast the bastard," Sarah had told Kim before she left. "I can't wait to get those girls on the stand and let them tell what this creep did to them."

That was an hour ago, and now Kim hurried her steps, surprised at how good she felt despite the heat, the lack of sleep, and the nightmares. She hoped she would feel even better when she reached her air-conditioned brokerage office.

She picked up a paper at the bus stop and glanced through it quickly, scanning the front-page story on the rally and march, smiling when she saw Sarah again prominently quoted. Once more, she marveled at Sarah's ability to manipulate the media, to use her good looks and quick mind to voice her outspoken views.

On page 3 of the Metro section, she found a lengthy piece on a possible strike by the transit workers. Great, Kim thought, looking up the street for her bus, which was already late. Just what I need. Below that story, a one-paragraph item, in a boldfaced box:

BODY FOUND IN RIVER
Foul Play Suspected

Authorities discovered the body of an apparent murder victim in the Mississippi River, near the University of Minnesota, Tuesday night. He was identified as 36-year-old Edward Hill, who police say lived at 3533 Pikely Avenue South. Police say they have no suspects. An autopsy has been scheduled for today, and police say they may have further information on the case after the autopsy has been completed.

Kim gasped. The name leaped out at her. Edward Hill? *The* Edward Hill? She couldn't believe it. Impossible. He's dead? Murdered? My God!

The nightmares became real again. The smell of him, like cough drops and Old Spice. The weight and *size* of him. The quick gasps for breath and the sickening gurgle in the back of his throat as he came.

It's over, she told herself as she sat back on the bus bench and closed her eyes. Her hand touched the side of her throat, just below the jawline. She fingered the tiny but jagged scar, felt again the steel tip of the knife. No, it will never be over.

She opened her eyes. Another waiting passenger looked at her curiously. "Are you okay?" he asked. "You looked like you were going to faint."

"No, I'm fine," Kim replied with a small smile. "I just get these spells now and then." Like every day, every night, she thought. And what happened to Edward Hill won't change that, will it, Kim? He may be dead, but what he did is still alive, isn't it? Take it easy, she told herself. Think.

Did Sarah know? Had she read the paper? Her thoughts were abruptly interrupted.

"Miss? Excuse me again." It was the same man. "Did you want to get the bus? It's almost here, you know. You sure you're all right?"

The bus pulled up in front of them, ten minutes late.

"Yes. I'm sure. Thank you. You're very kind."

It was the first time she had said that to a man in a long time.

Jessica woke up sweating, the heat of the morning permeating her small apartment. Her long T-shirt clung damply to her body as she padded from her bedroom into the kitchen, flipping on the coffeepot and the radio at the same time.

"Eighty-two degrees in the Twin Cities," the announcer said. "But the dew point is in the sixties, making for a very sticky morning."

Tell me about it, Jessica thought.

"Temperatures are expected to reach the upper nineties, and Northern States Power is expecting the heat wave to produce near-record power consumption from the intensive use of all of the air conditioners."

That I should be so lucky, she thought. Duluth was seldom like this; the breeze off the big lake had made even the warmest days seem cooler and had somehow blown the humidity away. It was the only thing she missed about the place.

The kitchen was just a few steps from the small living

room, separated by a tiny eating alcove, and just off a short hallway that led to her bedroom. Only slightly larger than the galleys of most airplanes, the kitchen provided barely enough room to turn around in, let alone cook anything. But it's too hot to cook, anyway, she decided.

"In national news, the battle over the federal deficit continues in Washington, with the president threatening to veto any legislation which would increase the deficit or raise the tax rates of the middle class. . . ."

That sure won't affect me, Jessica thought. She was still struggling with overdue college loans and the impact of two years of miserable wages in Duluth. While the money in Minneapolis was better, she knew it would take a long time to get back on her feet, to pay for the move and accumulated debts. There would be no quick end to her Spartan lifestyle.

Her apartment was on the second floor of a small brick building near the city's new convention center. The once-stable and proud neighborhood was in transition, still charming in its own semidilapidated way but clearly threatened by urban sprawl. She had quickly discovered that most of the people who lived there were, like herself, new to the area, either old or young, unable to afford more or better.

"In the local news, police have now identified the body of a man found murdered on the banks of the Mississippi River last night. He's thirty-six-year-old Edward Hill, of 3533 Pikely Avenue South. The police have released no other details pending an autopsy and will say only that the investigation is continuing."

Edward Hill? I knew it, she thought. That must have been his mother. She stored his name and address in her memory, then poured herself a cup of coffee and dialed the phone.

"Assignment desk. This is Laurie."

"Morning, Laurie. Jessica. Did you get my message?"

"Yeah, I got it, but I'm not sure we want to do much with this. It looks pretty routine to me. As far as we can tell, the dead guy's a nobody. His name certainly doesn't ring any bells around here."

Jessica listened, hesitant to argue.

"We can't follow up every killing that pops up or we wouldn't be doing anything else," Laurie continued. "But if you want to spend some time on it this morning, it's no skin off my nose. Just check in early this afternoon, okay?"

"Thanks, I'll talk to you later," Jessica said, wondering if she had made a mistake. Her first day on the job she had been warned by another reporter not to tangle with Laurie Sanders. "She's a tough lady," the reporter had said, "who's got her own ideas about what's news and what's not. She's good, and she's usually right, but she doesn't tolerate much argument."

When she first met Laurie, Jessica had been struck by her manly mien: hair cropped tight, wearing jeans and a button-down shirt open at the collar. No makeup, no jewelry. She had been polite but distant and suspicious.

Jessica had tried to reassure her. "I'm here to learn," she said. "I'm looking for all of the help I can get and for a chance to prove myself. That's all I want."

"That's something," Laurie responded, appraising her. "At least you don't come here thinking you know it all. We'll have to see how it goes."

"What have we got going, Laurie?"

The assignment editor looked up into the bearded face of George Barclay, the station's news director, who was making his routine check of the day's news agenda. Laurie handed him a computer printout of the assignments.

"Not much, I'm afraid. The dog days of summer have already set in, it seems. But it's still early." She ran her finger down the sheet. "We've got the hot-weather story . . . the governor's holding a news conference at the Capitol on some new appointment . . . that teacher accused of sexual abuse is going on trial . . . and Jackson's doing a follow-up on the storm damage. Hilliard is repackaging a piece on the 'Take Back the Night' rally, trying to see who some of these women are and what they really hope to accomplish."

"What's this murder follow-up?" Barclay asked idly, looking at the printout. "With Jessica?"

"I just talked to her. She and Kendrick covered that killing on the riverbanks last night, and Jessica's hot to pursue it, for some reason. I told her that it doesn't seem like much to me, but she's doing it on her own time. So what the hell?"

Barclay was a huge man, his body so large it blocked the sun coming through the newsroom window, leaving Laurie in his shadow. But almost everyone was in his shadow. He was considered a journalistic giant, known around the industry for his unbending dedication to the pursuit of news and to doing it with fairness and decency. He was also tough and demanding. Laurie could attest to that.

Three years earlier, Barclay had been brought in to help the station regain its ratings leadership and direction. Laurie knew he had almost left the year before—after management had tried to block Alex Collier's investigative report on a prominent local judge. They had won that battle, and both Barclay and Collier had stayed on.

"What do you think of her?" he asked. "Jessica, I mean."

Laurie took her time responding. "Too early to tell. She's bright enough and seems to have the right instincts. We need to give her a little more time . . . and a little more rope."

Barclay agreed. He had hired Jessica despite a gentle warning from her former news director in Duluth, who said that despite her potential she could get out of control.

In fairness to Jessica, Barclay had never shared that information with Laurie or anyone else in the newsroom. No sense in planting doubts before she had even started. But he wanted to be careful.

"Keep an eye on her," he told Laurie now. "I'd like to bring her along slowly."

Jessica turned the key in the door of her car. A '77 Chevy Impala. Two-tone, light blue on top, darker blue below, if you forgot the brown rust eating away at the fenders and the chrome molding below the doors.

She bought the car her last year at Northwestern from her roommate's brother, who also happened to be her first lover.

He was long gone, but the Impala was still with her. The odometer was now well on its second time around, and Jessica knew the old heap could collapse anytime.

Like her apartment, the Impala had no air-conditioning. That's why she kept her hair short, so the wind from the open windows would do a minimum of damage. As she started the engine, she tilted the rearview mirror down to give her face a final inspection. Not bad, she thought, considering the late night and the heat.

Pulling out into the traffic on LaSalle, she swore silently at the turn signal that wouldn't work, then tried to decide where to head first. She doubted Meecham would be back in his office this early or that Hill's autopsy would have yet begun. And she knew it was too early to show up at the station.

That left only one place. What had the radio announcer said—3533 Pikely Avenue South? Edward Hill's address.

Remember what they told you in school about invasion of privacy? You don't just walk in on the grieving relatives of a murder victim. Not the day after, anyway. Not unannounced. Hell, that was school. *Risk it.*

She pointed the Impala south and spread out the city map on the seat next to her as she drove. Next stop, Pikely Avenue.

SIX

The morning in court had not gone well for Sarah Andrews. First, the judge had been late, blaming an overnight attack of food poisoning. Sarah thought it was more likely a hangover. Then the attorney for Lowell Ingram, the alleged child molester, had filed two late and frivolous motions to delay the trial. Sarah had easily deflected both motions, but it was now the middle of the morning, and the first juror had yet to be selected.

The judge, a stooped and wizened man named Marcott, was impatiently eyeing the clock and suggested a conference in his chambers before lunch.

"I think we ought to resolve this matter without going to trial," he told the attorneys. "No matter how you look at it, it's going to be messy. For the defendant, for the young victims who must testify, for the entire community. It gives everyone a black eye, it seems to me."

Sarah was startled. She knew Judge Marcott lived in the same suburb as the teacher and that he had little patience with women prosecutors like herself or with cases like this one. But she was still bowled over by the suggestion.

"I strongly disagree, Your Honor," she said. "The victims are not only willing but eager to testify. The state can't agree to a plea bargain in this case; it would send an entirely misleading message to the community. That we're soft on sexual abuse."

"I object to that, Your Honor," said the defense attorney, a short, squat man by the name of Bernard Kippering. "Mr. Ingram's already paid a heavy price for this alleged indiscretion. His reputation, his—"

"Indiscretion?" Sarah was outraged. "He repeatedly squeezed the breasts and buttocks of three teenaged girls and forced one of them to hold his penis. For God's sake, that's an *indiscretion?*"

"Now, now, Ms. Andrews," Judge Marcott cautioned. "You're not on television here. Let's show a little restraint. Your strong feelings on this subject are well known in the community."

"My feelings have nothing to do with it, Your Honor. This is a clear violation of the law . . . a felony . . . and I think these children, and this community, should have their day in court."

"Have you two discussed a compromise in this matter?" the judge persisted. "Something that will satisfy the needs of both parties and save us the pain of this pending spectacle."

"No, Your Honor, we have not," Sarah said. "The state is not interested in bargaining this case. I suggest we proceed with jury selection."

"Have you spoken to your superiors about this, Ms. Andrews? If not, I suggest you do. I spoke to County Attorney Hamilton earlier this morning, and his opinion seems to differ from yours."

Sarah was stunned. Could Hamilton have screwed me over? Behind my back? She was dumbstruck.

"Well, Ms. Andrews?" The judge was studying her over his half glasses, a half smile at the corner of his lips.

"No, I have not spoken to Mr. Hamilton. Your statement takes me completely by surprise. I can't believe it, frankly."

"Then I suggest you speak to him over the lunch hour." And, to Kippering, the defense attorney, the judge added: "I would suggest that you discuss with your client a possible guilty plea to reduced charges . . . say, fifth-degree criminal sexual conduct . . . with a commensurate reduction in penalty."

Kippering nodded and got out of his chair, but Sarah stayed in hers. She was afraid her legs would not hold her.

"This meeting is over," the judge said impatiently. "We will reconvene at one-thirty and hopefully put this matter to rest."

Sarah finally managed to rise, turning from them, squeezing her eyelids tight to stop the tears of anger and to hide her rage.

As she walked slowly back to her office, Sarah tried to sort out what had happened. It didn't make sense. Hamilton had known she was going to come down hard on the teacher, to make an example of him. Something had gone wrong. She thought again about the faint smile on the judge's face.

She pushed past Molly, the receptionist, ignoring her "How'd it go?," and walked directly to the county attorney's corner office. It was empty.

"Where's Hamilton?" she yelled.

"Getting a sandwich," Molly replied. "Got a problem?"

"Bet your ass," Sarah said. "I need to see him right away." Then she went into her own office and closed the door.

The office was small. Sarah was one of about forty prosecutors in the criminal division, each provided with similar offices, side by side down opposite walls of two floors. Manila file folders were stacked on her desk and on the floor behind and beside it; all represented criminal cases in some stage of litigation, all assigned to Sarah.

Many would never come to trial. Some charges would be dropped, others would be dismissed, still others would be reduced through plea bargains. Without the bargaining, she knew, the criminal justice system would be overwhelmed and grind to a halt. She also knew you don't plea bargain some cases, and this was one of them.

Her office was bereft of many personal touches. Only her law diploma from the University of Minnesota hung on the wall, and only two pictures sat on the credenza behind the desk: one of her parents and younger brother back in Ohio, the other of Sarah and Gloria Steinem arm in arm at the head of a women's protest march years before at the university.

As Sarah stared at the picture, she wondered idly how many demonstrations she had taken part in over the years. More than she could count or remember, that's for sure. By now they all seemed a blur, with one exception, that day by the side of Steinem. She would never forget the exhilaration, the sense of strength, in that crowd of women to change the balance of power.

A sharp knock at the door brought her back. Before she could respond, Lionel Hamilton strode in, looking like the law-school professor he once was, slender, almost wimpish, with a blue bow tie, a Brooks Brothers suit, and thick, horn-rimmed glasses whose lenses were the size of two tiny fishbowls.

"Looking for me?" he asked. "Molly said you're pissed."

"What's going on here, Lionel?"

"You're talking about the teacher?"

"You mean the pervert," Sarah said, her voice rising as she rose from her chair. "Judge Marcott said he spoke to you . . . that you agreed we ought to bargain down the charges."

"We did have a discussion this morning, that's true."

"How could you . . . without talking to me first?" she demanded. "I'm trying the case, you know."

"Settle down, Sarah. I did look for you, but you were already in court, and I hoped the judge might reconsider. Marcott said he doesn't want the case to go to trial. Period. He said the teacher made a mistake . . . a bad mistake . . . but that he's read the files and thinks the girls are exaggerating, if not outright lying, on some points."

"For God's sake, Lionel, let a jury decide that. Don't you understand? Marcott could be the teacher's neighbor. Their wives probably play bridge or tennis together. It's a god-damned club out there."

"Then you should have gotten another judge."

"You know how easy that is," she protested. "I'd never be able to show my face in Marcott's courtroom again."

"Sit down and cool off. The reality is that Marcott tries ... what? ... twenty percent of our cases? Piss him off and we're in deep shit. We've got to compromise now and then."

"Compromise? Tell that to those girls," Sarah said. "Tell that to their parents. It's like they're being molested all over again."

"Make the best deal you can," Hamilton snapped as he started for the door. "Be reasonable, okay? Don't piss off the judge."

"How about the media?" she asked.

"Tell them anything you want. You're good at that."

Jessica passed the house on Pikely twice, squinting to see the faded house numbers between two huge evergreens that crowded the front yard, straddling a narrow sidewalk, almost blocking it. The house was a story-and-a-half Tudor, with gray shingles and green shutters, one askew, hanging on a broken hinge. The stucco siding was peeling and chipping like old paint.

She parked a half block away, tucking her car between an old Plymouth and a Pontiac, both so tattered they made the Impala look new. After one more glance at herself in the mirror, she started walking up the sidewalk, sidestepping the heaves and cracks in the cement.

She paused at the door of the Hill house, shaded by the towering pines, and listened for any sounds. There was nothing, inside or out. No neighborhood chatter of children's voices, not even the chirp of a bird hidden in the drooping boughs. Just the steady hum of a window air conditioner nearby. Before she could push the button, the door opened.

"Yes?" It was the woman from last night. Mrs. Hill. Wearing black, a one-piece dress that hung loosely from her slender shoulders, speckled with lint, smelling faintly of mothballs.

"I'm terribly sorry to bother you, Mrs. Hill. Especially at a time like this—"

"What do you want, please?"

"I'd like to speak with you, if I could," Jessica said. "About your son . . ."

"Are you from the police? They said it would be—"

"No, I'm not from the police. My name's Jessica Mitchell. I'm a reporter . . . from Channel Seven. . . ."

Mrs. Hill's expression didn't change. There was no angry outburst. She simply stepped back and began to close the door, quietly but firmly.

"Mrs. Hill? Please. It would only take a moment."

"I don't want to talk to reporters." From behind the door. "Can't you understand? Not now. Please leave me alone."

"I don't want to intrude, Mrs. Hill. Believe me. But I was there last night . . . on the riverbank. I felt very badly. I'd like to know more about your son, to understand how this could have happened to him. I thought you might want to talk with someone."

The door was still slightly ajar; she could hear the woman's quiet sobs through the screen door.

"Please don't shut the door, Mrs. Hill. I know this must be a terrible time for you, especially if you're alone." Jessica listened for other voices but heard none. "Maybe I could help in some way."

"No one can help now. Please go away. I want to be alone."

The door remained open a crack. "I understand," Jessica said. "But may I call . . . or come see you . . . later?" There was no response. "Let me leave this," she said, pulling a small business card from her skirt pocket, pushing it through the opening. "Perhaps you'll call me when you're feeling better, when you feel like talking."

The card was lifted from her fingers, and the door closed.

Jessica reached the sidewalk at the same time as Meecham's squad car reached the curb. She paused, ducking slightly to see inside the car. Hesitating, knowing she probably shouldn't be there but wanting to talk to him. Too late to hide, anyway.

Meecham was not alone. The lieutenant Jessica had seen the night before with Mrs. Hill sat next to him.

"What d'ya know?" Meecham said as he hauled his big body out of the car. "Jessica, right? The new girl reporter. Fancy meeting you here."

"Morning, Captain. I was going to call you later."

"Have you met Lieutenant Brinkman?" Meecham asked. "She works with us in Homicide."

Brinkman was standing almost at attention, ignoring Jessica's outstretched hand. "What are you doing here?" she demanded. "You've got no business here."

"Nobody told me," Jessica replied, surprised by her surliness. "I just wanted to talk to Mrs. Hill for a minute."

Brinkman was an imposing figure whose body stretched her carefully starched uniform. A full six inches taller than Jessica, her height was accentuated by a long, slender face and a pile of auburn hair knotted behind her head.

"You're interfering in a police investigation," Brinkman snarled. "To say nothing of intruding on a person's privacy. Don't you newspeople have any respect for the dead?"

"Hold on," Meecham said, walking around the car. "Let's not get all steamed. It's hot enough already." He stood next to Jessica. "Did Mrs. Hill talk to you? I can't imagine she would."

"Not really," Jessica admitted. "Maybe some other time. It's awful, you know."

"Spare us," Brinkman fumed. "All you want is a god-damned story, no matter what you have to do."

"How do you know what I want?" Jessica snapped back.

Meecham interceded again. "C'mon, ladies, cool off. Jessica, we can't prevent you from trying to talk with her, although we'll ask her not to. As you can guess, this isn't an easy time for her."

"What can you tell me?" Jessica asked.

Meecham chuckled. "Never stop trying, do you? Remember what I told you last night? We can't say shit, although I must tell you we don't know shit now, anyway. So why don't you take a breather. You must have other stories to cover."

At that, they pivoted and began to walk to the house. Meecham stopped a few paces away, turned back toward Jessica, cupped his nose, and delivered a mighty sneeze.

"Damned rain last night," he muttered. Then, in a whisper, he said, "Call me later, all right?"

Gladys Hill stood in the hallway as Meecham and Brinkman carefully picked their way through Edward's room. Opening drawer after drawer—first the desk, then his dressers—fingering the contents, pulling some out, flipping through notebooks and his calendar. Making a few notes, then moving on to the closet, emptying the pockets of his jackets and pants, shaking his shoes.

"Can we borrow your son's address book and his calendar for a while?" Meecham asked. "We'd like to spend more time checking the names, if that's okay."

"And any recent photos," Brinkman added. "Especially those with other people . . . friends, acquaintances . . . you know the kind of thing I'm talking about."

Gladys had trailed them as they searched the entire house, but when they'd reached Eddie's room, she was unable to follow. She hadn't entered it since the police first came to her door the night before.

"We appreciate your help and cooperation," Meecham said when the search was over, as they finally stood at the front door, ready to leave. "We'll return his things as soon as possible."

The screen door had closed behind them when Meecham stopped.

"Oh, yeah, almost forgot. I understand a reporter tried to talk to you just before we came."

Gladys nodded, her face in the shadows.

"You're obviously free to do as you'd like, Mrs. Hill, but I'd recommend that you not talk to anybody for a while. Not until we figure out what's going on and hopefully develop some leads. But it's up to you, of course."

When Gladys didn't respond, Meecham turned and walked toward the car, Lieutenant Brinkman hard on his heels.

SEVEN

Bill Kendrick was waiting by her desk when Jessica returned from Gladys Hill's.

"Hey, Jess. Laurie tells me you've been out playing reporter this morning. Find anything?"

She slumped into her chair. "Not really," she admitted, telling him of her closed-door conversation with Gladys Hill and her confrontation with Meecham and Lieutenant Brinkman outside.

"What do you know about this Brinkman?" she asked. "She chewed my head off when she saw me there."

Kendrick laughed. "Join the club. She's a real lady Rambo. Carries a chip the size of a stump on her shoulder and hates the media, especially television."

"Why?" Jessica asked.

"I'm not sure I know everything," Kendrick said, "but when she was a rookie, years ago, she and her partner got caught thumping a couple of guys on the street. Police-brutality stuff, you know. One of the TV stations happened to get the beating on tape and played it up big, a real exposé. An early version of the Rodney King thing in L.A., only not quite as brutal. The partner got busted, and the city got sued. Brinkman got off with a reprimand because she was a rookie, but she's never forgotten or forgiven. She's a tough broad, believe me. There are stories—"

Their conversation was interrupted by loud voices at the assignment desk, not ten feet away. Laurie Sanders was toe-to-toe with Jeff Hilliard, the reporter who had first warned Jessica to beware of Laurie.

"What's going on now?" Jessica wondered aloud.

"Another newsroom battle," Kendrick replied with a smile as he turned to walk away. "Happens all the time."

It was impossible to ignore the exchange. Jessica got up and sat on the edge of her desk.

"I'm telling you, Laurie, there's no follow-up there," Hilliard said, his voice tinged with anger. "You saw it all on the news last night. A bunch of women meet in a goddamned park, heard some speeches, and then got blown away by the storm. There's nothing new today."

"Listen, Jeff," Laurie retorted, "we need the story. We've got a newscast to fill, remember? And it's getting late."

"You're asking me to make chicken salad out of chicken shit," he complained.

Jessica edged closer, unseen by either of them.

"No chicken salad. Just a story, okay? Think for once! Do these women have a legitimate bitch? Are the streets really unsafe for them? What do the stats say? Use your head, for Christ's sake."

"We've done that story a hundred times," Hilliard groused.

"It's not every day five thousand women turn out to protest," Laurie countered. "Don't tell me there's no story."

On impulse, Jessica walked boldly into the middle of the argument, surprised at her own bravado, ignoring their angry reaction at the interruption.

"What do you need, Jessica?" Laurie demanded irritably.

She stopped short. "Sorry, I heard you arguing," she said. "I think I can help."

"That's all I need," Hilliard groaned. "More advice."

Hilliard was a tall and gangly transplanted Texan who had managed to lose his drawl in Minnesota but not his cowboy boots or the big brass belt buckle engraved with a Triple XXX brand.

He was staring at her stonily, but Laurie said, "Go on, Jess."

"I covered part of that rally last night . . . before I got sent to the murder. I did the interview with that woman—Sarah Andrews—the one with the STOP RAPE T-shirt."

"We know who she is," Hilliard said testily. "So what?"

"She's impressive," Jessica replied. "She's got all the facts at her fingertips. She'd be a great resource for a quick follow-up."

Jessica noticed they were both looking at her less irritably so she forged ahead. "If you want, I could help Jeff put something together in a hurry."

"He sure as hell needs the help," Laurie said.

"Wait a minute," Hilliard objected. "Is it my story or not?"

"You didn't want it a minute ago," Laurie fumed. "If you'd gotten off your ass this morning, you wouldn't need help now. It's almost noon, and we're still talking about it."

"Bullshit. I wasn't—"

"Look," Jessica said, "I don't want to get in the middle of this. It's Jeff's story. I was just trying to help."

"Relax," Laurie said, her anger ebbing. "We need the piece. You two work it out. Maybe you could try to get to Andrews again, Jess. She's handling that sex-molester trial and may not be available, but it's worth a try."

Hilliard was still pouting but agreed.

Kendrick was behind the wheel of the news car, Jessica by his side, heading for the Government Center to find Sarah Andrews. The downtown offices were emptying out for the noon hour, and Kendrick had to maneuver through the crowded crosswalks, dodging pedestrians who were ignoring the Don't Walk signals.

"I made a couple of calls," Kendrick said. "While you were in the middle of that squabble in the office."

"What calls?" she asked.

"I've got this friend who's some kind of a flunky at the medical examiner's office, an old high school buddy whose family owned a mortuary that went broke. He's ended up cleaning up the cadavers at the morgue. Horrible job. I can barely stand to shake hands with him."

Jessica groaned. "What did he say?"

"That our friend from the riverbank was pretty badly mutilated. Cut up something fierce. Stab wounds all over."

"No kidding," she whispered.

"That's not the worst of it," Kendrick added.

"There's more?"

Kendrick took a deep breath. "He was castrated. They cut off his balls. They're still missing."

"What?" she demanded. "Are you serious?"

"This guy wouldn't kid me. He said he'd get his ass fired if anybody knew he'd told me."

Suddenly, Jessica felt a thousand miles from Duluth.

Lowell Ingram sat across from his attorney in a darkened corner of the restaurant, caressing the edge of his martini glass, dipping one finger into the gin and stirring it.

"I don't know," Ingram mumbled, finally fishing the olive from the glass. "I don't like the idea of pleading guilty."

Bernie Kippering scowled. "You don't have much choice. Face it, you're dead meat if this goes to trial. That prosecutor, Sarah Andrews, is out to get you. You're just lucky we found a hometown judge who's willing to apply some pressure in the right places."

Kippering was getting impatient. They had been sitting there for a half hour, ever since he left the judge's chambers. He watched his client put away two martinis and saw that he was close to finishing his third.

He had only taken Ingram on as a client as a favor to his

law partner, who represented Ingram's school district. "I don't like the son of a bitch," Kippering had told his partner earlier that day. "Makes me feel like dirty laundry."

Ingram was in his forties and would have gone unnoticed in any crowd. Average height, average weight, with a sharply receding hairline and bushy eyebrows. His lower lip protruded slightly, giving him a perpetual pout, and his cheeks bore the faint pockmark traces of childhood acne.

He had taught at the school for a dozen years, an average teacher but active and well known in the community. While the molesting charges had shocked his neighbors, it had not come as a total surprise to school administrators; there had been whispers about his behavior before.

"He's apparently a real Jekyll and Hyde," Kippering's partner had told him. "Most of the time, he seems like a decent guy. Only he's not. He's got a nasty temper, especially when he's drunk. And he seems to have a constant hard-on when he's around young girls."

Sitting across from him now, watching Ingram grow surlier with each drink, Kippering could see what his partner was talking about. "Look, Ingram," he said, "take my advice. If a jury convicts you, you're guilty of a felony. You'll go to prison, maybe for a long time. When you get out, you can't vote, you can't do a lot of things other people can do. You're a half citizen, at best."

"But I could get off," Ingram argued. "The jury may not believe those girls. They're all prick teasers, anyway."

Kippering, who had a teenage daughter himself, was tempted to reach across the table and smack him. But he kept his cool. "That's a long shot. They may doubt one girl but not three. If you cop this plea, you'll get off with a gross misdemeanor. At most, you may spend a couple of months in minimum security, have a few treatment sessions, and put in some time in a halfway house."

Ingram drained the final drops from the glass. "What about my family?" he asked. "My job? All the lawsuits I'll be facing?"

Kippering again held his tongue. He knew Ingram's wife

had already tossed him out of the house and that there was no chance in hell that he'd be back teaching at the school. "Let's just get past this for now."

"Okay, okay," Ingram said grudgingly. "Do what you have to do. Let's get this shit over with."

Jessica sat on a hard leather chair in the waiting area just inside the county attorney's office. A parade of people—mostly lawyers, she guessed—passed through a swinging gate in the wooden railing.

"Ms. Andrews is free now," Molly told her. "You can go back. Third door on your right."

Sarah was waiting by the door and shook Jessica's hand. "Come on in," she said. "Sorry that I've only got a few minutes."

Jessica was taken aback. She hardly looked like the same woman she had met at the rally the night before. She seemed wilted and dejected. The buoyancy, the confidence, were gone.

"How's your trial going?" Jessica asked.

"Don't ask," Sarah said. "Off the record, it doesn't look like there's going to be one."

"Really? What happened?"

Sarah hoisted herself up in the chair, the fire coming back into her eyes. "You really want to know? Men run the world, that's what happened. They watch out for one another."

Jessica was shocked by the rancor in her voice.

"Sex crimes just aren't taken seriously in this system," Sarah went on bitterly. "Essentially, it's men who see the problem mostly as 'boys will be boys.' They can't deal with it. Think about it. Who makes the laws? Who sits on the benches? Men, mostly, jerks like Judge Marcott, who for years have treated predators with kid gloves. Men dispense the justice; women pay the price."

What did I walk into? Jessica wondered. This woman—who was so composed, so together, at the rally—now seemed on the edge of hysteria.

"How many convicted rapists in Minnesota do you think actually go to prison?" Sarah demanded, not waiting for an answer. "Three out of ten, maybe fewer. And how about this? Nationally, half the rapists who do go to prison rape again within three years of getting out. And those are only the ones they catch."

As she paused for breath, Jessica said, "Those are pretty scary statistics, but—"

Sarah cut her off. "That's not the worst of it. In this state, more than three thousand—hear that?—three thousand sex criminals are walking around free, on probation, ready to rape again. Fewer than six hundred are actually doing time. If that doesn't scare the hell out of you, nothing will."

She sank back into the chair. "Sorry for the tirade," she finally said, calmer now. "Nothing personal, you know. You just walked in at the wrong time."

"That's okay," Jessica said. "You obviously have strong feelings—"

"So would you if you see what I see every day. Slime slipping through the cracks and nobody doing anything about it."

Jessica glanced at her watch, then quickly explained her mission, to obtain additional information for use in a follow-up story on the rally.

"Are you doing the story?" Sarah asked.

"No, another reporter is, Jeff Hilliard. I'm helping out."

"Should've figured that," Sarah said with a slow shake of her head. "They always assign a man to do the stories on crimes against women. Like they can't trust a woman to get it right . . ."

"Wait a minute," Jessica protested.

"What does this Jeff Whoever know about women? The kind of fear and anger we're all feeling? How can he relate to us except through a bunch of statistics?"

"I'm told he's a good reporter."

"That has nothing to do with it," she insisted. "He's never felt afraid to walk the streets at night . . . or venture into a parking ramp alone. Or to turn the lock and walk into a dark apartment."

"I don't feel that afraid," Jessica said.

"You're new here, that's why. But you will. Damn near three million people live in the Cities, including hundreds of weirdos just itching to get their hands on a woman and thousands of jurors who still think rape victims are somehow at fault."

Sarah's voice had turned shrill again. "Tell this Jeff guy to talk to the three girls who were abused by their teacher and who are now getting screwed by the system. Will they ever trust a man or the courts again?"

"I can see what you're saying," Jessica mumbled, and then, almost in defiance, added, "But you're part of the system."

"You're right, and some days—most days—I'm ashamed to admit it." Sarah picked a folder from her file drawer and handed it to Jessica. "All the facts and figures you'll need are in here. Molly will make you copies if you'd like. Sorry to dump on you like this, but it's not been a great day."

There was a rap on the door, and a young man, not much older than Jessica, rushed in. "Sarah, I've got to talk to you about the Ripley case—"

He stopped short, sensing the tension still in the air and embarrassed to discover that Sarah was not alone. "Sorry," he blurted out. "I didn't know you were busy."

"It's okay, Jack. She was just leaving."

Jessica stood by the desk, her exit blocked by the breathless figure in the doorway. After an awkward moment, she moved toward the door. "Thanks again for your time, Sarah."

"No problem," she said. "We'll talk more another day. I'll give you a call."

The young man didn't budge, openly and admiringly appraising Jessica as she approached him. His momentary embarrassment had disappeared. "I didn't get your name," he said, holding out his hand.

Before Jessica could reply, Sarah spoke up. "This is Jessica Mitchell, Jack. She's a new reporter at Channel Seven." Jessica felt his hand, warm and firm, grip hers. "And this is Jack Tomlinson, Jessica. A fairly new addition to our prosecuting staff."

He wore a starched pinstriped shirt, open at the collar with a colorful paisley tie hanging loosely beneath it. The shirt-sleeves were carefully folded back to his forearms.

"Nice to meet you," Jessica said, politely trying to move past him and through the door, only to find Molly, the receptionist, in her path.

"Pardon me," Molly said, looking past her. "You've got a call, Sarah. Line One."

As Sarah picked up the phone, Tomlinson followed Jessica out of the office and down the hallway. "I don't think I've seen you on the news," he said.

"Not yet," she replied lightly, relieved to be free of the tense atmosphere of Sarah's office. "But keep watching."

He held open the railing gate. "You can count on it."

Sarah closed the office door, then returned to the phone and spoke impatiently. "What do you need, Kim?"

"Did you read the paper?" she asked.

"You mean Edward Hill?"

"He's dead, Sarah."

"I know. Real pity, huh?"

"Who could have killed him?" Kim asked.

"Who knows . . . and who cares? Important thing is he'll never bother you or anyone else again."

"But it doesn't really change anything, does it?" Kim said hesitantly. "It can't undo what's already done."

"C'mon, Kim. He got what he deserved. What's past is past and will soon be buried. This is the chance you've been waiting for . . . to put it to rest, to get on with your life."

Kim started to reply, but Sarah cut her off. "Kim, I can't talk anymore now. I'm up to my neck in problems with this teacher. I'll see you tonight."

Kim replaced the receiver and leaned back in her chair, staring at the ceiling tiles. Noticing for the first time how precisely, how tightly, the squares fit together. Forgetting, for the moment, the clutter on her desk. Wishing again that she had a window to see the sky and the clouds but knowing they were reserved for the managers.

Kim had been hired for the research department of Midwest Services the year before, after two years in the company's clerical pool and after finally finishing her business degree at the university. Not the most exciting job in the world, she thought, but God knows there's not much else in my life. No men. Not since that night. Few close friends, except for Sarah. And halfway across the country, a family which had grown further apart than the miles on the map.

Kim thought again of Sarah's words. "He'll never bother you or anyone else again." Not that simple, Sarah. Edward Hill may be dead, but what about the others just like him? By the scores or hundreds, still alive, planning to do to others what Edward Hill has already done to me.

What about herself? Despite her horrible experience and her fears, despite her heightened precautions, Kim knew she was not immune from another attack. Lightning can strike twice at women.

No, it's not quite that simple.

Sarah pressed through a group of reporters loitering outside the courtroom. They had waited all morning for Ingram's trial to begin and clearly were getting edgy as their deadlines approached.

"Hey, Sarah, what can you tell us?" one reporter called out.

"Is this show ever going to get on the road?" another asked.

Sarah paused for a moment. She knew she couldn't ignore them, but she was reluctant to say anything. "You'll have to be patient," she finally said. "Things are happening which I can't discuss. I may have a statement later on. That's all I can say."

She passed through the courtroom doors, heading for the judge's chambers. Lowell Ingram was sitting alone in the empty jury box, reading a newspaper. He looked up at her and grinned lopsidedly, giving her a broad wink.

The bastard's roaring drunk, Sarah thought as she walked by.

"Hey, Counselor. I hear we may have a deal, huh?"

Sarah stopped but did not turn; she couldn't stand the sight of him.

"May miss your big day in court, huh? Too bad. You'll have to save your shit for some other poor jerk."

His voice was barely above a whisper, but it seemed to echo in the empty courtroom. Sarah knew she should keep walking, but she was mesmerized by the virulence in the voice.

"You're a real man hater, aren't you, Counselor? A real ball-buster, they tell me. They say you'd like to crucify anybody who wears pants, especially if he has a loose zipper."

Then he chortled. She turned toward him. His face was buried in the newspaper, but his shoulders were shaking with laughter.

"You're an utterly disgusting human being," she said.

He looked up, the smile turning to a sneer. "You ever had a real man, Counselor? Or are you one of those lesbos?"

Sarah felt like vomiting. "You're drunk. Watch your mouth."

"Let me tell you something, Counselor, I better not come out of this deal with any jail time, understand? Or I'll find you and screw you until you could dock a boat up your crack."

"Don't threaten me, Ingram. It won't work." She was shaking with rage and frustration. "I've seen too many slimeballs like you. You mess with me and you'll pay."

His laugh was more of a snort. "Listen to the lady. Tough talk for a skirt. But don't forget what I said . . . or we'll just see how well you can take care of yourself."

"Let's get on with it," the judge said when Sarah and the defense attorney were back in his chambers. "What's the decision, Mr. Kippering?"

"My client is willing to plead guilty to fifth-degree sexual criminal conduct, as you suggested, Judge. He's hoping the court will be lenient and allow him to put his life back together again."

"You're suggesting no jail time, Mr. Kippering?"

"Yes, Your Honor, I am. Mr. Ingram has been a model member of the community until this unfortunate incident. Incarceration would serve no useful purpose."

"Ms. Andrews?"

"With all due respect, Your Honor, I can't believe what I'm hearing. The man's a menace. Allowing him to escape a felony conviction is hard enough for me to swallow. Escaping jail time is something else. You can't seriously consider that."

"Who wears the robe, Ms. Andrews?"

"Sorry, Your Honor, but the state strongly believes this defendant must pay some penalty for his crime and that he must receive treatment. We have reason to believe this is not the first time Mr. Ingram has behaved in this manner.

"I object to that, Your Honor," Kippering said. "There's no evidence of any such prior behavior."

"Okay, okay. Settle down, both of you. We'll go back into open court, and I'll accept the guilty plea, but I'll reserve judgment on the sentence until next week. Is that satisfactory?"

Sarah could not remain silent. "There's going to be a significant public outcry over this, Your Honor. From citizens concerned about the sexual abuse of children and about leniency toward the abusers."

"From women like yourself?" Marcott said smugly. "It's your plea bargain, isn't it? I'm simply ratifying the agreement."

The small smile was back on his lips. "I would offer one piece of advice, Ms. Andrews. I trust I will not hear your voice among the howling chorus."

Sarah wanted to kick him in the balls.

EIGHT

Jessica was back in the newsroom, helping Jeff Hilliard prepare his follow-up report, paging through the material Sarah had given her.

"Look at these statistics, Jeff," she said, leaning over Hilliard's desk. "Last year, reported rapes in this country topped one hundred thousand for the first time. And they say only one in ten rapes is actually reported. That means there could be a million rapes a year!"

"Those are pretty soft figures," he warned.

"How so?" she asked.

"It's guesswork, mainly. Nobody really knows for sure."

"But listen to this," Jessica said, using her pencil to circle one of the paragraphs. "Of the rapes reported, only five percent or so actually result in criminal trials. That means a hell of a lot of rapists are going free."

"I don't doubt that," Hilliard admitted. "The question is, What to do about it? Victims get scared, witnesses back off, investigations get botched. The system's overloaded. Not enough cops, not enough judges, not enough tough laws."

Jessica straightened up. "That's the whole point, Jeff. That's what all of those women at the rally were trying to say."

Hilliard scoffed. "That's no way to solve it, ranting and raving about it on television. It's too big, too complicated. Those women would be better off lobbying their legislators than standing around in Loring Park screaming about it."

Jessica shook her head sadly. "Sarah Andrews was right. Men just don't get it."

"What are you talking about?" he demanded.

She leaned over, in his face. "Think about it. Most of the legislators are men; so are most of the cops and judges. Sexual assault is an issue that mainly affects women, yet it's mainly men who are trying to solve it. And most of them can't get past the arrogance of their power."

"Who are you to lecture me?" Hilliard snapped. "And save the feminist crap. Sarah Andrews has you brainwashed. It's not just a woman's issue; it's society's issue, for Christ's sake."

"It's women who are getting hurt," she argued, "and men who are doing the hurting."

Exasperated, Hilliard said, "Careful, Jessica. You're starting to sound like one of *them*."

"One of them?" she said. "Who's them? Women? What's wrong with women trying to do something about a problem that affects women?"

She stalked back toward her desk, half-annoyed and half-wondering why she suddenly felt so cornered. "I'm just beginning to understand what this all means," she shouted over her shoulder.

As she passed the television monitor on the assignment desk, Jessica paused to watch Alex Collier's afternoon news update.

"Something of a surprise today," Alex reported. "There will be no trial of Lowell Ingram, the suburban schoolteacher accused of sexually molesting three of his female students. Ingram has agreed to plead guilty to fifth-degree sexual conduct, a gross misdemeanor, instead of facing trial on more serious felony charges. Judge Irving Marcott will sentence Ingram next week. No comment yet from either Ingram or his attorney or from Hennepin County prosecutor Sarah Andrews. We'll have a full report on the six o'clock news."

So Sarah was right, Jessica thought. A plea bargain. No trial. Another predator goes free. No wonder she was so upset. Hard to argue with her words: "Men run the world . . . They watch out for one another."

Jessica's phone was ringing as she reached her desk. It was Kendrick, still at city hall. "I can't find Meecham anywhere around here," he told her, "and nobody else is saying anything about the Hill murder. It's like a closed trap over here."

"He hasn't returned my calls, either," she said.

"If you really want to find him," Kendrick said, "you might try Barney's bar later on. That's his second home. Look in the back booth, near the air conditioner."

Sarah was standing in the lobby of the Government Center, where the reporters and cameras had gathered after Ingram's guilty plea. She was flanked by Ingram's attorney.

"C'mon, you two," one of the reporters shouted. "You've got to say something."

Sarah hesitated, then began. "I can only say that the county attorney's office has decided to accept Mr. Ingram's plea of guilty to a lesser charge. It will save the time, trouble, and expense of a lengthy trial, and it saves the young witnesses the anguish of testifying in open court."

"C'mon, Sarah," another reporter said. "That's not the way you were talking this morning. You could hardly wait to get at Ingram. You said you were going to make an example of him."

"Things change, that's all I can say. My hope is that this outcome will still serve as an example to others who might be tempted to take sexual advantage of youngsters."

"By letting him cop a plea? That's a great example."

Sarah stared at the reporter but made no response.

"Will he get any jail time?" the same reporter asked.

"I don't know," she said. "That will be up to Judge Marcott. It's certainly the state's belief that he should."

"How about Ingram? What does he say?"

Bernie Kippering stepped up to the microphone. "Mr. Ingram only reluctantly agreed to this arrangement. He was eager to save his family and friends the embarrassment of further proceedings. And, contrary to Ms. Andrews's feelings, we fervently hope he'll be allowed to return to his home and community."

Sarah couldn't listen to any more, turning on her heel, ignoring the reporters' questions. Kippering caught up to her before she reached the elevators.

"Listen," he said, "for what it's worth, and just between us, I think the guy's a creep, too. I'll personally be sorry if he doesn't get the slammer for a while, but I've got to do my job."

Sarah pushed the elevator button. "He hasn't learned anything, and we haven't even sent the message that he'd better. But I'm not through with him yet."

Jessica had no easy time finding Barney's bar. Tucked away in a corner of an old warehouse on the seedy fringe of downtown, it was virtually impossible to see from the street. Only a small Miller Time clock hanging in a tiny window provided a clue to its location.

As she stood outside, Jessica was relieved the summer sun had not yet fully set. This neighborhood is no place to be wandering around after dark, she thought, nervously surveying the run-down buildings and the all-but-deserted streets. What had Sarah said? "You will be afraid."

Inside, it could have been the middle of the night, dim and smoky, smelling of Pine-Sol and stale beer. She stood for a moment just inside the door and allowed her eyes to adjust. The soft twang of a country tune was floating in the air with the smells. Randy Travis? She wasn't sure.

The place was long and narrow, like an old railroad dining car, with the bar to the left and a few small booths to the right. A few people sat at the bar, slouched on stools, hanging heads raising slightly as Jessica walked past them. She could feel their drooping eyes follow her.

"Looking for somebody, lady?" It was the bartender, a dark, swarthy man leaning across the bar ahead of her. Thick black hair matted his arms and pushed out of his shirt collar like a shock of oily wheat.

"Captain Meecham here tonight?"

The bartender pointed toward the back. She found Meecham where Kendrick had said he'd be, in the very back booth, just beneath an air conditioner gasping for its last breath and a few feet away from the jukebox. Meecham was alone, looking down into his glass. The stub of a gummy, well-chewed cigar sat in an ashtray at his elbow.

"Captain?"

He didn't seem to hear, or he was ignoring her.

"Captain Meecham?"

His eyes slowly rose from the drink, traveled the length of her body, and finally focused on her face. He nodded in vague recognition, then looked back into his glass. "What are you doing here?" he mumbled. "Can't you see I'm off duty?"

"I'd like to talk to you. I've left several messages."

His eyes didn't leave the glass.

"May I sit down?" she persisted.

He shrugged his shoulders. Jessica slid into the booth. "You do remember me, don't you?"

He looked up with a hint of annoyance. "How could I forget? The little lady reporter . . . who doesn't like to let a dead man rest in peace." He paused and rested his chin on his clasped hands. "My friend Jessica. Uhhh . . . Jessica what?"

"Mitchell."

"Right," he mumbled. "I should've remembered that."

Again, she was struck by the difference a few hours could make in a person. The friendly, outgoing Meecham of that morning had vanished, replaced by this morose character sitting across from her now. Credit the booze, she thought.

"How'd you find me?" he asked as he reached into his coat pocket for another cigar and then struggled to unwrap it. His fingers seemed stiff, almost arthritic.

"It wasn't hard," she replied, watching him closely. "I'm told you're here a lot."

"Is that right?" He managed to get the cellophane wrapper off the cigar and wet the end of it. Then he bit off the tip. "Why don't I give you a call in the morning?"

"I'm here now," she said stubbornly, wondering now if she should have come. He seemed so lost in this private back-booth world. "You told me to give you a call," she reminded him. "Remember? This morning. After you sneezed."

He chuckled and touched a match to the cigar, puffing quickly, watching with satisfactioni as the end flamed and the smoke rose. "That was a phony sneeze, you know. I learned it from my dad. He used to sneeze like that as an excuse to get away from my mother."

Jessica smiled. She liked this man. He seemed like a gruff but gentle old bear whose growl, she suspected, was far worse than his bite. She was sorry to see him alone like this and took courage from the fact that he had not yet ordered her away.

Then she surprised even herself. "Why do you drink so much?" she blurted.

"And why do you ask so many goddamned questions?" His growl was back. "Is that all you do? Just ask questions?"

Jessica was not cowed. "Is that all you do? Just drink?"

"I mind my own business," he groused. "Don't bother anybody."

"Believe me, I don't want to bother you," she said, shrinking back, knowing she may have stepped beyond the bounds. "I just want to ask you about Edward Hill."

"More questions, right? About good old Eddie. All-American Eddie. Let me tell you something, Jessica Mitchell. Don't weep for Edward. Weep for his old mother, maybe, but not for Eddie boy."

"What do you mean?"

"Just trust me, okay? Don't try to take advantage of an old off-duty cop who may have had a couple too many. Take my word for it. The world will not miss Edward Hill."

She leaned across the table, her eyes locked on his. "What are you talking about?" she demanded. "Was he in trouble with the law?"

Meecham couldn't hide his amused expression. "Nice try,

Jessica, but I've told you too much already. Now get out of here. I can't stand company when I drink."

She squeezed up and out of the booth. "He must have been a real bad character," she said. "Why else would somebody poke him full of holes and then castrate him?"

Meecham's head popped up. No bleary eyes, no slurred speech now. "How'd you know that?" he demanded. "Who told you that?" He waited for a reply but got none. "Forget it, Jessica. I'm serious. That's confidential police information."

Jessica nodded and walked away, convinced now it was all an act. He's no more drunk than I am, she thought. He's just sad and sorry for himself. And very lonely.

As she walked back through the bar, the same eyes from the same stools followed her. From somewhere behind her, she thought she heard a thin, halfhearted wolf whistle. Then a raspy cackle.

When she reached the door, it was already opening from the outside, and she found herself face-to-face with Lt. Freda Brinkman, staring at her.

"Well, well . . . who do we have here?" Brinkman asked.

"Hello, Lieutenant. I was just leaving."

"I see that. You and Matt have a nice chat?"

"Very nice, thanks," Jessica replied. "I like him."

"How sweet. Do you always chase down sources in bars?"

"When they don't return phone calls, I do."

Jessica noticed that all voices in the bar were stilled. The two women were being watched with interest.

"Excuse me, but I've got to go," she said, trying to push past Brinkman.

The lieutenant slid to the side, blocking her path. "Is he sober?" she asked. "Or drunk enough to talk?"

"A model of sobriety. Now please move aside."

Brinkman stood fast, leering down at her. "Leave him alone," she hissed. "He's an old man, hear? He sees the world through the bottom of a glass. Stay away from him."

"When I hear that from him, I will," Jessica said, not backing down. "But not before."

The street had turned dark by now, and she didn't notice the flat tire until she tried to pull away from the curb. The first hint was a balky steering wheel, the next a slight tilt of the Impala's front end. Damn, she thought, why tonight? Why here?

She got out and looked at the left front wheel. Despite the darkness, she could tell at a glance that the tire was flat against the pavement. She knelt down, only then seeing a knife protruding from the side of the tire. A Swiss army knife, the corkscrew portion of it imbedded into the rubber.

She stood quickly and looked around. No one was in view, but with the deepening shadows and the darkened doorways, that was scant comfort. The nearest streetlight was a half block away, and few of the windows in the nearby buildings were illuminated.

She felt a shiver pass through her body. Who would do this? And why? Probably kids, she told herself. But why would kids leave their knife in the tire?

Jessica's first instinct was to hurry back to the safety of Barney's and ask Meecham for help. But she quickly decided against it. Brinkman's there. Don't bug him anymore. You're a big girl. Fix the flat. You've done it before.

She retrieved the keys from the ignition and opened the trunk, her head swiveling in all directions, watching for any movement. She retrieved a small trouble light from next to the spare tire and quickly plugged it into the cigarette lighter.

Once she had jacked the front end up, it took all of her strength to loosen the lug nuts and get the tire off. And she still faced lifting it into the trunk and getting the spare out. Her hands were filthy, and despite the cool of the night, she could feel the sweat on her face and beneath her arms.

"Got a problem, lady?"

Jessica jumped. Where did he come from? She thought she'd been watching. Out of one of the doorways?

He was a giant of a man, wearing bib overalls and no shirt. The brass clasps on the overall straps shone like stars against his black skin.

"I'm afraid so," she said, trying to keep the fear from her voice. Would she feel the same if it were a white man? "Somebody's been fooling with my tire," she added, hoping it hadn't been him.

"Let me give you a hand." He picked up the tire with no more effort than it would take her to lift a shoe. Before he put the tire into the trunk, he held it close to his eyes, examining the knife. "Somebody don't like you," he said. "I don't think they was playing around."

His voice was soft and low, almost melodic. Jessica could picture him singing and swaying in some church choir.

"Did you see anyone?" she asked.

"Not me, lady. Don't pay to see too much around here."

He quickly exchanged the flat for the spare and in no more than a minute had the new tire securely tightened on the wheel and the jack back in the trunk. "That ought to get you on your way."

"May I pay you something?" she asked.

"Nice of you to offer, but no thanks. But if I was you, I'd watch myself. This ain't the best part of town."

She nodded and started to get into the Impala.

"Then again," he said, "not many folks around here carry knives like that. That's a honky knife. Maybe it's not the part of town you should be worrying about."

As he walked away, blending into the shadows, the door of Barney's swung open, and Freda Brinkman emerged. She stopped short when she saw Jessica.

"You're still here? I thought you left long ago."

"Had a little problem," Jessica replied. "But everything's fine now."

Brinkman moved toward her. "What kind of problem?"

"Somebody put a knife in my tire," Jessica said.

Brinkman said, "You should call a cop."

"I wouldn't want to do that. I'd hate to divert them from more important jobs, like solving murder cases. You can understand that."

She opened the car door and flipped the knife to Brinkman. "But since you're a cop and since you're here, why don't you hang on to that for evidence," she said.

Then she drove away.

Kim and Sarah had dinner downtown after work, then drove home together in Sarah's small Honda. They listened to the local news on the car radio but heard nothing further about the murder of Edward Hill.

"Why don't they say any more about it?" Kim asked as she switched off the radio.

"Because nobody cares," Sarah replied, "because he was a nobody himself."

"But he was murdered. . . ."

"Makes no difference, Kim. You know that. There are too many murders. If you're not very old or very young, or very pretty or very prominent, or if you're not killed in an especially dramatic way, you're old news before your body gets cold."

"Still, you'd think—"

Sarah pulled up at a red light and glanced at Kim, who was leaning back against the headrest, looking puzzled.

"Look," Sarah continued, "if somebody kills a baby . . . or a babysitter . . . or some old lady with lots of cats . . . or a banker or a politician . . . they'll be in the headlines and on television for days. But kill an Edward Hill and its forgotten in hours. Nobody gives a damn."

"I do," Kim said softly. "Right after the rape, I thought I could have killed him myself. But now . . . I don't know."

Sarah shook her head slowly as the traffic light turned green. "Really, Kim. He had more than his share of luck. Look what he did to you. And probably to a dozen other women. His luck just ran out, plain and simple."

"What happens now?" Kim asked.

"To the case? The cops will try to solve it, but they're not going to bust their butts. They know nobody cares. They'll make a show of it for a few days, but then somebody more newsworthy will get knocked off and they'll tuck the file away and forget it."

Their car pulled up in front of the apartment-building garage, and Sarah pushed her security card into the slot. The door opened with a metallic groan.

"Will you have a chance to look at the file?" Kim asked.

"Not if I can help it," Sarah said as she maneuvered the car through the bunkerlike garage and into its proper space. "I'm not interested in how he died, and you shouldn't be, either. He's history, and the sooner you forget about him, the better."

"I'd think you'd be a little more curious, knowing what he did to me," Kim said. "I'd certainly like to know how he died."

Sarah turned in the seat, resigned. "Okay, if I get the chance, I'll look at the file. I'll talk to the cops. But I don't know what it's going to prove. Do you really care whether he was shot or stabbed or beaten to death? What's the difference?"

"Why are you getting so angry?"

"I'm not angry," Sarah said, slowly getting out of the car. "I'm tired. Between Lowell Ingram and Edward Hill, it's been a long day. I need a cool shower and a couple of aspirin."

As Jessica drove home, still confused and unsettled by the knife in the tire and her encounters with Brinkman, she self-consciously kept an eye on the rearview mirror. But saw nothing. And as she approached her apartment building, she circled the block twice, studying each car parked along the street. All were empty. So were the sidewalks.

Relax, she told herself. You're being foolish. Still, after finding a parking place a few feet from the entrance, she again checked the street, then hurriedly locked the doors of the Impala and rushed into the building.

Two letters awaited her in the box just beyond the door. One was from her younger sister, Janie, who was working at a resort in northern Wisconsin, the other a bill from a credit-card company. And inside the apartment, she found the light blinking on her answering machine. She pressed the button and heard a whispered voice so soft Jessica could barely distinguish the words.

"Miss Mitchell . . . this is Gladys Hill. You stopped by my house earlier . . . and left your number." There was a long pause, and Jessica thought she might have been ready to hang up. Then the voice continued. "I'm sorry I was rude. You seemed like a nice girl, and I have no one to turn to. The police said I shouldn't talk to you, but I don't know what it could hurt now. Maybe you can call or stop by my house again."

Jessica walked to the kitchen and pulled a beer from the refrigerator, sipping it slowly while she considered the message. Why would Gladys Hill decide to talk to her now, even after the police warning? She must truly be lonely. And although Jessica felt some guilt about imposing on the lady's grief, using it to her own advantage, she knew she couldn't pass up the opportunity to speak with her. To learn more about her dead son.

She returned to the living room and picked up Janie's letter, the first she'd received from her sister since moving to the Twin Cities. It turned out to be ten days old, thanks to a forwarding delay, and contained a recital of Janie's adventures working at the resort, including the details of a new relationship with a young fishing guide there.

> His name's Charlie Bowser. You ought to see him, Jess. He's a hunk, and soooo nice. He's smart, too. But all he wants to do with his life right now is to go fishing.

Jessica laughed. She could just envision her sister spending her life in the north woods, cleaning fish. But at least Janie has someone she's interested in, she thought ruefully.

Aside from the brief fling with her roommate's brother in college, Jessica's life had been without a serious romance. She certainly had had her share of dates, but so far none of them had led anywhere. She knew many of her high school and college friends were engaged or married by now, some with babies, and she sometimes felt cheated, occasionally wondering if she would wind up alone in her later years, with only a career to cling to. She didn't really worry about it, but she couldn't always escape the doubts, either. Especially alone, late at night, like now.

NINE

Matt Meecham looked across his desk into the face of Freda Brinkman, who was sitting next to another Homicide detective, Bill Pierce, the one who had briefed Meecham on the riverbank the night of Hill's murder.

"So what have you got?" Meecham asked.

"You won't believe it," Pierce said.

"Try me," Meecham replied.

Pierce glanced uneasily at Brinkman, then continued. "A guy working Lock and Dam Three on the Mississippi noticed a big bottle floating downriver this morning. It had a big red bow on it."

"So?" Meecham asked impatiently.

"So he got curious and fished it out," Pierce said. "Then he threw up his guts."

"Threw up? What the hell are you talking about?"

"Hill's missing parts," Pierce said with a small gulp. "At least we think they were his."

It took a moment for it to register on Meecham. "You've got

to be kidding! You're telling me you found Hill's balls in a bottle? Floating in the river?"

"You got it," Brinkman said with a smirk. "Gross, huh?"

"And the bottle had a bow on it?" Meecham said.

"Like you'd wrap a Christmas present," Pierce said. "The M.E.'s trying to make a tissue match now. It's obvious the killer wanted it found, although it could have just as easily wound up down in New Orleans."

"Son of a bitch," Meecham muttered. "The press know about this?"

"Nope. The lock guy's sworn to secrecy. Nobody else knows."

"Let's keep it that way," Meecham said. "They'd make a circus out of it."

They sat quietly for a moment, considering the information and what it might mean.

"What else have we got?" Meecham finally asked.

"Not that much," Pierce replied. "No murder weapon, no suspects, and no real motive."

Meecham cut him off. "What do you mean, no motive? He raped a couple of women. That sure as hell seems like a possible motive to me, especially with what they did to him."

Pierce scoffed. "You really think one of his victims, some woman, stabbed the shit out of him, cut off his balls, and hauled him down that hill? You've got to be kidding. You were there."

"I've heard of stranger things," Meecham said. "Besides, it wouldn't have to be a woman. It could have been a husband or a boyfriend who's still pissed off by what he did."

"We'll sure as hell check it out," Pierce said doubtfully, "but I wouldn't count on it."

"What about the time of death?" Meecham asked.

Pierce checked his notebook. "A couple of hours before we found the body, before the worst of the rain. The M.E. still doesn't know if he died on the riverbank or was hauled there. Found some traces of oil in his hair, but that could have come from the river."

"Talk to the women he was accused of raping," Meecham

ordered. "See if it leads anywhere. I don't want to just walk away from this thing because Hill was an asshole."

"I'll talk to them," Brinkman quickly volunteered. "They'll probably be more comfortable talking to another woman."

While the meeting went on inside Meecham's office, Sarah Andrews sat outside, waiting to have a look at the Edward Hill file, as she had promised Kim. Ten minutes had already passed, and she was ready to leave when the office door opened. Bill Pierce was the first one out, followed by Freda Brinkman, who seemed startled to see her.

"Sarah! What brings you into the police-department trenches?"

"I need to check something with Matt," she replied, raising her eyebrows slightly.

"Anything I can help with?" Brinkman offered.

"No, thanks. I can talk with Matt."

Meecham was at his office door. "Ms. Andrews," he said with an exaggerated bow. "Come in, please. To what do I owe this honor?"

"Save it, Matt. I need to see what you've got on the Edward Hill murder."

"Really? We were just meeting about that. But we're hardly far enough along yet for the county attorney's office."

"I know, but I read about it in the paper, and I'm interested. Can I see the reports?"

"You must not have enough to do over there," Meecham said lightly as he handed her the Hill file. "There's not much in it," he admitted. "The guy was a creep, but even creeps don't deserve to die the way he did."

Sarah quickly scanned the reports as he told her about the discovery of the bottle in the river.

"You don't seem that shocked," he said. "It's not every day we get somebody deballed."

Sarah made a face. "What kind of priority are you putting on this?"

Meecham shrugged. "What we can afford, I guess. There's not exactly a public outcry over this particular murder."

"Keep me posted, will you?" Sarah said.

"If you say so, sure. But why?"

"I understand there's some history of sex offense here. I'd like to keep tabs on it."

She left Meecham staring after her.

Sarah was halfway through the tunnel linking city hall and the Government Center, returning to her office, when she heard hurried footsteps behind her. She paused as Freda Brinkman fell into step beside her.

"What was that all about?" Brinkman asked.

"I was checking on Hill's murder. Kim insisted on it. She wouldn't let it rest."

"That's what I thought," Brinkman replied. "Did Meecham tell you he's ordered us to interview Hill's rape victims?"

Sarah stopped in her tracks. "No," she said. "Why would he do that?"

"Thinks they could be suspects, I guess. It's silly, but I told him that I'd do it. I thought it would be easier that way. Talk to Kim, will you? I'd like to see her tomorrow morning, if that's okay. Get it over with."

Sarah resumed walking. "Kim's going to go crazy," she said, "but I don't know what harm it can do. She doesn't know anything."

"One other thing," Brinkman said, trailing behind her. "Some reporter's showing an unusual interest in Hill's murder."

"Who's that?"

"A woman, Jessica Mitchell, from Channel—"

Sarah turned, surprise on her face. "Really? I saw her at the rally and again in my office yesterday. Why would she care about Edward Hill?"

"Don't ask me, but she's always around. She's chasing after Meecham and even tried to talk to Hill's mother before we got to her."

Sarah thought again about the intense young woman who had sat across from her the day before. Wide-eyed and so naive. The small-town girl learning the facts of life in the big city.

"Is she getting in your way?" she asked.

"Not really. At least not yet. But she's persistent."

"Keep me informed, will you?" Sarah asked as she left Brinkman and got into the elevator to her office.

Gladys Hill was at the door at Jessica's first knock.

"I got your message," Jessica said. "Is this a good time?"

"Yes. Come in." She pushed the door open and stepped aside.

The interior was cool but stuffy. All of the drapes were drawn except for those covering the front windows. The pines kept the sun away from those.

"Perhaps I should have called first."

"No, no," Gladys said. "It's fine. I was just sitting here."

Jessica saw she was wearing the same black dress she had put on the day before. Today she also wore a strand of small white pearls and two tiny pearl earrings.

"Please come in," she said, leading Jessica into the house. "Maybe we should go into the kitchen. It's brighter there."

As she followed Gladys through the dining room, Jessica noticed a collection of bone-china cups in a corner hutch and, on the buffet, two pictures in identical gold frames. One showed an older man with wire-rimmed glasses and a thatch of gray hair. His half smile seemed forced, as though the photographer had demanded that he try to look happy. The picture vaguely reminded Jessica of her own grandfather.

The other photo was of a much younger man, thin-faced, with a slender nose and ribbon lips and eyes so penetrating they seemed to leap from the frame. That must be Edward, she thought. His hair was combed straight back and slicked down like an old-time matinee idol. Valentino? He would be handsome, Jessica decided, if his lips were fuller and his eyes gentler.

"He would have been thirty-seven next month," Gladys said, watching her from the kitchen doorway. "That picture was taken several years ago, before Herbert died. They went to the photo place together."

They walked into the kitchen, and Gladys took two cups from the cupboard. "Coffee or tea? I have both."

"Coffee, please."

The kitchen was bathed by the sun and cooled by a soft morning breeze through an open window. The enamel surfaces of the stove and the refrigerator gleamed in the light, but Jessica noticed they had started to wear thin in spots. So had the linoleum.

"Why did you agree to talk to me?" Jessica asked softly as she sipped her coffee.

Gladys hesitated. "I don't really know. I need to talk to someone, and the few friends I have seem too embarrassed. Even though you didn't know Edward and don't really know me, you still seem to care. I thought it might help me get through it."

"Tell me about Edward," Jessica urged. "What was he like?"

Gladys got up and stood by the window, staring out. "That's not easy to explain. When he was growing up, I thought he was like any other boy, although even then he acted like a loner. He played sports in high school but never seemed to make any friends. We went to most of his games, and he was always off by himself. Almost never had friends over and never went to parties or dances like the other kids."

"Did he ever talk about it?" Jessica asked.

"Not really," she said, returning to the table. "He'd go off to his room and shut the door. Herbert thought I was being foolish, that Edward was just taking longer to grow up than most. 'Quit fussing about the boy,' he'd say. 'Let him be. He'll come out of his shell when he's good and ready.' "

Jessica recalled Herbert's dour expression in the photo.

"I remember crying about it at night . . . after everyone else was asleep. Wondered what we'd done wrong, why Eddie wasn't like other kids. I used to blame myself, think I wasn't a very good mother, that I hadn't raised him right somehow."

Jessica hesitated before her next question. "Did you like your son, Mrs. Hill?"

"What? Of course," she blurted out, then paused and stared into her cup. "I loved my son, and I miss him. But now that you ask, I'm not sure I *liked* him, not for a long time. I don't know if I ever really *knew* him. We seldom talked, and he'd come and go like he was renting a room in a boarding-house."

"Was he ever in trouble with the law?" Jessica asked.

"Where did you hear that?"

"Was he, Mrs. Hill?"

"Is *that* what you're interested in? Was I wrong about you?"

Jessica leaned back in her chair, carefully choosing her words. "Mrs. Hill, I'm a reporter. You know that. I saw Edward's body when it was found. Like you, I'm trying to understand why he was killed. I have to ask some difficult questions."

Gladys studied her, debating. "They said Edward did some bad things, but I wouldn't believe it. He was a strange boy, but he wouldn't do the things they said."

"They?"

"The police. Edward was arrested twice and put in jail."

"For what, Mrs. Hill?"

She got up and walked back to the window, nervously fingering the pearls around her neck. "For attacking two women," she said finally. "For . . . assaulting them. But they never proved it. He was set free."

Jessica was taken aback. She had imagined everything but this. Now she understood what Matt Meecham was talking about in the bar. 'Weep for his old mother, maybe, but not for Eddie boy.'

"You're shocked, aren't you?" Gladys said.

"I'm surprised, yes," Jessica replied after a moment.

"I don't think Herbert ever got over the shame of it. Even

after Edward was released. We tried not to believe it, but then it happened again. Herbert was dead by then."

"Can you tell me more?" Jessica asked. "Who were the women? Why was Edward released?"

Gladys shook her head. "Not now, please. It's too painful. I've tried hard to put it all out of my mind."

Jessica got up from the table and put her cup into the sink. Then she turned back to Gladys. "Do you think his arrests could have had anything to do with his murder?"

"I don't see how," Gladys said. "It's been some time ago. I think Edward must have gotten mixed up with the wrong people, but I just don't know."

"May I come back again?" Jessica asked as she reached the front door.

"I'd like that," Gladys said. "Perhaps you'd come to the funeral tomorrow."

Jessica hesitated for a moment, then agreed, and walked out beneath the drooping pines.

As she pointed the old Impala toward the station, Jessica could not forget the image of Edward Hill's eyes staring at her from the picture. He may be dead, she thought, but those eyes seemed very alive. The eyes of a rapist. Another one.

She silently cursed her own inexperience. Most other reporters would know what to do next, she thought. Figure it out, Jess. You may be from Duluth, but you're not dumb.

She knew she still had to talk to Meecham and to somehow get access to Edward Hill's court records. Why had the rape charges been dropped? she wondered. Was Gladys Hill right? Had the cops made a mistake? Do they make mistakes like that twice?

There were more questions than answers.

TEN

The next day, Jessica attended the funeral for Edward Hill. She was almost alone. Her Impala was the last of only five cars in the procession to the cemetery, following the hearse, another mortuary limousine, and two other cars, each carrying elderly friends of Gladys Hill. Seven mourners in all, including Jessica. Not a great sendoff for Edward, she thought as she parked behind the others at the cemetery and started to walk toward the open grave.

The service at McPhearson's Mortuary a half hour before had been short and simple. Edward's casket had remained closed, and Gladys had sat stoically in the front row of the chapel as the minister recited words from the prayer book. An older woman had been next to Gladys, but her attempts at providing comfort had gone unheeded.

Three men Jessica assumed to be mortuary employees had joined the only three male mourners, including one with a cane, to serve as pallbearers. An unseen organist had played "Nearer My God to Thee" as the casket rolled down the aisle and past Jessica, who was sitting in the last row.

Looking back, it seemed surreal to her: a funeral with few mourners and no visible grief. She had not seen a single tear, even from Gladys. It was as though a body unknown to anyone had been found on the street and that simple decency required strangers to be recruited to sit through the ritual.

That changed at the graveside. Gladys finally began to weep quietly when the minister threw a handful of dirt on the lowered casket and said a final prayer for Edward's salvation.

At the mortuary, and again now, Jessica noticed a small book clutched in Gladys Hill's hand. At first, from a distance, she had thought it was a Bible. Now, standing across the grave from her, she had her doubts. Its exterior was of vinyl, and it was held closed by a gold clasp.

The grave site was shaded by a giant oak which must have taken root decades before the first grave was dug. A few feet away, almost covered by the grave's excavated soil, was the headstone of Herbert Hill. The epitaph said simply: "Husband and Father."

One by one after the service the mourners walked up to Gladys, whispered their condolences, and then moved off toward their cars. Jessica was the last.

"I'm glad you came," Gladys said as she took her hand and moved a few feet away. "I'll be here," pointing down, "right next to Herbert. We bought these three spots years ago."

"You'll be all right?" Jessica asked.

"I'll go on. I don't have much choice, do I?"

They walked slowly toward the mortuary's big black car, which would take Gladys home. A flock of grackles squawked from high in the trees, and as Jessica looked for them, she saw the long white contrail of a jet between the branches.

"I want you to have this," Gladys said, holding out the vinyl book with the gold clasp.

"What is it?" Jessica asked.

"Edward's diary. I found it behind some books in his room. The police must have missed it."

"You should give it to them," Jessica said, backing away.

"If you choose, you can give it to them."

"Have you read it?" Jessica asked.

"I'm afraid to. It may tell me things about Edward that I'd rather not know. Not now."

"Why not throw it away?"

"You said you were interested in finding out the truth about Edward. This may help."

The diary was still extended in her hand. Jessica hesitated.

"Mrs. Hill, I don't think this is right. I'm sure the police would want this. They're responsible for finding Edward's killer."

"Then give it to them, if you must," Gladys said, placing the book in her hand. "But you may want to read it first."

Gladys turned and slid into the backseat of the mortuary car. "Come see me when you can, Jessica. I've always wanted a daughter to talk to."

Then she shut the door, and the big black car pulled away.

Jessica held the diary with both hands. She unsnapped the clasp but did not open the cover. In a way, she wished the clasp had been locked. Damn, she thought, what do I do now?

She finally fanned the pages, too quickly to read but slowly enough to get a glimpse of the contents. There seemed to be writing on about half of the pages, in red ink.

As she walked to her car, Jessica glanced toward the grave they had just left. She stopped short when she saw someone standing there. A younger woman, but not one of those who had attended the service. Slim, with a skirt that blew in the warm July gusts.

She put the diary into the Impala and locked the doors. Then she walked slowly back toward the grave. The woman did not hear her approach and seemed startled when Jessica stepped into view.

"Sorry," Jessica said. "I didn't mean to frighten you."

The woman said nothing and simply stared into the hole.

"Were you a friend of Edward's?" she asked casually.

The woman's eyes moved from the grave to Jessica but didn't seem to focus. "Hardly," she said. "I was just curious."

There was something vaguely familiar about her, Jessica thought, but she could not place her. Plain but not unattractive, maybe a little older than she was, with sharply cut bangs across her forehead and a dark beauty mark just to the left of her lips.

"I didn't see you at the service," Jessica said.

"Excuse me," the woman said, and abruptly walked away, her steps taking her in the opposite direction of Jessica's car.

Jessica watched until she disappeared amid the tombstones.

It took Jessica about a half hour to drive from the cemetery to the station, stopping once en route to gas up the Impala. The old car now needed oil almost as often as it needed gas, and Jessica was beginning to feel embarrassed by the smoky trail she left in her wake.

"This baby needs some work," the young attendant told her as he poured the second quart of oil into the crankcase.

"Tell me about it," she replied. "But it's going to have to wait, unless you work for free."

"She'll freeze up on you someday," he warned.

"She wouldn't dare, not after what we've been through together. She knows the next stop is the junkyard."

The attendant laughed and walked away with her credit card. As she waited for his return, Jessica picked up the diary from the seat beside her. She again flipped through the pages, noticing now how tightly together the writing was spaced. No margin on any page was left unfilled, the words and sentences flowing together like an unbroken river of red ink. The penmanship was precise, but the characters were so tiny, she had trouble believing they had been written by a man's hand.

She fanned the pages until she reached the final entry. It was dated July 7, the day they found the body by the river.

"Just sign here, please." The attendant was back.

Jessica put the diary aside, relieved she had been interrupted before she was tempted to decipher the words. She needed to think more about that first.

She signed the credit slip and started the car, watching for the burp of blue smoke in the rearview mirror. She wasn't disappointed.

"About the car," the attendant said. "I can't fix it for free, but I do work cheap for preferred customers." Then he winked.

"I'll be back when I can afford to pay the full price," she said, giving him an exaggerated return wink before gunning the Impala and leaving him in a dark cloud.

"You did what?" Sarah asked.

"I went to his grave," Kim replied. "After the burial, after I thought everyone had left."

Kim was back in her office. She had taken an early lunch to go to the cemetery, then called Sarah as soon as she returned.

"Kim, what's wrong with you? Why would you do that?"

"I can't explain it, Sarah. To make sure he was dead, maybe. To see who would be there. I don't know. I knew I had to go, that's all, to see for myself."

"Did anyone see you?"

Kim paused. Sarah could hear only her slow breathing. "Kim?"

"I thought everyone had gone. I didn't see her until she was standing next to me at the grave."

"Her?"

"That reporter. Jessica. The one who's been interviewing you."

Sarah took a sharp breath. "What was she doing there?"

"She was at the service, but I thought she'd left with everyone else."

"Did she recognize you? She saw us together at the rally."

"I don't think so. She asked some questions, but I walked away."

Sarah wanted a moment to think, but Kim pressed ahead. "What's the difference, anyway? Why should I care who saw me? I have nothing to hide. I didn't kill him or know who did, for God's sake."

"The police don't know that," Sarah said.

"What?"

"They're going to interview you, Kim. You and the other

woman Hill raped. Freda Brinkman told me that she's been ordered to talk to you as part of the murder investigation. She's going to be at the apartment tomorrow morning."

"Tomorrow? You've got to be kidding."

"Kim, for your own good, forget about Edward Hill. Trust me on this. Put it behind you. There will only be trouble if you keep pursuing it."

"The police actually think I had something to do—"

Sarah interrupted. "They don't think anything yet, Kim. It's just part of their routine. But if they get the idea you're obsessed by his death, they might start wondering."

After she hung up the phone, Sarah thought again about Jessica Mitchell. She seemed to be everywhere. What was she up to? Why her interest in Edward Hill? It was strange.

When Jessica walked into the newsroom, still clutching the diary, she immediately headed for the assignment desk. She needed advice. Laurie Sanders was cradling a phone beneath her ear while talking to one of the news cars over the two-way radio.

Jessica saw that two other reporters were already lined up, waiting to buttonhole Laurie once she had resolved the immediate crisis. So she changed her mind and walked to her own desk.

Think it through yourself, Jess. You've got the diary, so you've got the decision.

She had faced few ethical choices in her brief career. Most of her reporting in Duluth had been routine: cover what's happening in front of your nose. There had been no investigative reporting and virtually no coverage of controversial issues that required moral judgments or ethical decisions.

It was different now, at a place like this. She had to be careful. One major mistake and she could be back in Duluth, or worse. There were plenty of other young reporters out there just waiting to take her place.

Think! The diary clearly could be evidence in a murder, and certainly the police would never let you read it if they'd found it. But they didn't. They missed it. You didn't steal it, you didn't even ask for it.

Jessica knew she would have to turn the diary over to Meecham eventually. The question was, Before or after she had read it? What'll I tell Meecham when he asks if I've read it? That it's none of his business. You don't work for the cops. You've got your job to do, they've got theirs. Sure. Piece of cake.

She thought again about Meecham, how friendly and kind he had been to her so far. Would she be jeopardizing their friendship? Breaking his chain of evidence? Tainting it? She didn't know the answers, but she did know what other reporters in the newsroom would do. They would read the damned thing and worry about the ethics later.

Jessica opened the diary to the first page.

ELEVEN

Jessica had to squint, eyes straining, as she held the diary inches from her face. The red writing was that tiny. The first entry was written more than two years before, but she immediately skipped ahead to the last page, which she knew was dated the day of Edward's death. The passage was only four lines long:

> Life has become unbearable. Mother hovers over me, the house closes in on me. Still no money, no job, no future. The past will not release its grip. The same person has called again, taunting me, challenging me. It's time to settle up, one way or another.

The rest of the page was blank. What the hell? They probably were the last words Edward Hill had ever written but were hardly the stuff murder is made of. "It's time to settle up, one way or another?" C'mon, Eddie. "The same person has called again, taunting me, challenging me." Who, Eddie?

Jessica returned to the first page. Two hours later she was

still reading, lost in the spooky world of Edward Hill, oblivious to the constant hubbub of the newsroom. She had been interrupted once to help write copy for the early news, but otherwise had been left alone with the diary.

She managed to read about half of it, discovering a collection of random, often irrational and meandering thoughts that began abruptly and seemed to lead nowhere. Some of the writing was indecipherable; many of the thoughts so obscure, almost ethereal, that they defied understanding. What she could comprehend was an angry harangue, spiteful attacks on his parents, on people whose names Jessica didn't know, on the police ("the Gestapo creeps") and assorted segments of society which he had grown to despise.

Edward Hill, she decided, was a very confused, disturbed, and unhappy young man.

He seemed especially bitter toward his mother, punctuating the diary with hateful references to her, written with unusual clarity:

She was just pounding on my door again, demanding to know if I was up and dressed and ready to look for work. Bitch! Can't she leave me alone? Always whining, always pushing. 'Eddie, what's wrong with you? Eddie, show some gumption. Eddie, when am I going to meet one of your girlfriends?' That same kind of shit drove Dad to his death, for Christ's sake. I hate her. I've always hated her. I'm suffocated by her.

Jessica thought again of Gladys Hill, the kind lady in the black dress. "I used to blame myself, think I wasn't a very good mother, that I hadn't raised him right somehow." Jessica was relieved now that Gladys had chosen not to read her son's diary. What little peace remained to her surely would have vanished.

The entries in the diary were made haphazardly. Sometimes weeks, even months, would pass between narratives. There was no thread, no linkage, between them, no references to past entries or experiences. Each entry was a separate, bizarre chapter in the life of a man teetering on the edge of madness.

Jessica guessed that Edward would write only when he felt compelled, when he had stored up enough anger and frustration that he could no longer hold it within. Then he would lash out in his red scrawl, befouling whatever target happened to be within his immediate sights.

Nothing seemed to be spared: religion, especially the Jews and Catholics, education (he'd quit the university after one year), the business establishment, unions, and politicians of whatever stripe.

So far she had found no references to Eddie's arrests or the time he had spent in jail. She could only speculate that the blank weeks in the diary included those periods, but she had no way of knowing for sure. Perhaps there'd be more in the unread pages.

Strangely, there were only sporadic and fleeting mentions of women and then never by name, only by initials. Most of the encounters seemed to end in rejection, although Edward never actually admitted that. He simply said nothing further about them.

Near the middle of the diary, dated the previous April, he did write at length about a woman he identified only as K.H. The tone was gentle, almost loving, and Jessica found the passage fascinating:

> I can see her walking up the street now, coming from the bus stop, wearing those funny-looking tennis shoes. I love to watch her walk, the way she bounces, the way her skirt swirls around her hips. She's always smiling, and tonight she's licking an ice cream cone, trying to keep it from dripping on her chin while trying to get the door unlocked. I should help her, but there's no time. And what would I say? What have I ever been able to say to a woman?
>
> She may not know I exist, but I know everything about her: where she works, where she eats, who her

friends are, what time she gets up, when she goes to bed. My time will come.

Jessica sat back in her chair and rubbed her eyes. The early news was only minutes away, and she didn't want to miss it. The rest of the diary would have to wait until later. Try as she might, she couldn't discount her disappointment. It was as though she had been inside Hill's head, rummaging around, sorting through the odds and ends of his thoughts, but was walking away empty-handed.

Clearly, he was a troubled, disagreeable person. The diary pages left little doubt that he was capable of committing the crimes he'd been accused of, but there was no admission, no clear evidence in what she'd read thus far.

Nor had she discovered anything that could help explain his death. Or point to his killer.

"C'mon, Jess, loosen up," Bill Kendrick shouted. "It's Friday night. Time to relax."

Jessica could barely hear Kendrick's words above the jukebox wailings of Billy Idol that ricocheted around the bar. She nodded and smiled in response, trying even harder to look relaxed.

Five of them were gathered around the small table in the middle of Gino's, a ramshackle bar a few blocks from the station. Gino's was housed in one of the few old buildings which so far had escaped displacement by new office towers that were transforming downtown.

But Gino knew his bar days were numbered—that sooner or later the wrecking ball would come crashing down—so he had done little to improve the place over the years, allowing the ceiling to sag and the floor to warp, the paint to blister and peel.

Still, Jessica had to admit, the place had a cozy, down-home charm about it, like a decaying back-country tavern. No potted plants or ferns here. Just a long bar, a few scattered tables, two pool tables, a small dance floor, and dart boards on either side of the door to the ladies' room. She had been warned to be damned careful going to the john.

Jessica had been to Gino's only once before but knew it was a favorite hangout for newspeople from all of the television stations. Especially for the grunts working the late shift who had formed a unique bond spanning station loyalty and the fierce competitive demands of the day. They gathered almost every night after the late news to drink beer, play pool, trade gossip, and bitch loudly about the business they all loved to hate.

She had nursed a Miller Lite for the past half hour, watching the traffic pass through the bar, aware that she was being leeringly studied in return. Two young guys from one of the competing stations had asked her to dance, but she had declined, blaming a slightly sprained ankle. The truth was she thought of herself as a clumsy dancer and didn't want to look foolish in front of this crowd.

She knew no one in the bar except for those at the table. Besides Kendrick, there was Jeff Hilliard, the transplanted Texas reporter, Nina French, a research assistant who doubled as newsroom librarian, and Rich Forcell, a director who orchestrated the camera cues and tape rolls on the late news.

Like Jessica, Nina French was young and relatively new at the station. A recent journalism graduate from the University of Minnesota, she hoped to break into reporting by first putting in time as a researcher. Part of her job was to maintain a computer file on every story that appeared on every newscast and to label, number, and store all of the videotape segments that had been aired.

When the barroom music ended momentarily, Jessica turned to her. "Let me ask you something," she said. "About business."

"Sure," Nina replied.

"No business now," Kendrick interrupted from across the table. "It's Friday night."

"Buzz off, Bill," Jessica said lightly, turning her back to

him, facing Nina. "Tell me how you and the computer keep tabs on all the murders that happen around here?"

"What do you mean?" Nina asked.

"How's the information filed? How does the system work?"

"It's pretty amazing," she said. "The software does all of the work."

Jessica watched her expectantly.

"We feed the basic facts into the computer: name of victim, name of suspect, if there is one, where it happened, and also by the type of murder. The computer cross-files everything and automatically updates the file if there's an arrest or some new development like a trial date or a verdict in the case."

"So, say a guy kills his wife or girlfriend in a fit of passion," Jessica said. "What will the computer tell me?"

"You punch up 'Murders, Domestic,' and the computer will list that murder and all others like it, chronologically, in the metropolitan area, with names, dates, and disposition of the case, if there is any."

"Is the file complete?" Jessica asked.

"Goes back five years, but I wouldn't swear we have every killing. Just the ones we've done some kind of story on or that have appeared in the newspapers. It's no police file, believe me, but it's a pretty good reference for us."

At that moment, the jukebox reignited. Madonna this time.

Jessica leaned over to Nina, shouting. "I don't want to be a pain, but can we talk more in the restroom, where it's quieter?"

Nina looked at her quizzically but got up.

"Watch your behinds," Hilliard warned as they walked past the dart boards.

"Why your sudden interest in the computer?" Nina asked once they were inside the restroom.

Jessica checked the toilet stalls to make sure they were vacant. "It may sound silly, Nina, but I'm trying to follow up on a murder that no one else seems to care about. I'm not sure where to go next and thought your computer might be a place to start."

Nina stood in front of the mirror, carefully watching Jessica's reflection while idly running a comb through her hair. She was a few inches taller than Jessica, with dark skin and eyes and jet-black hair tied in a tight ponytail. Jessica thought she might be part Indian.

"That depends on what you're looking for," Nina said.

Thinking of Edward Hill, Jessica said, "I'm looking for unsolved murders of males, maybe young ones, maybe with criminal records, like for rape or other assaults against women. I'm not really sure. It's a long shot."

As Nina started to reply, the door opened, and two other women walked in, laughing, weaving, each balancing a glass of beer.

"Man, do I have to go," one said to the other, then giggled.

"I spend more time in here than I do in the bar," the other shot back. Each entered an empty stall, still laughing, ignoring Jessica and Nina.

"What's this all about, Jessica?" Nina whispered. "I mean, do you know what you're doing?"

There was no mistaking the misgiving in her voice, but Jessica shook it off. "Of course," she said with all the confidence she could muster. "Will you help me?"

"Do you work tomorrow?" Nina asked.

"I'm not scheduled," Jessica said, "but I could come in."

"Why don't you. Saturdays are slow, and I should have time to sit down at the computer with you."

"Good."

"I don't know what we'll find," Nina said. "The computer's not programmed to do what you want it to do, but we'll give it a shot."

As they returned to the table, Jeff Hilliard motioned to Jessica. She walked to his chair and knelt beside him. He cupped his hand around her ear. "See that guy at the end of the bar," he said, "the one who's going bald?"

Jessica glanced at the bar, her eyes quickly traveling the length of it. The man was standing with one foot on the floor, the other on the foot rail, leaning back on his elbows and watching the women pass by. He was wearing a blue-and-white flowered Hawaiian shirt and baggy shorts, with blue stockings covering his calves.

"Looks like a creep," she said.

"Recognize him?"

She shook her head.

"That's Lowell Ingram, I'm positive."

"The fondler?" she blurted out.

"Right. The teacher who copped a plea and pissed off Sarah Andrews."

Jessica wasn't sure she'd ever seen the man, although he must have appeared on the news. "You sure?" she asked.

"I'd lay ten bucks on it."

"What's he doing here? I thought this was a news hangout?"

Hilliard shrugged and took a swig of beer, his attention diverted by a shout from across the table. Jessica continued to study Ingram, remembering Sarah Andrews's anger and the scene of her ducking away from the microphones.

As she was about to look away, Ingram turned quickly toward her. His eyes locked on hers. Jesus, Jessica thought, he felt my stare from across the bar. She ducked her head and returned to her seat, forcing herself to concentrate on the dart game and on Hilliard's story of his latest run-in with Laurie Sanders.

Why worry about it? she asked herself. He must expect to be recognized in a place like this. He doesn't know me, and I don't know him. Besides, he's a jerk. But how did he know I was looking at him? ESP? Eerie.

A few minutes later, the waitress arrived with a beer for Jessica. "What's this? I didn't order another beer."

"Compliments of a guy at the bar," the waitress replied.

Jessica knew before she asked. "Which one?"

"The guy with the flowered shirt and the shorts."

Jessica turned in her chair. Ingram had his back to her, talking to one of the young guys who had earlier asked her to dance. So much for him not knowing who I am, she thought.

"Know him?" the waitress asked.

Jessica shook her head. "Not personally."

"Didn't think so," the waitress said. "He looks like a geek to me."

"And I really don't want the beer."

"Somebody at your table will," she said, and walked away.

When Jessica left the bar with Kendrick a half hour later, she could feel Ingram's eyes follow her to the door.

TWELVE

Kim was awake by six in the morning, feeling no less fatigued than when she'd first climbed into bed hours before. The darkness had brought some sleep but little rest. The bedroom was cool, but her thin nightgown was sticky with sweat, and her hair clung to her head like a damp, disheveled crown. The nightmares had come again, only more grotesque, more terrifying than ever. They'd begun the same, the smothering weight of his body, the raw sandpaper of his beard against her breasts, the steel against her neck, the screams locked in her throat.

But suddenly looming over them in the dream was a huge lady sitting astride the biggest horse Kim had ever seen. She could feel the flecks of foamy lather from his flanks and could *smell* his horse sweat, could hear him snort as he reared over the bed, hooves high above her. It was horrifying. The horse seemed frozen in space, like a living, quivering statue.

Kim remembered little of the woman rider except that she wore the clothes of a man and carried a long lance whose tip glistened as menacingly as the knife at her throat. She had no face, no features, just a round outline in the darkness, with two circles of light where the eyes should have been.

Before the nightmare ended, she heard the woman's laugh, sharp as the cry of a circling crow, and the man's scream, as piercing as her own had been. And she saw blood on the tip of the lance.

Kim rolled over on the bed, burying her head in the pillow, trying to remember more of the dream. To understand it. What did it mean? Who was the woman on the horse? She could still hear the shrieking laugh, could still see the two circles of light. What about the lance? The blood?

Kim had no ready answers. Except that Edward Hill was now dead and that the scream must have been his. She thought of waking Sarah but quickly decided no, let her sleep. Let someone sleep, for God's sake.

Head aching, she got out of bed and walked quietly to the bathroom for an aspirin. She knew a return to the bedroom would only revive memories of the nightmare, so she tiptoed past Sarah's room to the kitchen and quietly prepared a pot of coffee. Decaf. Sarah insisted on it.

Kim sat at the kitchen counter, feeling the warmth of the morning sun penetrate the closed kitchen windows. She moved her stool slightly to avoid the glare, wanting to open a window to the fresh air but knowing it was simply too hot. The heat wave was unrelenting, one of the worst on record, and not even the early-morning hours would bring relief.

There were no signs of life on the streets outside. Inside, only the gurgle of the coffeepot and the low hum of the air conditioner broke the silence. Kim knew even the morning paper would be late; the delivery boy always slept in on Saturdays and got up only when he felt like it.

As she sat in the stillness, she could not escape her dread of the pending visit by Freda Brinkman. But why? After all, she knew nothing about Edward Hill's murder and had nothing to fear from the police. Still, she couldn't shake her sense of foreboding.

"My, we're up early, aren't we?"

Kim was startled by the voice behind her. "Jeez, Sarah," she said, looking back, "you scared the hell out of me."

"Sorry. I thought you'd heard me get up."

She was standing by the refrigerator, covering a yawn. Her hair was in disarray, and her eyes were still filled with sleep.

"Coffee done?" she asked, rubbing her eyes.

"Should be," Kim replied.

Sarah found two cups and poured the coffee. "More nightmares?" she asked. "I could hear you moaning from across the hall."

Kim nodded, momentarily resisting the temptation to describe the dream. Instead, she sipped the coffee, savoring the steaming bitterness of it, smiling as Sarah predictably grimaced at the taste.

"What'd you put into this? An old tire?"

It was the same each morning: Kim made the coffee, and Sarah complained about it. She refused to make it herself but delighted in finding new ways to insult it.

But today Kim had no time for morning rituals. "Sarah," she said suddenly, "you never did tell me how Edward Hill was killed."

The statement caught Sarah by surprise. "Is that what the nightmare was about? The murder?"

Kim said nothing, waiting for an answer.

Sarah got up and walked to the window; the streets were still deserted. "I don't know what difference it makes," she finally said, "but I did talk to the cops. Hill was stabbed to death and left on the beach."

Kim saw the glistening lance, the blood on its tip. "I knew it," she whispered.

"Knew what?"

"That he'd been stabbed."

"How?"

"From the dream." She described what she had seen in as much detail as she could recall. "I heard the woman laugh, Sarah, and I heard him scream. It was terrible."

"That's ridiculous. It was a nightmare."

Kim refused to be deterred. "It was too real."

"You mentioned a woman," Sarah said. "What'd she look like?"

"She had no face. Just two beams of light for eyes."

"Then how did you know it was a woman? You said she was dressed like a man."

Kim considered the question. "I don't really know. Maybe the way she sat on the horse. Or the sound of her laugh. I honestly don't know. She just was, that's all."

Sarah shook her head. "I don't know, Kim. It's too weird to even talk about. I'll be glad when this interview with Freda Brinkman is over so you can put an end to this. It's starting to get to me."

Across town, Jessica had left her apartment by nine, immediately rolling down every window of the Impala, pretending she had somehow magically transformed the old heap into a convertible. The wind which swirled around her as she drove toward the station made the air seem cooler. She knew the relief was probably imaginary, but that was all right, too.

She wore a pair of shorts, tennis shoes, and a loose cotton blouse that billowed around her shoulders in the breeze. Not exactly work clothes, but what the hell? It was her day off, and she knew the people who worked weekends in the newsroom were casual about their attire. Besides, she couldn't stand the idea of another day in sweaty panty hose.

Jessica had planned to drive to Madelia to see her parents for the weekend and was relieved when she found an excuse not to go. The prospect of a long trip in the heat, and of the suffocating parental attention when she got there, was more than she wanted to face right now.

She found a parking place just outside the station and wasted no time locating Nina French in a small area off the newsroom, surrounded by piles of video cassettes waiting to be labeled and filed. The computer was tucked away in a corner.

"Sure you have time for this?" Jessica asked.

"No problem. I'll get you started on the system."

The computer was similar to the one at Jessica's desk, but she had never used it before to search the archives. Nina showed her the access code and punched up the library menu. There was page after page of listings, ranging from "aerospace" to "zoos."

"How do you keep up with it all?" Jessica asked.

"I don't; the software does. We just let it know which stories we want to save, and it does the sorting and filing by key words and phrases. The work really came in setting up the system, but that happened before I got here."

Nina quickly brought the "Murder" file to the screen and scanned the subfiles: "Murder, Domestic," "Murder, Drugs," "Murder, Gangs," "Murder, Police," and on and on.

"As you can see," she said, "it's a big file."

Jessica studied the list, pondering where to begin.

Nina noticed her chagrin. "You said this murder is connected with rape or assault?"

"The victim was an accused rapist," Jessica said, glancing around to make sure they were alone. "But no one seems to know if that had anything to do with his death."

"What do you think?" Nina asked.

"I don't know."

"Why do you think there may be others?"

"I don't. I know nothing except that he was stabbed and castrated. It was such a horrid crime and doesn't seem to make much sense by itself. I'm just curious if there might be any similar cases, maybe some kind of bizarre serial killer on the loose."

Nina scoffed. "What do the police say?"

"They seem to know less than I do. They've got a lot of murders to cover."

"Start under the 'Domestic' file," Nina said. "See what you find. I'll come back when I get this tape filing done."

"Thanks," Jessica said. "Laurie's not that excited by the story, and I wouldn't want her to think I'm taking your time, too."

"Don't worry, I won't say anything. I think I see what you're trying to do, and I'd like to help."

When Kim opened the apartment door to Freda Brinkman, she expected to find a woman in a uniform. She was disappointed.

Brinkman wore light linen slacks and a poplin blouse open at the neck. Both were off-white, joined loosely at the waist by a dark brown sash belt. Sunglasses were propped atop her head, half-hidden by her hair, and she carried a reddish leather briefcase.

She was hardly Kim's image of a policewoman.

"Hope I'm not early." She held out her hand and smiled, but her eyes did not remain on Kim. They looked past her, quickly surveying the apartment, darting from corner to corner. Suspicious eyes, Kim thought. Cop's eyes.

Kim shook her hand and stepped back. "No problem, you're right on time."

"I'm amazed we haven't met before," Brinkman said as she followed Kim into the apartment. "Sarah and I seem to see quite a bit of each other, and I know how close the two of you are."

"Your jobs bring you together," Kim offered. "I'm just a clerk in a brokerage house and don't really mix in that part of Sarah's life."

"Oh," Brinkman said, looking around again. "I thought Sarah was going to be here."

"She'll be back in a minute. She got tired of waiting for the paper and went to pick one up at the store."

Kim led the way into the kitchen and offered Brinkman coffee.

"No, thanks, but I'll take a Coke if you've got one."

Kim never could understand people who drank pop in the morning, but she retrieved a Coke from the refrigerator and then poured herself another cup of coffee. Kim guessed that Brinkman was a few years older than herself and was surprised by her size. Tall and sleekly muscular, like she does weights, Kim thought. Not pretty but certainly striking. Statuesque. She would stand out in any crowd.

They were walking back into the living room when Sarah came through the front door, carrying the paper and a small bag of groceries. "You made it, I see," she said to Brinkman as she walked past them to the kitchen. "I'll be with you in a second."

Once they were together, the lieutenant took a small tape recorder from her briefcase. "Kim, I don't want to cause you any more pain, but I've got to ask you some questions about Edward Hill. Do you mind if I tape the conversation?"

Kim looked at Sarah, then shook her head. "No, that's okay."

"I've read the case record, but I wonder if you could tell me again what happened on that night, in your own words."

"Do we have to go over it again?" Kim protested. "What good will it do now? I've told the story to the police a dozen times."

"I haven't heard it," Brinkman replied. "Not from you."

Kim looked at Sarah again, this time with pleading eyes.

"Go ahead," Sarah urged. "Maybe it will help Freda in some way."

Brinkman turned on the tape recorder.

"I've tried so hard to forget it," Kim said, her voice almost a whisper, "but nothing seems to help. Not the therapy . . . not the group sessions. Nothing. People are wrong, you know, when they say time heals everything. They just don't understand. Every day there's something in the newspaper or on television to remind me of it. And now this murder. Why can't I just be left alone?"

Brinkman said nothing, but glanced uncomfortably at Sarah.

Kim closed her eyes and leaned back on the couch, resigned. "There was nothing special about that night. Except that I'd worked late. I was exhausted when I finally got home, I remember that. I made a quick dinner, took a shower, and was in bed by ten. Didn't even watch the news."

Kim opened her eyes but seemed unaware of the two women sitting across from her. "I lived on the ground floor of a duplex near Lake Nokomis. There was a small deck and a patio door just a few feet above the ground. Always worried about that, you know, living alone and all. But I was real careful about keeping the doors and windows locked. Even had a broom handle that I'd wedge inside the patio door to make sure no one could force it open."

A small shudder passed through her body. "Well, that night I forgot it. The broom handle, I mean. I've thought about it a thousand times since. A million times. If I'd just remembered to put the broom in the door! But I didn't. Maybe I was too tired, I don't know."

"He got in through the door?" Brinkman asked.

Kim was startled by the interruption. "He cut out a piece of glass by the handle, then reached inside and unlocked the door. Just like that. A hole just big enough for his hand. The glass was sitting neatly on a table next to the door, as if he didn't want to leave a mess."

"You didn't hear anything?"

"Nothing. I slept hard in those days. The first thing I knew he was on top of me, tearing at my nightgown. I was half asleep, you know. I didn't know what was happening. At first . . . I guess . . . I didn't believe it. Like one of those horrible nightmares you wake up from, sweating, and discover it was only a nightmare. But this was real."

Sarah left for the kitchen. She always found a reason to leave when Kim got to this part of the story.

"Go on," Brinkman said.

"Do I have to?"

"Please."

"It's hard now to know what was real and what I've imagined since. It's all mixed up in my mind. It was spring and already warm, and I had only a sheet covering me. By the time I knew what was happening, the sheet was off me, and my nightgown was up around my hips. He was straddling me, one hand over my mouth, the other holding a knife—one of those curved hunting knives—at my throat. I can still feel the tip of it sticking into my skin.

"And he kept calling me by name. 'Kim, be still,' he said. 'Kim, don't move, don't make me hurt you. Kim, open your legs.' "

"He knew you?"

"He must have, although when I finally saw him in court, I knew I'd never seen him before. He must have been following me."

"How did you see the knife?" Brinkman asked.

"I always left the bathroom light on; it made me feel more secure somehow. I guess enough light must have spilled into the bedroom for me to see the shape of the knife."

"But you couldn't see him?"

"Not his face. He kept his head down . . . kept rubbing his cheeks on my breasts while he tried to spread my legs and get inside me. His one hand was big and strong enough to hold both of my wrists together. I couldn't do anything. I was so scared my whole body felt weak. I tried to remember what I'd heard you should do: If there's no escape, don't struggle, don't get killed. Comply. Live. But I kept struggling. Until he cut me."

Kim turned her head toward Brinkman, displaying the two-inch scar at the side of her neck. It had reddened with her telling of the story. In fact, her whole face and neck were flushed, her breathing more labored.

"When I felt the knife cut, I went limp. He was inside me by then, and I felt him come. It was like he had stabbed my whole being. I knew I was going to die . . . and, for a second, I didn't care, I didn't want to live. Can you believe that? I thought dying can't be worse than this."

She shuddered again, eyes closed. "But when he saw the blood on my neck, he actually sobbed. 'God, I'm sorry, Kim,' he said. It was more of a croak, really. He was crying."

She got up and walked to the window. Only the muted cries of a child from the sidewalk outside broke the silence. Her back was to Brinkman, who leaned forward, straining to hear her.

"I saw the blood on the pillow, a trickle of it only a few inches from my eyes. Bright red, soaking in. Know what I thought? The pillow's ruined." She turned from the window. "Can you imagine? Lying in my own blood and worrying about the pillow. It was all so . . . I don't know . . . unreal."

"You must have been in shock," Brinkman offered.

"Maybe so, I don't know."

"Is that when you saw the tattoo?" Brinkman asked.

"How'd you know about that?"

"It was in the report, Kim."

"Was all of this in the report?"

"Some, but not all of it."

Sarah returned from the kitchen, coffee in one hand, a cookie the size of a small saucer in the other. She was nibbling at the edges of it as she sat down.

"The tattoo was on the inside of his arm," Kim said. "I saw it when he pulled the knife away. A snake or serpent, curled up as if it was ready to strike. I'd seen pictures like it before."

"Then what happened?"

"He made me roll over on my stomach, and he put something cold on my back. It was a chain, a couple of feet long. He told me that if he heard the chain rattle, he'd come back and get me. He said to just lie still and don't call the police. Then he was gone."

The room was quiet. Both women watched Kim, but she avoided their eyes, staring at the window, wanting to flee, to go comfort the wailing child on the sidewalk. Instead, Kim buried her head in her hands and cried herself.

THIRTEEN

Jessica had been at the computer for three hours. Her eyes were weary from the task, and she wondered if there was that much to show for the time and effort. From the scores of cases she'd examined, she had compiled a list of six murders of young males which, on the surface, didn't seem to fit into any convenient category. The murders had all occurred within the past four years, and all remained unsolved. But Jessica realized the newsroom system might have missed updating some of the cases. Still, it was a beginning, and half of the computer file remained to be searched.

She got up and stretched, sorry now that she had worn the shorts and the light blouse. The newsroom air-conditioning system had made the small computer room uncomfortably cool, and she could feel the goose bumps pop up on her bare arms and legs. She turned off the computer and walked into the newsroom in search of a cup of hot coffee. She was surprised to find Laurie Sanders sitting at the assignment desk. And Laurie seemed as surprised to find Jessica in the newsroom.

"Don't you ever get tired of this place?" Laurie asked.

"I could ask you the same question."

"Just shows what kind of social life we both must have," Laurie said, grinning. It was the first time Jessica could recall seeing her smile.

She was going to let the exchange lapse, but Laurie persisted. "Seriously, Jess, what brings you in on a Saturday morning?"

"I was just doing a little research on the computer," Jessica said, moving away toward the coffeepot. "On the Edward Hill murder. It's all on my own time, Laurie."

"You're still working on that?"

"Consider it therapy. Makes me feel like a real reporter."

Laurie grinned again. "Tell me about it," she said.

Jessica returned with her coffee and quickly sketched out what she had learned so far from the computer. She neglected to say anything about Hill's diary; that would have to wait until later.

"So you think there's a castrating madman on the loose?" Laurie asked skeptically.

"I don't know what to think. Anyone could have killed Hill. I'm just grasping at any idea."

"Sounds pretty unlikely to me. The cops must have thought of the same thing."

"Don't be too sure," Jessica said. "They're overloaded, and Meecham's the only one over there who seems to give a damn about solving this case. Besides, if there was more than one murder, they could have happened in different jurisdictions over several years. I'm not sure the various cops talk to one another that much."

Laurie remained unconvinced, but she now seemed resigned to Jessica's persistent pursuit of the case. "I still think it's a wild-goose chase," she said, "but I can see you're not going to give it up. You need help?"

Jessica was surprised by the offer but responded quickly, before Laurie could reconsider. "Nina said she'd like to give me a hand when she has the time. I'm going to need help checking on these unsolved murders. Most of it would be telephone work."

"I'll talk to Nina," Laurie said. "But don't forget that we've still got to cover the rest of the news."

Jessica nodded, feeling some hope for the first time since she had stood on the river bluff in the rain.

Kim had stopped sobbing. She sat unmoving on the couch, drained of all energy and emotion. She had no strength to get up, yet no stomach to stay where she was. Everything around her seemed to stop. When Sarah took the cup from her hand to refill it, she appeared to move in slow motion. Even the tiny pendulum on the mantel clock seemed to pause at the arc of each swing.

"I'm sorry I made you go through that, Kim," Brinkman finally said, "but it's important that I heard the story from you."

"Why? I still don't understand."

"Because I'm supposed to be investigating Edward Hill's murder. I need to know what he did to you."

"He raped me and got away with it. That's what he did!"

"I know."

"Because the cops botched the investigation," Sarah added bitterly.

Brinkman ignored the jibe, returning to Kim. "Have you seen or had contact with Edward Hill since you last saw him in court?"

"No."

"He never bothered you again?"

"No."

"Do you know of anyone who bore a special grudge against Hill? Who hated what he did to you and might have wanted to get even?"

Kim glanced at Sarah, who stared back impassively. "No one but Sarah and the police know what he did to me. Not even my family. I once wanted to get even myself, but I didn't, and I don't know of anyone else who would."

"Where were you the night Hill was killed?" Brinkman asked.

"You're not serious?" Kim was disbelieving.

"I have to ask the questions, Kim."

"I was with Sarah at the 'Take Back the Night' rally and march," Kim said tiredly. "Lots of people saw me there."

"Why'd you go to the cemetery yesterday?"

"How did you know that?" she snapped, turning quickly to Sarah. "Did you tell her?"

"No, Kim," Brinkman said. "We had our own people there."

"I don't know why I went, okay? I shouldn't have gone. It was stupid. It was as if I couldn't be sure he was dead until I saw him put into the ground. He made a mess of my life, and maybe I wanted to see that what goes around finally came around for him."

"Why were you talking to that reporter?" Brinkman asked.

"I didn't talk to her, for God's sake. I walked away."

"Are you glad Hill's dead?"

"What kind of question is that?" Kim demanded.

"Just curious."

"No, I'm not glad he's dead. But I am glad he can't hurt anyone else now. I just wish the cops and courts had done that instead of some killer. I was taught that two wrongs don't make a right. As much as I hated him, I didn't wish him dead. Does that answer your question?"

Brinkman glanced at Sarah again but didn't respond.

As Jessica sat alone in her apartment that night, she looked again at the list of names she had retrieved from the newsroom computer earlier in the day. She had found two more unsolved murders that seemed to fit her criteria, making eight in all. But who knows, she wondered, how many others she or the computer may have missed? The task seemed impossible.

She put the list aside and again picked up Edward Hill's diary—opening it to the page where she'd left off in the newsroom the day before. Where Hill was writing about the woman K.H.

> She doesn't even know I exist, but I know everything about her: where she works, where she eats, who her friends are, what time she gets up, when she goes to bed. My time will come.

It was the first time Hill had written at any length about any woman, and Jessica quickly paged ahead to find the next reference to her. She found it in an entry dated two weeks later:

> I rode on the bus with her today. To her building. Got in the same elevator with her. She paid no attention, even when I brushed against her. The elevator was crowded. I stood behind her. My God, she smells so good! Cinnamon and jasmine, maybe. Her hair looks so soft, her skin so smooth. I wanted to touch her. I couldn't. Not then. There's a small mole on the back of her neck, just below her ear. I wanted to push against her, to let her know what she was doing to me. But people were getting off the elevator, and she moved away. She never even gave me a glance when she got off.

His next mention of the woman came five pages later, following a lengthy diatribe about two jobs he had lost in two weeks. One was loading trucks at a grocery warehouse; the other, pumping gas at a neighborhood station. He was fired from one for mouthing off to his supervisor ("the son of a bitch asked for it, called me a lazy bastard") and was laid off from the other when the station went fully self-service.

His words were filled with bitterness and hopelessness, and for the first time, his venom spilled over on K.H.

> She's no different from the others. Fuck 'em all. Nobody gives a shit. She wouldn't tell me the time of day if I gave her the goddamned watch. So fucking uppity. I

smiled at her on the street, and she looked right through me. Like I wasn't even there. Mr. Invisible, that's me. Well, we'll see about that. We'll just see about that.

Jessica closed the diary, but not before she felt a chill run through her body. And a pang of sympathy for K.H., whoever she is. One of Hill's victims? Probably.

Putting the book aside, she got up and walked through the darkened apartment, stopping at the window to look down on the quiet street below. Nothing was moving, and she suddenly found herself overcome by an intense sense of solitude. Here it was, Saturday night, and here she was, alone again in another strange city. With only Edward Hill's diary for company.

It had been the same during her first few weeks in Duluth, occasional gnawing periods of isolation and loneliness. Her answer then, as now, had been to work longer and harder, to bury herself in her job, to allow friendships to develop slowly, to let the loneliness quietly slip away.

But that took time, and it wasn't always easy. Tonight she'd considered and rejected a half-dozen different possibilities, a movie, a concert, a drive, because in every case she would have had to do it alone. She had thought about calling someone from the station, Kendrick or Nina, perhaps, maybe even Hilliard, but realized she didn't know any of them well enough to justify a lonely call out of the blue on a Saturday night.

At a loss for anything else to do, she put in a call to her sister, Janie, stuck away in the woods of northern Wisconsin. The phone was answered immediately.

"Goose Bay Resort," said a man's voice at the other end.

"Is Janie Mitchell around, please?"

There was a pause. Then: "She's not here now."

"When do you expect her back?" Jessica asked.

Another pause. "Who's calling?"

"Her sister. From Minneapolis."

"I'm sorry, I don't know when she'll be back."

Strange, Jessica thought, but then remembered Janie's letter. Must be out with her new flame, she decided, or maybe she went back to Madison for the weekend. "Do you know where I can reach her?" she finally asked.

"Sorry, I don't," the voice replied. Same hesitation. "Can I take a message?"

What's going on? Jessica wondered. "She's all right, isn't she?"

"As far as I know." Impatient now. "Was there a message?"

"Tell her to call Jessica," she said, giving him her number.

"I'll leave word," the man said. Then the line went dead.

She stared at the receiver. Forget it, she told herself. Janie's a big girl; she can take care of herself. Still . . .

She had barely put the phone down when it rang. Must be Janie, Jessica thought, instantly relieved. But it wasn't.

"This is Jack Tomlinson. Remember me?"

The man in Sarah's office. The prosecutor with the blue pin-striped shirt.

"Sure," Jessica said, already puzzled. "How'd you get my number?"

"From Information," he said. "It's listed, you know."

Jessica said nothing, waiting for the hustle she knew would be coming.

"I was wondering if you'd like to have a drink . . . or dinner, sometime," he said.

"Thanks, but I don't think so."

"Why's that?" he asked. "I'm single, respectable, come from a good family, practice safe sex, and am told I'm not especially ugly. What more can you ask?"

She laughed, but was mildly irritated. "I don't even know you," she said, "and I'm really busy at work. . . ."

"You're home on a Saturday night," he interrupted. "You can't be that busy."

Before she could reply, he pressed on. "You're not attached, are you? I didn't see a ring that day in Sarah's office."

He's not going to take no for answer, she thought.

"Look, Jack, I'm not attached, but I'm new in town. New in my job. I'm not dating anyone for a while. But when I do, I'd like to know who I'm going out with."

"I'll be happy to provide references," he said.

She laughed again, not wanting to be rude and unable to forget the loneliness she had been feeling. Was she going to spend every Saturday night alone?

"Okay, all right," she relented. "When?"

"I'll call you next week to set something up," he said. "You won't be sorry."

FOURTEEN

Meecham had already gone through two cigars and it wasn't even noon on Monday. Keep this up, he thought, and you'll smoke the whole goddamned box by the end of the week. Wind up dead, a rotting corpse surrounded by a heap of ashes and a pile of stinking cigar butts.

His mouth felt like the inside of a burned-out trash barrel. He was tempted to wash the taste away with a swig of brandy from the bottle in his bottom drawer but decided against it. He hadn't had a drink in almost a week, and he hated to spoil the record for the sake of a mouthwash.

Instead, he put a stick of gum in his mouth. He hated gum; it made his jaws tired and didn't taste worth shit. Give it a couple of minutes, he thought, and it had about as much flavor as an old rubber band.

Meecham also hated Mondays. He blamed his grumpiness on the long, lonely weekend. Especially a weekend without a few drinks to help pass the hours. In desperation, he ended up smoking even more of those fucking cigars.

"Christ, what the hell died in here?" Freda Brinkman asked as she walked through the door, holding her nose.

"It's my goddamned office," Meecham said defensively.

Brinkman sat down across the desk from him, shoving the filled ashtray to his side. "You know that you're not supposed to smoke in here, Matt. There's a sign right outside your door."

"Fuck 'em," Meecham said.

Brinkman grimaced and opened her briefcase.

"Did you talk to the women?" Meecham asked.

"Only one of them. The other's on vacation."

"Which one did you see?"

"Kim Hawkins. Says she hasn't seen Hill in more than a year and has no idea who might have killed him." She took out the tape recorder. "Want to hear the interview?"

He shook his head. "Not now. I took the old Hill file home over the weekend and—"

Brinkman cut in. "You actually took a file home?"

"Screw you, Lieutenant. I learned something I didn't know before."

"What's that?"

"The report said a diary of Hill's was confiscated at the time of his arrest, after the Hawkins rape. That it was returned to him after the case was thrown out of court."

"So?" Brinkman said impatiently.

"Did we find a diary when we went through his mother's house?"

"Of course not. You know that."

"Well? Where the hell's the diary?" Meecham demanded.

"Maybe he threw it away."

"People don't throw away diaries. They're like old picture albums. You keep 'em around."

Brinkman started to get up to leave.

"I want you to find the diary," Meecham ordered. "Search the house again if you have to. The name of the killer could be staring us in the face."

"What if the old lady doesn't want me to search again?"

"Then get a warrant. This is a goddamned murder case."

Brinkman was out the door when Meecham called after her. "One other thing. Someone told me that Sarah Andrews is this Kim Hawkins's roommate. Did you know that?"

Brinkman nodded. "Sarah was there during the interview."

"Why didn't you tell me? Now I know why she was over here pounding on my door."

"I didn't think it was important," Brinkman replied.

Jessica had the diary in her purse when she walked into the newsroom that afternoon, still debating what to do with it. She knew she would eventually have to give it to Meecham, but when and with what explanation were still open questions. When she reached her desk, she found an envelope addressed to her, except the writer had misspelled her last name. There was no return address, either.

Dear Ms. Mitchel:
I'm sorry we didn't have a chance to meet at Gino's.
Despite what you may have heard, I'm not the ogre
they make me out to be. If you'd like to hear my side of
the story sometime, I'll give you the exclusive
interview. I'll be in touch.
Lowell Ingram.

Jessica reread the letter. Lowell Ingram? The sex pervert. Why me? Because he caught me staring at him? she wondered. Why do I attract all the weirdos?

Still puzzled, she put the letter aside as Nina French walked up to her desk. "Laurie tells me I'm free to give you a hand if you need it."

"You're sure you have the time?"

"I can make the time," Nina said as she sat down. "If it's mostly telephone work, it shouldn't be a problem."

Jessica retrieved her notes from the computer search. "I found eight cases on Saturday which I would classify as possibles." She ran her finger down the page. "All males, Nina, all murdered in the past four years for no apparent motive in various locations in the metro area. Most of them were young, in their twenties and thirties, and according to the computer, all of the murders are still unsolved."

Nina took the list from her. "Let's see," she said, "two of the murders were in Minneapolis, including Edward Hill's, two in St. Paul, one in Bloomington, one in Maple Grove, and one each in Brooklyn Park and Fridley."

"Does that strike you as strange?" Jessica asked. "That so many are in the suburbs?"

"Not really. It's a myth that the suburbs are some kind of safe haven. But one thing does seem a little strange. Five of the eight murders happened during the summer months and four of the five in July. Maybe the hot weather pisses people off."

"Especially if they don't have air-conditioning," Jessica said ruefully.

"So what do you want me to do?" Nina asked.

"Let's divide the list in half. I'll take Minneapolis and St. Paul, you take the suburbs. Call the cops and try to get an update on each of the murders: cause of death, suspects, arrests, convictions, criminal history of the victims, if any. That kind of thing, as much as you can get."

"What if they don't want to cooperate?"

"Then we'll go out and look at the records ourselves," Jessica said. "They should be public."

"Not necessarily," Nina countered. "They may stonewall us by claiming it's an ongoing investigation, even if they're sitting on their asses, doing nothing on the case."

Jessica frowned. "Maybe so, but let's give it a try."

As Nina walked away to make a copy of the list, the phone on Jessica's desk buzzed.

"Jessica?"

She immediately recognized the frail voice. "Mrs. Hill?"

"The police came for the diary, Jessica. That lady lieutenant. I had to tell her I gave the diary to you. I'm sorry, but she was quite insistent and rude. She threatened to search the house again, accused me of hiding the diary from them."

"Take it easy, Mrs. Hill. When did this happen?"

"She just left a minute ago. She seemed quite angry, Jessica, more at you than me."

Jessica winced; she wasn't looking forward to the encounter she knew would be coming. "Did she say how they found out about the diary?"

"No. She just showed up at my door and demanded it. She was really quite pushy."

"Thanks for the call, Mrs. Hill. I'll take care of it."

"Will you give them the diary?" she asked worriedly.

"I may have to, yes."

"Did you read it?"

"Yes, I did. You were right not to read it, Mrs. Hill."

There was silence at the other end of the line.

Jessica didn't have long to wait for the confrontation.

"You have a visitor in the lobby," the receptionist said over the phone. "A Lieutenant Brinkman."

"Have her wait, please," Jessica said.

She put the diary into a large envelope and handed it to Jeff Hilliard as she passed his desk. "Hold on to this, will you?"

"What is it?" he asked, barely looking up.

"Personal. Keep your nose out of it."

Brinkman was striding back and forth in the lobby, in uniform, hands clasped behind her back. Like she's inspecting the troops, Jessica thought. Patton without his riding crop and jodhpurs.

"What can I do for you, Lieutenant?" Jessica asked, her tone pleasant, controlled.

Brinkman stopped in mid-stride. "You've got something we're looking for," she said, trying to keep her voice low.

"Really?" Jessica said.

"Edward Hill's diary. His mother said she gave it to you."

Brinkman stood straight and stiff, hands still behind her back, looking down on Jessica.

"Did Mrs. Hill say I should give it to you?" Jessica asked.

"She said you had it."

"That's not what I asked."

"Let's not play games, huh. You have no business with the diary, you know that."

"No one told me."

"I'm telling you. It's part of a murder investigation. Meecham wants it now."

"Then I'll give it to him," Jessica said, and started to turn away.

"You'll give it to me!" Brinkman's voice was icy, filled with menace.

"Fraid not, Lieutenant. Sorry. Have the captain give me a call and we'll arrange a meeting."

Brinkman stared at her. Her neck was at Jessica's eye level, and she could see it redden. Her hands came from behind her back, fists clenched. Jessica moved back a half step. "Sometimes it pays to be nice to reporters, Lieutenant."

"Fuck you," Brinkman said, no longer keeping her voice low. "You're all alike."

Then she strode out the door, with Jessica watching her and the receptionist staring at them both, mouth open.

Meecham was livid. He paced; he snarled; his hand shook as he tried to hold a match to the stub of the cigar. He yowled when the heat from the flame singed the tip of his nose.

"What do you mean, she won't let you have it?" he shouted.

"She wants to give it to you," Brinkman said from the door of Meecham's office. "Personally. Says you should call to arrange a meeting."

Meecham flung the cigar into a corner wastebasket, recoiling slightly when the sparks flew. "You know what that means, don't you? She wants to make a deal, a little tit for tat. Sweet Jessica is a shrewd young lady."

"That's what happens when you're nice to those people," Brinkman said. "I've told you a hundred times. All they care about is a story."

Meecham looked across the room at her as he picked up

the phone. "Maybe you're right, maybe I misjudged her." He paused before dialing, waiting for Brinkman to leave, seeing her scowl as she did.

Jessica answered on the first ring, guessing who it would be. "Hello, Captain," she said pleasantly, before he spoke.

"What the hell's going on, Jessica?" She could hear the quaver in his voice.

"Nothing. I was just sitting here waiting for your call."

"I need the diary—now."

"You can have it. But we should talk first."

"Have you read it?"

Jessica hesitated for a moment. "I finished it this weekend."

"Son of a bitch," he muttered.

"I didn't ask for it," she protested. "Gladys Hill gave it to me, almost pushed it on me. I told her she should give it to the police, but she insisted I take it."

"It's potential evidence in a murder case, Jessica. I thought I could trust you."

"This has nothing to do with trust. I was going to give it to you, but what good reporter wouldn't read it first?"

He sighed. "When can I get it?"

"Depends," she said.

"On what?" He could see the deal coming, plain as day.

"I want to see Edward Hill's criminal record. Under the counter, if need be. And I want to check out another murder in Minneapolis . . . a guy by the name of James Largo, who was killed about two years ago."

"What's he got to do with Hill?"

"Probably nothing, but I'd like to see what you have on it."

"Okay, but I can't let you see Hill's record. He was never convicted."

"He's dead, Captain. What harm can it do?"

"Dying didn't deny him his right to privacy, Jessica. That's the law."

"Think about it. It could take you a long time to get that diary from me. Courts don't like newsroom searches."

Jessica was bluffing and suspected he knew it, but she guessed—hoped—that Meecham wouldn't be spoiling for a fight.

"You know the pavilion at Lake Calhoun?" he asked.

"I can find it," she replied.

"There are some benches near it, right along the water. Meet you there tonight at seven. But bring the diary, Jessica."

"This is potluck, Matt. You have to bring something, too."

She heard him exhale loudly and was sure she smelled cigar smoke wafting through the phone line.

After she had hung up, Jessica spotted Bill Kendrick standing near the assignment desk. She waved him over.

"What's up, Jess? You look puzzled."

"Sit down, Bill, and tell me about Matt Meecham."

"What do you want to know?"

"Everything you know. I've met him a couple of times, but I can't quite figure him out. Is he really a drunk?"

Kendrick shrugged. "He was, but I'm not sure he still is."

"What's the story on him?"

Kendrick leaned back in the chair. "Way back in the sixties and early seventies he was the bright light of the department. Before the booze got to him. I'm told he still holds the record time for passing all of the promotional exams and has more official commendations than anyone else on the force.

"But then life went sour on him. Ten or twelve years ago, he got passed over for chief, thanks to politics at city hall. That's when he started the serious drinking. A year or so later, he lost his wife in a car accident up north. He was driving drunk and rammed a tree while trying to miss a deer in the road. The department managed to get the DWI charge dropped but never could get him into treatment."

"They try to fire him?" she asked.

"No, but they wrote him off as a lush. They couldn't take his rank away, and he refused to quit, so it's been a standoff since. He still runs Homicide and still has a lot of respect from the cops on the street, but now he spends most of his time at Barney's."

"Would you trust him?" she asked.

"When he's sober, yes. When he's drinking, I don't know."

FIFTEEN

Jessica had trouble finding a place to park near the Calhoun pavilion. People had apparently come from all over the city to stroll the paths around the lake, using the light breeze off the water as a fan to escape the evening heat.

Ten minutes late, she spotted Meecham on a bench a few feet from the water's edge, idly flicking popcorn to a small flock of ducks that squawked noisily nearby, fighting for the handouts. She sat down next to him, but he seemed to take no notice.

"Hey, Captain," she said. "Sorry I'm late. Had to park blocks away."

"Forget the captain," he said, holding the popcorn toward her but keeping his eyes on the ducks. "My friends call me Matt."

"Thanks," she said as she plucked a few kernels from the bag and chewed them quietly while waiting for him to speak. The sun still hung above the trees across the lake, the glare bouncing off the ripples in the water and directly into her eyes. She retrieved her sunglasses from her purse and waited.

Unlike their previous meetings, Meecham actually appeared tidy tonight: suit coat pressed, shirt fresh and tucked in, tie tight at the collar. Even his hair was combed.

"You're looking almost human," she finally said, breaking the silence.

"I should. I haven't had a drink since that night I saw you at Barney's."

"No kidding? What prompted that?"

He shrugged his shoulders. "Decided it was time, that's all."

Several more minutes passed before he finally turned to her again and spoke. "You have the diary?"

"It's in the car," she said.

"Why wouldn't you give it to Brinkman?"

Jessica didn't hesitate. "Because she's a bitch. She's been in my face since that first morning."

"She hates reporters," he said with a sigh. "But don't let it bother you. She doesn't much like anybody, including me. Chewed my ass something fierce that night at Barney's. She thought I'd given away the store."

"But you're her boss," Jessica protested.

"On paper. But to her I'm a hopeless drunk. She has no respect, no time, for me. Can't blame her for that, I guess."

Jessica winced at his self-abuse, but he took no notice.

"Normally, she couldn't care less what I do or who I talk to," he continued, "but for some reason, she's all uptight about this case. She doesn't like you nosing around or me talking to you."

"So why are you willing to help me?" she asked.

"Good question. First of all, you've got the diary, and I need it. But you also seem like a decent kid. And you're sure as hell persistent. Keep snapping at my heels. You remind me of some good young cops I've known."

Jessica smiled and leaned back on the bench. "That's nice to hear, but I didn't come here for compliments. I need information."

Meecham took a deep breath. "James Largo, the guy you

asked about, was a white male, aged thirty-nine, who died of a single stab wound in the chest two and a half years ago. He was killed in his apartment, where he lived alone. He was a homosexual but had no steady partner. He moved around a lot."

He recited the facts in a staccato monotone—as though he were reading from the official report—while staring, squinting, into the distance.

"The autopsy revealed he was afflicted with the AIDS virus. No one was ever arrested, although we believe Largo may have been killed by a gay acquaintance who had either contracted AIDS from him or feared he would. The case remains open, but we have no real hope of solving it. It would be a fluke, or pure luck, if we did."

Then he turned to her. "What does Largo have to do with Hill?"

"Probably nothing. He doesn't fit." Jessica quickly told him of her newsroom computer search and the names that had emerged. "Largo was one of the names. We're trying to check the rest of them now, but who knows how many we may have missed."

"You think Hill's murder had some connection to others? Some kind of serial killer? C'mon, Jessica, that's out of the movies."

"Maybe so, but at least we're checking. That's more than you're doing, Matt."

Meecham scowled but held his tongue.

"Think about it, Matt. I'm a novice, but from what I know, Hill's murder was clean, almost professional, and terribly brutal. Whoever killed him must have wanted to make a point, to leave a message. It doesn't seem like the work of some amateur killing for the first time in a fit of vengeance."

"You do think you're a cop, don't you?" he said with amusement and a hint of respect.

"I've read the diary," Jessica said. "Hill was a pathetic, angry loner, but there's nothing in the diary that indicates he was into drugs or crime or that he mixed with unsavory characters who might want to kill him."

"But he raped at least two women," Meecham interjected.

"Right, but his diary doesn't admit that, doesn't even mention his arrests, for that matter. He seems to have put them out of his mind. But I figure his murder must be connected to the rapes because no one else seems to have known him well enough, or hated him enough, to kill him. At least not the way they did."

"We're checking out the rape victims now," Meecham admitted.

"Does one of them have the initials K.H.?"

Meecham looked startled but did not respond.

"The diary talks about her," Jessica said. "Not the rape but about watching her, admiring her. Until the last entry."

"I need that diary, Jessica."

"And I need to know more about Edward Hill."

Meecham threw the last few pieces of popcorn into the water and then crumpled the empty bag into a tight ball. "I can't show you the records, but I'll tell you as much as I can. His first victim was a local actress and model. We had Hill cold. He was arrested a few blocks from her apartment, and she identified him in a lineup. Hill had a tattoo on his arm identical to the one she described on the rapist. But a week before the trial, she decided not to testify. She was terrified he might come after her later and go for her face. Said it could ruin her career."

Jessica moved closer to him on the bench, straining to hear every word over the squabbling of the ducks.

"The second rape happened about a year ago, to the woman Hill apparently talks about in the diary. She saw the same tattoo on Hill's arm during the attack, and some bright young cop in the sex-crimes division put the two rapes together. They went after Hill, found him at his mother's house, along with a knife and the diary. Problem was, the bright young cop didn't bother to get a search warrant, and a judge threw the case out for illegal search and seizure."

"So Hill went free," Jessica said.

"Twice."

"Must have made a lot of people angry."

"I'm sure it did."

"Would you let me talk to the women?" she asked.

"Of course not. You know better than that."

Jessica rose from the bench. "Okay, Matt. I guess you've done your part. Let's go get the diary."

While Jessica sat on the park bench with Meecham, the ringing phone on her newsroom desk went unanswered. But her voice mail captured the three incoming messages:

The first was from Sarah Andrews, who said she would like to meet with Jessica as soon as it was convenient, to continue their discussion of the media and women's issues.

The second call was from Lowell Ingram. "Did you get my letter? Are you interested in the interview?" His voice was low and husky. Hesitant. "I'm supposed to be sentenced tomorrow at two, and I'll be free to talk after that. Can you be there? My attorney says I shouldn't talk to reporters, but screw him. I think you'll be interested in what I have to say."

The third message was from Jessica's mother. "Have you heard from Janie? We've tried to get her at the resort twice, and she hasn't returned our calls. If you talk to her, Jessica, please have her call home. Take care of yourself, dear."

The next morning, Jessica waited until Laurie Sanders was free of the early assignment hassle before approaching her. She showed her Ingram's letter and told her of the message she'd found on the voice mail. "I don't even know the guy, Laurie. I saw him across the bar at Gino's, and now he seems to think I'm his confidante. It's weird."

"You seem to have that effect on men," Laurie mused aloud. "Even the perverts."

Jessica grinned. "Thanks a lot. What do you want me to do?"

"Cover his sentencing, I guess. I'd planned to send Hilliard, but you might as well play this out."

"Do you want an interview with him?" she asked.

"Why not? See what he has to say. We can always throw it out."

As Jessica walked back to her desk, her thoughts shifted from Ingram to the two other messages she'd found on her machine. Her mother's was the most troubling. What the hell's going on with Janie? She had not returned Jessica's message from the weekend, either. Had she taken off somewhere? Or was she simply showing her independence? She had always had a wild streak, but it was not like her to ignore messages, especially from their mother. Jessica vowed to call her again and get to the bottom of it.

The other message, from Sarah Andrews, struck her as slightly odd. True, she had casually mentioned getting together again after their heated conversation in Sarah's office, but Jessica had not expected her to pursue another meeting so quickly.

Nina French was waiting by her desk, a sheaf of papers in her hand. "Got a minute?" she asked. "I've run down a couple of those cases."

"Already?" Jessica said.

"Didn't take long for the two of them," Nina replied, sitting down and spreading the pages on the desk. "The deaths in Maple Grove and Fridley were drug related. One was a young college kid who was a small-time dealer. He apparently got greedy and ended up dead. The other one, in Maple Grove, was a simple overdose. It took them a couple of weeks of tests to decide that his death was an accident and not a homicide."

"That leaves two," Jessica said.

"Still working on those. All I've learned so far is that they're still unsolved and that there's no apparent motive in either murder."

"How'd they die?" Jessica asked.

Nina appeared puzzled. "That's what's strange. The cops won't give any details. They claim the information is integral to their investigation. Makes you wonder."

"Yes, it does," Jessica agreed.

* * *

Only a few seats in Judge Marcott's courtroom were occupied, most of those by reporters slumped lazily in their chairs, stifling postlunch yawns. One television artist sat in the empty jury box, sketch pad on her lap. She, too, seemed to be nodding off.

Much of the media interest in the Ingram case had dissolved with the plea bargain; the reporters who were there now knew the sentencing would likely get no more than a mention on the back pages of the newspaper or as a thirty-second item on television. Still, it was an event that had to be covered.

Marcott's courtroom was indistinguishable from others in the Government Center: a large, modern box whose contents were all constructed of slightly bleached oak—the judge's bench, the lawyers' desks, the jury box, and the spectator seating. It was stark and cool, well lit but lacking any of the character or architectural uniqueness of the courtrooms of earlier decades.

Jessica sat in the front row behind the railing, with Bill Kendrick by her side. Cameras were not allowed in Minnesota courtrooms, so Kendrick had stowed his equipment outside, ready for quick use if necessary.

None of the principals had yet appeared, but an elderly court clerk shuffled stiffly between the courtroom and the judge's chambers while the bailiff shuffled papers at his small desk, trying to look busy. Jessica glanced at her watch. Ten to two.

The doors at the rear of the courtroom swung open, and all heads turned. Three young women and several adults walked in, followed by Sarah Andrews. Grim-faced, none of them spoke as they sought seats in the rear. The three girls were huddled together, heads down, avoiding the eyes of the reporters.

Sarah stopped briefly and whispered to them, chucking one beneath the chin before making her way to one of the desks in front, ignoring everyone else in the courtroom.

"I didn't know the kids would be here," Jessica whispered to Kendrick. "Wonder what Ingram will do when he sees them."

The answer came a moment later when Ingram and his attorney walked through the same door. Ingram kept his eyes straight ahead until he reached the lawyer's table. Then he turned and glanced behind him. He saw Jessica first, and there was the flicker of a small smile.

Then he saw the girls and their parents. Ingram's face paled so quickly that Jessica thought he might faint. There was a sharp grunt of surprise, an embarrassed gasp, as if he had just walked blindly into a glass door. He pulled back, grasped a chair for support, and quickly turned away.

Before he could sit, the bailiff stood and called out: "All rise, please."

Judge Marcott strode to the bench and quickly surveyed the courtroom as the bailiff finished reading the preliminaries. "I've carefully considered the facts in this case," the judge said once everyone was seated, "including the presentence investigation and the arguments of opposing counsel regarding the appropriate and just sentence for this defendant.

"I am fully cognizant of the serious nature of the charges to which Mr. Ingram has pleaded guilty. However, I am also aware that this is a first offense, that until now the defendant has been a model citizen and an important contributor to his community."

Jessica looked up from her notes to see Sarah Andrews shift uneasily in her chair. The artist in the jury box was sketching quickly, her eyes moving from the pad to the girls and their parents in the back of the courtroom. The other reporters were leaning forward in their chairs, pencils poised.

"The state sentencing guidelines provide the court with some latitude in a case such as this," the judge continued, "and I plan to use that discretion to serve the interests of justice and the community as I see them. Any final comments from the parties before I pronounce sentence?"

Sarah stood quickly. "May it please the court, and without presuming to predict your decision, I can only repeat as forcefully as possible what I wrote in my brief."

"I didn't request the brief, Ms. Andrews . . ." the judge interjected.

"I understand that, Your Honor, but I believe the issues represented by this case are vital. The defendant has admitted molesting three young women while in a position of authority and responsibility. He was their teacher, Your Honor, a person the law and society says these girls should be able to trust, a man who was expected to nurture and educate them, not to violate them."

"Ms. Andrews," the judge said sharply, "we are not trying this case. There is no jury to hear you make a final argument."

"You requested final comments, Your Honor," Sarah countered. "I can only appeal to the court for the harshest possible penalty allowed by the guidelines for this defendant. Anything less than a prison sentence will make a mockery of the statute and render future prosecutions of similar cases extremely difficult."

There was applause from the girls and their families in the rear which a stern glance from the judge quickly quieted. "Are you finished, Ms. Andrews?" he asked.

"No, Your Honor, I'm not. For too many years society has winked at this kind of crime, too often blaming the victims, too often forgiving the perpetrator because he held some kind of lofty and trusted position within the community. I trust the court will not perpetuate that medieval myth. Thank you, Your Honor."

"And I trust the press has recorded your words accurately, Ms. Andrews," Marcott said sarcastically before turning to the defense attorney. "Mr. Kippering, any response?"

Kippering stood next to his client. "With all due respect to opposing counsel, I believe the court has summarized the situation fairly: My client made an unfortunate mistake which already has cost him dearly. It is his first offense, and it would serve no useful purpose to him or to society to inflict severe penalties upon a man whose prior record in the community is unblemished."

"Put him behind bars, Judge!" one of the girls' fathers stood and shouted.

"It wasn't the first time!" a mother yelled.

"We'll have quiet in this courtroom or I'll clear it," the

judge commanded. The bailiff stood and walked toward the railing, but paused when the parents sat back down, muttering.

"Now, then," the judge said, "if the hysterics are over, would the defendant please rise."

Ingram stood slowly, half-leaning against Kippering.

"Lowell Paul Ingram, you have pleaded guilty to the charge of fifth-degree criminal sexual conduct, a gross misdemeanor under Minnesota law. I order you to pay a three-thousand-dollar fine, to serve five years' probation under the supervision of this court, and to receive treatment from an agency authorized to counsel sexual offenders."

A chorus of boos rang out from the rear of the courtroom. Ingram's three young victims slumped in their seats and cried. Sarah turned her head aside, staring at the courtroom wall, while Ingram pumped the hand of his attorney.

"This concludes the business at hand," Marcott said loudly. "Court is adjourned." With that, he rose and walked through the door to his chambers, followed by his clerk and the court reporter. The bailiff stood guard by the bench.

"Lowell, let's get out the other door," Kippering said, eyeing the angry parents by the main door.

"In a minute," Ingram replied. He walked to the side of Sarah, whose face was still averted. He leaned down and growled into her ear: "Better luck next time, cunt."

Her head pivoted. "Get away from me, Ingram," she snarled.

He smiled and backed away. "No hard feelings, Counselor. You win some, you lose some."

Jessica could not hear the exchange from her position behind the railing, but she stepped forward as Ingram started to walk away. "Mr. Ingram," she said, "I'm Jessica Mitchell. You left a message for me."

He turned to her and held out his hand. "Ahhh, yes, Jessica. Nice to finally meet you."

"This is Bill Kendrick, one of our photographers," Jessica said as Kendrick stepped forward. "We have our equipment outside if you'd still like to do the interview."

"I've thought more about it, Jessica. Not now. My attorney says I should say nothing for a time. I'll call you when I'm ready."

"But you seemed eager—"

"That was yesterday, when I thought I might be going to prison. I need more time to think about it now."

"It won't take a minute to set the gear up," Kendrick offered.

Ingram shook his head. "I'll call you," he said, and then followed Kippering toward the back door of the courtroom, ignoring the parting catcalls from the girls' parents.

"You'd do an interview with that piece of shit?"

Jessica turned quickly at the voice and found Sarah a step away, looking past her at Ingram's retreating figure.

"Why not?" she said defensively. "He's news."

"You'd just make a hero of him to all of the other perverts out there," Sarah replied tiredly. "Not only do they see another molester escape the system, but he gets his face all over the TV set, claiming his innocence. That's all we need."

"This is my job, Sarah."

"Hope you do yours better than I do mine," she said bitterly.

Jessica saw the other reporters moving toward Sarah, so she quickly reminded her: "Your message? You still want to talk?"

Sarah's eyes turned back to her. "Sure. The sooner the better, as a matter of fact. Several things have come up that we need to discuss. How about lunch tomorrow?"

"Fine with me," Jessica said.

"There's a little place called Eddie's Grill just down the street from the Hyatt. Meet you there at noon."

As she walked away, Kendrick asked Jessica, "What's that all about?"

"I wish I knew," Jessica said.

SIXTEEN

Eddie's Grill was an unpretentious little place that reminded Jessica of one of those Parisian sidewalk cafes she'd seen in the movies. A green awning, emblazoned with a big golden E, stretched across the front, shading a few tables outside while keeping it cool and dark inside.

To Jessica, Eddie's Grill looked as if it might cater to people more interested in privacy than convenience, a place where shadowy deals and illicit affairs could be arranged.

A waiter stood by the door, a cloth napkin draped over his arm, breathing in the first whiffs of the cooler, fresher air flowing in from the Rockies. The heavy heat and humidity of the past several days were in retreat, and Jessica felt as though a great weight had been lifted from her body.

"Great day, huh?" the waiter said as she walked up.

"And how," Jessica replied, glancing inside. Two of the tables were occupied by couples, but she saw no sign of Sarah.

"Looking for someone?" he asked.

"I'm supposed to meet a woman here, but I guess I'm early."

"Get you something while you wait?"

"A diet something," Jessica said, sitting down at one of the shaded outside tables. While waiting, she thought again of Sarah's words of the day before: "Several things have come up that we need to discuss." What the hell's that about? she wondered.

Jessica couldn't shake her mixed feelings about Sarah. She was obviously quick and bright and committed to her job and to women's issues, but Jessica found her stridency unsettling, her quick changes of mood and flashes of anger unnerving.

She had met her what? Three times? But already she had seen several different sides of the woman: buoyant and confident at the rally, composed and literate on camera, depressed but defiant in her office, angry and cynical in the courtroom. A complicated lady, Jessica decided, whom I barely know.

The waiter returned with a diet Coke at the same time Jessica spotted Sarah striding up the street. She was wearing a light paisley cotton dress, a small purse slung carelessly over her shoulder, bouncing off her hip as her pace quickened.

"Sorry I'm a little late," she said, holding out her hand.

"No problem," Jessica replied, returning the handshake. "I've only been here a few minutes myself."

They chose another table outside, far to one side, and spent the first few minutes exchanging small talk and ordering lunch.

"I didn't expect to hear from you so soon," Jessica said.

"I had a trial scheduled for today, but we had to drop the charges," Sarah explained, and then went on to tell Jessica the story of a battered wife's decision not to testify against her abusive husband. "It happens all the time. Women get the crap beat out of them, over and over again, but still won't send the jerks to jail. It's maddening, but what can you do?"

"Sounds like a pretty good story," Jessica said. "Would any of these women be willing to talk on camera?"

"I doubt it. If they're too frightened to testify, I don't think they'd be eager to go on television."

The conversation lapsed when the waiter delivered their salads and then hovered over them, assuring himself everything was satisfactory and—Jessica was sure—trying to get a look down Sarah's open dress collar.

"You said you had things to discuss with me," Jessica said when he left. "Something specific in mind?"

"As a matter of fact, I do. Might as well not beat around the bush. I'm told you have an unusual interest in one of our recent murder cases. Edward Hill's, to be precise."

Jessica's forkful of salad stopped halfway to her mouth. "Where'd you hear that?"

"Our office works closely with the police. I've heard about your talks with Mrs. Hill and about the theft of the diary."

"What? Did Freda Brinkman tell you that? I didn't steal the diary, Sarah. Mrs. Hill gave it to me, insisted I take it. I don't like to be accused of theft."

"If it's not theft, it's tampering. You knew the diary could be evidence in a murder case, that keeping it could screw up an eventual prosecution. You should have turned it over to the police immediately."

"I debated that," Jessica admitted, "but I finally decided it wouldn't hurt to read it first."

"That wasn't your decision to make," Sarah snapped.

Jessica shrugged. "Maybe not, but what's done is done. Certainly I'm not the first reporter to cross that line. I don't understand why you're so uptight."

"And I don't understand why you're so intent on this particular case," Sarah shot back.

"It's none of your business, frankly," Jessica said, "but I'll tell you, anyway. I was there when Edward Hill's body came up from the river, the first murder victim I'd ever seen. It may seem strange, but I can't make myself forget it. I'd like to know how and why he died."

Sarah stared, her expression a mixture of skepticism and confusion.

"Don't look so puzzled," Jessica said. "I'm sure you remember every detail of the first major case you prosecuted. You probably lived with it, slept with it, for weeks. That's happening to me with this story. I've met Hill's mother; I've read his diary. I feel like I know the man."

"Then you know he was a class A jerk," Sarah muttered. "A lousy predator. God knows how many women he may have raped and assaulted. Maybe even killed."

Jessica's eyes widened. "So that's what this is really all about."

"That's part of it, sure. You're wasting your time on a dirtbag," Sarah said. "If you do a story on him, you'll end up glorifying him. Poor old Edward Hill."

"Are you saying he deserved to die?" Jessica asked. "Maybe he could have gotten treatment?"

"Do you know what the treatment record is for predators like Hill? Most of these guys are incorrigible. They thumb their noses at the system. They'll fake their way through treatment, then rape or kill again the first chance they get. The whole thing's a joke, and everybody knows it."

"So what's *your* answer?" Jessica asked.

"There *is* no answer. There aren't enough jails to hold them all, and even if there were, society's not ready to put all of them away for life."

Jessica went back to her salad, considering what Sarah had told her. "So what are you suggesting I do?" she finally asked.

"Forget about Edward Hill. Leave his killer to the cops. Don't screw up our case, and don't make a martyr of him."

"What case?" Jessica demanded. "The cops don't have a case, and you know it. I think I know more than they do, and I know almost nothing. I have suspicions, that's all."

"What suspicions?" Sarah demanded.

Jessica was about to answer when she heard tiny alarm bells sound in her head. "Nothing important," she said.

"I'd like to hear them," Sarah persisted.

"So you can run back to Brinkman?"

Sarah did not disguise her annoyance. "Look here, Jessica, one more time. Leave it to the cops and to our office. We know what we're doing. You're only going to get in the way, and it could be dangerous for you. After all, Hill's killer is still out there somewhere."

"Why are you worried about me?" Jessica asked. "Because

I'm a woman?" She delivered the words with a perverse relish, and they drew the expected response.

"That's ridiculous!" Sarah exploded.

"What, then? Everyone seems eager that I forget this case. The newsroom's not excited by it, Freda Brinkman's constantly in my face, and now you're trying to steer me away. It strikes me as a little curious."

"I'm not trying to 'steer you away,'" Sarah said. "I just don't want you getting in the way."

"Not to worry," Jessica said with a small smile. "I'll be careful not to step on any flat feet."

After leaving the restaurant, Jessica retrieved her Impala from the parking ramp and headed east across the Mississippi River toward St. Paul. She was there to check on another name on her computer list, one Eduardo Priaz, a young Cuban immigrant whose body had been found along the railroad tracks near Shepard Road. He had been tied across one of the tracks at night and sliced neatly in half by the wheels of a passing train.

What had caught her attention, however, was the elaborate preparation taken by the killer or killers. Poor Eduardo had been gagged, his eyelids taped open, and his head bound in such a way that he had to face the approaching train.

To kill someone like that, she decided, you not only had to hate him, but hate him enough to make sure his death was as frightening and agonizing as possible. Like castrating someone before you killed him.

She found a parking place a block away from the Ramsey County Courthouse, an imposing stone structure which housed both the city and county offices. Inside, an aging janitor polishing the already-gleaming marble floors directed Jessica to the office of Homicide detective Jeremiah Jenkins.

Jenkins was so tall he had to bend over to get through the office doorway to greet her, walking with a chronic stoop, the result—Jessica was sure—of years of ducking under all manner of things normal-sized people sailed through. He had blond, almost white, hair and skin so pale it appeared the sun had never touched him. An albino, she thought, or close to it.

As a favor to Jessica, and without asking why, Matt Meecham had agreed to arrange her meeting with Jenkins. Although years younger than Meecham, they had become friends during their combined investigation of a serial killer who had stalked Native-American women in both cities three years before.

"So you know Matt, huh?" Jenkins said once they were sitting in his office. He had a quick and easy smile, and his legs poked out from under her side of the desk.

"Yes, but not that well," Jessica said.

"He's a hell of a cop when he wants to be."

"He's been very helpful to me," she said. "I'm new in town, and I think he feels sorry for me."

"He likes to put himself down," Jenkins said, "but he's one of the best investigators I've ever known. Did he tell you about the case we worked on together?"

"Only a little. Something about a weirdo who went around killing Indian women."

"Did he tell you how we finally got him?"

Jessica shook her head.

"Just like him. Well, this particular weirdo not only liked to kill people but to taunt the cops. He'd write us a note after each murder, calling us bumbling idiots or ignorant assholes, among other things. Matt figured out that one of the notes was written on the back of the flyleaf from a Gideon Bible, the kind they leave in hotel rooms. Except this page was filthy dirty."

"What did he do?" she asked.

"The two of us went to every flophouse and two-bit hotel in both cities, searching every room for a Gideon Bible with the flyleaf missing. We finally found it, in a place called the Empress Hotel on Hennepin Avenue. We arrested the guy who'd had the room the week before and tied him to the notes and the murders."

"Pretty impressive," Jessica said.

"It was classic police work. No fancy technology, no DNA tests, just a good eye, common sense, and a lot of footwork."

Jessica hesitated a moment, unsure how to begin. "Matt said you might be willing to help me, although he doesn't know what I'm looking for. I'd like to keep it that way."

Jenkins gave her a puzzled look.

"I'd like to know everything you can tell me about the murder of Eduardo Priaz."

"Eduardo? Around here we call him Half-and-Half."

"That's awful," Jessica said, but with a grin.

Jenkins began reciting details of the murder while pulling a manila folder from a file drawer. Most of what he told her she already knew from the newsroom computer.

"Any suspects?" she asked.

"No, sorry to say. Pretty slick killing, actually. Nobody saw him get tied to the tracks, and no real clues were left behind. Footprints or fingerprints or that kind of thing. We worked the case hard but came up blank. The file's still open, but there's been nothing new recently."

"What kind of guy was he?"

"A loser. He'd been in and out of jail most of the time since he'd emigrated from Cuba. Burglary, armed robbery, sexual assaults . . ."

Jessica straightened up. "Sexual assaults? He was a rapist?"

"Among other things. Fancied himself as a real ladies' man, but he got most of his sex at the point of a gun." Jenkins studied the contents of the manila file. "Arrested four times for sexual assault but convicted only once. He'd rob women, then rape them. A couple of the rape charges got bargained away when he pleaded guilty to other counts."

Jessica considered the information, then asked to see the file. When he handed it to her, she turned the pages slowly, trying to form a mental picture of Eduardo Priaz. "You must have some idea who killed him?" she finally said.

"Not really. He hung around with a tough crowd, made lots of enemies. Could have been anybody."

Jessica flipped another page of the file, then turned her head quickly away.

"Came to the pictures, huh?" Jenkins said. "I should have warned you. They're pretty gruesome."

Jessica quickly closed the file and handed it back to him. "I appreciate your help, Detective . . ."

"Call me Jerry. Did it really help?"

"Everything helps, but I don't know where it's leading."

After escorting Jessica out of the office, Jenkins put the folder back into the file, debated a moment, then reached for the phone and dialed. "Is Meecham there?" he asked.

"No, he's not" came the reply.

"Can you take a message? This is Jenkins from the St. Paul P.D. Tell Matt that his friend Jessica was here asking about the Eduardo Priaz murder, if that means anything to him. Okay?"

There was a pause at the other end. "Got it," said the voice.

"Who's this, by the way?" Jenkins asked.

"Lieutenant Brinkman. I work with Matt."

"You'll give him the message then."

"You can count on it," Brinkman said.

SEVENTEEN

Jessica first saw the figure huddled on the steps of her apartment building when she parked the Impala down the street. Huddled like a baby in the womb, head down, legs up to her chest, arms clasped around her knees. The sun was in Jessica's eyes, but she had taken no more than a half-dozen steps before she knew who it was. She had seen her in that same position hundreds of times over the years. Her sister, Janie.

Jessica hurried her pace and was slightly out of breath when she reached the steps. "Janie, what the hell are you doing here? Where have you been? We've been trying to call you!"

Only then did Janie raise her head, looking startled, as though she had been awakened from a deep sleep. "I was wondering when you'd get home," she mumbled. "Seems like I've been sitting here for hours."

"Why didn't you call?" Jessica demanded, fishing in her pocket for the apartment key. "I had no idea you were coming."

"I didn't, either, not until a couple of days ago."

It was only when Janie stood up and faced her that Jessica noticed the redness around her eyes and the pallor of her skin. "What's wrong with you, Janie? You look terrible. Are you sick?"

"That's why I'm here," she replied as Jessica fumbled getting the key into the lock. "I need help."

Jessica finally got the outside door open and led her sister up the steps to her apartment. Her feet dragged, and she paused at every other step. Jessica steadied her while trying to slow her own spinning mind. What could have happened? What's going on?

Like the day itself, the inside of the apartment was cooler. Still uncomfortable but tolerable. She helped Janie to the sofa, then opened all the windows wide to take advantage of a slight breeze squeezing between the buildings.

"Have you eaten? Can I get you something to drink?"

Janie shook her head. "I'm not hungry, but I could use a glass of water." Her words were a raw whisper. "I think I'm going to kill myself, Jess. Honest to God."

"What?"

"They'll never understand."

"Who? Who won't understand what?" Jessica demanded.

"Mom and Dad."

"Just sit here while I get the water," Jessica said. "Then we'll talk."

When she returned, Janie was still slouched in the sofa, chin down. The tears had begun again. Jessica propped her chin up and held the glass to her lips, just as she had done when Janie was a toddler and she played the big sister.

Almost eight years younger than Jessica, Janie was a trailer whose arrival had surprised even their parents. They had long since given up hope of having another child. A miracle baby, they called her, and had raised her even more protectively than Jessica.

For sisters they bore remarkably little resemblance to one another. Janie was taller than Jessica and more angular, not really gawky but not graceful, either. Long-faced, with drooping eyelids and a full mouth, she had a sleepy but sexy look. Like Jessica, she never had trouble attracting men.

Janie drank most of the water, and some color seemed to return to her cheeks, but her skin was feverish, and the tears continued.

"Can you talk now?" Jessica asked. "Can you tell me what's going on?"

Janie tried to straighten up, but the effort proved too great. "You've got to promise not to tell the folks," she said. "Not now, not ever!"

Jessica nodded, unwilling to argue.

Janie closed her eyes and leaned back, her face filled with pain. "I just had an abortion, Jess. This morning."

"You what?"

"In St. Paul. At the clinic. There were no problems. They say I'll be fine. I just need to rest. I was hoping I could stay with you for a while until I decide what to do."

Jessica was speechless. Of all the possibilities she had quickly considered, this was not one of them. It simply didn't fit Janie.

"Start from the beginning," Jessica urged.

"There's no beginning, no end. I got pregnant, Jess. I tried to say no, I tried to stop him."

"Who?"

"The guy I wrote to you about, the one at the resort."

"The fishing guide?"

"Yes. Charlie Bowser."

"He raped you?" This can't be, Jessica thought. Not here, not now. The image of Edward Hill flashed through her mind.

"I don't know," Janie sobbed. "Not exactly. It must have been my fault. I let him go too far. Then he wouldn't stop. Said I led him on. But I didn't, Jess. I swear. No more than I've done with other guys. But he wouldn't stop, he just kept going."

Jessica was overwhelmed by a seething anger and by the enormous irony of the situation. It was beyond belief. As she pursues the story of one rapist, her own sister becomes the victim of another. She told herself it just couldn't be true.

"When did this happen?"

"A month or so ago, just after I wrote you that letter. We'd gone canoeing and stopped to swim at an island."

"Why didn't you call me?" Jessica demanded. "I would have come right away, you know that."

Janie shook her head and tried to wipe the tears away. "I was too ashamed. I thought it was my fault, that I should never have put myself in that position. He'd been so nice to me, so polite and gentle. I thought I could trust him."

"The dirty bastard," Jessica muttered.

"I was going to try to forget about it, to stay away from him and try to get through the summer. But my period was late. I took one of those drugstore tests, and it turned out positive. I didn't know what to do."

"Did you tell him? That you were pregnant?"

"Yes. He just laughed and said tough shit, that it was my own fault for leading him on. He *laughed*, Jess!"

Jessica sat next to her and held her, mind racing, stomach churning. She didn't realize she was crying herself until she tasted the salt of her tears. "I'm sorry, Janie, so damned sorry. I don't know what else to say."

"Don't say anything. It's over, it's done. I didn't call you before the abortion because I didn't want to argue about it. I got myself into this mess, and I had to get myself out."

"You didn't get yourself into anything!" Jessica shouted. "He had no right to do what he did. It's called date rape, Janie. They put people in prison for that."

"I could never prove it, Jess. Who'd believe me? He lives up there. Everybody knows him, likes him. To those people I was just a round-heeled college girl."

They sat together for several minutes without speaking. Despite her anger, Jessica knew Janie was probably right about retribution. It was too late. There was no proof, no evidence of rape. The passage of time and the abortion would probably make prosecution impossible. It would be strictly her word against his.

"You can stay here," Jessica said finally, tiredly. "We'll make room. I'll call the folks right away, tell them you got fed up with life in the north woods and are spending some time with me. You can talk to them yourself when you're up to it."

"I'll never be able to face them," Janie said, sobbing.

"Yes, you will. Once you get your own head straight. We'll get you some help, some counseling. You'll do fine."

"I don't need counseling," Janie protested.

Jessica held her sister close. "Janie, please. Trust me on this, okay. After what you've been through, you need to talk to someone who knows what they're doing. I'll set it up and go with you if you want. You've got to get past this."

When Jessica dialed her parents' number, she hoped her father would answer. He'd be in a hurry to get somewhere and wouldn't ask as many questions. No such luck. Her mother's voice greeted her.

"I got your message, Mom, and I'm sorry I haven't gotten back to you sooner. It's been really busy."

Her mother got right to the point. "Have you heard from Janie?" she asked, urgency in her voice.

"That's why I called," Jessica replied. "She's here, with me."

"In Minneapolis?"

"In my apartment, just down the hall, sleeping."

"What's she doing there?" The urgency had turned to alarm.

"She got tired of the resort. Too much work, too little pay. Plus, the people weren't very nice. So she packed up and left. She's going to stay here for a while."

"That doesn't sound like Janie," her mother said suspiciously.

"She's growing up, Mom." And how, Jessica thought.

"Why did she come to you and not to us?"

"Because we're sisters, I guess, and because I don't think she thought you'd approve."

"Let me talk to her, Jessica."

"She's sleeping, Mom. She was really beat when she got here. I'll have her call you later."

"Your voice sounds funny, Jessica. What's going on up there?"

"Nothing," she lied. "Just what I've told you."

"Maybe your father and I should drive up."

"Don't, Mom. You know how Dad hates to drive in the Cities. I'll have Janie call you. Maybe we'll drive down this weekend."

Her mother reluctantly agreed, but Jessica knew this was not the last of it. She hoped Janie would be up to it.

Despite the misgiving in her mother's voice, Jessica knew her folks would never suspect the truth. If she hadn't, they wouldn't. The truth would seem even more impossible to them than it had to her.

She lay down on the lumpy couch, noticing for the first time its many sags and bumps. Stretched out, she felt as if her body were draped across a mountain range, sinking into every valley, being poked by every peak.

It was twilight, and she could hear the starlings squabbling outside the kitchen window. One of the neighborhood cats must be on the prowl, she decided. In the distance, there was the warble of an ambulance siren, and closer, the clatter of a trash can being rolled to the street. Somewhere, neither near nor far, the cry of a hungry baby.

Jessica knew the first task facing her was to help Janie get back on her feet. Physically and emotionally. Get her some rest, find a counselor, and eventually perhaps, help her find a job. In the meantime, they'd have to fit two people into an apartment that was barely big enough for one.

She got up and stretched, then padded quietly to the kitchen, careful not to awaken her sister down the hall. She made coffee, then leaned against the counter as the pot began to perk. Aside from the crisis with Janie, there was still the matter of Edward Hill to deal with. Something was strange about the whole situation, and she was starting to feel threatened and overwhelmed by it.

Jeremiah Jenkins, the St. Paul cop, had struck her as honest and forthright enough; he certainly didn't seem to be hiding anything. It was clear the murder of Eduardo Priaz was not at the top of his priority list and that she would get little additional help from him without revealing more of her own, maybe silly, suspicions. She wasn't ready to do that yet.

Sarah Andrews was something else. Why would she take the time and trouble to confront Jessica about Edward Hill? It still puzzled her. Sarah's concern that Jessica would interfere with the police investigation or make a hero of Hill rang hollow. But maybe she was misjudging her, she thought. Maybe she was warning her for her own good.

EIGHTEEN

The sun had dropped behind the stately homes along St. Paul's Summit Avenue but still touched the tops of the giant elms and maples that towered over the broad boulevard. Beneath the trees, the sidewalks lay in the dusky shadows of approaching darkness.

They came at intervals of fifteen minutes. Four women, all on the younger side of forty, all dressed casually and coolly. Each had parked her car a block or two away and approached the house from a different direction. They walked with the unhurried gait of a summer-evening stroll, but their eyes were never still, sweeping the unlit yards, probing the gaps between houses and behind every tree and bush.

In one hand, three of them carried bags of varying sizes and descriptions, each filled with the tools and materials of her particular craft: needlepoint, knitting, sewing. One even lugged a partially finished quilt. In the other hand, held loosely, was a tiny can of Mace.

They were not afraid, just cautious. The fourth woman, Freda Brinkman, carried nothing.

Their common destination was a modest two-story brick home tucked between two of the mansions for which Summit Avenue was famous. A century before, the house had served as a guest cottage for the adjoining estate of a lumber baron but was later split off and sold, with a succession of owners over the intervening years.

The present owner was a history professor at Macalester College, Patricia Sample, a short, bulky woman who stood at the door and quietly greeted the four visitors, one by one, as they arrived. She ushered each through the living room and into a larger oak-trimmed library filled with hundreds of volumes.

One wall of books allowed space for a small stone fireplace, its interior blackened from the flames of uncounted winter fires. In front of the hearth were two leather couches facing each other, flanked by two matching chairs.

The women chatted quietly until the last had arrived and the library door was closed. That's when Freda Brinkman rose slowly from one of the chairs and stood next to the fireplace. Her face was grim. The emergency meeting of the Craft Club was about to begin.

Brinkman wasted no time on preliminaries. "I'm glad you could come on such short notice," she began. "You'll understand why it was necessary in a few moments."

There was a slight stirring in the seats and an exchange of curious glances. Five years before, the women were strangers; they had slowly come together in an ever-expanding circle, with Brinkman at its center. Three things besides gender bound them: Each had been scarred in some way by the violence of rape, all were filled with a deep rage at society's inability or unwillingness to deal with sexual predators, and all had come in search of vengeance.

The last to join—the year before—was Sarah Andrews, after Kim's rape, after seeing Edward Hill, like so many other predators before him, go free to rape again and again. Recruited by Brinkman at a time when Sarah's anger and frustration at the system were at their peak. Like the others, she was bound by an oath of secrecy which each felt as deeply as her own womanhood.

The women seldom saw one another outside of these meetings, covertly held under the guise of an innocent group of friends interested in chatting and working on their crafts. In truth, none of them ever touched the bags they so dutifully carried.

As Sarah surveyed the group, she marveled at how ordinary they all appeared. None of the women would stand out in a crowd; any of them could be a next-door neighbor or someone who worked across the office or behind the department-store counter. Yet, Sarah knew, each had blood of predators on her hands.

Next to her, on one end of the couch, was Nancy Higgins, a blond thirtyish accountant who had been raped twice within two years by the same man, the second attack only two days after the rapist got out of jail from the first assault. Sarah knew that Higgins's marriage, battered by the emotional effects of the rapes and the trials, had ended months later.

Across from Higgins sat Teresa Johnson, an attractive, dark-haired mother of three who ran a local day-care center. Sarah had been told that five years before, the woman's youngest child, a girl of seven, had been kidnapped, raped, beaten, and left for dead by a walkaway from a halfway house for sexual offenders. The child was brain damaged and was now confined to a wheelchair in a semivegetative state.

Next to her was the professor, Patricia Sample, whose runaway teenaged daughter had been kidnapped on the streets of Minneapolis and transported to New York City to work as a prostitute. Her body had been found two years before in a seedy Times Square hotel, sexually battered and dead of a drug overdose.

And then there was Freda Brinkman herself, who now stood in front of the group, looking down on them. "We've discovered a possible threat to our security," she said. "One that we may have to deal with."

"What are you talking about?" Nancy Higgins demanded.

"For reasons I can't explain," Brinkman said, "a reporter at Channel Seven has taken a special interest in the death of Edward Hill. Her name's Jessica Mitchell. . . ."

"Never heard of her," said Teresa Johnson.

"I don't doubt it," Brinkman responded. "She's new at the station. But that hasn't slowed her down. She's pressing for information on the Hill murder. She's gotten to know Hill's mother and has managed to get hold of Hill's secret diary.

"By itself that might not be a problem," Brinkman continued, "but I learned today that she's also poking around in St. Paul, asking about the murder of Eduardo Priaz. That has to be more than coincidence or mere chance; she's somehow stumbled onto what she sees as the beginning of a pattern."

Teresa Johnson had moved to the edge of her chair, a tremor in her voice. "I thought you told us Hill's death would be forgotten in a few days."

"It would have been without this reporter," Brinkman replied. "She's a factor we had no way of anticipating or predicting."

Sarah jumped in. "I know her. I've talked to her. She admits her fixation is strange, that no one else seems interested in the case. But that hasn't deterred her."

"So what can we do?" the history professor asked.

Brinkman shook her head slowly. "I'm not sure. We hope she'll get frustrated and drop it. We're going to keep a close eye on her, but we wanted you to know we may have to deal with her."

"What do you mean, 'deal with her'?" Higgins asked.

"I don't know," Brinkman said. "It depends."

"We're talking about a woman here, not some rapist, for God's sake." Teresa Johnson was on her feet. "I hope you're not suggesting what I think you're suggesting."

"Relax," Sarah interrupted. "Freda's talking about simple persuasion, maybe scare tactics. Nothing more, right?" She looked at Brinkman for confirmation, but she stood stoically, saying nothing. "Right?" There was still no response.

"I don't like the sound of this," the professor said.

"Listen to me," Brinkman said. "We can't tolerate a possible breach of security. There's too much at stake for all of us. We can't risk exposure. It's that simple. As the founder of this group, I will do everything in my power to prevent it."

No one spoke, and Brinkman sank back into her chair. Sarah studied her with fascination, awed by the power she exerted over the group. She was an enigma, her face a mask that revealed almost nothing. As Sarah thought about it, she realized she had never seen Brinkman smile, had never seen her features relax. The mask, like the woman behind it, seemed impenetrable.

What little Sarah did know about Brinkman had come to her in bits and pieces over the past year. Freda had revealed some of it herself in a rare, unguarded conversation with Sarah months before, but most of the information came from the other women in the group or from Sarah's sources in the police department or the county attorney's office.

What had slowly emerged was the portrait of a hardened, vengeful woman whose brutish adult life had been forged in the fires of an abusive childhood. As a young teenager, her only relief from the repeated physical and sexual pummelings of a drunken stepfather were those periods when he was in jail or in a stupor at the detox center.

"When he wasn't fucking me, he was beating me," she had told Sarah. "Or vice versa. I decided then that no man would ever do that to me again."

"What about your mother?" Sarah had asked. "Didn't she try to stop it?"

With a bitter laugh, Brinkman said, "Hell, no. If he was pounding on me, it meant he wasn't pounding on her. Courage was never my mother's strong suit."

Sarah decided that in many ways, Brinkman's childhood paralleled those of the victims, and some of the predators, she saw pass through the system.

Before she turned fifteen, Freda fled her house of horrors for the streets but found life there no happier or less threatening. Alone, broke, hungry, and constantly hassled by the pimps and assorted other street scum, she finally retreated to a refuge for runaways operated by Catholic Charities.

Then, after a few weeks, it was on to a foster home, where the foster father happened to be a Minneapolis cop and the only decent man she would ever know. He died a year after her graduation from high school, but not before convincing her to become a cop, too.

But her afflictions were not over yet. As one of the first women on the police force, she found herself subjected to endless harassment from other cops who still thought a woman's place was at home, in bed, and not in a squad car. By refusing to submit to the bullying and sexual badgering, she became an outcast in the department, a bitter loner who managed to rise through the ranks despite the obstacles but whose contempt and hatred of men now bordered on the obsessive.

Sarah was told that attitude only intensified during Brinkman's years in the sex-crimes unit, where she saw women and children victimized again and again by men no different from her stepfather or others of those who had scorned and abused her over the years.

When, like Sarah, she finally had seen enough, the club was born, and its first victim, the monster who had terrorized Teresa Johnson's daughter, had died. That was five years ago, and Sarah knew that the other women were increasingly worried at the pleasure Brinkman seemed to take with each additional death.

"I don't think it matters to her anymore who he is or what he's done," Pat Sample confided to Sarah recently. "She just enjoys the killing."

As the newest member of the club, Sarah felt uncomfortable challenging Brinkman in front of the others, but she suspected that such a confrontation was inevitable. Even now she realized some calming words were necessary.

Sarah said, "Rest easy. We'll be in close contact with you regarding all of this. We're not going to go off the deep end, but we may need to meet again on short notice."

Sarah's reassurance seemed to quell the grumbling, but tension could still be felt as the women reached for their bags and prepared to leave.

"There's one more item on the agenda," Sarah said.

"What's that?" Higgins asked, already halfway to the door.

"Lowell Paul Ingram," Sarah said.

"The teacher?" Higgins again. "We saw you on television. What happened, anyway?"

Sarah explained the background and disposition of the case, including a verbatim account of her venomous encounter with Ingram in the empty courtroom. "He got away with probation and counseling, which he'll ignore. He's learned nothing, and it's only a matter of time before he's back at it."

"Especially now that he doesn't have a wife to get off on," Brinkman added. "He's an unrepentant prick of the first order."

"What are you going to do?" Higgins asked.

"Teach the teacher a lesson," Sarah said.

"What kind of lesson?"

"One that he'll remember."

"Is this wise?" the professor asked. "Shouldn't we back off for a while? Especially considering what you've said about the reporter. So far, I've agreed with every decision and action this group has taken, but this gives me the willies."

"This won't be like the others," Sarah said.

"Still . . ." the professor persisted.

"What if your daughter—"

"I don't have a daughter anymore," she said bitterly.

"I know," Sarah said. "I'm sorry. But you should understand the need."

She became quiet. No one else protested.

"All in favor?" Brinkman said.

Every hand was slowly raised.

The next morning, Sarah awoke feeling tense and grumpy. Even after a cool shower, two aspirin, and her first cup of coffee, she could not shake the sour mood.

By contrast, Kim was in unusually good spirits, bouncy and eager to chat. "How was the Craft Club last night?" she asked from across the breakfast table.

"Same as always," Sarah answered vaguely, buttering her

toast with more attention than it deserved. "More gabbing than crafting, I'm afraid."

"You never cease to amaze me," Kim said lightheartedly. "You're the last person I'd expect to find in a group like that. What's it been now, a year or so? And I've yet to see anything you've done there."

"That's because I'm a klutz. Knitting's not my strong suit."

"Then why do you keep going?" Kim pressed. "It seems strange."

Sarah wiped the crumbs from her lips and forced a smile. "It's a diversion, I guess. Something different, and I like the women." She picked up her dishes and began to stack them in the dishwasher, hoping to divert the conversation.

But Kim persisted. "You've never told me who all attends."

"Nobody you'd know," Sarah lied. "Just a bunch of women I've gotten to know through work. We talk about everything but work."

Sarah had always suspected Kim was slightly miffed that she had never been invited to one of the Craft Club meetings. But until now they'd never really talked at length about it. Sarah preferred to keep it that way.

"How's your job?" Sarah asked, changing the conversation.

"Dull," Kim replied. "Summer's always slow. Everybody's on vacation, and the market's in the doldrums. I keep busy, but I have to work at it. How about you?"

"The files are still stacking up. Three more murders last week alone. The hot weather seems to bring out the worst in people."

Kim picked up the morning newspaper from the table and pointed to a front-page article. "I see the number of rapes is up again."

"I know. Twenty-seven percent in the first six months of the year," Sarah replied. "It's amazing. Rapes are way up, but arrests and convictions aren't."

"What's the problem?"

"Same old thing. Ninety-five percent of the rapes are the so-called date rapes, and they're tough to prosecute. Juries like to believe that if a woman knows the guy, there has to be consent. It's nonsense, but until we change some attitudes, it's going to be an uphill battle."

"What do you hear about that Ingram guy?" Kim asked as she grabbed her purse and walked to the door.

"His attorney says he's on cloud nine, delighted to be a free man. But, trust me, he'll get his someday."

"Are you ready to go?" Kim asked.

"In a minute," Sarah said. "I have to brush my teeth."

As Kim listened to the water running in the bathroom, she glanced down at the shopping bag Sarah had dropped by the door after the Craft Club meeting the night before. The yarn was there, and the knitting needles. But not a stitch had been cast on.

NINETEEN

When Jessica emerged from the apartment building that morning, she was surprised to find an unmarked squad car sitting behind her Impala. Matt Meecham was at the wheel, holding a stub of a cigar in one hand, a steaming cup of coffee in the other.

"Matt?" she said, shielding her eyes from the sun as she approached the car. "What're you doing here?"

"Waiting for you," he said. "I was about to come and knock on your door."

Jessica walked around the car and climbed into the front seat, studying him curiously. She again noted the tidiness of his appearance. "Is someone dressing you these days?" she asked lightly.

Meecham laughed. "Hardly. I'm saving myself for you, Jessica."

She smiled and leaned back in the seat, waiting. He flicked the cigar into the street and blew on his coffee before turning to her. "What does Eduardo Priaz have to do with anything?" he asked.

The question caught Jessica by surprise. "Jenkins called you? I asked him not to."

"What can I say? We're friends."

She shifted in her seat, saying nothing.

"What about it?" Meecham pressed. "Jenkins gave me the details of the case. He said you seemed to be especially interested in this guy's record." Then he grinned. "Is this part of your serial-killer theory?"

"Do I amuse you, Matt? Is that why you're here? To humor me?"

"No, Jessica," he said more seriously. "I'm here because I'm interested in what you're up to and because I happen to like you."

She leaned across the seat. "When Jenkins told you about Priaz, did any bells ring?"

"You mean Edward Hill."

"Could be, Matt. Think about it. Repeat rapist who was killed brutally, almost professionally, with what I'd call a vengeance. Made him suffer, that's for sure. No clues, no suspects. It could be a coincidence, but it makes me wonder."

It was Meecham's turn to study her. Was that a hint of respect in his eyes?

"Anything else?" he asked.

"Maybe, but we've got to get something straight first."

"What's that?"

"This is a murder case for you, but it's a story for me. I'd like to see us help one another, if that's possible, but I don't want to lose the story in the process. Everyone tells me to keep my distance from the cops, that they'll screw me over without a second thought. If we work together on this, you've got to guarantee me you won't get in the way of my story."

Meecham considered her words. "I don't see a problem," he finally said, "as long as you don't spoil any possible prosecution."

"Fair enough."

"Now, what else do you have?" he asked.

"There are two other murders we've discovered that could fit the pattern. And there may be more. Both victims were men, both murders are unsolved, both happened in different years and in different suburbs."

"So what do you want me to do?"

"So far the cops in Bloomington and Brooklyn Park are stonewalling us. Won't even give us a cause of death. I thought you might pry it out of them, all of the details you can get."

"That shouldn't be a problem," Meecham said. "We trade that kind of information all the time."

"Good. Will you call me?"

"As soon as I know something."

Jessica reached into her briefcase and gave Meecham all of the information she had on the two killings. "Keep it to yourself for now, will you?" she asked, getting out of the car.

"Yes, ma'am. Anything you say, ma'am."

He was still smiling when she got into the Impala.

When Jessica reached the station and walked into the newsroom, she found people scurrying in every direction, bumping into one another, cursing, shouting instructions and questions that were drowned out in the hubbub. The reasons quickly became clear.

A freight train had collided with a school bus carrying children to a summer camp in the wilds of northern Minnesota, and first reports indicated there were a number of dead and injured. The station helicopter had been dispatched with two news crews, one to fly to the crash scene, the other to be dropped off at a hospital where the injured kids were being taken.

At almost the same time, police in the suburb of Minnetonka confirmed that the wife of a local bank president had been kidnapped. The woman had actually been taken two days before, but the abduction had been kept quiet while the negotiations with the kidnappers continued. Those talks had now broken off, with the million-dollar ransom still unpaid, and the police and FBI decided to go public with an appeal to the kidnappers.

Jessica was surrounded, almost lost, in the confusion.

Laurie Sanders stood on a chair behind the assignment desk, trying to make herself heard above the babel. "Where the hell's the satellite truck?" she yelled. "Is it on its way north yet?"

One of the technicians shouted back, "It's leaving the garage now, but they've got to gas up."

Laurie's head drooped. It was a standing order that the satellite trucks and all of the news vehicles would never be parked without a full tank of gas. She knew it could mean the difference in getting a live report on the news, or worse, getting beat on a story like this by competitors who didn't have to stop for fuel.

Jessica edged closer to the assignment desk, hoping to get Laurie's attention. Before she could, a desk assistant grabbed Laurie by the arm. "The network's on Line Three," she said. "They want to know what we've got on the bus crash."

"Tell 'em it just happened, for Christ's sake, and that it's in the middle of nowhere. We'll get back to them."

The assistant whispered into the phone, then turned to Laurie again. "Now they want to know about the kidnapping." Laurie was irate. She grabbed the phone away and shouted into it. "Get your own crew up here. We're knee-deep in shit, and we don't need you on our ass." She slammed the phone down without listening for a reply.

Jessica took advantage of the momentary pause. "What can I do, Laurie?"

Before she could respond, the radio on the assignment desk blared, "This is Minicam two. We're set up and ready to go from the FBI news conference. It's set for twenty minutes from now. You want it live?"

"Does the pope have balls?" Laurie spit into the mike. "Of course we do. We're setting up in the studio now. Get back to us in ten minutes."

Her attention returned to Jessica. "Have you ever anchored?"

Jessica was startled by the question. "A couple of times in Duluth, but that was months ago."

"Were you any good?"

"I was all right, I guess." What was she supposed to say?

"Good. You're all we've got. We can't get hold of Collier or Barbara, and everybody else is off on one of the stories. Go see Barclay in the studio. He's running the live cut-in on the kidnapping. He'll fill you in. Move!"

Jessica dashed across the newsroom and down the hall. When she reached the studio, her legs were shaking from fear. Technicians hurried to set the lights and get the cameras into position. George Barclay sat to one side, his bulk balanced on a small chair behind a makeshift desk where he had plugged a portable computer into the system. He had a phone in one ear, listening, while also talking to the floor director. "All we need is two cameras. Single talent. Not complicated. Okay?"

He was surprised to see Jessica rush up to the desk. "Laurie says I'm supposed to report to you. She wants me to anchor the cut-in. No one else is available, she says."

"Can you do it?"

"I think so," Jessica said.

"Good. All you have to do is read what's on the PrompTer. I'm writing that now. Hilliard's at the news conference, and he'll carry most of the load. Feel free to ask him a couple of questions when he's done, but listen for the director's cues in your earpiece. We may have to interrupt Hilliard if the news conference drags on and if we need to do an update on the bus crash."

As she settled in at the anchor desk, Jessica was both excited and frightened. Forget that you've been picked from the bottom of the barrel, she told herself. Make the most of it. You've been waiting for a chance. Don't blow it.

Forgotten in the exhilaration of the moment were all thoughts of Edward Hill or Eduardo Priaz or Matt Meecham.

"Stand by! Ten seconds to air. Five, four, three . . ."

The earpiece felt as if it would fall out, and she was sure a frog was creeping up her throat, ready to croak. But Jessica knew the moment had arrived, for better or worse.

". . . three, two, one . . . cue!"

"Good morning everyone. I'm Jessica Mitchell with a special report from Channel Seven News. Two major stories are developing at this hour: a train-school bus collision in northern Minnesota, in a remote area near Ely, has killed at least four children and injured another dozen. Details are scarce, but we're told the children were en route to a church camp when their bus was hit by a freight train at an unguarded crossing. None of the dead or injured has been identified, but Channel Seven news crews are en route to the scene, and we will bring you further details as they develop."

The studio lights were intensely hot and bright, leaving Jessica blind beyond the TelePrompTer. She could feel the sweat trickle down the back of her neck, and she desperately craved water to moisten her mouth. But she forged ahead:

"Closer to home, a startling announcement. Minnetonka police and the FBI revealed this morning that Darlene Carlstrom, the wife of prominent local banker Eugene Carlstrom, was kidnapped two days ago and is still missing. Jeff Hilliard is standing by . . . live . . . at the FBI offices, where a news conference is now under way. Jeff?"

She glanced at the studio monitor and saw Hilliard's face pop up on the screen, replacing hers.

"Jessica," Hilliard began, "the special agent in charge of the Minneapolis FBI office, Jason Albright, is at the podium now, explaining that efforts to meet the kidnappers million-dollar ransom demands have failed. He's urging the kidnappers to reestablish contact with authorities and the family and to do no harm to Mrs. Carlstrom."

The camera zoomed slowly past Hilliard to the podium to pick up part of the FBI agent's statement. In the studio, with the microphones off, George Barclay edged close to the set. "You're doing fine, Jess. Feeling okay?" Jessica nodded but pointed to her mouth. "Water?" Barclay signaled to the floor director, who quickly handed her a cup.

Hilliard was back on camera, explaining that the missing woman had been working in her garden when two men wearing ski masks had emerged from the adjoining woods, gagged and blindfolded her, and carried her off. A maid working on the second floor of the banker's house had seen the abduction take place but was so shaken she could provide no real description of the kidnappers or their car.

The screen was then filled with a live picture of the gate of the Carlstrom estate with police and reporters milling outside on the street. Then Hilliard was back on camera.

"Jessica, the FBI has gone public with this out of obvious concern for the safety of Mrs. Carlstrom. It's been twenty-four hours since they've spoken to the kidnappers, whom they fear may have been panicked by their unsuccessful attempts to collect the ransom. They're hoping for the best but clearly fearing the worst. Back to you in the studio."

"Jeff, no leads at all to the woman's whereabouts?"

"I'm afraid not. She's simply disappeared without a trace. Years ago, the kidnapped wife of another prominent local businessman was found alive, tied to a tree in a state park near Duluth. However, in that case, the ransom had been paid."

"What's the problem with the ransom?" she asked.

"Authorities say they have the money, but they've run into snags trying to get it to the kidnappers. They won't say any more than that."

Jessica thanked Hilliard and then signed off the special report, promising viewers frequent updates on both the kidnapping and the bus crash throughout the day. There was a smattering of polite applause from the crew as her mike was cut and the lights dimmed. Jessica blushed slightly.

"Nice job, Jess," Barclay said from beyond the set. "Just like a veteran. Why don't you stick around the newsroom in case we need to do another one."

When Jessica returned to the newsroom, it was quiet, almost deserted. Virtually every reporter and photographer on staff had been sent to one of the two stories. Those not on duty were being called into the station to cover the other news of the day. Jessica walked to the assignment desk and stood to one side as Laurie Sanders huddled with several newscast producers.

"The helicopter should arrive at the scene of the bus crash

in about forty-five minutes," Laurie said, glancing at the studio clock. "They'll get some quick video there, pick up the hospital footage, and head back. They'll transmit as much tape as they can from the air—once they get within range—so watch for it. We'll do an update with the first video as soon as we get it."

One of the producers nodded, quickly jotting notes on a yellow legal pad.

"The crew will stay at the scene," Laurie continued, "and wait for the satellite truck to get there. They'll use the bird to feed the finished pieces for the early newscasts. We need to book the satellite time now."

Another of the producers headed toward a phone.

Laurie looked up and noticed Jessica. "Good job, Jess. Just like Duluth, right?" Jessica smiled gratefully as Laurie returned to the producers.

"Hilliard will do the package on the kidnapping, using video from the Carlstrom estate, the FBI news conference, and—"

The newsroom intercom interrupted. "Jessica Mitchell, phone please, Line Four."

Who could that be? she wondered as she walked to the phone.

"Jessica?"

It was Matt Meecham. "Don't say anything, don't mention my name," he said. "Just listen."

She did as she was told.

"The Carlstrom lady is dead. They just found her body."

"What?"

"You won't hear anything on the police radios, and you're not hearing this from me, okay?"

Jessica listened.

"The body is in an old railroad car parked on the Soo Line siding in northeast Minneapolis, just off Central. A railroad dick found it while looking for bums trying to boost a free ride. No other newspeople know, Jess. Nobody. They're hushing it up."

"You're sure it's her?" she whispered.

"Positive."

"Does the family know?"

"Not yet, but they will soon."

"How soon?" she asked.

"Why?"

"Because we can't put the story on the air until they do."

"I'll call you," he said.

"Why are you doing this?"

"Because I want you to trust me, Jessica. If we're going to work together, we need that. All cops aren't out to screw you over."

"I could be in big trouble if you're wrong on this."

"Trust me, Jessica. But you don't know where you heard it. I'm trusting you on that."

The line went dead.

Jessica put down the phone and raced back to the assignment desk. Laurie was still in the midst of her briefing with the producers. ". . . we're trying to get the FBI guy to appear live on our five o'clock show," she was saying, "but it's not definite . . ."

"Laurie!" There was a trembling in Jessica's voice.

The assignment editor looked up, startled.

"I need to talk to you, quick."

"Can't it wait?" Laurie barked. "I'm not finished here."

"No."

Laurie frowned and stepped away from the circle of producers, joining Jessica a few feet away.

"They found the woman's body," Jessica whispered to her. "Mrs. Carlstrom."

Laurie's expression changed to disbelief. "How do you know?"

"Just got a call," she replied, telling her the essence of her conversation with Meecham but without mentioning his name.

"Who's the source?" Laurie demanded.

"I can't say. I promised."

"Tell me," Laurie insisted. "I need to know."

"Sorry, I can't."

Laurie stared at her, her annoyance showing. "You'd better

be right," she said, then scurried back to the assignment desk to pick up the radio microphone. "Car two, stop at the nearest phone and call me. I've got an assignment that I don't want pirated off the radio."

As she waited for the phone call, George Barclay walked into the newsroom. He glanced at Laurie, then followed her pointed finger to Jessica. "What's going on?" he asked.

Jessica told him what she'd already told Laurie. "She's dispatching a cruiser to the railroad yard now. We could have this all by ourselves."

"If it turns out to be true," Barclay said doubtfully.

"I'm certain it is. I trust the source."

"Certain enough to go on the air with it?"

Jessica could sense he was testing her. "We have to be sure the family knows first. I'm waiting for another call."

"The hell with the family!" Barclay shouted. "This is no highway fatality. This is big news. If you're that sure it's true, let's go with it now."

Barclay's orders were contrary to everything Jessica had been taught. Was he testing her again? "You don't really want them to find out on television, do you?" she asked. "I didn't think we'd ever do that." Was she crazy, arguing with the news director?

Barclay smiled, but before he could respond, Jessica was summoned to the phone again.

"The family knows now. They've all been told." Meecham's voice again, in a husky whisper.

"You're absolutely sure?" she asked.

"Would I lie to you, Jessica?" Then he hung up.

Would he? Not Meecham. Then she remembered his anger over the diary. Was he drinking again? Of course not; she'd just seen him an hour before. Jessica knew if he was right, she'd be an instant hero. If he was wrong . . .

She made her decision. "The family knows," she told Barclay. "I think we should go with it now."

Laurie had rejoined them. "Not without knowing your source," she said. "We could look like jerks."

Barclay peered at Jessica expectantly.

Jessica shook her head. "I gave my word."

"Our car will be at the railroad yard in ten minutes," Laurie said. "I say we wait until they confirm it."

"Ten minutes could cost us the exclusive," Barclay said.

"Going with it now could cost us our reputation!" Laurie argued. "We need a second source on something like this."

Jessica felt as if she were watching a tennis match. "It's up to you," she said.

Barclay looked at her steadily, then turned and shouted to a technician. "Light up the studio. Now! We're going with a bulletin."

For the second time in less than a half hour, Jessica was back in front of the camera. This time, there was no Tele-PrompTer. It would be strictly ad-lib.

"Don't give the exact location of the body," Barclay shouted from behind the cameras. "We don't want the competition showing up before they get the corpse out of there."

The countdown went as before, and suddenly the red light flicked on above the camera.

"I'm Jessica Mitchell with a bulletin from Channel Seven News. We have learned that Minneapolis police have discovered the body of Darlene Carlstrom, the kidnapped wife of Minnetonka banker Eugene Carlstrom, in a railroad boxcar in northeast Minneapolis."

Steady, she told herself. Keep going.

"We have no details on how the woman was killed or how long she has been dead, but we're told the body was found by a railroad detective who was checking empty boxcars for transients.

"Ironically, the grim discovery came at about the same time the FBI publicly appealed to the kidnappers to reestablish contact with them so the million-dollar ransom could be delivered. The FBI had said they were afraid the kidnappers might have panicked when earlier attempts to deliver the ransom went awry. It now appears that their fears were justified.

"Repeating: Channel Seven News has learned that the body of kidnap victim Darlene Carlstrom has been found in northeast Minneapolis. Stay tuned to Channel Seven for the

latest details on that story and on the train-school bus collision in northern Minnesota. I'm Jessica Mitchell, Channel
Seven News."

The studio darkened and became deadly quiet. Word had
spread quickly; everyone seemed to understand the risk.
Jessica was sure she could hear George Barclay's whispered
prayers.

The crew slowly withdrew from the studio, leaving Jessica
sitting at the now-darkened anchor desk and Barclay perched
uncomfortably on his tiny chair. Neither spoke, waiting. Then
the studio door burst open. It was Laurie Sanders. "The FBI's
on the phone, jumping mad. They say we're jeopardizing their
investigation. They say they're going to the FCC . . . that
they'll have our license."

Barclay ignored the warning. "Was it her?" he asked
tiredly. "Was the body Mrs. Carlstrom's?"

"They won't confirm or deny," Laurie replied, almost choking, "but our crew at the scene says it is. No question. And
we're the only TV crew there."

Barclay got up from his chair and walked over to Jessica.
He took her hand in his and said simply, "Good work, Jess."
Then he walked out of the studio with Laurie, and Jessica
heard him say something like "How's that for giving her
enough rope . . ."

When they were gone, Jessica put her head in her hands.
Thank you, God. Thank you, Matt. I owe you both one.

TWENTY

For the rest of the day, Jessica had little time to worry about anything but the breaking news. After Alex Collier and Barbara Miller relieved her at the anchor desk, she helped prepare the kidnapping story for the evening newscasts. She tried to call Matt Meecham to thank him but was told he was out of the office for the day and couldn't be reached. She didn't leave a message.

The newscasts went well; the satellite feeds from the bus crash came off without a hitch, and they had the exclusive tape of Mrs. Carlstrom's body being recovered and hauled away from the railroad yard. The FBI was still angry that they had broken the story but was no longer talking about going after their license.

Perhaps it was her imagination, but Jessica sensed she was now viewed differently in the newsroom, accorded a certain respect and deference, even by some of the senior reporters, who had all but ignored her until then. There were the small, almost imperceptible smiles and nods, the way people would politely step aside for her.

Amid great speculation about her secret source, she had become the whispered talk of the newsroom. Only Bill Kendrick had dared to confront her. "It was Meecham, wasn't it?" he asked quietly.

Jessica had laughed. "You know better than that, Bill. I've never heard you talking about *your* sources."

"Wait a minute. Who told you about Hill's castration?"

"That was different," she said. "You volunteered it."

"I won't say a thing to anybody," he promised, "but just between us, I'm right, aren't I?"

"Forget it," she said with a grin, and walked away.

By the end of the day, Jessica was exhausted. Like everyone else, she had worked twelve hours straight, with only a short break for a sandwich. She was already dreading the prospect of another night on the lumpy couch.

"Hey, Jess, we're heading to Gino's for a quick one." It was Jeff Hilliard, standing, smiling, a few feet from her desk. "Come along and bask in your glory."

Jessica craved a cold beer, but the thought of sitting around the noisy, smoky bar—fending off hustles and questions about her secret source—had no appeal. Besides, she knew she had to get home to check on Janie. "I think I'll pass, Jeff, thanks. I'm beat."

As she walked out of the station, however, she remembered that she should make one quick stop first.

Jessica found Meecham in the same back booth at Barney's. She sat down across from him without a word and without invitation. She picked up his glass and sipped from it. Straight tonic water.

"Surprised?" he asked with a grin. "I thought you trusted me."

"Just checking," she replied.

"Can I get you something?" he asked.

"I'd love a beer, if it doesn't bother you."

"No sweat." He heaved himself out of the booth and walked to the bar, returning with a frosty mug of Michelob.

She hoisted the mug in a small toast and took a deep swallow. "I just came by to say thanks," she said, savoring the taste. "You did me a big favor, and I appreciate it."

"I'm glad I could help."

"How'd you find out about the body?" Jessica asked.

"We've known about the kidnapping since it happened, but it wasn't in our jurisdiction, and the feds were handling it, so we kept hands off. But when the report of a dead lady came into the office, I knew it had to be her. Instinct, I guess. As soon as I confirmed it, I called you."

"You made a hero out of me, that's for sure. People don't seem to regard me as the rookie reporter anymore."

"Don't let it go to your head. I like you the way you are."

Jessica smiled and sipped her beer, feeling the exhaustion of the day seep through her body. They sat quietly for a few minutes, surrounded by the soothing voice of Natalie Cole on the jukebox.

She felt comfortable with Meecham, as at ease with him as she was with her own father. Yet he was still a virtual stranger to her. He had never volunteered anything about his private life, and until then she had been hesitant to ask.

"It's none of my business, Matt, but what do you do when you're not at the office or sitting here?"

He looked at her warily, knowing she was crossing a new and personal threshold in their relationship. "Mostly sit at home with the cats," he finally said. "Read some, watch TV, fish when I can."

"You have cats?"

"My wife got them years ago, when they were kittens. Siamese twins, Tippy and Tyler, Too. Loved history, my wife. They're a pain in the ass, but they're company and damn near as old as I am—in cat years."

"I heard that your wife died," Jessica said. "I'm sorry."

"Then you probably know I killed her," he said bluntly. "Driving drunk." He looked away but hardly paused. "I don't know why she died and I lived. I never have understood that. It's so unfair. She was a sweet woman, and I was an asshole, yet she was the one who died."

He spoke matter-of-factly, as though he had long since expended all emotions. "She was a lot like you, Jessica, when she was younger. Bright and curious. Loved concerts and museums and would read more in a month than I'd read in a year. I'm still amazed that she actually saw something in me."

"I'm not," Jessica said. "You're a nice man." And then: "Any children?"

He looked away, hesitant. "A boy. Scotty. But I haven't seen or heard from him in years. He's never forgiven me for . . . for what I did to his mother. I don't blame him. He took off after the funeral and never came back. I think he's in California. It's like I killed him, too."

Jessica leaned closer. "You've never tried to reach him?"

"Nah. I don't know how, and even if I did, I don't know what more I'd say to him. What's done is done, and I'll never be able to undo it." He wiped the back of his hand across his eyes. "I'm doing okay. I live with it every day, and I know it will never get any better. Actually makes it easier to be a cop. I have no fear of death now. In fact, I'm kind of looking forward to it. I just hope I'll see her again then, to say I'm sorry."

"Is that why you kept drinking?" she asked. "To forget?"

"Because I'm a weak son of a bitch, Jessica. Because the hours sometimes seemed like days. Because there didn't seem much left to live for. But I never drank and drove after that. Never. What I didn't spend on booze, I spent on taxi fares."

She took a final sip of beer. "May I come see the cats someday?"

"Sure," he said, smiling, "but let's get your serial killer first."

"It's a deal," Jessica said as she rose to leave.

When Jessica got back to the apartment, she found Janie curled up on the couch, a throw pillow clutched to her chest, staring vacantly at the flickering TV in the corner of the room. Only when the door clicked shut did she glance in Jessica's direction.

Jessica stood for a moment with her back to the door. "Janie, you okay?"

Her sister sat unmoving, except to hug the pillow even more tightly against her body.

"Janie?"

Jessica walked across the room to switch on a small table lamp, then to the TV, lowering the volume. Janie paid no attention.

"Hey, sis," Jessica said. "Talk to me."

Janie's eyes remained fixed on the TV screen. "Do you always work this late?" she asked quietly.

"Not always," Jessica said, crossing to her and kneeling down beside her. "But it's been a busy day. I'm sorry I'm so late."

"It's okay," Janie murmured. "I watched your reports."

Jessica saw that she was still wearing the same T-shirt pajamas that she'd had on that morning. "Have you even gotten dressed today?" she asked.

Janie shook her head, eyes still on the TV.

"What have you been doing all day?"

"Sitting here. Thinking. Sleeping. Watching the tube."

"Have you eaten anything?"

"I wasn't hungry."

"Nothing?"

"An apple, that's all."

Jessica straightened up. "C'mon, Janie. You can't do that to yourself."

Her sister threw the pillow aside and glared at Jessica. "I don't need any lectures, Jess."

Jessica grabbed her hand and pulled her up, leading her toward the kitchen. "I'll make us both an omelet," she said.

Janie shook free. "I told you I'm not hungry!"

Jessica stopped and turned, anger in her eyes. "Look, Janie. I know you've had a tough time. I wish like hell it hadn't happened. But starving yourself and sitting here in the dark like some mummy isn't going to change anything."

"I just need time," Janie said plaintively, tears welling.

"You need *help*," Jessica replied. "I'm going to find a counselor tomorrow. Set up an appointment."

"No, Jess . . ."

"Yes, Janie. No more arguments, please."

Janie started to walk down the hallway toward the bedroom.

"Did you call the folks?" Jessica asked her retreating figure.

"No, not today. But Mom called and left a couple of messages. They're on the machine along with another one for you. From some woman, I don't remember her name. She says it's important."

Jessica strode to the answering machine and hit the button, listening first to her mother's pleas for Janie to call, then to the voice of Nina French, almost in a whisper.

"Jess, this is Nina. Call me first thing in the morning. I've found something really strange. I'll be in at eight."

TWENTY-ONE

The street and sidewalk were wet and steaming, the gutters still flowing like small streams, as Jessica walked out of the apartment building the next morning. She had been shocked awake during the night, first by the booming thunder, then by the spray from the slashing rain that swept through the bedroom window. The night had exploded around her. Guided by the flashes of lightning, she groggily stumbled through the darkened apartment, closing the windows and quickly checking on Janie, who slept on, undisturbed. How can she do it? Jessica wondered as another burst of thunder shook the building.

It was the first storm since the night on the river bluff, and she knew no thunderstorm would ever seem the same again. By the time her alarm buzzed in the morning, the rain had slowed to a steady drizzle, and now, as she walked to the Impala, the sun emerged, leaving a hazy, humid mist hanging over the city.

When Jessica reached the station, she found Nina French in her small computer room, sorting through several stacks of tapes collected from the two big stories of the day before.

"I got your message, Nina. What's up?"

Nina seemed surprised to see her. "I didn't mean to bring you in. You must be beat after yesterday. You should have just called."

"Forget it. I couldn't sleep, anyway," she said.

Nina walked to the door and closed it. "Here's the deal. After we talked last time, I started thinking more about all four of the murders happening in July of different years. That seemed too strange. So I started checking further."

"How?" Jessica asked.

"I went back into the files again to see if I could find some, I don't know, thread, I guess."

"In each year?" she asked.

"Right. Because each of these guys died on a different day in July, depending upon the year."

Jessica waited expectantly, impatiently.

"I discovered something else was happening the same week they found each of those bodies. The same thing—every year, without fail, including this year."

"What are you talking about?" Jessica demanded.

"The 'Take Back the Night' rally," Nina whispered.

Jessica was stunned. "You've got to be kidding."

"I couldn't believe it, either, but it's true. Every year, for four years straight. There has to be a connection, Jess. It can't be pure coincidence."

"You wouldn't think so," Jessica mused aloud. "Still . . ."

"You know what I think?" Nina said. "That somebody's trying to make a statement by killing one of these perverts each year, the same week as the rally."

Jessica looked at her admiringly. "That would be a hell of a story, wouldn't it? Still, we don't know anything about two of the murders. A cop friend is supposed to be checking on those for me."

"Hope he has better luck than I did," Nina said.

"Do we still have the tapes from this year's rally?" Jessica asked. "The night Edward Hill was killed?"

"Sure. I'll get them."

When Nina returned with three cassettes, Jessica took

them to a vacant viewing room, closing and locking the door
behind her.

She had no idea what she was looking for, but she wanted
to view the tapes again more carefully in light of Nina's discovery, maybe jarring her memory. The first cassette contained general footage of the rally: wide shots of the crowd,
close-ups of protest signs and of women chanting and singing.
An all-woman musical group performed on the long stage,
with some of the protesters dancing and parading on the grass.
Jessica had forgotten just how festive it had been.

She viewed the tape once, then again, searching for any
familiar faces, for anything that seemed out of the ordinary.
She could spot nothing.

The second cassette included short excerpts of several
speeches from the platform, including the mayor and the police chief promising greater efforts to protect women and to
make the streets safer for everyone. Their remarks were dry
and predictable, drawing more catcalls than applause from
the audience.

Several women also spoke, including Sarah Andrews, who
delivered a fiery denunciation of the city's meager efforts to
curb violence against women.

Looking directly at the mayor and the chief, Sarah shouted:
"Women in this city are sick and tired of the same old promises, the same old bullshit. We want . . . no, we DEMAND
. . . action, and we won't wait until one of your wives or daugh-
ters is raped or killed to get it."

The camera swung to the crowd, on its feet, cheering
wildly. The mayor and the chief sat stone-faced.

"Until the men who run this city understand what it's like
to be a woman, to feel the same fear, to know the same shame
and degradation we are forced to feel, nothing will ever
change."

Jessica again marveled at the woman's charisma, at the flu-
ency and power of her speech, at her sway over the crowd.
Watching it again on tape, Jessica had to admit she was as
captivated and moved by Sarah's words as were the women at
the rally. She ought to be in politics, Jessica thought.

The third cassette contained only her interview with Sarah. She was about to fast-forward through it when she suddenly stopped. What had she seen? At the top of the tape, Jessica was standing next to Sarah, waiting as Bill Kendrick focused the camera.

As they stood there, with the camera lens still wide, Sarah turned aside to whisper something to another woman. Jessica punched the pause button, then moved the tape ahead, frame by frame, to get the clearest image.

The woman Sarah was talking to was the same woman Jessica had met standing next to Edward Hill's grave.

She stared at the picture of the woman on the TV monitor. No question, it was her. Jessica wouldn't forget the bangs and the beauty mark. No wonder she had seemed familiar at the grave. She couldn't remember speaking to her at the rally, but if she had, it was only in passing.

What did it mean? Simply that one of Sarah's friends must have known Edward Hill. Or at least been curious enough about him to come to the cemetery to stand by his grave.

So what?

Hadn't Sarah tried to talk Jessica out of pursuing the Hill murder? Hadn't that struck her as strange? Did Sarah have some personal connection to Edward Hill?

The key, Jessica knew, was to find the mystery woman by the grave and talk to her. But how? She certainly couldn't ask Sarah, not now. And she didn't know anyone else at the rally who might know who she was.

There was a knock at the viewing-room door. "You've got a phone call," Nina told her when she'd unlocked the door. "Line Three."

She walked into the newsroom, hoping the call might be from the rape-crisis counselor confirming an appointment for Janie two days hence. It wasn't. It was Jack Tomlinson, the hustling young prosecutor.

"I promised you I'd call," he said. "Am I catching you at a bad time?"

"Kind of," she replied warily.

"I'll make it quick," he said. "I know it's short notice, but how about dinner tonight?"

Jessica hesitated.

"C'mon," he urged, "what can it hurt? I know a great place by the lake. We can have a little wine and walleye while we watch the boats come in. You'll love it."

Jessica thought for a moment. What could it hurt? He seemed nice enough, certainly no ogre. And she had been working hard enough to deserve a night off. How long had it been since she'd had a real date? And don't forget, she suddenly realized, Tomlinson works with Sarah Andrews. He might know some of her friends, like the woman at the rally, the woman she saw at the grave.

"Okay," she suddenly said. "Tell me when and where."

He gave her directions to the Cove, a restaurant on one of the bays of Lake Minnetonka. "I'll meet you there at seven," he said.

Jessica was secretly pleased with herself. She had accidentally found an inside source who could possibly provide more information about Sarah Andrews. Only later did she realize, with a start, that it could also work the other way around. Jack Tomlinson could be Sarah's inside source to learning more about her.

Jessica spent the rest of the day covering two routine news conferences and a taxpayer protest at the state Capitol. In between assignments, she had managed to confirm Janie's appointment with the counselor and, finally, to reach Janie at the apartment late in the afternoon.

"I took your advice and got off my butt," Janie told her. "I've been out all day looking for a job . . . and I think I may have found one, downtown at Dayton's. Clerking in women's wear."

"Are you sure you're ready for that?" Jessica asked cautiously.

"It's better than sitting around here. And besides, I need the money."

Jessica told her that she would be out for part of the evening and wanted to be sure that she would be all right.

"Of course," Janie said. "You've really got a date?"

"Something like that," Jessica replied. "But don't get all excited. I'm not."

Jack Tomlinson was waiting on the deck of the Cove when Jessica arrived a half hour late. "Sorry," she apologized, "I got held up at the station and had no idea it would take this long to get out here."

"No problem," Tomlinson said as he pulled out a chair for her. "I should have warned you about the traffic."

The Cove was situated on a small bay of Lake Minnetonka, some twenty miles west of Minneapolis, the last few miles following a narrow two-lane road which hugged the shoreline and was always clogged late in the day by homeward-bound commuters.

The deck overlooked a marina jammed with boats ranging from sleek runabouts to small yachts, some of which were now backing out of their berths and heading for a sunset cruise on the lake. A dozen sailboats floated by their moorings in the bay, going nowhere, lying motionless in the dead calm of dusk.

"Nice place," Jessica said, looking around. "I love the smell of the water and the way the sun glistens on the lake."

"Beautiful evening to be here," he agreed. "But it'll be packed in another couple of hours when all of the boats come back in off the lake."

Their table was shaded by a large red-and-white umbrella that drooped in the heat. Tomlinson had loosened his tie and collar and rolled up the sleeves of his shirt. His suit coat was thrown over a nearby chair.

A head and a half taller than Jessica, he had closely cropped sandy hair, a broad forehead, and a nose that was slightly bent, as though it had once been broken. The rest of his features were smooth and regular, not handsome in any classic sense but ruggedly goodlooking.

"I'm glad you decided to come," he said. "I wasn't sure you'd actually show up."

"You shouldn't have worried," she replied lightly. "I don't stand people up."

They each ordered a glass of wine and spent the first half hour trying to get to know one another, slowly—almost shyly—revealing bits and pieces of their lives: their families, where they had grown up and gone to school, and more about their jobs. The conversation was quiet and relaxed. Jessica felt at ease with him, but she was also on guard, careful about what and how much of herself she divulged.

He seemed to have no such reservations. He was open and talkative, by turns both serious and funny, as interested in hearing about her as he was in talking about himself. He smiled easily and often, creasing his cheeks, revealing teeth that were straight and even and a brilliant white. His eyes were a deep brown and seemed to be smiling, too. Jessica now regretted resisting his earlier advances.

Tomlinson told her he had spent a couple of years in private law practice before joining the county attorney's staff to get more trial experience. For the moment, he said, he was assigned to the department's white-collar-crime unit, a task he found satisfying because the cases were so complex and the criminals so cagey and tough to collar.

"It's like a jigsaw puzzle," he said. "I'm always trying to fill in the missing pieces, to make sure they eventually fit."

"Funny," she said quietly, "that's my job, too. But right now too many pieces of my puzzle are still missing."

After they had ordered dinner, she tried to delicately turn the conversation back to his job and to his relationship with Sarah Andrews. "In what you do, do you work closely with Sarah?" she asked as casually as possible.

"Not really," he said. "She mainly works homicides and sex crimes, but occasionally we do get together on a case. Like the day I met you in her office."

"She seems like a fascinating woman," Jessica said, watch-

ing him closely for any reaction. "Smart, outspoken. I'm thinking of doing a special feature on her."

"Really? Well, she'd love that."

"How well do you know her?" she asked, again keeping her
voice neutral.

"Not that well, actually. We graduated from law school a
year apart, and as I say, we haven't worked together all that
closely."

"Tell me what you do know," she pressed. "I need another
perspective."

For the first time, he seemed slightly suspicious, pausing
briefly before responding. "She's brilliant, I can tell you that,
one of the top two or three students in her class. And a great
trial lawyer, I'm told, although I've never seen her in action."

"What was she like in law school?" Jessica asked.

Again he paused, searching his memory. "Kept pretty
much to herself. Never socialized much. Seemed shy except
when she got involved in the women's protests on campus.
Then she came out of her shell and was a real activist, maybe
even a fanatic. I remember we used to talk about the two sides
of Sarah Andrews. Since then, as you know, she's become a
real media darling, always good for a juicy quote. Causes quite
a stir in the office sometimes."

"Interesting . . ."

"What's this *really* about, Jessica?"

"Just what I told you. I'm thinking of doing a story."

He seemed unconvinced. "Then you ought to talk to people
who know her better than I do."

"Like who?" she asked, taking a deep breath. "I need a
personal viewpoint. You happen to know any of her friends?"

"Not really. I'm not sure she has that many. I did meet her
roommate once, six months or so ago, when I ran into them on
the street."

"Her roommate? A woman?"

"Yeah, but I don't remember her name."

"Did she have bangs?" Jessica tried to keep the excitement
out of her voice.

"What?"

"Did she have bangs in her hair? A beauty mark on her cheek?"

"Hell, I don't know," he said impatiently. "Maybe a beauty mark. I remember wondering at the time if it was real."

Jessica's mind whirled. What does it mean? First, a woman who may be Sarah's roommate shows up at Edward Hill's grave; then Sarah tries to discourage me from pursuing Hill's murder. Was it a bizarre coincidence?

"You don't remember her name?"

"No chance. Why don't you ask Sarah?"

"I'd rather not," Jessica said vaguely.

"What's going on here, anyway?" he demanded, plainly puzzled. "Why do I have the feeling I'm being grilled?"

Jessica laughed. "You know reporters. We never rest."

Tomlinson appraised her. "Is the name really important?"

She nodded.

"If I get it, will you tell me what this is all about?"

"Not now," she replied. "Someday, maybe."

"Give me a minute," he said as he got up and walked across the deck to a pay phone on the restaurant wall.

He returned a few minutes later. "Her name is Kimberly Hawkins. She works for a brokerage firm downtown, Midwest Services. She and Sarah have lived together about a year."

"Who'd you get all of that from?" Jessica asked.

"A friend who knows Sarah better than I do," he said.

Jessica made a mental note of the name and information and then tried to steer the conversation in other directions, hoping to deflect his curiosity from her intense interest in Sarah Andrews and her roommate. It seemed to work, helped along by the arrival of their dinner and by the activity surrounding the boisterous return of several large yachts to the marina.

The remainder of the evening passed pleasantly and all too quickly, reaffirming Jessica's earlier impression that Jack was not only bright and quick but fun to be with. It had been ages since she had actually enjoyed a date, and she was sorry to see the evening end. She could only hope that he felt the same way.

Not until she was driving the narrow road back to town did her thoughts leave Jack and return to Sarah Andrews. Then it suddenly struck her. The name of Sarah's roommate. Kimberly Hawkins. K.H. As in Hill's diary.

Now she understood.

TWENTY-TWO

Lowell Ingram was groggy with sleep when he thought he heard a soft but persistent rap at the door of his motel room, where he had been staying since his wife kicked him out of the house weeks before. He raised himself up on his elbow and stared into the darkness, ears straining. Was it a dream? He heard nothing now but the distant sounds of a TV, the canned laughter permeating the thin walls.

He lay back down, the sheets damp and smelling of his sweat, rumpled from his restless sleep. He crammed the pillow beneath his head and raised his arm. The luminous dial on his watch said 3:20.

Then he heard another knock. Sharp but soft, knuckles against the metal of the door. What the fuck? he thought. Probably some whore selling her wares door-to-door. There certainly were enough of them hanging around this place.

Ingram switched on the bedside light and walked quietly to the door, pressing his ear against it, the place too cheap for a peephole. Another knock, no louder but now ringing against his ear.

"Who's there?" he said.

"The hotel clerk, sir," said the voice from the other side of the door. A woman's voice? "Someone down the hall smelled smoke, so we're checking all the rooms."

"There's no fire in here," Ingram replied irritably.

"Sorry, sir. We have to check. Fire code requires it."

"Just a minute," Ingram said as he searched for his pants. Then he unlocked the door.

He saw only the blur of a ski mask before the intruder pushed past him into the room. "Close the door and don't say a fucking word," the figure said in a soft, menacing voice.

Then Ingram saw the gun, the biggest he had ever seen, pointed directly at his heart. The long barrel seemed to fill the distance between them. "What the shit . . ." he sputtered.

"*Quiet!*"

"I don't have any money, for Christ's sake."

"We don't want your money, pervert. Get dressed."

It was a woman's voice.

"Wait a fucking minute," he protested.

The gun barrel moved like a whip, the tip slashing him across the nose. He could see the blood spurt, could taste it as it dripped onto his lips. The pain came a moment later, but a hand covered his mouth before he could cry out.

"Now get dressed," she ordered.

Ingram was in a car; that's all he knew. Sitting on the edge of the backseat, his hands numb from the handcuffs cutting into his wrists behind him, a blindfold tight around his head. Someone was driving, and someone else was beside him. The steely tip of the gun barrel against his temple told him that. But no one spoke. He had been hustled quietly out of the sleeping motel, gun against his side, blindfolded and cuffed when he had reached the car in the darkened parking lot.

The gash on his nose had stopped bleeding. He knew now that it wasn't a horrible nightmare from which he had suddenly awakened. What had she called him? Pervert? He shuddered at the hatred in her voice.

They had been driving for what he guessed to be fifteen minutes when the car slowed and stopped. The back door opened.

"Out!" said the same harsh voice.

He was pulled from the car and led across a gravelly surface. A parking lot? After no more than ten feet, he was stopped. He heard the scratchy sound of a key in a lock and the squeak of a door opening. He was pushed inside. Warmer here, musty. There was an echo to their footsteps.

"Take three steps up," the voice said.

He climbed the steps and stopped. His hands were uncuffed.

"Take off your clothes," he was ordered. "All of them."

"What are you doing?" he asked, his fear almost choking him. The gun was in the small of his back.

"Do it."

Still blindfolded, he slowly removed his clothes, feeling the eyes on him. He tried to cover himself with his hands.

"Not much size to him, is there?" Then a small chuckle.

"Fuck you!" he blurted.

"Now you know how those girls felt, teacher." A new voice, muffled, but familiar.

His hands were pulled behind his back, this time tied around a what? A post? Then his ankles. And his chest. He could not move. His blindfold was pulled away. The space was dark but not pitchblack. In front of him, some kind of curtain, translucent. He could see dim light but no movement beyond it.

"Where the hell am I?" he demanded, trying to keep the fear from his voice.

There was a chuckle from behind him, then the first voice again. "You'll know soon enough, teacher. We want you to be surprised."

A gloved hand came from behind him, holding a big piece of cardboard. It was hung around his neck with what felt like a thin piece of wire, covering his naked chest. He assumed it was a sign of some sort, but a thin ridge on top of the cardboard kept him from reading whatever might be on it. Then a gag was stuffed into his mouth. Ingram fought against the ropes, but there was no give.

"Don't waste your energy," said the same voice. "You aren't going anywhere, at least not for a few hours. If you have to piss, just piss on the floor."

More muffled laughter, then the second voice. Disguised, but . . . it had to be her!

"If you ever, ever touch another woman, another girl, without her permission, we'll hang you bareass from a lamppost. You get the message, teacher?"

Then he heard the door behind him close; leaving him naked and alone.

The shrill ring of the phone brought Jessica instantly awake.

She looked at the clock on the dresser: 6:30 A.M. She reached the phone before the third ring, before it could wake Janie in the next room.

"Hello." She knew her voice was foggy.

"Jessica?" Laurie Sanders, sounding harried. "Can you make it down here, quick?"

"I guess so, Laurie. What's happening?"

"Not sure. We just got an anonymous call. Something about Lowell Ingram. Said we should be near Seventh and Marquette in an hour with reporter and camera. It sounds too weird to be phony."

"Lowell Ingram?" Jessica was not sure she had heard it right.

"Yes," Laurie said. "Don't ask me any more because I don't know anything more."

"I'll be there as quick as I can," Jessica said, reaching for her clothes.

Bill Kendrick was waiting for Jessica outside the station, camera already hoisted on his shoulder. It was 7:20 A.M., and Jessica knew she must look as ragged and disheveled as she felt.

"Nice hustle, Jess," Kendrick said, falling into step beside her. She gave him a wan smile in return.

"You know what's going on?" he asked.

She shook her head.

They covered the four blocks to the corner of Seventh and Marquette in less than five minutes. They found most of their competitors already there, milling near the intersection, asking one another what it was all about, trying to keep out of the way of the pedestrians crowding the sidewalk on the way to work.

It was 7:30 A.M.

No one gave the curtained window of the vacant store a second look until they heard the scream of a woman passing by. Piercing, like an owl making a moonlit kill, rising above the noise of the traffic and the commotion of the rush-hour crowd.

All eyes turned in her direction. More screams now, a small crowd forming in front of the store window. Hands covering mouths, or pointing. Some people turned away, others gawked, a few laughed. Cars stopped in their tracks.

The reporters and photographers joined the surge. Jessica was swept along, pushed by Kendrick, whose camera was already high above his head, tape rolling. They elbowed their way through the crowd, shouting apologies, hearing curses. Jessica had no idea what they'd find. She couldn't believe what she finally saw.

Ingram's head was pressed to his chest, eyes unwilling to look at the crowd, his body still struggling to be free. The bold black letters of the sign on his chest were starting to run from the sweat and tears that dripped from his face. But it was still perfectly readable:

I AM A CHILD MOLESTER!

On either side of Ingram in the window, several women mannequins, as naked as himself, stood staring at him, plastic smiles on their faces, apparently enjoying the show. Jessica would later learn that the curtain covering the window had been pulled aside by an automatic timer. Promptly at 7:30 A.M.

"Get him out of there!" someone in the crowd shouted.

"Cover him up, for God's sake," said a woman who looked as if she might faint.

The photographers were jockeying for position, trying to frame their shots to avoid what they knew would never be used on the air. One of the reporters shouted questions at Ingram through the window, but the gag was still stuffed in his mouth.

A cop who had been directing traffic at the intersection was wading through the throng, speaking urgently into his walkie-talkie. Jessica could hear a siren in the distance, coming closer. When he reached the window, the policeman sought to break up the crowd, but it was like pushing back the tide. The human circle had now spread out into the street, blocking the little traffic that was still trying to move.

Jessica could do little but watch, caught up in what was now almost a mob scene. Any crowd interviews would have to wait until later. And then what would she ask them?

More policemen arrived, some scurrying into the building, others trying to spread a blanket across the outside of the window. When they found nothing to attach it to, they valiantly tried to hold it high enough to cover Ingram's not-so-private parts.

Jessica followed the cops into the building, staying back but watching as they worked to force open an inside door of the store. Something heavy had been pushed against it from the inside, and the door would not budge.

"Try the back door," one of the officers shouted.

"We did," another replied. "It's tight as a drum."

"Then let's cut through the front window," the first one said. "We've gotta get that guy out of there."

By the time Jessica was back outside, the police had cordoned off a wide area around the window. One of the officers used a glass cutter to remove a piece of the window large enough for a man to crawl through.

Ingram had raised his head, ignoring the crowd and cameras, focusing instead on the progress of the glass cutter. He looked stricken, drained of blood, conscious but unconscious. Jessica hoped he might glance her way, that she might catch his eye, but she knew that would be impossible in this crowd of gawkers.

The glass was finally cut, the piece carefully removed from the window. Another officer climbed through the hole, lifting the sign from around Ingram's neck, trying his best to shield Ingram's naked body from the window. The policeman quickly wrapped Ingram in a blanket and led him through the door behind the store window. The newspeople rushed to the door of the building but were blocked by a police line.

"Leave the poor son of a bitch alone," one of the cops shouted.

"We want to talk to him," a reporter replied angrily.

"Not now, you don't," said the officer.

Jessica found Kendrick loading another tape into his recorder.

"Can you believe all of that?" she blurted out.

"It's bizarre, the poor bastard," Kendrick said. "Shouldn't happen to anybody, I don't give a shit what he's done."

"Maybe so," she mused aloud, "but I wouldn't tell that to those three girls he molested."

As they prepared to interview some of the policemen and spectators, Jessica happened to glance across the street just as a bus passed by. Through the cloud of black exhaust she was sure she had caught a glimpse of Freda Brinkman and Sarah Andrews disappearing into a building.

TWENTY-THREE

The story of Lowell Ingram's store window captivity created a sensation in the media and became the dominant topic of office-cooler conversation. Curious crowds continued to gather by the window long after Ingram was gone, dispersing only when police boarded it up and roped off the area.

One newspaper headline read:

LIVING MANNEQUIN STARTLES
RUSH-HOUR CROWD

Another used a small play on words:

CONVICTED MOLESTER EXPOSED IN PUBLIC

Each of the newspaper and television stories recounted the details of Ingram's earlier plea bargain, including the fact that he had eluded a prison sentence. Speculation abounded as to who was responsible for his abduction, but neither Ingram, who was in seclusion, nor the police would provide any useful information.

Suspicion immediately focused on the families of the three girls Ingram had admitted molesting. They adamantly denied any involvement but didn't hide their satisfaction, suggesting that this punishment might have been more fitting than the prison term Ingram had avoided.

Jessica spent most of the day working the story, piecing together all of the elements, including interviews at the scene, at the homes of the girls' families, and with police investigators. Ingram was the missing link, but he was nowhere to be found.

Late in the day, Jessica decided to place a call to Sarah Andrews. "Any reaction to the Ingram incident?" she asked.

"Off the record?" Sarah replied.

"If you like," Jessica said.

"I think he got what he deserved. Whoever did it should get a medal. He's a pervert who should be in prison, not out on the street."

"On the record?" Jessica asked.

Sarah laughed. "On the record, I think it's an outrage. Someone was taking the law into his own hands. It looks like a vigilante at work, and that's an affront to the judicial system. But appalling as it was, it may be a lesson to men who prey on women and escape their rightful punishment."

"You seem almost pleased," Jessica offered.

"Don't put words in my mouth, Jessica. I would be less than honest if I said I felt any great sympathy for the man. Down deep, I don't believe it's any worse for a man to be ridiculed in public than it is for a woman to be violated in private."

Jessica tried to be her casual best. "You didn't happen to be there to see it, did you?"

There was only the slightest hesitation. "No, I was in the office. Why do you ask?"

"I thought I might have seen you and Freda Brinkman across the street. I must have been mistaken."

"You were," Sarah snapped.

After Jessica hung up, she sat for a moment and stared at the phone. Another lie, she thought.

Once the police had rescued Lowell Ingram from the window, they took him to the hospital to stitch up the gash in his nose and to question him. He could see their half-hidden smirks as he described the degrading details and their open disbelief when he told them he thought his abductors were two women.

"You let a couple of broads do this to you?" one of the cops asked, aghast.

"They had a gun the size of a fucking cannon," Ingram said. "What was I supposed to do? Stick my finger in it?"

He had not told them that he thought he recognized one of the voices. He wanted to keep that information to himself for now, and he knew they wouldn't have believed it, anyway.

The police promised they would follow up and get back to him if they came up with any leads. But Ingram could tell from their expressions that they viewed him with little sympathy and thought of his abduction more as a joke than a serious police matter.

Once free, Ingram had returned to the motel only long enough to check out, pick up his few belongings, and retrieve his car from the parking lot. He knew he couldn't spend another night there, but he had no idea where he would go next.

After driving around aimlessly for the rest of the day, Ingram had finally found a small, shabby apartment in a run-down area near the university. The landlord had not recognized him, had not asked any questions, and had accepted only two weeks of rent in advance. Ingram had not left the place since except to buy a few groceries and two liters of gin. He had a lot of thinking to do.

Freda Brinkman got a fresh whiff of cigar smoke and knew Meecham was still in his office. It was after six in the evening, and she had been waiting for him to leave for more than an hour. Usually, he would be long gone by now, off to Barney's to while away the hours. But things had been different lately, and his change in habits continued to worry her.

She was even more concerned over the conversation she happened to overhear the day before. Meecham telling another detective that he'd be gone most of the day, talking with the Homicide cops in Brooklyn Park and Bloomington.

Now, while waiting for him to leave, she watched the TV coverage of the Ingram story on the small set in her office, chuckling to herself as she saw the chaos around the store window and the public humiliation of Lowell Ingram. It couldn't have gone better, she told herself proudly.

Then she turned the TV off. Finally, she heard Meecham's office door close and the rattle of his key chain, along with a deep, raspy cough, as though he were choking on his own cigar smoke. The hacking continued, more faintly, as he walked away down the hall.

Brinkman waited five minutes, then strode the few steps to Meecham's office. The door was locked, but one key opened all the offices in Homicide. Leaving the door ajar, she stepped quickly inside and rummaged through his desk—flipping open file folders, shuffling through papers, opening drawers, searching for any clue of what he'd been up to. She stopped often to listen, tiptoeing twice past the door, glancing down the hallway. There was no one.

She resumed the search, heart pounding, underarms wet. More minutes passed. The file cabinets were locked, and she had no key for them. She went back to the desk, pushing papers aside, then a butt-laden ashtray which sat atop a battered desk pad. A manila folder was underneath the pad, the name "Jessica" scrawled across its front.

She flipped it open and found two sheets of paper, each containing computer printing and handwritten notes. Two names stared back at her: Ezra Scott and Michael Amery. Then she heard the footsteps in the hallway. Frantically pushing the folder back beneath the pad, she was halfway to the office door when Meecham suddenly filled it.

"Hey, Matt," she said, trying to disguise her distress. "You're back."

"Freda. What the hell are you doing here?" He sounded more surprised than suspicious.

Brinkman fought to breathe and act normally. "I tried to catch you before you left," she said. "I wanted to take a look at Hill's diary. I didn't think you'd mind."

"Couldn't you have waited until tomorrow?" he asked, more cautious now.

"I had the evening free, and I thought . . ."

Meecham walked to one of the file cabinets and unlocked the top drawer. He lifted the diary out and handed it to her, his eyes wary. "Here it is," he said, "but next time, ask before you look, will you?"

"Sorry, but I didn't think you'd mind. We've got no secrets around here, do we?"

"I don't know, do we?" he answered, escorting her out of the office, locking the door behind them.

Brinkman tried her best to appear calm as she caught up with Sarah walking across the plaza of the Government Center.

"What's the problem now?" Sarah asked, eyes straight ahead.

Brinkman quickly told her of her foray into Meecham's office. "The folder had Jessica's name on it. She must have given it to him."

Sarah stopped and faced her. "How could she know about Scott and Amery?" she demanded. "Those cases have been dead for years."

Brinkman said, "Who knows? The names were on some kind of computer printout. Not one of ours. I would have recognized it."

Sarah resumed walking slowly, but her mind raced. Who cares how they found out? The important thing is that they now know about all four of them. But what's the difference? They don't know who killed them or why. Relax.

"I think we should cool it," Sarah said. "Let's not panic."

"Cool it? Are you serious? They're in our fucking footsteps!"

Sarah suddenly remembered Jessica's phone call and her troubling questions about the Ingram incident. It had struck her as strange at the time, but in light of this, even more worrisome.

"Maybe you're right," she finally said. "Let's get the club together and talk about it."

"Screw the club," Brinkman said. "You heard them the last time. They just want to bury their heads."

"We're all in this together," Sarah argued.

Brinkman grabbed her by the arm, wheeling her around. "Look, it's one thing to have a reporter nosing around, but now she's got Meecham involved. That's getting too close to home."

Sarah shook her arm free. "Don't muscle me, Freda. Get the club together. You can't go off half-cocked."

Brinkman backed away. "Okay, but it'll be a goddamned waste of time, watch and see." Then she stalked off.

TWENTY-FOUR

Jessica found Meecham on the same bench by the lake. The ducks were once again gathered by his feet, at the water's edge, crabbily competing for the pieces of bread he would occasionally flick in their direction.

"Sit down, Detective," he said wearily as she walked up. "We've got a lot to talk about, you and I."

Meecham looked as though he hadn't slept. His eyes were swimming in red, the only color in his face. His skin sagged beneath his cheekbones and around his neck. His shirt was badly wrinkled, and his suit looked as if it had just come out of the dryer.

If he has slept, Jessica decided, it must have been in his clothes. "You look like you've been on a bender," she said, only half-joking, hoping she was wrong.

"No such luck," he said. "I just have a lot on my mind."

Jessica came to the lake after finding an urgent message from Meecham on her desk that morning.

"What's going on, Matt?" she asked now.

"I paid a visit to the cops in Bloomington and Brooklyn

Park," he said, "and found out about your other two victims, Ezra Scott and Michael Amery."

Jessica leaned forward.

"I hate to admit it, but you may be on to something," he said. "Scott, the one in Brooklyn Park, burned to death. Someone tied him to a stake in an old, abandoned barn out there in the middle of the night. Piled bales of hay around him and set it on fire. Just like Joan of Arc, for Christ's sake. He was charred meat by the time the cops found him. At the time, they only said that he'd died mysteriously in a fire."

"Was he a rapist?" Jessica asked.

"Right again. He'd been in and out of jail since he was a kid, most of the time on sex charges. Flunked treatment a couple of times and was missing from a halfway house when he was killed. No suspects, no clues, no nothin'."

Jessica listened with rapt attention, allowing Meecham to go on without interruption.

"Bloomington was a little different. This Amery guy had no record, but the cops think he was one of the key people in the 'Minnesota Connection.' Know what that is?"

She shook her head.

"A prostitution ring. An underground railroad of sorts. They used to ship young Minnesota girls—mostly blond and pretty, a lot of them runaways—to New York to work the streets as prostitutes. Dozens of them, maybe scores, were recruited in the Twin Cities and sent out east. Many of them never came back.

"The cops said they were about ready to make an arrest when they found his body floating in a lake."

"He drowned?"

"With help," Meecham said, slowly shaking his head. "Somebody tied him to one of those surfing boards you pull behind a boat. Laid him out flat, bound his hands and legs around the board—so it looked like he was riding the thing. But they somehow propped his mouth open, which kept him from yelling and let the water pour into him like a funnel when they hauled him behind the boat."

"In broad daylight?" she asked.

"Just before dark, I guess, although they didn't find his body until the next morning. People on the lake remembered seeing the boat and board but had no memory of the people in the boat."

"People? More than one?"

"At least two, maybe more. The boat was stolen in Wisconsin a couple of days before and left on shore with the body bobbing on the board behind it."

"I knew it," Jessica whispered. "There had to be some connection."

"You may be right. Looks like somebody out there is going after rapists or other predators, somebody who likes to see them suffer and die."

"I'm not surprised there was more than one person in the boat," Jessica said. "One person couldn't have done any of these murders alone. They're too complicated, too elaborately staged."

"Maybe so, but we have no proof in the other—"

"C'mon, Matt," Jessica interrupted. "Could one person have done what they did to Eduardo? Or to Ezra or to Hill?"

Meecham threw the last piece of bread to the ducks.

"There's something else you should know," Jessica said.

Meecham turned to her. "What's that?"

"We've discovered that each one of these guys was killed in the same week as the 'Take Back the Night' rally was held. Each year, four years running. It must be more than simple coincidence. Seems like somebody is trying to make a point."

Matt was clearly impressed. "How did you learn all that?"

Jessica told him of Nina's newsroom computer search. "It was just a hunch on her part, but it turned out to be right."

Meecham sat quietly, digesting the information.

She smiled. "It's a hell of a story, Matt. And it looks like I'm getting close to the point where I can tell it."

"What do you mean?" he demanded.

"We know that at least four sexual predators are dead, that they died in particularly horrible ways, that they all died in July of different years, and that all of the murders are still unsolved. That's not bad, Matt, even without knowing who did it."

"You can't report that," Meecham said in disbelief and anger.

"Why not?"

"Because it'll screw us up."

Jessica was taken aback. "What are you talking about?"

"Listen, all we know for sure is that we've got four unsolved murders that may be, okay, probably are, connected. But we don't have the slightest idea who's responsible for them. If you report the story now, we may never know. It'll queer the investigation."

Jessica started to protest, but Meecham cut her off.

"Besides," he said, "everything I told you about the murders in Brooklyn Park and Bloomington is strictly off the record. I barely managed to get the information out of those cops myself. They'd have my ass if they were to see it on television."

"You didn't say anything about it being off the record," Jessica protested.

"We were trading private information, Jessica."

"Where does that leave me?" she argued. "Do I have to wait until you solve the case? That could be forever."

"You've got to give me some time," Meecham said. "Maybe not forever, but a few weeks, anyway. Besides, face it, it'll be a hell of a lot better story if you can report that somebody's in jail."

Jessica knew he was right. But she also knew the longer she waited, the more likely there would be leaks and she would end up getting beat on her own story. That would be an unforgivable sin, one she was not about to commit.

"I don't know, Matt. This could be the biggest story of my life, and I don't want to mess it up. Besides, the public's got a right to know if some screwy serial killers are on the loose."

"And have the shit scared out of them? C'mon. We agreed to work on this together, Jessica. I promised not to get in the way of your story, and you promised not to screw up our investigation. I think we can both keep our promises, but it's going to take a little time."

"How do I know the story won't end up on the front page of the newspaper or on some other television station?"

"You have my word," Meecham said.

"What if Brinkman or someone else in your office leaks it?" she asked. "I don't know or trust any of them."

"Let me worry about that. I've got the files from Bloomington and Brooklyn Park, but I'll be working alone for a while. Until I can figure out what's going on."

"Can I see the files?" she asked.

"I can't do that, Jess. They don't even belong to me."

"I thought we were working together," she said.

Meecham shook his head. "We'll see. Give me some time."

Jessica rose from the bench and walked up the shore of the lake. The ducks trailed behind her, splashing and squawking. She ignored them, staring across the lake, trying to decide. After several minutes, she walked back to Meecham.

"Okay, Matt. I'll go to my boss. I hope he'll agree to give us the time. But I'm going to keep pressing myself. I want to get this story on the air."

"Fair enough," he said. "But be careful, Jessica."

The door to George Barclay's office was open, and he was at his desk, head bowed, poring over the latest rating books. The newsroom grapevine said the news numbers were up, and Jessica hoped she would find Barclay in a good mood.

She knocked lightly, and he glanced up, smiling. So far, so good, she thought.

"Sorry to bother you," she said from the doorway, "but I need to talk."

"Something Laurie can't handle?" he asked.

Jessica hesitated. "Maybe she should be here, too. But I think you ought to hear it as well."

"Sounds serious," he said as he put aside the rating books and picked up the phone to call Laurie. "Grab a chair."

Once Laurie had joined them, Jessica said, "I need some advice. I may be into something over my head."

Neither of them spoke but watched her intently. Jessica

began from the beginning. She knew they were aware of part of the story, but she was determined to tell it as completely as she could, leaving nothing out: Edward Hill's diary, the details of the other, connected murders, and the ties to the "Take Back the Night" rallies. And, finally, about Matt Meecham.

"He was my source on the Carlstrom lady's body," she admitted. "We've become good friends. I trust him, and he trusts me. I wouldn't be where I am in this thing without him. He wants me to hold off on the story, to give him time to solve the case."

Barclay and Laurie exchanged glances. They had sat quietly during Jessica's entire recitation, resisting the temptation to interrupt. Jessica could sense they had many questions.

"You know I don't like working with cops," Barclay finally said. "They've got their jobs to do, and we've got ours. And our job sometimes includes going after them."

Jessica nodded. "I feel the same way, but Meecham's different. He's honest and decent. He wouldn't screw me over, I know that."

"Forget about Meecham for a minute," Laurie said. "What about the story? You've got a theory, that's all. I admit it makes some sense, but there's nothing concrete."

"C'mon, Laurie," Jessica protested. "How do you explain all of the murders happening during the same weeks as the rallies, four years in a row? Is that just a crazy coincidence?"

"I suppose stranger things have happened," Laurie said, "but the problem is, you've got to have somebody in authority confirm that a serial killer, or killers, is on the loose. Who's going to do that? Not Meecham, certainly. And from what you say, no one else even suspects it yet."

"I could just present the facts," Jessica argued, playing devil's advocate, "and let the public come to its own conclusions."

"Laurie's right," Barclay said. "You're going to need more. Everything's too sketchy now. You don't even have the details of the Brooklyn Park and Bloomington murders on the record at this point. And what about the video to help tell the story? You've got practically nothing on tape."

Jessica had to confess a certain relief. Meecham would get his time; she could keep on digging.

"I'll free you up from other assignments," Laurie said, "and give you any more help you need. But I don't want to go with the story until we've got it all."

"I don't want to get beat," Jessica said.

"Neither do we," Barclay said, "but we want to do it right."

The ball was back in her court.

Jessica stayed at the station late that night, and when she left, she found the air outside suffocatingly hot and heavy. Traffic was light, and few people were left on the street. Probably home by their air conditioners, she thought with a touch of envy. As she neared the opposite curb, walking toward the parking ramp, she glanced to her left and noticed a car parked about thirty feet away. Its interior was dark, but she could see the outline of a person sitting behind the wheel. Probably waiting to pick someone up from work, she thought.

While waiting for the traffic light to change, a bus roared across the intersection, its headlights momentarily bathing her and the parked car in their bright glare. Jessica turned quickly—in time to see the person inside the car duck down, away from the light and out of sight.

She stood stock-still on the curb, narrowing her eyes, willing them to penetrate the dark insides of the car. She could see no shape, no movement. She took a few tentative steps toward the car. It was like an explosion. The engine roared, the headlights flared and immediately were flicked to bright. Jessica was blinded, frozen in place. The car roared past her. She could feel the brush of a fender against her skirt, the heat of its exhaust against her face. It was gone before she could do more than gasp.

For a moment she was paralyzed. Then she raced for the ramp, heart pumping, the stench of the car's fumes still filling her nostrils. A close call, the careening car missing her by no more than inches.

Who could it have been? Were they waiting for her?

It was so dark, and had happened so quickly, that she didn't even know whether the driver was a man or woman, let alone the make or model of the car. It was black or dark blue with a white stripe down the side, that's all she knew.

What the hell's happening?

Relax, she told herself. It must have been some kook playing games. She knew weirdos liked to hang around television stations, hoping for a glimpse of the stars. It must have been a mistake.

But then she remembered the knife in her tire. Somehow she knew it wasn't a mistake.

TWENTY-FIVE

Jessica wasn't sure what she expected the rape counselor to be like, but from her phone conversation with the woman, she had pictured someone gray-haired and matronly, with half-glasses propped on her nose.

Marjorie Collins hardly fit her vision. Not much older than Jessica, she was clad in washed-out jeans and a Hard Rock Cafe T-shirt, with dangling gold earrings and a Mickey Mouse watch on her wrist. Her auburn hair was cropped even shorter than Jessica's, and her face was absolutely bereft of makeup. Maybe it was the slight crook in her nose that reminded Jessica of Meryl Streep.

"Afternoon, you two," Marjorie said, rising from behind an old battered desk heaped with papers. "Jessica, right? And Jane?"

As they shook hands, Jessica quickly surveyed the office. No more than ten by twelve, it was fully as cluttered as the desk: stacks of file folders and magazines everywhere and, on every wall, shelves overflowing with books and video cassettes. A battered placard leaned against one corner, a poster of the kind Jessica had first seen at the "Take Back the Night" rally: YES MEANS YES, NO MEANS NO.

The counselor noticed her inspection. "Sorry for the mess," she said with a smile. "I keep meaning to clean it up, but there's never the time."

As Jessica and Janie sat down, Marjorie cleared away some of the scattered papers. "Before we get started," she said, "I should tell you about myself. So you know who you're talking to."

Jessica sneaked a sideways peek at Janie, hunkered down in her chair, looking agitated and angry. Only Jessica's persuasion and persistence had brought her here, and she was making no effort to disguise her discomfort.

"For the record, I grew up in Minneapolis, have my M.A. in social work from the university, and am working on my Ph.D. That's not important," she continued, eyeing Janie. "But what is, is that I'm a rape victim just like you. Happened at the university, in the dorm. By a guy who lived down the hall whom I'd dated a few times. I'll spare you all of the sordid details, but I think I know where you're coming from, what you've been through."

Janie straightened up in her chair. "Did you have to get an abortion?" she blurted.

Marjorie shook her head.

"Then you don't know what I've been through," Janie said angrily. "Let's get that straight."

The counselor looked at her sympathetically. "You're right. I shouldn't have presumed to put myself in your place. Every case is different, but I wanted you to know I'm not just some do-good academic."

Janie sank back into her chair.

"Jessica told me something about your experience over the phone," she continued, "but I'd like to hear the whole story from you, if you're up to it."

"What good's that going to do?" Janie protested. "You can't turn back the clock, you can't undo what's already done. I'd just like to get on with my life."

"Can you?" Marjorie asked quietly.

Janie's defiance turned abruptly to tears. "I have to," she said, sobbing. "It may take some time, but I've got to get over it." Then, looking squarely at Marjorie: "You did, didn't you?"

"Not without a lot of help," the counselor replied. "That's what made me get into this business. Hoping to repay the people who helped me by helping others. But you have to want the help."

They sat quietly for a moment, waiting for Janie to decide. Then she began, suddenly and without preamble, telling the whole story in more graphic detail than even Jessica had heard: from first meeting the fishing guide to the rape and on to the eventual abortion. It took an hour in all, broken by long pauses as she struggled through her tears and chest-heaving sobs to relate the details she had already tried to block.

"I tried to stop him, God knows. I pleaded with him, begged him. Screamed. But he kept tearing at me, ripping at my swimsuit, laughing at me when I tried to fight him off. He was a madman. Called me a 'fucking tease.' I got away once, tried to run, but he tackled me. I can still taste the sand in my mouth, feel it in my eyes. Then I think I blacked out."

Jessica found herself weeping with her sister, seeing herself on that remote island beach, feeling Janie's pain and humiliation.

Throughout the rending recitation, Marjorie Collins said nothing, watching them both steadily and soberly. Only once, when Janie spoke of the trauma of the abortion, did the counselor show any emotion. Her blinking eyes could not stop the escape of a single tear that rolled down her cheek.

When it was over, Janie leaned back in her chair, eyes fastened blankly on the ceiling.

"What are you feeling now?" Marjorie asked.

Janie shook her head slowly. "I don't know. Anger, I suppose, and guilt. But mostly just sad. So fucking sad. Like I watched someone die and it was me. Life was so great, you know . . . until then." She glanced at Jessica. "I guess I've led a pretty protected life. I never dreamed something like this could happen to me. To other people, maybe, but never to me. And then it did."

"It happens to thousands of women, Janie," the counselor said. "More every year. It's an epidemic. To women just like you. And . . . me. Caught off guard. Too trusting, maybe too innocent. Women who believe that because we happen to know a man, he's incapable of violating us. Or betraying us.

"And do you know what happens?" she continued. "Because it's someone we know and trust, we start doubting our own judgment. Blaming ourselves, figuring it must have been something we said or did that caused it."

As Jessica listened to the woman, she recalled Janie's words the day she found her on the doorstep. "It must have been my fault. I let him go too far . . . he said I led him on."

"But whenever you start having those doubts, Janie, just remember that rape isn't about sex. It's about power and control. This guy probably could have gotten as much sexual satisfaction by masturbating in a corner, but he wanted to control you, to dominate you. He's a sick man, and you can never forget that. Never."

Janie got up from her chair and turned away, staring at the placard in the corner. "I hear what you're saying," she said, "but it doesn't make me feel less dirty. I feel like someone else now. Another person. Everything that seemed so important to me before seems unimportant now. School, friends, the future, even my family." She turned to face them. "It's like I'm floating in some big black hole. Like nothing's real. It hasn't been since that day."

"I suspect you've thought about suicide, haven't you?" the counselor asked.

Jessica came out of her chair. "What are you saying—"

"Several times," Janie said, interrupting her. "Especially when I thought about facing the folks. It often seemed like the best way out."

"Jesus, Janie, are you serious?" Jessica said, alarm in her voice.

"Calm down, Jessica," Marjorie said softly. "Many of us think those thoughts. The trick is to get rid of them, to talk them out." Then, to Janie: "We've got to get you out of that black hole."

"How do you do that?" Jessica asked.

"With therapy, if Janie's willing. With some group sessions, where she'll be with other women who are also trying to recover. She's got to come to terms with what happened, to get rid of her guilt and to get on with her life. It won't be easy, but I don't have any other ideas."

They both looked at Janie, who slumped back into her chair.

"I'll try," they heard her whisper.

After dropping Janie off at the apartment, Jessica headed back downtown, stopping first at the station to check in, then walking a few blocks to the building that housed Midwest Services. Where Jack Tomlinson had said Kimberly Hawkins worked. The K.H. in Hill's diary.

As she stood outside, Jessica debated whether to confront the woman inside or catch her by surprise after work. With a glance at her watch, she decided on the latter tactic. Not only was it close to quitting time, but she guessed that if she showed up at her office, Kimberly would probably refuse to see her, anyway.

Jessica didn't relish the idea of an ambush interview, but what the hell? The woman could always just walk away. It was crucial to talk to her. Kim was, after all, the link between Sarah Andrews and rapist Edward Hill, the one person who might be able to shed light on Sarah's role in all of this. With nothing more than her suspicions at this point, Jessica desperately needed an inside track to Sarah's thoughts and actions. Kim might fill that void. What did she know about Hill's murder? About the ties between Sarah and Freda Brinkman? About Sarah's fanaticism and her efforts to squash Jessica's investigation?

But would she talk? That was the biggest question now.

Jessica spotted a small coffee shop across the street from Kim's building and took a table near the window. She didn't have long to wait; within twenty minutes the exodus from the office buildings began.

Slipping out of the shop, she strode across the street, trying to appear inconspicuous as she stood waiting. After fifteen minutes, she was ready to give it up; the sweltering late-afternoon heat and the oily exhaust from the street choked her, nauseated her.

That's when Kimberly Hawkins walked quickly past her.

No doubt it's her, Jessica thought, following a few paces behind, hoping for a break in the crowd on the sidewalk. When it came, Jessica moved next to her. "Ms. Hawkins. Kimberly," she began. "I don't mean to bother you."

If Kim was startled by the voice, she was even more shocked by the sight of Jessica. Her mouth opened, and her face seemed to freeze in surprise. But her legs were not frozen; almost without pause, she hurried her steps to a near jog as Jessica tried to keep pace.

"Ms. Hawkins, please," Jessica panted. "I need to talk to you. It won't take long."

Kim ignored her and plunged straight ahead, dodging others in her path, forcing Jessica to do the same. "C'mon, Kim," Jessica shouted, "this is silly. I don't want to race you, I want to talk to you. Give me a break."

Kim glanced over her shoulder and finally slowed to a stop, facing Jessica. "I can't talk to you," she said. "Leave me alone."

"Can't talk or won't talk?" Jessica asked.

"Both. I have nothing to say to you."

"Can't we stop someplace?" Jessica pleaded, desperate to detain her. "Let me buy you a cup of coffee. There's a place just down the block."

"No, I've got to get home."

They were standing almost nose to nose in the middle of the sidewalk, causing curious glances from others passing by. "I know now why you were at Edward Hill's grave, Kim. I need to talk to you about him, about what he did to you."

"How dare you ask me about that?" Kim replied angrily. "What possible business is that of yours?"

"Aren't you curious about who killed him?" Jessica demanded, trying to keep her voice low. "That's all I'm interested in."

Kim started to back away. "I know nothing about that. I've already talked to the police."

"Then talk to me," Jessica pleaded. "Why were you at the grave? Why would Sarah try to discourage me? Was she trying to protect you, Kim?"

Kim stopped, her anger replaced by confusion. "Sarah talked to you about this? When?"

"A few days ago. I didn't know you were roommates then."

Kim shook her head. "I don't understand any of this," she said. "Leave me alone."

Then she hurried away without looking back.

Sarah was the last to arrive at Freda Brinkman's second-story duplex in south Minneapolis. She found the other members of the Craft Club gathered around a large mahogany dining-room table, exchanging few words as they waited for the meeting to begin. The silence spoke to the tension in the room, which was reflected, too, by the taut expressions on each of their faces.

Their bags of knitting and needlepoint sat on the floor next to their chairs, again untouched. Each had grumbled mildly when Brinkman called to arrange the meeting on short notice, but hearing the urgency in her voice, none had failed to heed the summons.

As Sarah looked around the apartment, she was struck by its dinginess. The furniture was old and nondescript, the carpeting was worn, smelling faintly of mildew, and the walls were devoid of all but a couple of faded paintings, one of an old Dutch windmill, the other of a skinny horse by a barn. They looked as if they had been left by the previous tenants.

A large television set stood against one wall, with VCR and stereo equipment attached. On top of the TV were several police marksmanship tropies and a color picture of Brinkman at the firing range, pistol proudly in hand. The place was cheerless, without color or personality or sense of style. And certainly without any feminine frills. A reflection of the austere woman who lives here, Sarah thought.

Brinkman opened the meeting with a quick description of Ingram's abduction but then got to the real purpose of the gathering. "We told you last time about the possible threat posed by a young television reporter, Jessica Mitchell. Well, I'm afraid it's gotten worse."

The women stirred in their seats but never took their eyes off Brinkman.

"We now believe she's also linked the . . . ahh . . . cases of Michael Amery and Ezra Scott to the others and has managed to convince Matt Meecham that she's on to something."

"Who's Meecham?" one of the women, Nancy Higgins, asked.

"My boss," Brinkman replied. "The head of Homicide."

"God Almighty," someone else muttered.

"How could she put them together?" Teresa Johnson asked sharply.

"Damned if we know," Brinkman said with a shake of her head. She then told them of finding the hidden folder on Meecham's desk and of being discovered in his office. "Matt hasn't said anything to me or anyone else about this, and I don't dare ask him now."

"I can't believe this," Johnson said. "Everything was done so carefully. You assured us—"

Brinkman cut her off. "There were no assurances, you know that. There were only precautions."

Sarah rose and spoke for the first time. "It may be my imagination, but I think this Jessica also believes Freda and I were involved in the Ingram thing."

Brinkman was as shocked as anyone. "Why's that?" she demanded.

"Because she thought she spotted us across the street from the store window and took the trouble to ask me about it. I denied it, of course, but I'm not sure she was convinced."

Nancy Higgins leaned forward, elbows on the table. "What

can she prove about the murders that the cops haven't been able to prove?"

"No one's ever put them together before," Brinkman replied. "Until now they've been separate, unsolved killings, a few among many. Once the cops think they've got serial murders on their hands, they'll never let go."

"I knew it was going to come to this," Higgins said, her voice little more than a frightened whisper. "I knew we couldn't get away with it forever. What the hell are we going to do?"

"We're not going to panic, for sure," Brinkman said. "But we're not going to sit back and do nothing, either. We've got to sidetrack them somehow. Meecham's a drunk at heart and should be less of a problem than the reporter. She's the one who worries me."

"What are you proposing?" Johnson asked hesitantly.

Sarah and Brinkman exchanged glances. "We hope you'll leave that to us," Brinkman said. "We don't want to take drastic action, but we'll do what's necessary to protect ourselves."

Patricia Sample, the professor, stood up, the quaver in her voice unmistakable. "I think this is getting out of hand! I said so at the last meeting, and I'll say it again. We should just disappear for a while, let things cool off."

"I agree," Higgins said. "We're asking for more trouble."

"The problem's not going to disappear by itself," Sarah interjected. "They've gotten too close, too quick. I think Freda's right. We have to do something to discourage the investigation."

"It's the 'something' that bothers me," Johnson argued. "Our enemies are the predators, not reporters and cops. I don't want any part of this. It's not why I joined this group."

"C'mon, get real," Brinkman said. "We're talking about murder here. This is no fucking parlor game. Each one of you has blood on your hands. I'm not going to simply watch while they tighten the nooses around our necks. We've got to eliminate the threat. And if I have to do it alone, believe me, I will."

The women stared at their hands, no one saying anything for several minutes.

"Are we going to take a vote?" Higgins finally asked, meekly looking around the table.

Brinkman stared back at her, eyes afire. "You can vote from now until midnight for all I care," she said. "It won't mean shit to me. I'm not going to risk a prison sentence because you're all too chickenshit to act."

Sarah wanted to intercede, to restore calm, but one glance at Brinkman told her the discussion should end. More talk would only bring more trouble, she thought.

"I think it's time to adjourn," she said.

No one disagreed. The women quickly and quietly picked up their bags and walked out the door.

TWENTY-SIX

Kim was sitting tensely on the edge of the couch, hands clasped in her lap, when she heard the key turn in the lock and saw Sarah standing in the door of the darkened apartment.

"Where have you been?" Kim demanded angrily from the shadows.

Sarah didn't move, startled by the rancor in the voice and momentarily confused by the darkness. She quickly scanned the room, struggling to see in the gloomy interior. A single shaft of light from the kitchen crossed the living-room floor like an arrow, ending at Kim's feet, giving her upper body a ghostlike glow.

"Kim?" Sarah slowly closed the door behind her and took a tentative step inside. "What's going on? Why are you sitting here in the dark?"

"Waiting for you."

Sarah stood for a moment in silence, then walked to one end of the couch and flicked on a standing lamp, bathing Kim in light. Kim quickly covered her eyes. "Turn it off," she shouted.

"No," Sarah replied. "Look at me. What's going on?"

When Kim looked up, her eyes welled with tears. Her body was tense, strung out. "She was waiting for me, Sarah, outside the building . . . that reporter . . ."

Sarah felt her legs sag, and she knelt down, the rough tweed of the carpeting scraping her knees.

"How did she know who I was?" Kim whispered. "How did she know where to find me?"

Sarah reached for Kim's chin and gently pulled her face toward her. "Calm down, Kim," she said, her own mind whirling.

"She ran after me, for God's sake. I tried to get away." Kim's eyes were desperate. "Why would she want to talk to me?"

"I don't know, Kim. But she did see you at Hill's grave, remember."

"But I didn't tell her my name. I barely talked to her."

Sarah took a deep breath. "What did you say to her, Kim?"

"Nothing. But she knew about Edward Hill, what he had done to me. She said you'd talked to her. Did you tell her, Sarah?"

"Of course not."

"Then how does she know?"

Sarah got up and sat next to her. "I really don't know, Kim. She has a friend in the police department; she's read Hill's diary. She must have figured it out somehow."

"What did you say to her?" Kim asked.

"I told her to forget Hill's murder. I warned her that she was going to screw up the investigation. She didn't know about you then, Kim. She didn't know we lived together. I was just a prosecutor talking to a reporter."

"She knows now. She thinks you were trying to protect me," Kim said.

"I suppose I was," Sarah replied, "but I didn't let her know that. I said nothing about you."

"Then why is she following me?"

"She's just a nosy, persistent reporter who's trying to play cop. Forget about her, ignore her."

"Does she think I had something to do with Hill's murder?"

"Who knows what she's thinking?" Sarah sighed.

They sat, unspeaking, for several minutes. By carefully watching Kim's face, Sarah had learned to read her thoughts and emotions. She saw confusion and worry, but to her relief, no sign of suspicion.

"So where were you?" Kim finally asked again. "I've been waiting a long time."

Sarah shot her an irritated look and got up. "I had to work late," she said. "Since when are you keeping track?"

"What?" Kim was taken aback. "Don't we usually check in with one another? What's gotten into you?"

"I need some space," Sarah said, her voice harsh. "You're not the only one with problems."

Kim began to weep, quietly. In more than a year, since that first day at the crisis center, Sarah had never spoken to her that way before. Something was wrong.

The next morning, Jessica was at her desk in the newsroom when she received two phone calls. The first was from Jack Tomlinson. "Are you up to another dinner?" he asked.

This time there was no hesitation. "Sure, I'd love it."

"How about tonight?" he asked. "Let's meet at the Loon, downtown. About seven?"

She agreed, not bothering to disguise her eagerness. The second call came a moment later and took her totally by surprise. Sending a shiver through her body.

"Jessica?"

It took only a fraction of a second to recognize the voice. Lowell Ingram.

"Yes," she said, trying to keep her own voice level.

"This is Lowell Ingram."

"I know." Steady as she goes.

"I'd like to talk to you," he said. His voice was low and husky. And close. As if there were no telephone, no distance, between them.

"Where are you?" she asked.

"In a shitty apartment."

Jessica tried to choose her words carefully. Don't frighten him, she told herself, don't scare him off. Soothe him. "You've had a rough go of it," she said, forcing herself to sound sympathetic.

She heard a short grunt, a hollow chuckle. Then: "Those bitches!"

"What?"

"Never mind. When can we talk?"

"Anytime," she said. "Name the place. I'll be there."

"Know the Skyway Theater?"

"Downtown?"

"Right. *The Firm* is playing on one of the screens. I'll be in the third row from the back at two o'clock. Meet me there."

"Can I bring a photographer along?" she asked.

"No!" he shouted. "Just you. No camera, no one else. Deal?"

"Deal," she replied, knowing there was no other choice.

When she replaced the receiver, her hand felt clammy.

She arrived at the Skyway ten minutes early and followed the ticket taker's pointed finger down a hallway to one of the small theater auditoriums. She had hoped to find it still lit inside but instead walked into a dark cavern illuminated only by the images on the screen and by a small row of lights that lined the floor along both sides of the center aisle.

Jessica stood in the rear, allowing her eyes to adjust from the glare of the midday sun. The theater was nearly empty; the outlines of only a few heads were etched against the giant screen, and no one was sitting in the third row from the rear.

She hesitated, debating whether to wait where she was or to go ahead and take a seat. What the hell? I'm early, she reminded herself, sliding across the empty seats to a spot in the middle of the third row.

The prospect of being nearly alone in a darkened theater with Lowell Ingram was frightening, but Jessica knew it was worth whatever risk might be involved. And what could he do?

Grope her? Unlikely, even in a near-empty theater. Besides, she could always scream and flee. Still, knowing Ingram, it did give her the creeps.

The previews of coming attractions filled the screen, but Jessica paid little attention. She continued to glance over her shoulder, watching the doorway, knowing that in the murkiness she would see him before he could see her.

Ten minutes passed. Then fifteen. She held her watch close to her eyes. Ten past two. The feature film had begun. Would he stand her up? Then why go to the trouble of getting her here?

Suddenly, a dozen rows ahead of her, she saw a figure rise from his seat, a shadow against the screen. He looked in her direction, then began walking slowly up the aisle toward her. It was Ingram, she knew it. He'd been there all along, watching her as she looked for him.

He stopped in the aisle, quickly glanced toward the door, then made his way down the row of seats. "Glad you could make it," he said as he slipped into the seat next to her. "And that you came alone."

He leaned close, his words soaked in gin, bubbling on his lips. She pulled back, repelled by the smell and by his haggard, haunted features. His eyes were watery pools, surrounded by deep purplish circles that drooped to his cheekbones, blending into the dark stubble of his beard.

"Where have you been?" she asked. "I tried to find you after—"

"Were you there?" he asked.

"Yes. Along with everyone else."

He gave a short, bitter laugh. "The whole world now knows Lowell Ingram intimately, doesn't it? They know how to get even, that's for sure."

"They?"

"The ones who did it to me."

Although there was no one within twenty feet of them, he spoke in a whisper, telling her every detail of the abduction. Jessica had to strain to catch his words over the dialogue on the screen.

"So you know who they were?" she asked when he'd finished.

"One of them, I'm sure. That's why I wanted to talk to you." She edged closer.

"I've done a lot of thinking," he said. "At first, I thought I'd go after her."

"Her?" Jessica was astonished. "The police didn't say—"

". . . but I knew it would only get me in more trouble, and I don't need more trouble. Not now. I hate the bitch, but I don't want to go to prison. I want to get out of town, start over somewhere else. I can't face anybody here anymore."

"Who are you talking about?" she demanded.

He ignored the question. "The cops think I'm some kind of fucking joke. They could barely keep from laughing in my face."

Ingram hunched over in his seat, head hanging. Then he took a deep breath and raised his head again, looking directly at her.

"Then I thought of you. I figured you'd want to know who it was, that maybe you could expose them on television, humiliate them, hurt them like they hurt me. It's all I could think of."

"I'd have to have more than your word," Jessica said. "I'd need proof."

"There is no proof. One wore a ski mask, and I never saw the other. But I heard her."

"You told the police they were women?"

"Yeah. They thought I was a wimp. You probably do, too."

"Nonsense," she said, quickly losing her patience. "So who do you think it was, Lowell?"

"I don't know about the one in the mask, but I'm sure the other one was that bitch prosecutor Andrews. I'll never forget her voice, never."

Though Jessica knew she shouldn't be surprised, having spotted Sarah and Brinkman at the scene and then hearing Sarah lie about it, still a chill swept through her. Too much was coming together, and she was frightened.

"You're absolutely sure?" she asked.

Ingram was adamant. "As sure as you're sitting there."

"What about the other one?"

"It was too quick; I didn't get much of a look. But she was big and fast with her hands. She used that gun like a whip."

"And you say she handcuffed you?" she whispered.

Ingram nodded in the darkness, rubbing his wrists.

Brinkman, Jessica thought. It fit.

"Would you tell your story on camera?" she asked.

"Everything?"

"You can't name Andrews," she said. "She'd be suing us before the news was off the air. But everything else, yes."

Ingram sat back in the chair, pondering. "I don't know. It would only stir things up again."

Jessica suspected he was right, but she was determined to get his story on tape. An exclusive interview with Lowell Ingram, revealing for the first time that he'd been kidnapped by two women. A hell of a story, she thought, and if he was right, one that would put the pressure on Sarah Andrews and Freda Brinkman.

She persisted. "Right now, Lowell, all people know about you is what they saw in the store window, what they may have seen or heard about the charges against you. Maybe if they saw you up close and heard your story, they'd think differently. And maybe the cops would take the whole thing more seriously."

"Big deal," he said. "There's no future for me here no matter what I do or say."

"What can it hurt, Lowell?" she said, pressing him. "If you're really out for revenge, it could help."

"How?"

"By making the two women squirm, maybe forcing them to make a mistake. Who knows? It'd be better than just walking away."

"Let me think about it," he said. "I'll call you."

Jessica was relieved. No definite commitment, but a chance, however remote. "One more thing," she said. "Will you sign a statement, an affidavit, saying you believe one of the women was Sarah Andrews?"

"Why?"

"I don't know," she admitted. "At least we'll get it on the record. Could be helpful later on."

Ingram thought for only a moment. "Hell, yes," he said. "If it will help hang that bitch, sure."

By the time Jessica left the theater, a slight drizzle had begun to fall. More of a mist, really, but enough to dampen the sidewalks and to send pedestrians scurrying for the skyways. Darker skies to the west and distant streaks of lightning promised even heavier rains to come, so Jessica quickly joined the race for cover.

She had left Ingram inside the theater, content to watch the rest of the movie, admitting he had nowhere else to go. And while he refused to tell her where he now lived, he did promise to call about the interview and the affidavit.

Jessica knew the affidavit would be of little use and of no probable legal consequence, but she was comforted by the prospect of having something in writing, something substantial, which would tie Sarah Andrews to a part of the puzzle. God knows I have nothing else, she thought.

The notion of working with a creep like Ingram was not particularly pleasing to her. But what the hell? He was in the news and a possible link in an incredible chain.

A prosecutor and a police officer involved in the abduction and humiliation of a convicted molester. An activist, feminist prosecutor who happens to be the roommate of a woman raped by one of a string of murder victims, all of them sexual predators. And a police officer who happens to be a friend of the prosecutor's and one of the cops responsible for a murder investigation that's going nowhere.

There was that chill again. "Goddamnit," Jessica whispered to herself, "is this really possible? What am I doing?"

Jessica moved through the skyway system, oblivious to the stream of shoppers surrounding her. She was on automatic pilot, weaving unseeing, unthinking, through the pedestrian traffic, her mind now fully absorbed by the implications of her suspicions. She plunged straight ahead, looking neither to the right nor to the left. And certainly not to the rear, where Freda Brinkman followed at a safe distance, part of the anonymous skyway parade.

TWENTY-SEVEN

Jessica wished now that she had arranged to meet Jack Tomlinson somewhere else. She felt awkward, standing alone just inside the doorway of the restaurant, unable to spot him in the crowd. She had purposely come a few minutes late to avoid this situation, and she wasn't quite sure what she should do next.

The Loon was a favorite yuppie hangout, located just off Hennepin Avenue on the edge of the downtown warehouse district, situated amid art galleries, small jewelry and leather stores, and other bars and restaurants fully as yuppified. It was not Jessica's favorite kind of place, especially when she knew no one and was already drawing stares that blatantly tried to undress her.

"Can I help you?" asked a young woman with an armful of menus.

"Thanks, I'm just waiting for someone," Jessica replied.

"Why not grab a spot at the bar," the hostess suggested.

Jessica followed her pointed finger, choosing a barstool closest to the door, sitting atop it as primly as possible. After a lot of thought, she had chosen to wear a light cotton sundress with a halter front and a low-cut back. She now regretted the bare back; she could almost feel the eyes behind her caressing her skin.

She had been there for about five minutes when she heard, "What brings you here, Jessica?" The voice was to her side, a woman's voice. She turned, startled to find Sarah Andrews facing her. Holding a glass of white wine.

"Just waiting for a friend," Jessica said after a moment's hesitation. She momentarily debated mentioning Jack's name but decided against it. "How about you?"

"Taking a break from work," Sarah said. "No rest for the wicked, you know."

Jessica gulped at the Freudian slip. It was hard to hear in the hubbub of the bar, so they said nothing for a minute or two, filling the void with polite smiles and glances around the room.

Was this truly a coincidence? Jessica wondered. How could it be anything else? Jack was the only one who knew she would be here. So where the hell was he? Conveniently late? C'mon, Jess, she told herself, ease up. Things like this do happen.

Finally, Sarah leaned close to her ear, and any façade of politeness disappeared. "I hear you came after my roommate," she said. "It shook her up, being chased like that."

Jessica was taken aback but refused to be cowed. "Chased? I just wanted to talk to her."

"That's not what Kim said," Sarah replied.

"Sorry to hear that."

"People have a right to avoid reporters."

"Not if I can help it."

"Don't give up easily, do you?" Sarah said.

"How so?"

"Just that. You're persistent. Kim knows nothing about Edward Hill's murder. She was his victim, for God's sake. Leave her alone. Any mention of him brings it all back."

"She wasn't too upset to go to his grave," Jessica countered.

"Listen," Sarah said. "I warned you once about interfering in a police investigation. I don't know what you're trying to prove, but I'm told you're still pushing it."

"Told by whom? Freda Brinkman?"

Before Sarah could reply, Jessica felt a light tap on her shoulder. "Hi, Jess. Sarah?" It was Jack Tomlinson. He had arrived unseen by either of them. "Am I interrupting something?" he asked, smiling mischievously.

"Perfect timing, Jack," Jessica said. "We just finished our discussion."

"Is this the friend?" Sarah asked Jessica, appearing genuinely surprised to see Tomlinson. "I didn't know you two were an item."

Tomlinson laughed. "We're hardly an item. We've barely gotten acquainted."

"Be careful, then," Sarah whispered to him. "She doesn't trust lawyers."

With that and a curt nod of the head, she was gone.

"What kind of windmill did I walk into?" Jack asked once they were seated and had ordered a beer. "It looked as if you were ready to trade blows."

"It wasn't that bad," Jessica replied, smiling. "But it was getting a little tense."

"What the hell's going on?" he asked.

"I told you at the Cove. Sarah's involved in a story I'm working on. She doesn't like it much."

His brow furrowed. "That's not exactly what you told me."

Jessica shrugged. "Things change," she said.

"You also said you'd tell me about it sometime."

"I'd like to, but not right now."

"At the Cove, you wanted her roommate's name. Does this involve her?"

"Obliquely, yes. That's what the argument was about."

"Sounds mysterious, Jess."

She had to be careful. She hardly knew Tomlinson, certainly not well enough to put her full trust in him. As much as she liked him, she couldn't forget that he worked with Sarah.

Still, she desperately needed to talk to someone not directly involved in all of this, someone who had no personal or professional stake in it. Someone who would be neither skeptical nor judgmental, a friend who would help her weigh the facts and sift through her suspicions.

Jack seemed like a perfect candidate, but she knew it was too soon, at least for him to know the full story. But perhaps, she thought, he would be willing to help in a way that didn't directly involve Sarah or point to her. Doing so could also serve as something of a test.

"Would you be willing to do me a favor?" she asked. "A big one?"

"Like what?" he asked.

"It'll sound strange," she warned. "You'll have to trust me."

He was plainly puzzled.

"I need information," she continued. "Information I don't have access to myself."

"For what?"

"For a story I'm working on," she replied vaguely.

"The story on Sarah?"

"Not directly, no." A small lie, but a lie nonetheless.

"Where's this going, Jessica? Why do I have the feeling I'm being used again?"

Jessica laughed. "Because you are. But you can always say no."

"So what is it you want?" he asked.

"I'd like to learn everything I can about one particular Minneapolis cop, a lieutenant by the name of Freda Brinkman. Her background, her record, even her psychological profile, if you could get it."

"Man, Jessica. That's real private stuff."

"I know. But I don't know how else to get it."

She had first considered asking Meecham for the information but then decided against it. She didn't want to raise his suspicions and knew that he would probably say no, anyway.

"I could get my ass fired," Jack whispered.

"Not if you're careful," she said, silently challenging him.

She could see the doubt in his eyes. "You'll have to tell me more first," he finally said. "It's too big a risk when I don't know what it's about."

"Not first," Jessica said. "After. You get me the records and I'll tell you everything. Fair enough?"

"I'll have to think about it," he said doubtfully.

"I told you that you'd have to trust me," Jessica said.

"I'm sorry we both have our cars," Jack said as they stepped out of the restaurant. "I'd love to drive you home."

"Maybe next time," she said, hoping for a next time.

"At least let me walk you to your car," he said, taking her arm lightly, letting her steer them in the right direction.

His hand was cool, nonpossessive. Jessica felt comfortable next to him, arms swinging slightly, surrounded by the warmth of the night and by the faint, spicy smells from the restaurant kitchens still lingering in the air.

The dinner had only reinforced her strong first impressions of Jack at the Cove. He was an engaging companion: bright and funny but with a serious side as well. He was never at a loss for words but was also a willing listener. She couldn't remember being more quickly or strongly attracted to any man.

To her relief, he had not pressed her further about her mystery story, instead turning their conversation to more personal topics. On their first meeting, Jessica had told him nothing about Janie or what she had gone through. Tonight, feeling more comfortable with him, she'd related the whole story, including details of their meeting with the counselor. He listened intently, reacting first with anger, then with sympathy.

"Is she going to be okay?" he asked, genuine concern in his voice.

Jessica had shrugged. "I wish I knew."

The Impala was parked in a small lot about two blocks from the restaurant. As they approached it, he said, "I've really enjoyed tonight. I'd like to do it again."

"So would I," Jessica said as she reached into her purse for the car keys.

Before she could retrieve them, he leaned over and kissed her softly on the lips. The movement was unhurried but still caught her by surprise. She drew back slightly, and their lips parted. She studied him for a moment, their eyes no more than an inch apart.

She knew this was an important moment. She allowed her lips to return to his. And linger. Her back was against the car door, and she could feel the slight pressure of his hips against hers. Not insistent but there. His tongue was on her lips, caressing, tasting of mint. Their tongues touched. She felt her breath quicken.

Then he pulled back and looked down on her, the back of his fingers lightly brushing against her cheek, stroking it with the gentleness of the softest feather.

"I think I'd better go," he said softly. "Before things get out of hand."

Jessica slowly opened her eyes and looked around the darkened parking lot. "It is kind of public, isn't it?" she murmured.

"So I can see you again?" he asked.

Jessica smiled. "I think I just gave you your answer."

Then she kissed him again lightly and got into her car.

Jessica could hear the phone ringing as she stood outside the apartment door, fumbling for the right key in the gloom of the hallway. Where the hell's Janie? she wondered, silently cursing her sister's absence and her own hurried clumsiness. She tried one key, then another. When the lock finally turned, the ringing stopped.

Strange, she thought. She'd called Janie before leaving the restaurant but had gotten a busy signal. Maybe she'd just run to the grocery store. Still . . .

Jessica pushed the door open slowly, tensing as the grating squeak of the hinges sliced through the emptiness. The standing lamp by the couch illuminated one corner of the room, but the rest of the apartment was in darkness. She stood just inside the doorway, listening. She heard the faint hum of the radio in the kitchen but no sounds of movement, no voice from within.

As she was about to call out, the telephone rang. She closed the door and hurried across to it.

"Janie?" A man's voice, gruff and close. She could hear the sharp intake of his breath.

"No. This is Jessica."

"Let me talk to Janie."

"She's not here."

There was a long pause.

"Who's calling?" she asked, already knowing, ready to hang up.

"Never mind," said the voice, and the line went dead.

"Was that him?" A shout from the end of the hall. Janie's shout. High-pitched, frightened.

Jessica was startled. She was sure the apartment was empty. "Where the hell were you, Janie?"

"In the bedroom," she said, now coming into view. The apartment was warm, but her arms were clutched tightly around her chest. "He's been calling all night, Jess. He won't stop."

Jessica put her arms around her sister. "Did you talk to him?"

"Only the first time. I didn't know what to do."

"What did he say?" Jessica asked.

"That we should give it another chance. He says he loves me and wants me back."

"And what did you say?"

"To leave me alone. I called him every name I could think of, told him I'd call the cops if he kept calling."

Janie buried her head in Jessica's shoulder. "Do you think he's here, Jess?" she whispered. "In town? If he knows the number, he must know where we live."

"I don't know," she replied, walking to the window to peer out, "but I doubt it. It's easy and safe to pester you by phone, but I don't think he'd risk facing you now."

"You don't know him!" Janie cried.

Jessica suddenly had a thought. "Let me check with Matt Meecham," she said. "Maybe he can talk to a sheriff or somebody in that part of Wisconsin. Maybe put a scare into Charlie Bowser."

Janie seemed unconvinced. "I don't start work till next week, Jess. I'm going home for a while. I need to get out of here, away from the phone."

"What will you tell the folks?" Jessica asked.

Janie flopped on the couch. "I don't know. I'll have to face that when the time comes."

TWENTY-EIGHT

Matt Meecham sat in his small office, door closed, a stack of files piled high in front of him. His cigar smoldered in an ashtray that teetered on the edge of the desk. He carefully read each page of each report.

Meecham had persuaded his police buddies in Brooklyn Park, Bloomington, and St. Paul to provide him with copies of the full files on each of their predator murders. But they had complied only after Meecham had promised to fill them in as soon as possible.

So far the files had told him little more than he already knew. Each department appeared to have done a competent job of investigating the murders, and at first glance Meecham could discover nothing the police had not already looked into.

He was on his second reading of the reports when he was startled by a rap on the door. Before he could hide the files, Freda Brinkman pushed the door open. "Hey, Matt," she said, "hope I'm not interrupting anything."

"Matter of fact, you are," he replied, not masking his irritation. "What do you need?"

"We're all a little worried about you, Matt. It seems like you've been stuck in here for days. You okay?"

As she spoke, Brinkman moved inside the door and approached the desk, glancing down at the stack of files.

"I'm fine," Meecham said, closing the cover of the top folder. "I've just got a lot of work to do."

"Anything we can help with?"

"You don't have enough work of your own?"

Brinkman laughed. "Hell, yes, but nothing like this," she said, pointing to the stack of files. "What's going on, anyway?"

"Nothing that should concern you," Meecham replied vaguely. "A private project of my own."

"Sounds mysterious. I thought we didn't keep secrets."

Meecham didn't respond, and when Brinkman made no move to leave, he switched topics. "You ever talk to Hill's other rape victim? The woman who was on vacation?"

"Yeah, I did," Brinkman said, "but she had nothing to add. She says she hadn't seen or heard from Hill since the rape and sure as hell knows nothing about the murder. There's no indication that she's lying. Like Kim Hawkins, even talking about it again really upset her."

"So where does that leave us?" Meecham asked.

"On the Hill murder? Nowhere. The diary certainly doesn't tell us anything except that he was planning to meet someone who'd been pestering him that night. We have no idea who the 'someone' was."

"We're at a standstill?"

"I guess so. We haven't closed the file, but nothing's jumping out at us, either."

"I don't want the file closed," Meecham said sharply. "I want it solved."

"Then wish us luck," she said. "We're not exactly overrun with leads."

"You won't solve it standing there, will you?" he said irritably. "And I'm not going to get my work done if we keep jawing about it."

Brinkman took the angry hint, retreating quickly from the

office as Meecham returned to the files on his desk. The files she desperately wanted to see.

When the door closed, Meecham leaned back in his chair and relit the stub of his now-dead cigar. He wanted to think.

What the hell's going on?

First, Brinkman had confronted him in the back booth of Barney's when she had been so upset because he had talked to Jessica. He had chalked that up as strange, but not that unusual, knowing her hatred of reporters. Then he found her rummaging around his office. Again, strange, but she did have a right to see Hill's diary. What was it, then? Maybe she looked more guilty than surprised.

And now her sudden interest in his files and his work load. Was it, as she suggested, a genuine concern for his welfare? If so, it was the first time she had ever shown it. He knew she had long since written him off as a lush and a drunken bum, an embarrassment to the force.

Finally, there was her apparent indifference over the Hill murder. She was going through the motions but didn't seem to give a damn if they ever did find his killer. He remembered her words about Hill: "This guy was a real piece of shit."

It didn't make sense to Meecham. He was tempted to take his concerns to the chief, but he knew that would be futile. The chief had no more respect for Meecham than Brinkman did and would almost certainly brush off his misgivings as nothing more than an old drunk's paranoia or senility.

Meecham decided he could only wait it out. Wait and watch.

As it turned out, and although he would never know it, Meecham picked the wrong time to take a piss. The Homicide secretary was off on a similar mission, leaving their office empty.

Except for Freda Brinkman.

So when Meecham's phone rang, she was there alone to answer it. "Homicide. Brinkman here," she said.

"Where's Meecham?"

"Gone for the moment, I guess."

"This is Detective Shear in Bloomington. I need to double-check the time of our meeting."

"What meeting is that?" Brinkman asked, now alert.

"The meeting on Wednesday. I didn't write down the time."

"Hold on. Let me look at his calendar." She walked the few steps into Meecham's office and flipped open his date book. "Meeting, Registry" was scrawled in the space opposite 2:30 P.M.

"Looks like it's 2:30 at the Registry," Brinkman said when she returned to the phone.

"That's what I thought," Shear said. "I'll see him there."

"You think the others know the time?" Brinkman asked, fishing.

"Probably. I just forgot to jot it down."

Brinkman returned to her office and shut the door. She knew immediately what the meeting was about. She also knew she didn't have much more time to waste.

Sarah was already waiting on the small bench in the Government Center courtyard when Brinkman came down the escalator and out the door. The leaves of the locust tree overhanging the bench were wilted from the heat of the midday sun, hanging limp, unstirred by even the slightest breeze. Sarah was fanning herself with a yellow legal pad but seemed to find little relief from it or the shade of the locust.

"Why can't we talk inside?" Brinkman asked as she walked up. "Out of this damned heat."

"Too many people inside," Sarah said. "The less we're seen together these days, the better."

Brinkman sat next to her, loosening the top button on her uniform shirt. "Then I'll make it quick," she said, hurriedly telling Sarah of trailing Jessica the day before to the Skyway

Theater. "I don't know what the hell she was doing there. I couldn't follow her in, and she wasn't there long enough to see any movie. She must have met someone."

"What else?" Sarah asked.

"Nothing else. She went back to the television station and stayed there, as far as I know. I had to get back to work."

"Why meet someone in a theater?" Sarah wondered aloud.

"So somebody like me wouldn't see her, I suppose. We meet snitches like that all the time."

Sarah stared across the courtyard, watching bare-chested, helmeted workers crawling on the girders of a new office building. They seemed to be sweating less than she was.

"One more thing," Brinkman said. "I walked in on Meecham this morning. He was hunched over a stack of files—"

"Let me guess," Sarah interrupted. "Murder files. Four of them."

"That's my guess, too. But there's more."

"What?"

"I took a call for him from a cop out in Bloomington. Meecham's set up some kind of meeting for Wednesday. Ten to one it's about those files. It's getting too close for comfort."

"What are we going to do about him?" Sarah asked.

"I told you. Leave it to me," Brinkman replied.

Her smile made even the hot day seem cold.

TWENTY-NINE

The message light on Jessica's telephone was blinking when she sat down at her desk. She picked up the phone, punched her voice-mail access code, and listened.

"Jessica, this is Ingram. I'll do your interview. Bring your camera to the Holy Angels Cemetery at three this afternoon. I'll meet you by the gate. Shouldn't be many people around."

She couldn't believe it. The son of a bitch was actually going to talk.

"What canary did you just eat?" Jeff Hilliard asked, watching her from the next desk.

"What?"

"You were grinning like the cat—"

"Was I really?" she asked, embarrassed.

"So what's going on?" he asked.

"I just got some good news." She pushed her chair closer to his, her voice low. "Lowell Ingram's agreed to an interview."

"No shit. When?"

"This afternoon. An exclusive."

Be careful, she told herself. You don't have him on tape. He might change his mind, might not show up. He's already backed out of one interview, remember.

But she had a feeling this would be different. He certainly had been angry enough when they'd met in the theater, and although he'd been drinking then, he sounded sober enough now.

She listened again to his message. Holy Angels Cemetery? Why there? she wondered. Certainly solitary enough, if that's what he wants. No sweat, she thought. She wouldn't be alone this time.

Jessica and Bill Kendrick found Ingram where he said he would be, by the giant stone arch that marked the entrance of the cemetery. He was leaning against the side of an old Plymouth station wagon that sagged on its springs, its lower body mostly eaten away by rust, leaving jagged holes in the fenders and doors.

A small chapel, built of the same gray stone as the arch, sat to the right, behind a small fountain and inside a tall steel fence that went off in either direction. A car was parked by the chapel, but there was no other sign of people or activity. Not a banner day for funerals, she thought.

Kendrick pulled in next to Ingram as Jessica rolled down her window. "Glad you made it," she said. "Hope we're not late."

"No problem," he replied brusquely. "I was early." Then he got into his car. "Follow me and we'll find a nice, quiet spot."

Kendrick trailed the old Plymouth under the arch and along a narrow, winding road that led them through a forest of granite gravestones and marble monuments, some of the spires nearly as high as the trees that shaded them.

An entire grassy slope was covered, as far as one could see, with perfectly aligned rows of small white crosses. Many of the markers were chipped and gouged, almost crumbling from the passage of too many years, too many winters, too many wars. Small flags stood by each, at attention, as if on guard.

The slow pilgrimage continued for about ten minutes before Ingram's car pulled to the side of the road, next to a small, open area in the cemetery. Ingram got out, looked around, and stretched. "This ought to be okay," he said.

Kendrick began to retrieve the camera gear from the car and search for a place to set up the equipment. "Want to do the interview sitting on the grass?" he asked.

"I guess so," Jessica said dubiously. "I don't want to do it on a tombstone."

Ingram was paying no attention. He had wandered away, to the edge of the clearing, studying the etched inscriptions on nearby gravestones. Jessica joined him. "How did you happen to pick this place?" she asked.

"My mother's buried here," he said, pointing toward the west. "I knew we wouldn't be disturbed. I've had my fill of being seen in public."

"All set!" Kendrick shouted from across the way.

Jessica and Ingram walked back and settled on the grass, staring at the camera until Kendrick had made all of his final adjustments.

"We're rolling," he said.

Jessica looked at Ingram. "Now, Mr. Ingram, I'd like you to start from the beginning. Tell us what happened to you on the morning you ended up in the store window. . . ."

Sarah got home late that evening. She found Kim curled up on the couch, reading Tom Clancy's latest bestseller, just out in paperback. Kim barely acknowledged her entrance.

Sarah walked into the kitchen and rummaged through the refrigerator. She had eaten nothing since lunch but had little appetite. She finally settled on an apple. The juice sprayed as she bit into it.

"Mind if I turn on the news?" she asked when she returned to the living room. "It'll be on in a few minutes."

"Won't bother me," Kim said without taking her eyes from the book.

Sarah picked up the remote control and switched on Channel Seven. The final network prime-time program had just ended, and anchorman Alex Collier's face popped on to the screen.

"Next on Channel Seven News," Collier said, "an exclusive interview with Lowell Ingram, the man who was forced to stand naked in a downtown Minneapolis store window. Jessica Mitchell will tell you his astonishing story in a moment. . . ."

Sarah felt the blood rush to her head, and she quickly sat down on the edge of a chair. She fought the dizziness, breathing deeply. She wanted to put her head between her legs but knew she couldn't, not with Kim there.

"Did I hear him right?" Kim asked, her book now in her lap, staring at the TV set. "Did he say Lowell Ingram?"

Sarah nodded, not daring to speak, hearing again Collier's words: "Jessica Mitchell will tell you his astonishing story . . ."

Jessica pushed her chair tight against the anchor desk and adjusted the small microphone on her blouse. They were in the midst of the commercial break just before the news, and she was working hard to settle her nerves. She would be first up, the lead story. Calm down, she told herself. You're a big girl. Just look into the camera and tell the story. Ingram's the star, not you.

The studio lights seemed brighter and hotter than ever. An island of heat. It was a far cry from a few weeks before, when she had stood huddled and hidden in the cool darkness by the studio wall, watching the late newscast unfold with anonymous admiration. Now she was here, under the lights, about to lead off the station's major newscast of the day.

Collier and coanchor Barbara Miller both gave Jessica reassuring smiles as the floor director counted down the final seconds to the show's opening.

"Good evening, everyone," Collier said as the camera

zoomed slowly in on him. "Just a few days ago, during the heart of the morning rush hour in downtown Minneapolis, Lowell Ingram was found standing bound and gagged—and naked—in a vacant store window."

Sarah was now sprawled on the floor of the apartment, transfixed, as the pictures of Lowell Ingram in the store window flashed on the screen. Her dizziness had disappeared, but she still felt weak and breathless.

"Ingram had earlier pleaded guilty to child-molestation charges but had avoided a prison term." Barbara Miller was reading from the TelePrompTer. "Police have revealed few details of the kidnapping and have made no arrests. Lowell Ingram has been in seclusion. Until now."

Sarah saw the tape of Ingram in the window dissolve to a wide shot of the studio. Jessica was sitting to one side, at the edge of the anchor desk.

Collier was speaking again. "Channel Seven reporter Jessica Mitchell, who covered the original story, was able to arrange an exclusive interview with Ingram—who told her, for the first time, the startling details of his abduction. Jessica?"

There she was, her face filling the screen. The face Sarah had grown to fear.

For an instant, a heartbeat, Jessica thought she might panic. The studio seemed to whirl around her, the colors and images changing with the speed of a spinning kaleidoscope. Then it was over; balance was restored. And her first words broke free.

"Lowell Ingram revealed to me today what the police have never made public: that he believes his two abductors were women, one of them wearing a ski mask and brandishing a large pistol. He was blindfolded before he could see the second person, but he heard a voice and is convinced that it was also that of a woman."

Ingram's face then appeared on the screen, tightly focused. "I don't think the cops believed that it was two women," he said. "But I know it was, I heard them. The one I saw was big and strong and knew how to handle the gun. She hit me across the nose with the barrel when I tried to resist."

Ingram went on to relate, in a tightly edited narration, the rest of his story, starting with the knock on his motel room door and ending with his rescue by police.

"It's outrageous that people can get away with this kind of thing. The cops think it's a joke, but they weren't in that store window like I was. I trusted our system of justice, I put my faith in it. I pleaded guilty under pressure and was ready to take my punishment when this happened. I think the whole thing stinks."

Jessica reappeared on camera. "Police have refused to comment on Ingram's story but have denied that they consider his abduction a joke. They say their investigation is continuing.

"One other thing, Alex," she said as the camera went wide. "Ingram is convinced he knows who one of the women was, that he recognized her voice. That claim cannot be proved, of course, and we cannot broadcast it until it is. But Ingram has signed an affidavit, which I have in my possession, naming the woman."

"Will you turn that over to police?" Collier asked.

"That's yet to be decided," Jessica replied vaguely.

"Do you believe that?" Kim cried out from the couch when Jessica's report was over. "That's incredible! Two women did that to him?"

Sarah had not moved from her spot on the floor. She was spellbound, paralyzed. Jessica's words echoed in her mind: "Ingram has signed an affidavit . . . naming the woman."

Kim got up and turned off the TV. "Sarah," she said, waving her hand in front of Sarah's eyes, "can you hear me?"

"Of course," Sarah replied irritably. "I was just thinking."

"Well, what do you think?" Kim persisted.

"I'm as amazed as you are," she said as she got on her feet

and took another bite of the apple. "The cops haven't told our office anything about it. But knowing Ingram, he could be lying through his teeth, making the whole story up."

"He didn't look like he was lying," Kim offered.

"You don't know him like I do."

"Think she'll turn the woman's name over to the police?"

Sarah could think of little else. "Who knows? Legally, it won't mean much," she said, thinking aloud. "Ingram says he didn't see the woman, just heard her. And that won't be worth much to the cops or in court."

"You'd think the police would try to get it from her, anyway," Kim said. "Even if she doesn't want to give it to them."

"Maybe so, but my guess is she won't give it up. Reporters like to guard things like that."

The conversation was interrupted by the ring of the telephone.

Kim answered it. "It's for you, Sarah. Sounds like Freda Brinkman."

"I'll take it in the bedroom," Sarah said, and walked swiftly down the hall, not noticing—or ignoring—Kim's quizzical stare.

Why, Kim wondered, would she be calling this time of night?

The kitchen was warm from the morning sun when Sarah stumbled from her bedroom, still in her boxer pajamas, eyes filled with sleep. She was surprised not to find Kim there. The coffeepot was cold and empty, the morning paper still rolled up, lying outside the front door.

Strange, she thought. Kim's always up before I am.

She picked up the newspaper and walked back down the hall, stopping outside of Kim's bedroom door. "Kim, you there?" she called, rapping lightly on the door. She thought she heard a mumbled reply but no movement. She knocked again and then pushed the door open. "Kim, you okay? It's late."

She could see the outline of her body beneath the sheet, one arm hanging over the side of the bed. "Are you sick or something?" she asked from the doorway.

Kim's head slowly emerged from beneath the cover. "Go away," she said in a groggy voice. "I'm not going to work. I'm staying here."

Sarah walked around the bed and knelt beside it. Kim's eyes were closed, her breathing shallow. Sarah waited.

"I had the nightmare again," Kim said as her eyes slowly opened, staring past Sarah. "Only it was worse this time. I saw the woman on the horse, the one with the bloody lance, Sarah. She had a face now. It was horrible."

"It was a nightmare, Kim, for God's sake. A bad dream. Get up and move around. You'll feel better."

"Don't you want to know whose face it was?" Kim's eyes were closed again, her face grimacing—as if she were seeing the apparition all over again.

"I don't care whose face it was. You had a nightmare. It wasn't real. Can't you understand that?"

"It seemed real," Kim continued. "Just like the last time. But I saw her now, I saw her face."

"Okay, Kim," Sarah said tiredly, reluctantly. "Who was it?"

Kim pulled the sheet back over her head, and Sarah could barely hear her whispered response. "You won't believe it, but it was your friend, that lieutenant, Freda Brinkman. She was smiling, Sarah, holding that bloody lance and smiling."

Sarah got up and backed away. Her face was pale.

"What does it mean, Sarah?" Kim's voice was still muffled, beneath the covers.

"It means nothing," Sarah said, retreating. "Sleep it off, Kim. You scare me. You're getting crazier all the time."

Once Sarah had left for work, Kim got out of bed and padded into the kitchen, making coffee, in no mood to face the demands of her job. She was confused and worried. Things were happening which she didn't understand; she couldn't shake her uneasiness or escape the feeling that she was missing something.

No question, Sarah was acting strangely. Her edginess, her flashes of temper, her unpredictable schedule, were all peculiar, unlike the Sarah that Kim had known for the past year. She had continued to treat Kim's nightmares as some kind of crazed aberration, almost blaming her for having them. There had been no attempt to comfort, to counsel, to even understand. Just ridicule. Again, not like the Sarah that Kim had known.

And how could Kim forget the almost-hypnotic spell cast on Sarah by Ingram's television interview? It was more than fascination. Kim also detected a touch of fear in Sarah. She had been almost paralyzed by it. And then the call from Freda Brinkman immediately after. What was going on?

Kim picked up the morning newspaper and reread its story on Ingram, storing the details in her mind. It was not until later, however, as she walked around Lake Harriet, that Kim finally realized, with a start, what should have been obvious before, that Ingram had been abducted the same night Sarah said she was going to be out of town.

Suddenly, Kim didn't feel so dumb.

THIRTY

Jessica's story caused a storm. Both daily newspapers and the Associated Press carried long stories on Lowell Ingram's televised revelations, quoting heavily from Jessica's interview. Several radio stations sought permission to use audio excerpts, and the local *City* magazine told Jessica it planned to do a major article on her, profiling the rookie reporter who had scooped the city.

The station's television competitors scrambled to catch up on the story, but they had no chance without Lowell Ingram. And they couldn't find him.

Nor could the police. An embarrassed deputy chief was on the telephone to Jessica the first thing in the morning, demanding to know the whereabouts of Ingram.

"Got me," she told him. "Ask his probation officer."

"We tried. He doesn't know, either."

"I can't help you," Jessica said.

"You don't know where he's living?"

"Sorry. He met us for the interview."

"Then we want a copy of that affidavit," the deputy chief said. "We need the name of the woman."

She hesitated. "I don't know about that," she finally replied. "I'd have to check with my boss first."

"We need the name now," he growled.

"Then your cops should have asked Ingram when they had him," she said, growing irritated. "He gave that name to me. I don't have his permission to give it to you."

"We'll see about that," the officer grunted, and hung up.

That was the storm's first thunderclap. When Jessica looked up from the phone, she found George Barclay hovering near her desk. He did not appear happy. She was about to hear the second rumble.

"Need to talk to you," he said gruffly, motioning toward his office. Laurie Sanders was already there, waiting.

"Jess, that was a hell of a story," Barclay said. "You should be proud of yourself. But why didn't you tell us about this damned affidavit?"

"I did. Laurie saw it. I showed it to her."

"You didn't tell me you were going to use it on the air," Laurie protested.

"I didn't think it was that important," Jessica admitted. "It was just a footnote to the story, really."

"It could cause us all kinds of shit," Barclay groused.

"I understand that now," she said. "I just talked to some deputy police chief. They want the affidavit. I told him I'd have to speak to you first."

"I knew it!" Barclay exploded. "The assholes will probably take us to court to get it."

Jessica was cowed. "Then give it to them. I didn't promise Ingram that I wouldn't."

"It's not that simple, Jessica," Laurie said. "If we give it to the police and the word somehow leaks that it names Sarah Andrews, she could possibly sue our ass for libel."

"Ingram says it was Sarah, we don't," Jessica argued.

"But we solicited the document from him," Barclay answered. "That could make us part of the libel if it ever becomes public. I'll have to talk to our lawyers."

"I'm really sorry for all of this," Jessica said. "I didn't know what I was getting us into. I didn't even want the affidavit for this story. It was for possible future use."

"What do you mean?" Barclay asked sharply.

"I'd rather not go into it now," she said. "It's only a theory, and it may be too far out."

"I'd like to hear it," Barclay persisted.

Jessica glanced at Laurie, then back to Barclay, swallowing hard. "It'll sound ridiculous, but I think Sarah Andrews and that police lieutenant, Freda Brinkman, not only put Ingram in that store window but may also have something to do with the string of murders."

Barclay was beside himself. "C'mon, Jessica. You think a couple of women are knocking off these guys? A cop and a prosecutor, to boot? That's crazy. Putting some pervert in a store window is one thing, but a string of murders?"

"I told you it's only a theory," Jessica said, pulling back. "I have no proof. But too many strange things have been happening."

"Like what?" Laurie demanded.

Jessica recited the attempts by both Sarah and Brinkman to blunt her pursuit of Hill's murder. "Everywhere I go, one or the other seems to be there, in my face, threatening me or trying to persuade me to pull back. I was damn near run over, and somebody put a knife in my car tire. Something's screwy, I'm convinced."

Barclay and Laurie stared at her, surprised at the conviction in her voice. "Why haven't you told us about those things before?" Barclay asked.

"Because for a while I couldn't believe it myself. And I didn't want to bother you with my wild ideas. But if Ingram's right . . . if Andrews and some other woman, probably Brinkman, were involved in his abduction, then it makes their participation in the other stuff more plausible."

"But Ingram didn't get killed," Laurie argued.

"You're right," Jessica replied. "And I can't explain that. Maybe they just do one killing a year. That's been the pattern so far. Every July. Maybe they decided Ingram didn't deserve to die but just needed a lesson. I don't pretend to have all of the answers."

"If you're right," Laurie said, "someone could argue that they're doing us all a favor. Killing off these scumbags. Who the hell's going to miss them?"

Jessica stiffened. "You don't really believe that, Laurie. And, besides, that doesn't make it less of a story, does it?"

Barclay said, "You've got to be careful, for your sake and ours."

"I won't do anything without telling you," she promised. "But don't pull me off the story. I'm too deep into it, and I know something's there. It's just going to take more time."

That evening, after work, Jessica barely had time to get home to shower and change before Jack Tomlinson was at her door, looking cool and comfortable in a pale blue polo shirt, white shorts, and sandals. He'd called earlier in the day, telling her he had the information she was looking for. She asked him to stop over and she would fix a pizza.

"Not late, am I?" he asked.

"Not this time," she said, smiling. "C'mon in."

He didn't move. He stood back, staring. "Wow," he whispered, followed by a low wolf whistle. "You look terrific."

"Really?" she said, glancing down at herself, feeling a slight blush begin to rise. But she was secretly pleased. She'd been too rushed to worry much about what she would wear, grabbing the jade silk tank top and tapered white slacks because they were the only clean clothes in the closet. But he would never know that.

Jessica stepped aside as he walked in carrying a narrow sack in one hand, a small bouquet of daisies in the other, and a thin manila folder tucked beneath his arm.

"That's sweet of you," she said as he handed her the flowers.

"Don't thank me, thank my mother," he said, laughing. "I stole 'em out of her garden."

"They're wonderful."

Jack stood in the middle of the living room, surveying the small apartment and its sparse furnishings. Jessica suddenly felt embarrassed, slightly ashamed, wishing now that she had arranged to meet him somewhere else.

"Nice place," he said. "Cozy."

"Who are you kidding?" she replied. "It's dumpy. But it's better than I had in Duluth, and it's all I can afford."

"And here I thought all of you television people made big money," he said slyly.

"Think again. I may be on food stamps next month."

Jessica walked toward the kitchen. "Make yourself at home while I try to find a vase."

Jack followed her. "I picked up some wine on the way," he said, taking a bottle from the sack. "Hope you like chardonnay. It's nice and cold."

"Love it," she said as she retrieved a vase and two wineglasses from the cupboard and a corkscrew from a kitchen drawer. It took him only a moment to uncork the bottle.

"To the future," he said, raising his filled glass, his eyes gently locked on hers. She nodded and smiled but said nothing as she brought the glass to her lips.

The future? Who had time to think about that? She had enough trouble making it through each day. Her life was moving too quickly, in too many different directions. And whose future was he talking about? His? Hers? Theirs?

They returned to the living room, sitting together but slightly apart on the lumpy couch. The curtains billowed around the open window, the breeze blessedly cool and smelling faintly of steaks cooking on somebody's outdoor grill.

"Where's your sister?" he asked.

"Back home in Madelia for a few days. She got some weird phone calls from the guy who attacked her and wanted to get away for a while. She also decided it was time to finally face the folks."

"What about the phone calls?" he asked.

"I hope that's handled. I talked to Meecham, who has a cop

friend of a friend who knows the sheriff in Sawyer County, Wisconsin, where this guy lives. Apparently the sheriff got the word to him to back off or face trouble. I just hope it works."

"How is Janie doing otherwise?"

Jessica shrugged. "I don't really know. She's attending the therapy sessions but doesn't say much to me. Still seems to be holding it all inside. I just wonder what she'll tell the folks. They won't be easy to lie to."

As they talked, Jessica could not take her eyes off the manila folder he had dropped on the coffee table when he came into the apartment. "Is that it?" she finally said, pointing to the folder. "The file on Freda Brinkman?"

Jack nodded and reached for it. Jessica moved closer to him, stretching her neck to see.

Before he opened the folder, he looked at her. "At the restaurant," he said, "you asked me to trust you. By doing this, I hope you realize how much I am. I could get my ass in a sling for having this, for taking it out of the office."

"I understand," she whispered. "I was being straight. You can tell me later if you think I'm crazy."

He opened the folder and flipped through the pages. "I haven't really studied this, but I must say nothing jumps out at me. According to this, Brinkman's a pretty good cop. Joined the force almost fifteen years ago, after a couple of years at a community college. One of the first women cops to hit the streets. Worked hard, had a good record, got a handful of commendations. Had some problems with some of the men on the force in the early years but toughed it out, never filed a complaint. She had a reputation as tough and dependable. Didn't take shit from anybody, on the force or on the street."

He paused, apparently studying one entry. "Only major problem during those early years was a brutality complaint filed against her and her partner."

"I heard about that," she said. "Some television cameraman got it on tape."

"Right. The partner got busted, and the city got sued. Brinkman was reprimanded for not intervening, for not reporting it to her superiors immediately. She was shifted to a desk

job for a while and eventually was transferred to the sex-
crimes unit."

"When was that?" Jessica asked, leaning in.

"Six, seven years ago. Stayed there until she got moved to
Homicide two years ago. Never missed a chance to take a promotional exam and slowly built up rank. She's now one of the
top women in the department, although it's still not that large a
group."

"What about her years in sex crimes?"

Jack turned back two pages. "Good arrest record. Concen-
trated on rape cases. Worked closely with the victims. Her supervisor says she was the hardest worker in the unit. Never
seemed to take time off. Unbending in her pursuit of the bad
guys. Obsessive, almost, it says here."

Jessica considered what she had heard. Certainly no smoking guns there. A record she guessed most cops would be
proud of. Tough, ambitious, persistent, her only major reprimand for not squealing on a partner. Not exactly a badge of
shame among policemen.

"What about the psychological profile?" she asked.

"That's a little more interesting," he said. "Grew up in a
tough neighborhood. Parents split when she was still in grade
school. Father disappeared, mother remarried, apparently to a
real jerk. The report's not very specific, but apparently the
stepfather was pretty abusive to both the mother and daughter.
Brinkman hated him, got out of the house before she was
through high school. Lived with a foster family. She never
married. Has few other interests or hobbies."

"Doesn't sound like much of a life, does it?" Jessica offered.

"From what it says here, her job is her life."

Jessica took the file and thumbed through it, looking for
any item that Jack might have missed. She found nothing until
she turned to the final page. There was a handwritten note
with a signature she couldn't make out.

Brinkman has often demonstrated a private and public
hostility toward the news media. For the sake of depart-

mental public relations, it is recommended that she be
kept at a distance from the press until and unless there
is a demonstrable change in that attitude.

No kidding, Jessica thought.

"Okay," Jack said, reaching for the file. "I've done my
part. . . ."

She took a deep breath, then a small swallow of wine.

"You're probably not going to believe any of this," she
said, "but I want you to hear it all."

Jack made her pause twice in the story while he went to the
kitchen to refill their wineglasses. Otherwise, he listened
without interruption.

Forty-five minutes later, when she had finally finished, he
cupped his hands behind his head, leaned back, and stared at
the ceiling. "That's it?" he asked.

"That's it," she acknowledged. "All of it."

"Then it's pizza time," he said, getting up. "I'm starved."

"That's all you're going to say?"

"I need to think about it awhile. And I can't think on an
empty stomach. Besides, I'm tipsy from all the wine."

So was Jessica, although she didn't realize it until she tried
to follow him to the kitchen. She sat back down, feeling the
wooziness wash over her. "You're not the only one," she said.

She could hear him fumbling around in the kitchen, opening and closing the freezer and microwave, poking in drawers
and cupboards, setting the silverware on the table. She wanted
to help, but two attempts to find her legs failed.

She finally made it on the third try, joining him just as he
was slicing the pizza. "Sorry," she said. "Wine doesn't usually
do that to me."

"Me, either," he said, piling the pizza on her plate. "Must
be the lack of food."

They said little as they each consumed three large slices of
the mushroom and sausage pizza. Jessica couldn't remember

ever eating as much, but it did quell the queasiness from the wine.

"So what are you going to do now?" Jack asked as he picked the last crumbs from the plate.

"I don't really know. Keep going, I guess. It's too late to turn back."

He arched his eyebrows. "If what you suspect is true, it could get real risky."

"You're telling me?"

"Can I help?" he asked.

"You can tell me I haven't lost my goddamned mind."

He chuckled. "I'm serious. I don't know if you're right about any of this, but I'm willing to help you find out, one way or the other."

She studied him across the table. Could she trust him? He had certainly kept his part of the bargain, supplying the Brinkman profile. Then why the lingering doubts? Jessica couldn't forget that he worked with Sarah Andrews and that she knew nothing about him except what he had told her. Any good reporter would have checked him out by now. So would any woman feeling what she was feeling.

Her mother's words came back to her again. "Small-town girls like you are just too trusting."

Still, he had done nothing to earn her distrust. And it couldn't hurt to have someone like Jack on the inside, available for help and advice.

"You sure you want to get involved?" she asked.

He got up and came around the table. He lifted her chin and found her lips. His tongue tasted of spice. But sweet.

"Yes, I'm sure," he whispered.

This time he didn't walk away.

Maybe it was the wine. Or her years of abstinence. Perhaps the weeks of pent-up tension. Whatever it was, Jessica found herself helpless after that first lingering kiss.

No, not helpless. She would never admit to that. Open. Willing. Even eager.

She was still sitting at the table, head back, feeling the

chair tilt slightly. His tongue caressed her teeth, then moved slowly across her lips. Sucking at them gently. Then on the tip of her nose, her eyelids, the lobes of her ears.

His breath was soft and warm against her skin. Then the nape of her neck. She could feel her nipples begin to harden. Tingle.

Eyes closed, she slowly clasped her hands behind his neck, her thumbs tracing, massaging, the taut muscles of his neck. Feeling the beat of his pulse, the flush of his skin.

She clung more tightly as the chair tilted farther back. "Hey," she whispered. "I'm falling."

She heard a small chuckle, then felt one of his arms beneath her knees and the other behind her back. She opened her eyes as he picked her up without apparent effort, cradling her body as loosely but snugly as her father once had, carrying her to bed as a child.

"Where to?" Jack asked with the smallest of smiles.

She hesitated. He was leaving the choice to her. The uncertainty of only minutes before had not disappeared, clinging to the edge of her consciousness. But that was then. This is now.

"Take a right," she said, burying her head against his neck, allowing her own tongue to roam, tasting the saltiness of the sweaty mist that clung to him.

He placed her gently on the top of the comforter, then sat on the edge of the bed. He gently touched her cheek, running a finger to her neck, pausing at a half-moon birthmark. "What's this?" he asked, leaning over to examine it.

"I was born with it," she whispered. "You think it's ugly?"

He kissed it. "I think it's beautiful. You're beautiful."

His hand moved down, touching her breast, his finger circling the nipple, feeling it grow even harder through the brassiere and the fabric of her top. She closed her eyes, absorbing the wonderful sensation. His hand moved to her other breast, then back, his touch so light as to be almost no touch at all.

Without willing them to, she felt her hips move, arching slightly, then higher as his lips and tongue again found hers. His hand was beneath her tank top, on the flatness of her stomach, moving down, under the top of her loose-fitting slacks.

Then it was there. Tracing the triangle. Cupping her. Finding her open, wet, and waiting. She could hear his breath quicken, his own body move.

My God, how long has it been?

His lips left hers, but his hand stayed, softly massaging. She slowly opened her eyes, found him looking down at her.

"Are you sure you want this?" he asked quietly. "It's not too late to say no."

At that moment, hearing his gentle question, seeing his eyes, she found it impossible to escape the horrifying picture of Janie struggling in the sand, fighting off a madman determined to do violence to her body. Unlike Jessica, Janie was given no choice and because of that, she feared, might never have the trust to experience what she was feeling right now.

Jessica reached down and put her hand on top of his, pressing it into her. "Do I act like I'm saying no?" she asked.

In the end, it was the most wondrous, erotic hour of her life. Gentle and unhurried. Lingering. Exquisite. So different from the guilt-ridden rushes to completion in the college dorm or the acrobatics in the back of the Impala. In a real sense, Jessica had considered herself still a virgin and had willingly allowed Jack, and her body, to guide her through the marvelous intricacies of lovemaking.

She felt no shame, no regrets, no shyness. Not at the beginning, not now. Only a deep, warm satisfaction. From the center of her, the glow touched every nerve, every pore. Her body had been reborn; she had never felt more alive.

They lay spent, on top of the comforter, their bare bodies bathed by a cool breeze wafting through the window, caressing them as they had caressed one another only minutes before.

For the first time in weeks, Jessica felt at peace.

THIRTY-ONE

Freda Brinkman sat slumped behind the wheel of her dark blue Pontiac outside city hall. She had been there for twenty minutes now, waiting for Matt Meecham to walk out. She knew that his car, a white Ford Crown Victoria, was parked just down the block—in a police zone—and that he couldn't get to it without coming into her view. The trick was not to be seen by him.

Brinkman had left the Homicide office early, blaming an aching tooth, and had quickly taken up her position. She didn't know how long she would have to wait, but she was determined not to miss him. She had changed from her uniform into a light blouse and slacks, freeing her bundled hair and allowing it to fall down over her neck. At first glance, she hardly looked like the same woman.

The sun had sunk behind the towering downtown office towers as the rush-hour traffic crawled past her, a steady, unending stream heading for the freeways and the slow, bumper-to-bumper journey home. She watched and waited impatiently. She was counting on the crush of cars for cover.

Brinkman had been planning for this moment since the day she had been caught in Meecham's office, the day she found the hidden folder. She knew then that she would have to deal with Meecham in some way, somehow. Yet now her plans were dependent on Meecham doing what he always did, following his familiar routine.

She had told no one, including Sarah, the details of the plan, asking only that Sarah stand by for a call later that night. She knew the scheme was not foolproof, that it could go terribly wrong, but she tried to build in as many safeguards as possible. Still, there were risks.

By the time Meecham finally emerged from city hall, twenty more minutes had passed, and traffic had thinned. His suit coat was slung over his shoulder, and Brinkman could see, even from this distance, the small gun and holster tucked into the belt at the back of his pants. He stood on the steps for a moment, as if debating, then slowly ambled toward his parked car. He never glanced her way.

Meecham drove straight down Fifth Street, past the Nicollet Mall and Hennepin Avenue. Brinkman was four cars behind him, taking her time, growing more confident—and relieved—as he followed the expected route. She became absolutely sure when he took a right on Third Avenue, deeper into the warehouse district, and then swung into the small parking lot next to Barney's.

Pulling to the curb a half block away, within sight of the bar's front entrance, Brinkman watched as Meecham walked around the corner of the building and through the door. She glanced at her watch: 6:14. Still three hours until darkness.

Despite being on the wagon, Meecham held to his old habits. That meant being at Barney's on Tuesday night for the weekly cribbage tournament. Brinkman knew that Meecham invariably took part, almost always winning, seldom leaving the place before ten. He talked about it often enough so that she knew the chances were great that he would be here again tonight. She was not disappointed.

* * *

She waited in the same spot for almost an hour to make sure Meecham didn't make an early exit. Knowing that the cribbage games started promptly at seven, she felt relieved when that hour had passed and he was still inside. She put the car into gear and began what she knew was a twenty-eight-minute drive to Meecham's home in suburban Arden Hills. Give or take a minute or two.

Craving the safety and anonymity of darkness, Brinkman wished it were winter, when the sun would have long since set. But this was July, when daylight lingered far longer, and the sun was still hanging ten degrees above the horizon.

Meecham's house was set well back from the road, secluded within five acres of birch and scrub oak, overgrown with thickets of aspen seedlings and wild roses and blackberry bushes. Meecham and his wife had bought the land decades before, when it was still surrounded by rolling, wooded countryside, before the developers had come along with their bulldozers and truckloads of sod.

The Meechams had rejected all appeals to tame their property, to groom and manicure it like those who now lived around them. As a result, their place still stood as a small and wild island in a sea of expensive homes with putting-green yards, curving concrete streets, and ubiquitous cul-de-sacs. Meecham could not see his nearest neighbor, nor could they see him. He liked it that way.

However, with only his cats to share the space, Meecham now found the house much too large for his needs, increasing his sense of isolation and loneliness. Since his wife's death, he had often been tempted to sell, but each time he had backed away, unable to part with the last vestige of a life he had erased in a searing, drunken instant.

Brinkman had been inside the house only once, two years before, when Meecham had reluctantly hosted a retirement party for one of the Homicide detectives. But she had driven around it often in the last week. She knew the area well by now.

She circled again, twice, before parking her Pontiac four blocks away, close to a small shopping area that included a drugstore, a bakery, a hardware store, and a boutique dress shop. The car would draw no special attention there.

She opened the trunk and pulled out a small, collapsible baby stroller and set it up. From the front seat, she retrieved the most lifelike doll she had been able to find at Toys 'Я' Us two days before: a plastic infant with clicking blue eyes, its head covered by a white bonnet, its body by a dainty pink kimono.

After glancing casually around her, Brinkman gently carried the doll to the stroller, shielding it with her body before tucking it into the stroller seat and covering it with a thin white blanket. Then back to the trunk of the car. Out came a canvas bag, already heavy with the tools she would need. Into it she put a fifth of brandy, wrapped in a narrow brown paper bag, which fit neatly beneath the row of diapers. Brinkman and her baby were now set for their evening walk.

"Fifteen two, fifteen four, and a pair is six."

Meecham watched absently as his opponent, an old geezer he knew only as Jackie, moved the pegs up Third Street on the cribbage board. Meecham was having trouble concentrating. He was twenty-three holes ahead and had the crib on the next hand. What's more, Jackie was working on his fourth beer and having trouble getting the pegs into the right holes. He was hardly a threat.

As he dealt the cards, Meecham looked up at the old Grain Belt beer clock above the bar. 8:20. He had already knocked three opponents out of contention, but four other games were still in progress. That would mean another hour at least.

His heart wasn't in it, but he couldn't leave now. Not until he had won it all or was beaten himself. The latter was unlikely, considering he was the only sober one in the bar. And he couldn't throw a game. The others might be drunk, but not drunk enough to miss that. And that would put a permanent end to his cribbage at Barney's.

"C'mon, Jackie," he said irritably, "put your fucking cards in the crib. Studying them isn't going to make 'em any better."

"What's your hurry, copper?" the old man asked. "I've got a hell of a hand here. Takes time."

"Sure," Meecham muttered, lighting up his second cigar of the night.

Meecham had been taking part in these weekly games for more years than he could remember, since a year or so after the accident, at least. They had become an important part of his meager outside life, the only event that could bring him out of his solitary back booth. But he understood now that playing without drinking was in itself a sobering experience, not nearly as much fun as it had been with a slight buzz on. He yawned, yearning for the games to be over, to be home with his cats in the silence of the house in the woods.

Sporting sunglasses and a silk scarf tied loosely around her head, Freda looked like any young mother on an early-evening stroll with her child. She walked slowly, the diaper bag slung on her shoulder, stopping now and then to adjust the doll's blanket, giving wide berth to children in the streets or to people in their yards. No one seemed to give her or the "baby" a second glance.

She sauntered by the driveway of Meecham's house twice. Like the house itself, the drive was hidden from the view of anyone but those who happened along the road. On her third pass, when she saw no sign of an approaching car, she calmly pushed the stroller into the shadows of the towering trees.

She waited in the trees and underbrush, out of sight of the road, for five minutes. Ignoring the mosquitoes that swarmed around her in a feeding frenzy, she remained absolutely still, listening. She knew this was a dangerous moment. If Meecham were to drive in and find her here, she would have no plausible explanation.

When she heard and saw nothing, she picked up the stroller and carried it still deeper into the woods, covering it with underbrush and broken branches. If she could pick it up later, fine. If not, no one would likely find it there, let alone connect it to anything that had happened. She picked up her bag and began to work her way toward the house.

Sarah continued to pace back and forth in her small office. She had tried to sit at her desk and work, but it was useless. She couldn't concentrate on anything but the phone call she thought would be coming. Knowing that Kim would be at the apartment, she had decided to stay here to await the call. She didn't want to do anything more to further what she already sensed was Kim's growing confusion and suspicion.

Brinkman had told Sarah virtually nothing except that she planned to deal with Meecham tonight and that she might need a ride later on. Sarah had tried to press her for details; when that failed, she had urged her to use caution and common sense.

"We just want to take him out of circulation for a while," she reminded her. "Nothing more, remember? This is a cop we're talking about."

Brinkman had smiled. "Just stick by the phone," she said.

As she got closer to the house, Brinkman emerged from the cover of the trees and walked boldly up the driveway to the front door. She pressed the bell and waited. No sense in trying to break in, she thought, if someone's here already. She knew that was unlikely, but she didn't want to take a chance. She had a story ready if somebody else was there. And if Meecham drove in, she would simply run like hell.

After pressing the button for the third time and hearing the chimes sound inside, she stepped back and looked toward the front window. She found two sets of eyes staring back at her. Cat eyes.

Meecham's Siamese twins were sitting on an inside window ledge, heads tilted slightly, watching her with unblinking curiosity. Brinkman knew they would be in the house, but finding them now, watching her with the intensity of guard dogs, was unsettling.

She walked slowly around the house, checking each window. She knew the house was air-conditioned but hoped Meecham might have left one of the windows open to give the house—and the cats—some fresh air. If not, she would have to crack one open. The cats followed her progress, their heads poking up in almost every window she checked. They were beginning to get on her nerves.

Darkness was settling in. The crickets were a chorus at her feet, and from the woods she could hear the deep-throated call of the whippoorwill. The luminous dial on her watch told her it was ten after nine.

At the back of the house, she found what she was looking for, a window, at waist height, open about ten inches behind a screen. She quickly slit the screen with a knife from her bag and raised both it and the window. She squeezed through the opening, pulling her bag in behind her.

Brinkman found herself inside what she guessed was a pantry. Shelves, mostly empty, lined the walls on either side of her, and a door stood ajar opposite her. On the floor in front of her, the cats' litter box, which one whiff told her needed cleaning. No wonder he leaves the window open in here, she thought.

She didn't think Meecham had a security system, but she held her breath as she pushed past the pantry door and walked through the house, using a small flashlight to guide her way. No alarm sounded, and she breathed easier. Time to get ready, she decided, opening her bag, ignoring the two cats winding around her legs.

It was down to two of them. Meecham and a hulk of a man with a shiny dome and protruding ears, known around the bar as Matburn. A professional wrestler in the early seventies, Matburn's sole claim was serving as Vern Gagne's tag-team partner in a match which no one now remembered. They had won, of course—Gagne never lost—but not until after one of their opponents had forgotten to pull his punch. Matburn had sailed over the ropes and out of the ring, landing on a steel chair that had been hurriedly abandoned by its occupant.

Matburn was in traction for six months and still walked with a bent back. His wrestling career was quickly over, but he remained a hell of a cribbage player.

Meecham was eight holes away from winning, Matburn fifteen, when the final cards were dealt. But it was Matburn's turn to count his hand first.

"Maybe you just want to concede," Meecham suggested tiredly.

"Fuck you," Matburn replied, picking up his cards.

The two were at a table in the center of Barney's, surrounded by a dozen players who had already lost, most of them perched on barstools or slumped against the wall. The bartender held the bets. Most of the money was on Meecham.

Meecham pegged three, but Matburn pegged four. Matburn was eleven holes out, Meecham five, when the cards were all faceup. There was stunned silence. Then groans. Matburn had an eight, two sevens, and a three in his hand. The turn card was a six. Fifteen two, fifteen four, and a double run of eight makes twelve.

Meecham had lost. By a single point. Most of the bystanders had never seen him lose before. Matburn was up, whooping, holding his hands high above his head, as though he had just been crowned world wrestling champion.

Meecham wanted to knock him on his ass, bent back and all. Instead, he muttered, "Nice game," and started to walk out. "Sorry, boys," he said to those who had bet on him, who now stared morosely after him. "I've got to go feed the cats and get some sleep."

Then he looked at the clock. Almost ten. Jesus, he was tired.

THIRTY-TWO

Brinkman saw the head-lights of Meecham's car sweep into the driveway, penetrating the dark tunnel of trees that led to the garage behind the house. The glare blinded her for an instant, and she quickly turned away, forcing her eyes to readjust to the pitch-black room.

In the past half hour, she had wandered the house in darkness, memorizing the placement of every table and chair, of every lamp and throw rug. She had learned to avoid the darting movements of the cats, to know where they were by the soft glow of their eyes. She knew such preparations might be unnecessary, but she wanted to minimize the risks if something went wrong.

Brinkman pulled a ski mask over her head and adjusted the eye and nose slots. The mask was black. So was the running suit which now covered her blouse and slacks. No one would ever know whether she was a man or a woman, especially in the dark. And it would remain dark. She had loosened the bulbs in the kitchen light fixture.

The garage door opened with a creaking groan; a moment later, it closed again. There were twenty-five steps from the garage to the kitchen door. Brinkman knew; she had walked it twice.

The cats had heard the garage door, too. They stood at her feet, behind the kitchen door, softly meowing in anticipation. The night-stick weighed heavy in her hand.

Meecham could barely keep his eyes open as he walked from the garage to the house. He had narrowly avoided falling asleep at the wheel on the drive home, and he could already feel the soft comfort of his big double bed. He only hoped he could stay awake long enough to feed the cats, who he knew would be hungry as hell by now.

Why am I so tired? he wondered. Because you're getting old, he told himself. Because you don't have the booze to keep you awake. Shit, he thought, if this is the way I'm going to feel, I should start drinking again.

He could hear the soft cries of the Siamese twins from the other side of the door before he put the key into the lock. The door swung open, and he reached for the light switch. He flicked the switch. Nothing happened. The cats were at his legs, but the kitchen remained in darkness.

Strange. Power out?

He stepped into the room. Everything went from dark to black.

It was easy. Brinkman carefully placed the blow at the base of his skull, where it would kayo him but not kill him. She had practiced the swing, measured the impact. Good police training. She had even moved the kitchen table back so when he fell, he would fall freely, cleanly. She watched his knees buckle, his body slowly crumple like the collapsing springs of a Slinky. He made no sound when he finally sank to the floor and lay sprawled facedown on the tile.

One of the cats had to leap sideways to avoid being caught

beneath him. Now both cats were nuzzling Meecham's neck and cheek, trying to lick him awake. Their soft cries were the only sounds in the house.

Brinkman stood with the nightstick raised high, ready to strike again if he moved. He didn't. She checked his pulse. It was strong. She quickly pulled a pair of handcuffs from her bag and bound his hands in front of him. Another pair of cuffs went on his ankles, and a blindfold was tightened around his eyes.

She felt no regret, no sympathy for the man lying at her feet. A drunken bum, she thought bitterly, too stubborn or stupid to let go of a job he was no longer fit to handle. If he had quit when he should have, she thought, or if he had stayed in his back booth, he wouldn't be where he is now.

As she looked down at him, she knew the tough part was yet to come. She had to get him to his car.

First, she screwed the kitchen light bulbs back into their sockets, then shut the window in the pantry. She could only hope no one would notice the slit screen. After propping open the outside door, she retrieved Meecham's keys from his pocket and grabbed him beneath the arms, working to pull his heavy body through the door.

My God! she thought. It's impossible. His dead weight amazed her. She had the strength but not the leverage. It took five minutes to move him five feet. She had known he would be heavy, but nothing like this! A flaw in the plan. She would have to move quickly.

Brinkman ran to the garage, using her flashlight to survey the interior. Various garden tools hung from one wall; a workbench was attached to another. A snow blower was parked just inside the door, a stepladder standing next to it. Panicky, she swung the light in a wide circle, finally seeing what she needed, a long length of heavy rope hanging from the garage rafters.

Meecham was lying just outside the kitchen door, inert, still unconscious. Brinkman wound the rope across his chest and beneath his arms in a kind of sling. She pulled again, and his body moved, more easily now. The crossed rope beneath his head cradled it inches above the ground.

It took fifteen minutes and all of her strength to drag him to the garage and get him into the front seat of the car. She recuffed his hands firmly behind the headrest and then returned to the house to get her bag and lock the door.

That's when she heard the first faint sound. After the door was closed and locked. Her head swiveled. She could see nothing. Then she heard it again. To her left, in the bushes near the house. Two eyes, wide open but impassive. She'd forgotten about the cats! One was outside.

Brinkman knelt down. "Here, kitty," she called out softly. "Come here, kitty." She held out her hand invitingly as she started to inch forward, duck-walking. The cat was wary, retreating farther into the bushes. "Now, now, kitty, let's not run away, okay?" Brinkman pleaded.

But she soon lost patience. Standing, she lunged toward the shrubs. The cat arched its back in fear and fled. The last she saw of it was its tail, heading for the woods.

Meecham didn't stir as Brinkman drove quickly but cautiously through the darkened neighborhood streets and then onto the freeway, easing into the fast-moving and anonymous flow of nighttime traffic. She had mapped the route carefully in advance, knowing the precise destination and the exact amount of time it would take to get there. She glanced at her watch. Ten minutes gone, twelve minutes to go.

Meecham remained blindfolded, wrists cuffed awkwardly behind the headrest. Breathing regularly, as though in a deep and untroubled sleep. I must have really hit him, Brinkman thought with relief and satisfaction.

Exit the freeway onto River Road. Six-point-three miles to go. Little traffic here. Few streetlights. An all-night gas station on the right, a Tom Thumb store on the left. Most homes were dark. The news was over; people were off to bed. Left on McKaskil. Only two blocks now. No streetlights here.

Brinkman slowed the car and doused its lights as she neared the spot. Here!

She sat quietly behind the wheel, allowing her eyes to adjust to the darkness. No late-night strollers. No cars. No houses within two blocks.

Five minutes passed. She retrieved the brandy bottle from her bag, opened it, and poured some of the liquid over Meecham's clothes. Careful, not too much! Just enough to leave a stain and a smell. Then she tilted his head back and to one side, pouring more of the brandy into his mouth. He began to choke. She clamped her hand over his mouth, forcing him to swallow, then poured more down his throat. More choking, more gagging and coughing. But he did not come awake. Her hand was wet from the liquor and his spittle.

Now the hard part. She put the car into gear and carefully nudged it over the curb, feeling the tug of the soft ground against the tires. Twenty yards. Out of the car and around it. Open the passenger door, nightstick at the ready. Uncuff his ankles and wrists.

Push!

With enormous effort, she moved his heavy body toward the middle of the seat. Her arms and shoulders ached; sweat dripped from her face, a sweet syrup to the mosquitoes who fought for a taste.

But finally it was done. The brandy bottle was in the car; the bag was in her hand. She leaned through the open window, turned on the ignition, and threw the gearshift into drive. Then she stood back and watched.

The telephone finally rang about 11:45 P.M. Sarah leaped for it.

"Yes?" The word was more of an exhaled breath.

"Come and get me." Brinkman's voice was calm, measured. "I need to get back to my car."

"Where are you?"

"At an Embers restaurant in Fridley, just off the interstate, at the River Road exit."

"Is everything . . . all right?" Sarah asked, feeling the familiar dizziness.

"Everything's fine, but I'm beat. I've walked a long way."

"How's—"

"No names!" Brinkman said. "The problem's taken care of."

Sarah collapsed into her chair. She knew her legs would not hold her. "Is he . . . okay?"

"Just come pick me up. I'll tell you about it then."

The dial tone was her goodbye.

Harrison Munson hated to jog. He found it exhausting and boring. He wouldn't be on the street now if he weren't thirty pounds overweight with a cholesterol reading that bordered on the danger level. Mild chest pains two months before had prompted his doctor to sternly order him on a low-cholesterol diet with regular, moderate exercise.

Harrison would never run in the Twin Cities Marathon, but he was up to two miles a day and building. Hating every step. If he had to run, he decided, he would do it in the early morning, before the heat of the day and before too many people were awake to see his flabby body bouncing down the street. Which is why he was now on McKaskil, along the river, just before dawn, moving slowly but steadily, listening for the waking birds over his own labored wheezing. He had a half mile more to go before he could turn around and head home for a nice cool shower.

Normally, Harrison ran with his eyes straight ahead and down, watching for potholes and cracks in the pavement. Since there was little traffic at this time of day, he could concentrate on the road ahead.

Later, he could not recall whether it was the sound of a bird or some other noise which had caused him to glance to his right. What was that? He went twenty yards farther before he stopped and looked back.

He ran this road every morning. Something wasn't right. He walked slowly back to the spot. The brush along the side of the road was bent over, almost matted down, and two low-hanging branches from a small maple were broken, hanging limp. He knelt down. Tire tracks? He walked to the edge of the embankment.

A crumpled white car—a Ford, he thought—was lying on its top halfway down the hill, hung up between two thick Norway pines. There was no sound, no movement, from it. He later remembered how out of place but peaceful it looked there. At rest, as though some giant hand had crushed it and then carefully placed it between the trees.

Harrison turned on his heel and ran for the nearest house. Faster than he had ever run before.

As Sarah drove to work in the morning, she listened intently to every radio news report, impatiently switching from station to station.

Had they not found him by now?

The past eight hours seemed a blur. As ordered, she picked up Brinkman at the restaurant, surprised to find her absolutely calm. She had told Sarah the story impassively, as though she were reciting the details of some routine case she'd been working on.

"Jesus, Freda, did you kill him?"

"Who knows?" she replied. "I wasn't going to climb down the hill to check. If he's not dead, he's close to it. The car rolled a couple of times. He never knew what hit him."

"You said you wouldn't kill him," Sarah had reminded her angrily.

"Wrong. You said that."

"Don't you feel *anything?*" Sarah couldn't believe the woman's dispassion.

"Relief, that's all. And who are you to talk? You knew I was going to deal with him. It had to be done. Now we've just got to worry about Jessica."

Sarah could not escape the chilling indifference in the woman's voice. She had known then that Brinkman was spinning out of control, but she felt helpless. What was done was done. There could be no retreat.

How has it come to this? she wondered again. Back then, it had seemed so simple, so right. So just. Her hatred of Edward Hill—of what he had done to Kim—had finally overwhelmed her. He had gone free, like so many others. Animals, all of them, snarling and vicious, with no more humanity than any creature of the wild stalking its prey.

She had seen them by the dozens, parading through the system, aloof, arrogant, oblivious or indifferent to the pain and suffering they had caused, to the lives they had ruined. She had watched their smug faces, heard their righteous denials, listened to their whining cries of abused childhoods, their self-serving pleas for treatment, and their empty promises to change. Only to see them back again, weeks or months later.

She had talked to their victims, from little girls to old women, sharing their anger and pain, only to discover time and again that she could offer them little comfort and, too often, little justice. The system, she had finally decided, was simply incapable of dealing with the repeat rapists and other sexual scum. That's when she'd met Freda Brinkman and was introduced to the other members of the Craft Club.

She thought about Teresa Johnson, whose daughter was now a drooling vegetable locked for life in a wheelchair. And Pat Sample, whose runaway child, her only child, ended up as a whore, dead in a New York hotel. And Nancy Higgins, raped once, then again, by the same man the day after he emerged from jail.

She couldn't bear to watch it all helplessly. But now the solution, which had appeared so simple and just at the time, had clearly cartwheeled out of control. And there seemed to be no stopping it.

As she neared the downtown exit, she finally heard what she'd been waiting for. The radio announcer's voice was flat, unemotional.

"An off-duty Minneapolis police captain was critically injured last night when his car went down an embankment along the Mississippi River, just inside the Fridley border. Sixty-three-year-old captain Matt Meecham was found, unconscious, inside the overturned car and is in a coma at the Hennepin County Medical Center. . . ."

He wasn't dead, she thought. That's good. Or is it?

THIRTY-THREE

Jessica had just stepped out of the shower when she heard the security buzzer sound from the front door. She hurriedly wrapped a towel around her body and walked to the intercom.

"It's Bill Kendrick, Jess. Let me in, huh."

She was startled. Bill Kendrick? Here? Now?

"I'm not dressed yet, Bill."

"Make it quick," he said.

"I'll buzz you in and leave the door open. Half floor up, first one on your right. Grab some coffee and I'll be out in a minute."

As Jessica retreated to her bedroom to slip on a pair of sweats, she was truly puzzled. Did she forget an assignment? Was he supposed to pick her up? No, she would remember something like that.

When she emerged, Kendrick was leaning against the kitchen counter, blowing on his coffee.

"What's going on, Bill? You're the last person I'd expect to see this time of morning."

"Bad news, Jess. I thought I should be the one to tell you."

"What are you talking about?" she demanded.

"Matt Meecham. He's in the hospital. In a coma. They're not sure he's going to make it."

"What?" She was disbelieving, shaking, her stomach heaving. "What happened?"

"He drove his car off the road and down an embankment along the Mississippi. They just found him a few hours ago."

She stared at him, stricken.

"No one saw it happen," he continued. "They're not sure how long he'd been there. The engine was cold, so it had to have been a while. He'd been drinking, Jess."

"I don't believe it," she said.

"He smelled of booze. His clothes smelled of booze. And there was a half-empty bottle of brandy on the front seat."

"He'd quit drinking," she murmured. "I know he did."

Kendrick was skeptical. "You know what they say about that. One day at a time."

"Where is he?" she asked.

"At the Hennepin County Medical Center. In intensive care. I don't know everything, but he's got head and internal injuries. A broken pelvis, maybe more. He's still unconscious."

Meecham hurt? Near death? Only then did she realize what the burly detective had come to mean to her. He had always been there. Gruff but reassuring. A friend, almost a father. She fought the tears, and her stomach heaved again.

"I've got to see him," she mumbled. "Will you wait till I get dressed and go with me?"

"Sure. I've already alerted Laurie."

Jessica and Kendrick were kept outside intensive care by a snooty nurse with a beaklike nose and a pointed chin. She told them haughtily that only members of Meecham's immediate family were being admitted.

"He doesn't have any immediate family around here," Jessica argued. "His only son's in California."

By then, Nurse Ratched had walked away. Kendrick shrugged his shoulders and sat down on a chrome-armed vinyl chair. "Won't do much good to see him, anyway," he said with a sigh. "Not if he's still in a coma."

As they sat waiting, two people in uniform strode into the room. One was Freda Brinkman, the other a man Kendrick recognized as a deputy chief of police. Before Jessica could get up, they brushed past with barely a glance and walked straight into intensive care.

"I'll be damned," Jessica muttered.

"What?" Kendrick asked.

"Nothing. I'm just surprised to see *her* here, that's all."

"Why? She may be a bitch, but she does work with Matt."

Twenty minutes passed before Brinkman and the deputy chief emerged. Jessica was ready this time, stepping in front of them, blocking their way. "What can you tell us about Matt?" she asked after identifying herself to the chief.

"I have nothing to say to the media," he replied brusquely.

"I'm not asking as a member of the media," she said. "I'm Matt's friend."

Brinkman snorted. "With friends like you—"

Jessica glared at her. "Back off, Lieutenant, I wasn't talking to you."

"He's still in a coma," the chief said, relenting. "The doctors say it's touch and go. The next seventy-two hours or so will be crucial."

"I was told liquor was involved," Jessica said. "I can't believe that. I know Matt was on the wagon. He wouldn't have been drinking."

"I can't talk about that," the chief snapped. "Not until we know more about the accident."

With that, he stepped past Jessica and walked out, Brinkman two steps behind.

* * *

"I still don't believe it," Jessica said as she got into Kendrick's car outside the hospital. "Matt would never have gone on a binge, not now."

"Why so sure?" Kendrick asked.

"He was in the middle of something important, something he cared about. He wouldn't have blown it like that."

"Want to tell me about it?" he asked.

"Sorry, I can't. Not yet."

"The Hill murder?"

"That's part of it. There's more."

Kendrick pulled away from the parking meter. "I'll bet you haven't known many drunks, have you, Jess?" She shook her head. "Well, I have, and believe me, they'll let you down damn near every time. My dad was a prize example."

"I'm not sure Matt was an alcoholic," she said.

"Maybe not, but how do you explain his ending up like this?"

He had a point, but it still didn't ring true. She had always taken pride in her ability to read people, to judge character, to spot the phonies. Matt Meecham was no phony. No way. Lonely, certainly. Maybe bitter. And, as he himself had admitted, weak at times in the past. But not now. Not the Matt Meecham she knew.

"Do me a favor, Bill."

Kendrick glanced at her, nodding.

"After you drop me off at the station, try to find out where Matt was last night. Check Barney's or any other place you can think of. See if anybody saw him . . . drinking."

"I'll try," Kendrick said, "but besides Barney's, I don't really know where to look."

"Neither do I," she admitted, realizing again how little she knew about the man.

It was not yet ten o'clock in the morning and Sarah had already received frantic calls from the three members of the Craft Club. Each had heard about Meecham's accident, and all of them demanded to know if it had been the work of Brinkman.

Sarah had been guarded and unresponsive. "We shouldn't be talking on the phone," she had told each. "We'll call a meeting as soon as we can and get a full report from Freda."

"I don't want another meeting," the last caller, Teresa Johnson, had screamed. "She scares the hell out of me. Always has. But before this, I believed in what we were doing. I want out!"

"Settle down," Sarah had told her. "It's too late to get out. We're all in this together, understand? Just keep your cool and wait for the next meeting."

None of the women had been placated, and despite her own calm on the phone, Sarah had found it hard to swallow her nervousness. She hesitated to call Brinkman but finally could wait no longer.

"I'm getting calls from the club members," Sarah told her. "They're worried. One of them even wants out."

"Which one?" Brinkman demanded.

"That's not important. They're all uptight."

"Fuck 'em," Brinkman said in a whisper. "We did what we had to do."

"And if Meecham makes it?" Sarah asked.

"I was at the hospital. He's still in a coma and looks bad. If he lives, he'll be out of commission for weeks, maybe months. And the top brass over here think it was just another drunken accident. He won't be back running Homicide, believe me."

"Meecham knows it wasn't a drunken accident."

"Even if he wakes up, he'll never convince them. It's only his word, and they don't trust him."

"How about the other cops?" Sarah asked. "The ones Meecham was supposed to meet?"

"I don't think they know anything, and with Matt half dead, I'd bet the whole thing gets forgotten."

"Hope you're right," Sarah said doubtfully, "but don't forget about Jessica."

"How can I?" Brinkman said. "I just saw her a few minutes ago at the hospital, checking on Meecham."

I should have known, Sarah thought.

When she walked into the newsroom, Jessica immediately sought out Laurie and George Barclay, arranging an impromptu meeting in Barclay's office. She quickly briefed them on Meecham's accident and condition.

"Where does this leave us, Jess?" Barclay asked.

"I wish I knew. I was depending on Meecham. He had the files, and I think he was planning to meet with the other cops. But I don't know any of them, except for Jenkins in St. Paul."

"Let's think about it," Laurie said, steepling her fingers beneath her chin. "We know Meecham's not going to be of any help for a while, if ever. And from what you've said, you sure as hell can't go to Brinkman."

Jessica snickered. "Hardly."

"Okay," Laurie continued. "The way I see it, you're going to have to cozy up to one of the other cops."

"Wait a minute," Barclay objected. "You know how I feel about that. Meecham was one thing, but—"

"Hold on, George," Laurie interrupted. "If Jessica's right about all of this, it could be a hell of a story for us. We're not going to get it by ourselves. She's going to need help."

"Let me try, George, please," Jessica pleaded. "Jenkins seems decent enough, and he had a lot of respect for Matt. Maybe he'd listen to me."

Barclay shook his head, muttering to himself, but made no further objection. However, as they rose to leave, he motioned Jessica back. "One more thing," he said. "I talked to our lawyers about that Ingram business."

Jessica nodded, waiting.

"They say we'd better turn his affidavit over to the police."

"Really?"

"They say that as long as Ingram didn't demand that we keep Andrews's name confidential we can't legally refuse to surrender it. They'll just subpoena it if we don't."

She slumped into the chair. "So the cops still haven't found Ingram?" she asked.

"Not yet, I guess. But they're worried that even when they do, he'll refuse to give them the name."

Jessica could just picture some cop marching into Sarah Andrews's office to question her. What the hell would she say? How would she react? She'll certainly know where they got her name.

"I didn't intend for this to happen," she said, more to herself than to Barclay. "Not now, anyway."

"Then you shouldn't have mentioned it on the air, Jess," Barclay said. "Chalk it up as a lesson learned."

Kendrick walked up to Jessica's desk just before lunch, appearing puzzled. "I talked to the bartender at Barney's, the same one who was working last night."

"And?" She watched him expectantly.

"Meecham was there, all right, till ten or so, playing cribbage. Plays every Tuesday night. The bartender says the only thing Meecham drank was mineral water. He remembers because everyone else was sopping up the beer and booze."

"I knew it," she said, exultant.

"Not so fast, Jess. Meecham left Barney's just before ten. They didn't find him in the car for another seven or eight hours. He could have done a lot of drinking in between."

Again, she knew Kendrick could be right. She was grasping at any straw. "What else did the bartender say?" she asked.

"Not much. Matt lost at cribbage, which he almost never does, then left. Said something about having to get home to feed the cats and get some sleep."

The cats! His wife's cats. Jessica had forgotten all about them. What had Meecham called them? Tippy and Tyler, Too.

"He wouldn't have gone off and left the cats," she said. "Not Matt, not knowing they'd be home alone and hungry."

"C'mon, Jess, drunks go off and leave their wives and kids,

for Christ's sake. Last thing he'd worry about are a couple of cats."

"I wonder who's taking care of them now?" she wondered aloud.

"Who knows?" Kendrick said. "Some neighbor, I bet."

Jessica could picture the cats, locked inside Meecham's house, probably frightened and hungry. For who knows how long. "What if they're not?" she said.

Kendrick gave her an exasperated look. "You're going out there, aren't you? How in the hell will you get into the house?"

She shrugged her shoulders. "Maybe a neighbor has a key. Maybe he leaves one under the doormat. I'll have to see."

Although she had never been in that part of town before, and despite its isolated position, Jessica had little problem finding Meecham's home. But before driving in, she checked the nearest neighbors, none of whom lived closer than a block and a half. She knocked on the doors of the two closest, but there was no answer at either. Have to try again later, she thought.

Meecham's driveway seemed to go on forever. When Jessica got out of the car, she thought she might be stepping into a wild forest glade. Smelling of moss and wildflowers, fresh and cool from the shade of the trees, it was serenely quiet except for the sound of the birds flitting among the branches. It wouldn't have surprised her to see a bubbling stream and waterfall, with trout rising.

He does like his privacy, she thought.

She walked first to the back door, then to the front, ringing the bell at each, then peering inside. She heard and saw nothing until she stepped away from the front door. That's when she saw the cat, sitting on the inside window ledge. It didn't move.

"Are you Tippy or Tyler?" she whispered, nose to nose at the window. "And where's your brother?"

The cat simply stared at her, black mask, pointed ears. When Jessica took a step back, she stumbled, almost falling. Catching herself, she saw a brown blur streaking from her feet.

After racing fifteen yards, it stopped and looked back at her over its shoulder. The other cat.

"What are you doing out here?" she asked, as though expecting an answer. "How'd you get outside?"

The cat lay down on the gravel driveway, stretching and rolling, watching suspiciously as she walked ever so slowly toward it. She talked quietly, soothingly, and was relieved when it allowed her to stoop and pick it up.

Why would one be inside, the other outside?

A glance at its collar told her this was Tippy, and a glance elsewhere told her Tippy was Tyler's sister, not brother. She put the cat inside the Impala, then searched for a key to the house. She looked in all of the predictable places without success. The house was locked up tight, and except for a torn screen on one of the rear windows, everything seemed to be in order. What do I do now? she wondered. She would have to find a key somehow and hope that the other cat would survive until then.

From the house, Jessica drove directly to the site of Meecham's accident, finding a lone squad car parked at the crest of the hill. A police officer was halfway down the slope, taking measurements and photographing some of the remaining debris.

Matt's car had been lifted out and towed away hours before, but she could still follow its broken path down the hill. It was clear the car would have gone another fifty feet into the river if it had not been caught and held by the two big pines.

She slid down the embankment, holding on to small trees and bushes for support and balance. The officer watched her progress curiously, gently grabbing her arm as she slid the final few feet.

"And who might you be?" he asked as she stood next to him, catching her breath.

She quickly introduced herself. "I'm a friend of the fellow who was in the car," she said.

"So am I," said the officer, who identified himself as Jason

Coolidge. "I worked with Matt in Minneapolis before taking this job in Fridley. He's a good guy. Too bad he couldn't keep his nose out of the sauce."

"I'm not so sure he'd been drinking," Jessica said, quickly explaining what they had learned about Matt's activities the night before. "He once told me that he never drank and drove anymore, not since . . . well, not for a long time."

Coolidge was dubious. "I was here, miss, when they pulled him out. He smelled like a still. And the bottle was still in the car."

"Did you do a blood test?" she asked.

"Not here. We just wanted to get him to the hospital. They probably did one there."

She watched as Coolidge completed his survey of the scene and took several more pictures. The bark on each of the pine trees was deeply gouged, with small, jagged pieces of broken metal and glass scattered around their roots. Off to one side, a torn shoe lay unclaimed.

When the officer was done, they struggled back up the hill together, pausing at the top. "There is one weird thing," Coolidge said, pointing toward the road. "We couldn't find any skid marks. Apparently he never tried to stop. He was either too sloshed or fell asleep at the wheel."

Before he got back into his squad car, Jessica stopped him. "I know you don't know me," she said, "but I'd like to ask a favor. For Matt, really."

"What's that?" Coolidge asked.

"Could you get me the results of his blood-alcohol test? It could be very important."

The officer shook his head. "Not me, lady. Sorry. That'd have to come from the higher-ups. I shouldn't have been talking to you at all."

Then he got into the car and drove off.

When Jessica returned to the newsroom, she put in a call to Jack Tomlinson. He answered on the first ring.

"Are you still willing to help me?" she asked.

"Don't be silly," he said. "Of course."

She quickly told him of Meecham's accident. "The police must have taken a blood-alcohol test," she said, "but I have no way of getting the results. Do you know anyone in the Fridley police department?"

"Not directly," he said after a moment. "But I should be able to find someone around here who does. Give me a couple of hours and I'll see what I can do."

"Be discreet," she said, thinking of Sarah Andrews just down the hall from him.

"I understand," he replied. "Don't worry."

"And thanks," she said, ready to hang up.

"Jessica? About the other night . . ."

"Yes?"

There was a momentary silence. "Never mind," he finally said. "I think you already know."

Another nurse was on duty when Jessica got back to the hospital that night. Younger and more accommodating, she checked Jessica's ID, listened to her explanation, then led her from the waiting room into the intensive care unit.

"He won't know you're here," the nurse warned. "He's still unconscious. But you can spend a few minutes with him."

"No change in his condition?"

"Afraid not," she said. "Still critical."

The beds in the intensive care unit were situated on either side of a wide hallway. On one side, where Matt lay, the beds were encased by glass walls but within easy view of the medical staff. A large computer screen at the nursing station kept constant track of the elaborate electronic monitoring equipment attached to each of the patients. Equipment which pulsed and glowed, reflecting the often fragile rhythms of life within the glass rooms. Sometimes the pulsing and glowing stopped.

Jessica and the nurse paused at the door of Meecham's room. Jessica was momentarily stunned. It could have been anyone lying there, a stranger, some unknown victim of random violence clinging to an anonymous life. But it was Matt. Looking like a mummy on life support.

His head was a turban of bandages. Tubes ran from his body to bottles and machines which Jessica didn't pretend to understand. His eyes were closed; his skin—the little still visible—was pallid. He seemed to be breathing regularly, though she could hear the hiss of oxygen being fed from the respirator into his lungs.

"Don't be surprised if his hands and arms move around a bit," the nurse warned. "Or if he reacts when you touch him. That can happen in lighter comas."

"What's that tube into his head?" Jessica asked.

"It's called a ventriculostomy," she replied. "It goes through his skull and measures the swelling of the brain."

"His brain's been damaged?"

"With a head injury like this, there's often some bruising of the brain, which causes the pressure and swelling. We're going to have to wait to see just how bad it is."

Jessica walked to the bed and leaned over him. "Hey, Matt," she whispered, "it's me, Jessica. C'mon, Matt, wake. Look at me, Matt."

She knew she was being foolish. She didn't expect a response, and none came. But she couldn't just stand there and say nothing. She had to urge him on, to will him awake and well.

Jesus, Matt, what the hell have you done to yourself?

THIRTY-FOUR

The phone call to Jessica's apartment the next morning caught her completely by surprise. And even now, walking into the restaurant a half hour later, she wasn't convinced it was for real. Until she saw the caller sitting at a table, staring into her coffee cup, stirring it absently. She didn't notice Jessica's approach. Just like the day at the cemetery.

"Kim?"

Her head bobbed up. "Sorry," she said, embarrassed. "I was watching for you, but then my mind kind of drifted away."

"No problem," Jessica said, slipping into a chair. "I got down here as quickly as I could. Your call caught me by surprise."

"Yes, and I'm sorry about that, too. I should have given you more notice. I got your number from Information."

Surprise was an understatement. Jessica had been flabbergasted when she'd realized it was Kim Hawkins on the phone, asking to meet as soon as possible.

"Now that you're here, I feel a little foolish," Kim said.

"But this morning, after I got up, I felt I just had to talk to you. It was impulsive, I'm afraid."

Kim wore a light cotton twill dress, sleeveless and pale green, with darker green buttons down the middle. Her skin bore only the faintest trace of makeup, and she was without jewelry except for a thin band of gold that hugged her neck. Her bangs fell to the middle of her forehead, the same dark brown as her eyes. The beauty mark was darker still, almost black.

"I'm glad you called," Jessica said, smiling. "And don't worry about the short notice. I'm just happy I don't have to run a race with you again."

Kim grimaced at the reminder, then glanced at her menu. She seemed hesitant to begin, and Jessica didn't push her. The waitress was waiting for their orders, anyway.

"I'd like to know what's going on," Kim said, once they were alone again. "Everything seems upside down, and Sarah won't tell me anything."

"I'm not sure I understand . . ."

"You must!" Kim said. "I know you're still investigating Edward Hill's death. Sarah did tell me that. And that's where this all began, with his murder. Nothing's been the same since."

"How so?"

"Everything's changed. Sarah's like a different person. She's, I don't know, secretive, suspicious, bad-tempered, just plain strange."

"Why are you telling me all of this?" Jessica was genuinely puzzled. "You wouldn't even talk to me before."

"I'm not sure," Kim said with quiet desperation. "I even thought about going back to the police, but I don't know anyone there except Freda Brinkman, and I don't really trust her. Sarah keeps telling me to stay away from you, but I want some answers. I'm tired of waiting. You're a reporter. You found out what happened to that Ingram guy. I want to know what happened to Edward Hill." She looked away, and her voice softened. "And I want to know why Sarah is acting so, I don't know, odd."

"I don't know any of the answers, Kim. But I have a lot of suspicions—about Sarah."

"Suspicions?"

Jessica studied her across the table, debating. Tell her more and she would run the risk of her going back to Sarah, of spilling everything. But Sarah seemed to know everything, anyway. And Jessica knew Kim could provide information about her roommate that she would have no other way of obtaining. Face it, she told herself, the way things are now, you're getting nowhere.

"Kim, you and Sarah are friends . . . roommates. I'm not going to sit here and tell you everything I suspect. That'd be stupid and not very fair to Sarah, I'm afraid."

"You think she's one of the women who got Ingram, don't you?"

Jessica was taken aback. "Why would you think that?" she asked sharply.

"Because I think so, too. It makes sense. The way she's acting, the way she reacted to your television story. Because she wasn't home that night, because of how much she hated that man. I know her pretty well, Jessica."

"You think she's capable of something like that?"

"I wouldn't . . . I didn't. But now I don't know. She won't talk to me."

Jessica leaned forward. "You've asked her about this?"

"Heavens, no!" Kim said. "It's just a feeling."

"And you don't trust Freda Brinkman?"

"No, but I'm not sure why." Kim thought again about her nightmares, about Brinkman's phone call to Sarah the night of the Ingram report. "She and Sarah are . . . friends, I guess, but I don't really know her. She questioned me about the rape and Hill's murder, but that's the only time I've seen her."

"So why the distrust?" Jessica pressed.

"It's hard to explain. She and Sarah seem so different that I can't understand their friendship. It doesn't make sense, like a lot of other things."

"What about Sarah's other friends?" Jessica asked.

"She doesn't have many," Kim admitted. "Neither do I.

Sarah's so tied up in her work that she doesn't have the time. She dates now and then, but they never seem to go anywhere. Other than that, there's only the . . ."

"The what?" Jessica asked.

"The Craft Club. A group of women Sarah knows. They meet once a month or so, a kind of social club, I guess. Sarah brings her knitting, the others bring handwork."

"Sarah knits? That's hard to picture."

Kim nodded in apparent agreement.

"Have you ever gone?" Jessica asked.

Kim smiled sadly. "Never been invited. Sarah doesn't talk much about it. It's her way of getting away from me, I think."

"Know any of the other women?" Jessica asked.

"Nope. Sarah's never said."

"You find that strange?"

"A little, I suppose, but I've never really pressed her."

Jessica knew her questions were going on too long, but she couldn't resist one more. "Do you know in advance when they hold these meetings?"

"Sometimes, but not always. Why?"

"Just curious," she replied. "Would you let me know when the next one happens?"

"I guess so, but I still don't understand."

"You're not alone, Kim. Neither do I."

They were interrupted by the waitress, who put their breakfasts in front of them and refilled their coffee cups.

"I'm not sure where we go from here," Jessica said as she picked at the food on her plate.

"Can't you tell me more?" Kim pleaded.

"I don't mean to frighten you, Kim, but this whole thing could be larger than Ingram or even Edward Hill," she said vaguely. "It could be very serious, and Sarah could be up to her neck in it. I'm not sure you'd want to know more."

She could see a small shudder pass through Kim's body.

"I want to know the truth," Kim said finally. "I can't go on living like this."

"Let's both think about it," Jessica said. "If I agree to tell you more, I'll expect your help in finding the truth. It could be painful, Kim, maybe even dangerous."

Kim seemed to shrink into her chair but said nothing more.

When everyone else was out of the Homicide office—at lunch or on assignment—Freda Brinkman calmly unlocked Matt Meecham's office door with one of the keys she had taken from his key ring the night before. She quickly opened his file cabinet with yet another key and hurriedly thumbed through its contents. She found what she was looking for in the bottom drawer: four thick folders, bound together with a heavy rubber band. Without studying the contents, she tucked the folders beneath her arm, closed and locked the file cabinet, and then left, locking the door behind her.

The Homicide office was still empty. She knew she'd have to get the keys back on Meecham's key ring in case he came out of the coma. But that was a minor problem. She had the files and would soon know exactly where the other three murder investigations stood.

To anyone else, it would have seemed to be a chance encounter, but Jack Tomlinson couldn't escape the sense that Sarah had been waiting for him to emerge from a meeting in the conference room. She was lingering near the receptionist's desk as he passed by and quickly fell into step beside him. As they walked, she asked about a case they had been working on together, then paused as they reached his office door.

"By the way, how's it going with Jessica?" she asked suddenly but with apparent innocence.

Jack knew Sarah was not one for small talk. "What do you mean?"

She looked at him coyly. "You still seeing her?"

"Now and then," he replied vaguely. "Why do you ask?"

"No special reason. Just wondering. After all, you did meet in my office, remember."

"I remember," he said, turning toward his desk, hoping the conversation would end.

Sarah followed him in. "I'm curious what you think of her."

"I don't really know her that well," he lied. "But she seems pleasant enough. And smart. And she's sure as hell attractive."

Sarah hesitated. "I don't suppose she's mentioned our differences, has she?"

Jack sat on the edge of the desk, facing her, feigning a puzzled expression. "No, although it was obvious that something was wrong the night I saw the two of you at the Loon. But we don't talk about business. It's off limits."

Sarah watched him closely, trying to read his eyes.

"So what's the problem?" he asked, returning her gaze.

"Nothing, really," she replied with a shrug. "She's been getting in the way of a murder investigation, and I'm afraid she's going to muck it up. We've had some words about it, that's all."

"It's news to me," Jack said. "But I'm sure the two of you can work it out."

Jessica stifled a grin as she watched Jeremiah Jenkins lope down the street. He looks like a giraffe, she thought, long legs, long neck, moving awkwardly, as though he had never quite reconciled where his center of gravity was.

When she had called the St. Paul detective the day before, he had readily agreed to see her again, although he was plainly curious about the topic. "You still trying to piece old Eduardo together?" he asked cheerfully.

"In a way," she said, ignoring his small joke. "With Matt in the hospital, I need to talk to you."

He suggested meeting her outside, at Rice Park across from the Ordway Theater in downtown St. Paul. "Sorry to hear about Matt," he said as he sat down, unfolding his long legs. "Is it true he'd been drinking again?"

"That's what they say, but I don't believe it," she replied, explaining what they knew about the accident. "Doesn't make sense."

"I was supposed to meet with him today," Jenkins said.

"Really? You and the cops from Bloomington and Brooklyn Park?"

His eyebrows shot up in surprise. "You know about them?"

"I knew Matt was working with all of you, yes."

"No shit. He told you that?"

"Matt and I are good friends. I know what he was going to talk to you about."

"I don't understand," he said.

Jessica began from the very beginning, telling him everything, including her suspicions about Sarah Andrews and Freda Brinkman.

Like Laurie and Barclay, Jenkins was openly disbelieving. "You're telling me another cop may be involved in this?" he asked sharply. "And an assistant county attorney? That's pretty hard to swallow, Jessica."

"You're not the first to say that," she admitted. "And, frankly, I didn't expect you to believe it. Not right off. But I know Matt was suspicious of Brinkman, too."

In all, it took her almost a half hour to finish the story, interrupted several more times by questions from Jenkins.

"That's remarkable," he said. "Matt wouldn't give me any details on the phone. He just said he thought he had found a connection among several murders, including Eduardo's, and that he wanted to talk about it. Said it was very hush-hush."

"Matt and I worked together on this from the get-go," she said. "If he was here, he'd tell you that. I want you to get the killers, but I don't want to lose my story in the process. You and the others have to keep the promise Matt made to me, that this is my story, that it won't get leaked to somebody else before I get it on the air."

"I can't speak for the others," he said. "I hardly know them."

"Tell them what I've told you, then let them decide. I'll have to trust all of you."

"I'll do what I can," he said, doubt written on his face.

* * *

A message was waiting for Jessica when she returned to the newsroom: Call Jack Tomlinson. He first told her about his brief encounter with Sarah at the office, then got to the real purpose of his call. "I'm afraid I have some bad news," he said.

"On the blood test?"

"Yeah. It was point-one-one. Over the legal limit. Matt was drunk when he drove over the edge."

"I'll be damned," she muttered.

"That would seem to seal it," Jack said.

"Not for me," she said stubbornly.

"What do you mean?"

"Think about it, Jack. If Matt was going to drink, why wait until after he'd left the bar? Because he'd lost a cribbage game? Hardly. Why no skid marks? Because he was too drunk to try to stop? Point-one-one isn't that drunk. Did he fall asleep at the wheel? A possibility, I admit, but again points to his drinking." She stopped to catch her breath. "And why would he forget his cats? They're all he had. Why would he leave one of them outdoors? The cat seemed scared to death."

"He may have just run out on him," Tomlinson offered.

Jessica would not be deterred. "If Meecham was still as bored and depressed as he once was, I could accept the fact that he might fall off the wagon. But, believe me, he wasn't. He was committed to this investigation."

There was momentary silence at the other end. "I'm not sure what more you can do, Jess. Not until . . . or unless . . . Matt wakes up."

Jessica thought for a moment. "Could this Fridley source do you one more favor?" she asked.

"Depends," Jack said, "but I suppose so."

"Do they still have the brandy bottle from the car?"

"Probably. It's evidence if they decide to charge him."

"Would your friend be willing to check it for fingerprints?"

"What?"

"If Meecham had been drinking from that bottle, his prints surely would be on it."

"What are you getting at?" Jack demanded.

"If Matt wasn't driving drunk, the only other explanation is that someone set him up. Caught him in the car somehow, poured the liquor down him and all over him, and sent the car over the edge."

"That's reaching, Jessica!"

"What can it hurt to check?" she argued. "If his prints are on the bottle, it only bolsters their possible DWI case. If they're not, we know something's screwed up."

She could hear a deep sigh at the other end of the line.

"C'mon, Jack. Please. At least ask the guy."

"I don't know, Jess. I'll get back to you."

As she left the station late that afternoon, walking toward the ramp, Jessica was startled to find Lowell Ingram hunched over on a bus bench, waiting for her. He kept his face partially hidden behind a newspaper until she was within a few feet of him. Then he rose to meet her.

Her face betrayed her surprise, and she took a step back. "Lowell? What are you doing here?"

"I need to talk," he said. "Can we get a drink?"

Jessica hesitated. "I'm running late," she said, edging farther away. "What do you need?"

"A few minutes of your time. You owe me that."

She glanced around. Relax, she told herself. The sun was still high in the sky, and plenty of people were on the street. And Ingram himself appeared sober, a far cry from the loathsome and drunken lout she had met in the darkened theater a week before.

"You're afraid of me, aren't you?" he said, squinting into the sun, reading her mind.

"No, of course not," she lied. "I'm just surprised to see you, that's all." Then she pointed to the new Hilton across the street. "Let's go over there. But we'll have to make it quick."

They found a table in the lobby bar. He ordered a Beefeater martini, while she asked for a Miller Lite.

"Did you give the cops her name?" Ingram asked as they waited for the drinks.

She nodded warily, fearful of his reaction. "We had no choice, Lowell. If we hadn't, they would have gone to court to get it."

"Doesn't make any difference," he muttered. "They won't do anything with it, anyway."

"How do you know that?" she asked, relieved at his calm.

"Because they're all in cahoots. The cops and the prosecutors. They watch out for their own. She'll come up with some alibi, and there's no way they'll take my word against hers."

At that moment, the waiter appeared with the drinks, which Ingram insisted on buying. "I'm not totally broke yet," he said.

"So is that what you wanted to see me about?" Jessica asked as she poured the beer into a glass.

"Not really. I think I know now who the other one was. The big one with the gun, the one who slashed me."

Jessica leaned across the table.

"I don't know her name, but she's a cop. I saw them together, Andrews and her, talking. I'd swear she's the one. Same size, big shoulders, moved the same way."

"Where'd you see them?" Jessica asked.

"Sitting outside the Government Center."

"How'd you manage that?" she pressed.

Ingram turned away, avoiding her eyes. Swallowing the last of the gin.

"Lowell?"

He turned back. "I've been following her a few days. Watching her come and go."

"Andrews?"

He nodded.

"Why in the world are you doing that?"

He shrugged, choosing not to reply. Instead, he asked, "Do you know who she is, the cop?"

This time, Jessica avoided an answer. What's going on here? Lowell Ingram on the loose, prowling, looking for revenge. Further mucking up an already complicated situation. Damn!

"I hope you're not ready to do something foolish," she said. "That would be real stupid, Lowell. Leave it to the cops."

"She is a cop, for Christ's sake!" he said. "They fucked up my life, made me a goddamned laughingstock. Don't tell me to leave it to the cops. Now, do you know who she is?"

Jessica decided she had to lie, that she couldn't be a part of whatever it was Ingram had in mind. Whatever she might feel about Sarah and Brinkman, she wanted no part of his vendetta.

"Sorry," she said, "I don't. And I'm telling you, Lowell, leave it alone. You can only get yourself in more trouble."

Ingram was ordering another martini as Jessica walked out.

THIRTY-FIVE

The weekend again passed slowly for Jessica. Janie was still at their parents' home in Madelia, and Jack Tomlinson was with his family at their lake cabin near Brainerd. He had invited Jessica to come along, but she declined, telling him she didn't want to abandon Matt in the hospital for two full days. She went to the hospital on both Saturday and Sunday, never staying long but hoping that Matt would know that someone was there and cared.

She also returned to Meecham's house, found a neighbor who had a key, and retrieved the second cat. Tippy and Tyler were both now safely and comfortably reunited at her apartment.

On Saturday, she met Meecham's primary physician, Dr. Bruno Wessler, who told her that Matt had survived a critical period and that his vital signs seemed to be strengthening. But he would not predict if, or when, Meecham might regain consciousness.

"We seem to have controlled the swelling of the brain," he told her. "But it's still too early to say when he'll come out of the coma or how much damage was done."

"Will he remember what happened to him?" she asked.

"Not likely. Most of these people have what we call 'a window of amnesia.' They seldom remember the accident or what happened immediately before it."

"Never?"

"Someday, maybe, but it could be weeks or months. The brain's a very fragile organ."

When she returned to her apartment on Sunday night, Jessica found Janie there, waiting. Back from Madelia, she looked relaxed as she cuddled on the couch, watching television.

"You look great," Jessica said, sitting down next to her. "Like a new woman. What happened, anyway?"

Janie held out the remote control, silencing the TV. "I told them the truth," she said, almost whispering.

"You what?"

"I told them everything, Jess, from start to finish. Once I got there, I found I couldn't lie to them."

Jessica had no words. She was awed.

"I realized if I lied then, I'd be lying the rest of my life. And I couldn't do that, not to Mom and Dad. Not to myself. So I just spilled it all."

"What'd they say?" Jessica asked, disbelieving.

"At first? Mom cried, and Dad got extremely angry. He paced around the house like a caged lion, growling and cussing. I'd never heard him really swear before."

"Angry at you?"

"Mostly at Charlie. He said he'd kill him if he ever saw him."

Jessica had trouble picturing her father angry. He was perhaps the most placid man she had ever known, the friendly small-town plumber who never said an unkind word about anyone.

"Later," Janie continued, "they both settled down, and we talked it out. We must have spent hours talking. They were wonderful, Jess. I'd never really appreciated them before this. They've always been, you know, just Mom and Dad."

"What about the abortion?"

"We cried a lot. It was very sad. But they were mostly concerned about me, about how I was taking it. Whether I'd be able to have more babies someday."

Jessica found herself groping for the right words. "I'm proud of you, Janie. I really am. You showed a lot of guts. More than I would have. I feel badly for the folks and what they're going through now, but you're right, it's a lot better this way."

"They asked about you, Jess. Wanted to know if everything was all right with you, when they'd see you. I told them you were involved in something fairly big and that I didn't know when you would be able to get there."

"I'll call them tonight."

"Any more calls from Charlie Bowser?" Janie asked.

Jessica shook her head. "That's over, I hope."

"What do you mean?"

Jessica quickly explained how Meecham had enlisted the help of the Wisconsin sheriff on Janie's behalf. "He supposedly scared the hell out of Charlie boy. Told him he'd throw him in jail if he tried to contact you again."

"Thank God," Janie said. "I just hope he listens."

Jack Tomlinson was wearing the same blue pin-striped shirt and paisley tie he had worn the day Jessica had first seen him, in Sarah's office. But now they were sitting across from one another at a sidewalk table outside a small Nicollet Mall cafe.

He had called her that morning, asking to meet for lunch. And he wasted little time on preliminaries. "You were right," he said. "I heard back from the Fridley P.D. There were a bunch of prints on the brandy bottle, but Meecham's weren't among them."

Jessica almost whooped. "I knew it."

Two women at an adjoining table glanced at her curiously, then resumed their own conversation.

"The bottle was pretty badly smudged," he said, "but the lab says one of his prints should have shown up somewhere. Others did, probably from some of the cops at the scene."

Before she could respond, Jack continued. "Don't go off the deep end, Jess. It doesn't change the fact that he was drunk. He could have been drinking somewhere else."

"Why would he have a half-empty bottle of brandy in the car if he hadn't been drinking from it?" she said, challenging him. "That doesn't make sense."

"Hold on," he warned. "Maybe somebody else was in the car, drinking the brandy before the accident."

Jessica knew that was a possibility, but who? "Could we find out who those other fingerprints belong to?" she wondered aloud. "Besides the cops?"

Jack shook his head. "That could take a long time, maybe forever. There are millions of prints on file, and making a match would be—"

She cut in. "Wait a minute. Remember the profile on Freda Brinkman you showed me?"

"Sure."

"Remember on the top page. There was a copy of her fingerprints. Remember? Along with all of the statistical stuff on her. Date of birth and all the rest."

"I guess so," he said doubtfully.

Jessica was visibly excited. "Could you see if her prints match any of those on the bottle?"

"Jesus, Jess."

"Please! That way we'd know one way or the other if Matt was set up, whether Brinkman was involved. Don't tell them whose prints they are. Just see if there's a match."

"Why Brinkman?" Jack asked. "Why zero in on her?"

"A gut feeling, I guess. She's certainly nasty enough to have done it. And who knows? She may have discovered that Matt was pressing the investigation of the four murders and decided to eliminate the risk."

"What about Sarah?" Jack asked.

Jessica shook her head. "I may be wrong, but I don't think she's capable of something like that."

"I don't know if I can get Freda's file again," Jack said, reluctance filling his voice.

Her pleading look brought him up short. "Okay," he said. "I'll try. But I'm not making any promises, Jess."

She blew him a kiss across the table.

The deputy police chief who greeted her was the same man she had met at the hospital. Barton Oates by name, one of five deputy chiefs who directed the various divisions of the Minneapolis police department. Homicide fell under him.

He led Jessica into an office that was sparsely and starkly furnished with a gray steel desk, file cabinets, and three matching chairs. Several plaques hung on the wall—police awards, she guessed—and two bowling trophies sat atop one of the cabinets.

"I assume this visit deals with Matt Meecham," he said.

Jessica nodded. "I'm concerned about him. And since he can't speak for himself, can't defend himself, I feel like I should."

Oates said nothing. He had a florid face with puffy eyes and a red-veined nose that seemed constantly to run.

"Have you talked to the Fridley police?" she asked.

Oates looked puzzled. "Not this morning. Why?"

When Jessica told him the results of the fingerprint check on the brandy bottle, his expression changed to one of surprise.

"Who requested the fingerprint check?" he asked.

"I did," she replied. "Through a friend. I think Matt may have been set up," she added quickly, reciting all of the facts in Meecham's favor. "It's the only logical explanation."

"I'd call that jumping to conclusions," Oates said. "As you know, Matt has an alcoholic history. And why in the world would someone want to set him up?"

Jessica had known it would come to this. She couldn't explain her suspicions, yet without them the setup charge sounded ridiculous. Be careful, she told herself.

"Let's just say that I know Matt was working on an important investigation that was a threat to some people . . . people who wanted to see the investigation end."

"An investigation I knew nothing about?" Oates asked, incredulous. "Who are you trying to kid?"

"Believe what you will," she said, "but it's true. It involves several other police jurisdictions, and I can only guess that Matt wanted to get a handle on it before he came to you."

Oates didn't pretend to hide his skepticism. "What other jurisdictions? This sounds like a goddamned fairy tale to me."

"Time will tell," she replied. "But right now I'm only asking that you don't make any hasty decisions about Matt. Don't assume that he was drunk. Talk to the Fridley police, please. And wait to see if Matt comes out of the coma."

"I don't make hasty decisions," Oates said. "But I don't believe in fairy tales, either."

THIRTY-SIX

Lila Bowie was the first to hear the rattle of the bedrails. A nursing student on her ICU rotation, she was already nervous after witnessing her first violent death the day before, a young Hispanic boy, no older than her little brother, who had been stabbed three times in the chest in a squabble over a Chicago Bulls jacket. It had taken her hours to recover, and she was still on edge.

She paused at the door of Matt Meecham's glass cubicle. Had she been mistaken? She stepped into the room. His eyes were still closed, his body inert. She listened and watched intently. There was only the hum of the equipment, the hiss of the respirator. She walked closer to the bed. Should she call one of the other nurses?

She was about to turn away when she saw his lips, dry and cracked, part slightly around the endotracheal tube. There was a moan, more like a growl, raspy and pained. Lila had heard it before, from patients in the recovery room emerging from the fog of anesthesia.

Meecham's hand shot out, grabbing the bed rail, shaking it.

His eyelids twitched, then fluttered open. His pupils seemed to swim, unable to focus. She leaned over him. The eyelids closed again, then slowly reopened. He seemed to see her now.

His lips parted again. He struggled to speak, then pointed to his throat as his tongue tried to find his parched lips. Water! Lila thought, he's awake and wants water. She turned quickly and ran for the nursing desk.

It was not until later in the afternoon that Jessica learned Meecham had emerged from his coma. The word came from an intensive care nurse whom Jessica had befriended on her visits to Meecham.

"How is he?" Jessica asked.

"Still guarded but awake," the nurse reported. "He can't talk yet. The tubes are still in him, and he's dopey from the drugs."

"I'll be right over," Jessica said.

"Take your time. He's not going anywhere."

Jessica was kept waiting for more than an hour before a doctor appeared. She recognized him as the same man she had spoken to during the weekend. A Dr. Bruno something, she remembered. He quickly reintroduced himself. Dr. Bruno Wessler.

"I know you're eager to see Captain Meecham," he said, "but I have to caution you about a few things. You'll be able to talk to him, but he won't be able to respond. We're going to keep his tubes in until tomorrow at least."

"He's going to make it?" Jessica asked.

"Looks that way," the doctor replied. "But we've got to keep a close eye on him. He can't get excited or agitated. He not only has the head injury but a broken pelvis and a couple of broken ribs. He'll be on a lot of pain medication and will be confused for a few days, maybe longer. Probably won't remember much even then."

The doctor went on to explain that once Matt's condition stabilized, he would be moved to another unit in the hospital so that therapy could begin. "He may have to learn how to swallow and talk again," he added. "Maybe even walk. We still don't know the full extent of the damage."

"May I see him now?" Jessica asked.

"Okay," the doctor said. "But only for a few minutes. And remember, don't get him excited."

Inside the glass room, nothing had changed. Meecham lay in the same position, his head still enshrouded in bandages, his body still harnessed by tubes and wires to the same equipment. But his eyes were now open.

Jessica stood over him, her hand softly touching his. Meecham's eyes never left hers. Detached. Curious. Like the eyes of his cats the first time she had seen them. Did he recognize her?

"Hi, Matt," she whispered, leaning down.

A cervical collar held his head rigid, but his eyes moved to the side, following her movement. Watery eyes, overflowing in small drops that trickled slowly down his cheeks. She dabbed them away with a tissue.

"You're going to make it, Matt. You're going to be okay."

She couldn't be sure, but she thought she saw his body relax slightly. She talked to him in hushed tones, never knowing if he understood or would remember a word she said. "You gotta get well soon," she whispered. "I can't do this thing alone, Matt, and besides, I'm running out of food for your cats."

Was there a hint of a smile? Jessica stayed by him for ten minutes, then quietly withdrew, promising to be back the next day. As she turned at the door, he was still watching her.

The members of the Homicide squad were somber as Deputy Chief Barton Oates faced them in the conference room. Three of them were off duty, called in from home for the meeting. They knew something was up, for they seldom saw Oates and rarely met as a unit.

"I just got word from the hospital that Matt's out of his coma," Oates told them. "But he still can't talk and may not remember much. Are any of you aware of some kind of special investigation that he was involved in?"

The detectives exchanged glances. Freda Brinkman unconsciously gripped the edge of the table.

"Well?" He was clearly impatient.

"We knew he was up to something," Bill Pierce volunteered. "He was closeted in his office with a bunch of files."

"But he didn't tell us anything," another of the detectives added. "You know Matt."

"What's going on, Bart?" Brinkman asked, carefully controlling her voice.

Oates ignored the question, studying the group. "So none of you knew what he was doing? He didn't tell any of you?"

Finally, Pierce spoke up again. "Whatever it was, he seemed pretty serious about it. I think he had even quit drinking. At least until, you know . . ."

"C'mon, Bart, what's up?" Brinkman asked again.

Oates hesitated. "I've been told Matt may have been working on something that involved other, unnamed police jurisdictions. Frankly, I find it hard to believe that he wouldn't have told me or one of you. But as you say, Matt is Matt."

"Who's your source on this, Chief?" Pierce asked.

"Can't tell you that right now," he said, and then paused. "There's also some question about his accident. No doubt he was drunk, but the Fridley P.D. can't find his fingerprints on the brandy bottle in his car. They think that's a little strange, and I must say, so do I."

Brinkman sank into her chair, feeling her stomach turn.

Oates went on to explain Jessica's theory of a setup, again without mentioning the source. "I know it sounds farfetched," he said, "but I think we owe it to Matt to follow up."

He couldn't miss the smirks on a few of the faces. "I can

see what some of you are thinking," he added, "but I want to take this one step farther. I would like to see Matt's files. Who has a key?"

Brinkman's grip on the table turned her knuckles white.

No more than an hour had passed before Sarah climbed into Freda Brinkman's Pontiac outside the Government Center, angry at being summoned on such short notice. "This better be important," Sarah said as she buckled up. "I had to cancel a deposition, and the other lawyer's all pissed off."

"The hell with your deposition," Brinkman said. "I'm not here for the fucking fun of it."

Sarah flinched at her anger.

"It's all coming apart," Brinkman said, clutching the steering wheel as she drove. "Like one of your goddamned balls of yarn."

Brinkman relaxed her grip on the wheel and pulled to the side of the street. "Meecham's out of his coma. Looks like he may make it. But that's not all." She took a deep breath and related every detail of the meeting with Oates and the other Homicide detectives.

"Who could have gotten to Oates?" Sarah asked.

"Take a guess," Brinkman sneered.

"Jessica?"

"I'd bet my badge on it."

"Son of a bitch," Sarah muttered. "What did Oates find in Meecham's file cabinet?"

"He couldn't get it open. I've got the keys and the important files."

Sarah put her hand over her eyes.

"He's going to check Meecham's keys at the hospital," Brinkman continued, "and if he can't find them there, he's going to get a goddamned locksmith to open it."

"But there won't be anything there," Sarah said.

"Yeah, but he won't stop with that. Everybody saw Meecham working on a big stack of files. He'll keep looking."

Sarah stared out the side window, allowing her mind to roam.

"Let's think for a minute," she said. "There's still nothing to connect us with any of this. Not with the murders, not with Meecham. We're getting excited over nothing. We've just got to relax."

Brinkman was not convinced. "Meecham's recovering. And Jessica is sure as hell not going to sit still now."

"Meecham won't know who hit him. Or why," Sarah argued. "Jessica may suspect we were involved with Ingram, but she has no proof. No proof of anything."

Brinkman pulled away from the curb, her anger and fear beginning to subside. Until Sarah spoke again.

"You mentioned the brandy bottle, said that Meecham's fingerprints weren't on it. I trust yours weren't, either."

Brinkman stared straight ahead.

Sarah glared at her. "We need to get the club back together."

"What the hell for?"

"I told you about their calls," Sarah said. "We've got to get back to them. We can't afford to split up now."

After more argument, Brinkman finally agreed to call a meeting for the next night. "But I'm telling you, I'm not going to take any shit from them. Their asses could be grass, too."

The late news had just ended, and Jessica was at home, in the bedroom slipping on her nightshirt, when the phone rang. She got to it by the fourth ring and for a moment thought no one was there. The voice was that hushed.

"Who is this?" Jessica asked for the second time.

"Kim, Jessica."

"Kim, can you speak up? I can barely hear you."

"I only have a minute," she said, still whispering. "Sarah's in the shower."

"What's going on?"

"The Craft Club. You said to call."

"What about it?" Jessica asked.

"They're having another meeting."

"When?" Jessica couldn't hide the urgency in her voice.

"Tomorrow night."

"Do you know where the meeting is?" Jessica asked.

"No."

"The time?"

"No. Just tomorrow night."

"I've got to think about this, Kim. I'll call you at your office tomorrow, okay?"

"Okay. But I don't like this, Jessica."

"It may be nothing, Kim, but thanks."

After she had hung up, Jessica retreated to the kitchen and grabbed a can of beer. She sat at the small table, staring at the fading yellow stripes of the kitchen wallpaper. Thinking.

She simply couldn't picture Sarah Andrews in a Craft Club, knitting. Any more than she could envision herself there. It just didn't ring right. What had Kim said earlier about Sarah? Something to the effect that she brought her knitting to the club but never did much.

THIRTY-SEVEN

Jessica waited until midmorning before calling Kim at work. Kim's voice, which was so hushed and excited the night before, sounded tired now, as though she barely had the strength to lift the phone.

"Are you okay?" Jessica asked.

"Yeah. Just didn't get much sleep again."

"Sorry," Jessica said. "You still want to go ahead?"

"I guess so."

"Did Sarah say any more about the meeting?"

"Just that she'd be home after work to change clothes and get her stuff."

"Her stuff?"

"Her knitting bag. She always takes it."

"Tell me about it," Jessica said.

"The bag?"

"Right."

"It's an open canvas bag, filled with yarn and needles and a couple of knitting books, I think. I've never paid that much attention."

"It's at your place now?"

"She keeps it in the closet."

"You have any plans for lunch?" Jessica asked.

"No. I was going to eat at my desk."

"I'll pick you up in an hour, outside your building. Look for an old Chevy that puffs blue smoke."

Kim was waiting by the curb, looking nervous, as Jessica pulled up. She slipped quickly into the Impala, her face averted from the passersby on the sidewalk.

"Where are we going?" she asked before Jessica could say anything.

"To your place. If you'll tell me how to get there."

"Why?" Kim demanded.

Jessica reached into her handbag and pulled out a tiny tape recorder, no larger than the palm of her hand. "To put this in Sarah's knitting bag," she said, her eyes on Kim.

Kim's mouth was agape. "You're kidding. Is that what I think it is?"

"It weighs only a few ounces but has enough tape and battery power to run for four hours. She'll never know it's there."

"My God," Kim muttered.

"We'll take it to your place now," Jessica said. "I'll show you how it works and find a spot for it in the bag. But you'll have to get home ahead of Sarah and turn the thing on. It'll only run for four hours, remember."

Kim slumped back in the seat, saying nothing.

"I'm driving blind, Kim. I need to know where your place is."

Kim reluctantly gave her the directions. "What if she finds it?" she asked. "She'll know I put it there."

"You said you didn't think she ever touched the bag."

Kim was clearly unconvinced. Her hands were clasped tightly in her lap, and Jessica thought she saw a tremor on her lips.

"When you get the chance, after Sarah gets back from the

meeting, just retrieve the recorder from the bag. I'll pick it up from you tomorrow."

"Where will you be tonight?" Kim asked.

"Trying to follow Sarah. To find out where the meeting is, to see who else is there. It's the only way we'll find the truth, Kim. The Craft Club could be just what it seems to be, but I've got a hunch that it's more. This should tell us one way or the other."

"It scares me, Jessica. Everything about it scares me."

Kim haltingly told her that she'd been thinking of leaving, of starting again somewhere else. "But I can't run away. The nightmares wouldn't stop, and Sarah would always be there, in the shadows somewhere. I have to find the truth."

"I've told you, we may never find the truth," Jessica reminded her. "But if we do, it could be painful."

"That's what I don't understand. . . ."

Jessica again faced a quandary. While she still couldn't tell Kim everything, she had to tell her enough to convince her this wasn't some bizarre wild-goose chase.

"Kim, I think Sarah may have gotten involved in something that's, well, impossible to understand. For me, anyway. Maybe it's out of her anger and frustration with the system's failure to deal with men like Edward Hill."

Kim appeared puzzled. "I don't know what you're talking about, but I do know Sarah hated Hill. Maybe even more than I did. When the case got thrown out of court, I thought she'd go crazy. . . . She blamed herself because the cops had screwed it up."

"What did she say?" Jessica asked, her eyes moving between Kim and the road.

"At the time?"

Jessica nodded.

"Can't remember, exactly. Something to the effect that he would eventually get what's coming to him."

Jessica drove on quietly.

"I know I'm not too quick," Kim said, "but are you suggesting that Sarah had something to do with Edward Hill's murder?"

Jessica offered no response.

"Are you?" Kim's voice was more demanding.

"She may have, Kim," Jessica said finally.

"She couldn't have. She's not capable of that. Besides, we were together at the rally that night."

"She may have known about it, Kim. Maybe helped to plan it."

"Is that what you've been talking about? You're crazy!"

"Did you see Freda Brinkman that night?" Jessica asked.

"At the rally? No, but . . ."

"Kim, listen to me. I told you I only had suspicions. But Hill wasn't the first predator to die that way. There have been others just like him over the past several years. All of their murders are still unsolved, unexplained. They all died especially horrible deaths."

"And you think the Craft Club had something to do with them?"

"Maybe."

"I can't believe any of this," Kim said.

"You're not alone," Jessica said as they pulled up in front of Kim and Sarah's apartment building.

Hours later, Jessica and Kendrick sat in the Investigative unit's van less than a block from the same building, within easy view of the wide garage doors that would open for Sarah's red Honda. They had been there for more than an hour, slouched in their seats behind the darkened windows of the gray Chevy van, its outside panels inscribed with phony faded lettering: Johnson's Plumbing.

The bright sun of earlier in the day had disappeared behind a bank of heavy, dark clouds moving in from the west, leaving the air sagging with the weight of impending rain. Even the laboring air conditioner could not eliminate the stickiness inside the van.

"Why didn't you use a wireless transmitter instead of the

recorder?" Kendrick asked. "We could have monitored the meeting from here in the truck."

Jessica had considered that option but had finally rejected it as too dangerous. The transmitter weighed slightly more than the recorder, and unlike the recorder, it had both a microphone cord and a transmitting antenna attached to it.

"It would have been too bulky," she told Kendrick. "I needed something as small and unobtrusive as possible. Besides, if we'd lost Sarah on the way there, we would never hear what was said."

Kendrick's camera equipment was ready to go in the rear of the van, sitting next to a small window that was used as camera portal. His assignment was to tape anyone who showed up for the meeting.

"Hope this rain holds off," he said, peering through the van window. "It's getting dark enough as it is, and with rain it'll be tough to get the kind of shots you're looking for."

"I don't know what else we can do," Jessica said with a shrug. "We can only follow along and see what happens."

She knew the whole thing was risky business. Not only could the recorder be discovered, but Sarah or one of the other women might spot the van and become suspicious.

Jessica had learned long before that secretly recording a conversation was permissible if one of the participants was aware of the recording. But, in this case, none of them would be, and Jessica knew she would be acting illegally.

For that reason, she had told neither George Barclay nor Laurie Sanders what she planned to do. She felt guilty, but she couldn't risk having them say no. Convincing herself that the end justified the means was one thing; convincing them was something else. And there wouldn't have been time to argue.

"Hey, Jess," Kendrick whispered, looking into the side mirror. "Your friend has arrived."

The red Honda passed them and pulled up to the garage doors.

* * *

Kim was busying herself in the kitchen, tossing a small salad and waiting for the bread to pop out of the toaster, when she heard Sarah walk into the apartment. She pretended not to notice, concentrating instead on the portable TV set on the kitchen counter. Dan Rather was describing a series of tornadoes that had devastated parts of the Oklahoma panhandle. She felt rather than saw Sarah standing in the doorway.

"Home early, aren't you?" Sarah said.

"What?" Kim said, turning quickly, feigning surprise.

The bread popped out of the toaster.

"I tried to get you at your office . . . to see if you needed a ride home. They said you'd already left."

"Had a headache," Kim said, returning to the salad.

"You're having a lot of those lately," Sarah said, moving next to her. "Anything wrong?"

Kim shook her head, avoiding Sarah's eyes, trying to hide the nervous flutter in her hands. Keep calm, she told herself. "Want me to make you a salad?" she asked as casually as she could.

"No, thanks. I've got to change and get going. You're sure you're all right?"

"Of course. It's only a headache."

Sarah stared at her curiously for a moment, then moved toward her bedroom.

Kim didn't want to even think about the tiny tape recorder hidden away in one corner of Sarah's knitting bag. She and Jessica had checked the weight of the bag with and without the recorder and had found no discernible difference. They had also tested the range of its reception from inside the bag, discovering it was effective up to about forty feet. Beyond that, their words turned to mush.

She glanced out the kitchen window but could see no sign of the van Jessica had said they would be driving. It must be on the other side of the building, Kim thought. Trembling, she sat down at the kitchen counter and slowly chewed her salad and toast. But she tasted only fear.

* * *

Jessica tried to relax. So far, so good. After following the red Honda for ten minutes, Jessica felt secure that Sarah had failed to spot them. She seemed to be in no particular rush, driving within the speed limit, signaling her turns, running no yellow lights. Hendrick kept the van well back, but close enough not to miss any of the turns or stoplights.

"She sure as hell isn't going to get a ticket," he muttered impatiently as they waited for another light to change.

They had traveled from the apartment near Lake Harriet across town to the new Lake Street bridge and into St. Paul, following Marshall Avenue. Then a right on Fairview and a left onto the broad sweep of historic Summit Avenue. A few blocks past Macalester College, Sarah's car slowed, and she signaled a right turn at Pascal Street. Kendrick pulled the van to the curb on Summit and watched as the Honda ducked into a parking place a half block away.

"Must be around here," Jessica said, surveying the nearby homes. Kendrick was already in the back of the van, hoisting his camera onto a tripod next to the window.

Sarah was out of her car, walking toward them, striding with purpose but with no apparent apprehension. The knitting bag was held firmly in one hand.

"Thank God," Jessica murmured.

Sarah walked past the van, glancing casually toward it without slackening her pace. Kendrick's camera followed her as she turned up a sidewalk leading to an old brick house thick with ivy climbing the walls. She paused halfway to the house, head turning. Jessica rushed to the back window of the van and carefully pulled aside the curtain. Kendrick could hear her drawn breath. Freda Brinkman was coming from the opposite direction.

"I knew it," Jessica whispered.

"What the hell are you doing?" Sarah demanded as Brinkman joined her on the sidewalk. "You know we're supposed to come separately."

"Don't get excited," Brinkman replied, glancing around. "Who's watching?"

They walked the final steps to the house and waited until Patricia Sample, the Macalester College history professor, answered the chimes and opened the door for them. There were no warm greetings. Sample led them, unsmiling, through the house and into the familiar library. "The others should be here soon," she said curtly. "I'll get the coffee."

Sarah took a seat, the knitting bag resting at her feet.

By the time the fourth woman arrived at the house, the rain had begun. Slowly at first, no more than light sprinkles, but then increasing in intensity. The raindrops were large, splattering on the metal roof of the van. Jessica felt as if they were being bombarded with buckshot.

"How many women are there?" Kendrick asked, hunched over behind the camera.

"Who knows?" she said. "Just keep shooting."

With the engine and air conditioner off, it was sweltering inside the van. Jessica wiped away the sweat running into her eyes and down the back of her neck.

"Better not be any more," Kendrick said. "Between the rain and the dark, we're not going to get much more on tape."

"I wish now that we had used the transmitter," she said. "We would be able to hear what's going on in there."

Kendrick said, "Depends on where they are in the house and how thick the walls are. This rain wouldn't help the signal, that's for sure."

Jessica returned to the cab of the van and cracked a window open, ignoring the rain against her face, breathing in the cooler air. "Let's wait another fifteen minutes, then move the van," she said. "We could get spotted if we stay in the same place much longer."

Kendrick left the camera and joined her in the front seat. "How long are we going to wait?" he asked.

"Until the meeting's over," she said. "Until they leave."

* * *

The anger inside the room was palpable, as heavy as the air outside before the rain. Fear, too, could be seen on the faces of the women, choking their voices. Evident even in the way they sat, turned half away from either Sarah or Freda Brinkman, unwilling to look squarely at either of them. Staring, instead, at the books on the library shelves or at one another.

Sarah found the atmosphere suffocating. She had tried to cut through the venomous cloud with casual small talk, but her efforts were rewarded with grim looks and grunted replies. Whatever unity had once bound the club had vanished. It was three against two, with Sarah and Brinkman in the minority. And it didn't take long for the anger to spill out.

"Why are we here?" one of the women, Teresa Johnson, asked.

"To be consulted, brought up-to-date," Sarah replied.

"Cut the crap, Sarah," Nancy Higgins said. "What we say or think doesn't matter, and you know it. You proved it. You and Freda do whatever you damn well please, period."

"Hold on!" Brinkman said, rising from her chair.

"No. You hold it," Higgins shouted. "You tried to kill a cop. You knew we didn't want that."

"He's not dead," Brinkman said.

"Through no fault of yours," Johnson replied sharply.

Brinkman was still standing, hands clasped behind her back, a satisfied smile resting at the corner of her lips. "Meecham's out of commission," she said, "and who knows if he'll ever recover. He's an old man with a pickled liver and a swollen brain. Even if he does get his memory back, he won't know what hit him."

At Sarah's side, no more than ten feet from Brinkman, buried by the yarn, the tape recorder rolled soundlessly on.

"You're missing the point, Freda," Higgins said. "We didn't join this club to kill or maim cops."

"He was a danger to us," Brinkman exploded, cutting her off. "He had to be dealt with, plain and simple. With Meecham out of it, I suspect his investigation will simply dry up and blow away."

"How about the reporter?" It was Patricia Sample. "Will she dry up and blow away?"

Brinkman's face tightened. "Probably not. She's still a major problem."

"That's what you said about Meecham," Sample snapped. "Are you going to try to snuff her out, too?"

"Settle down, all of you," Sarah said. "Like it or not, Freda's right. Jessica's a growing threat. She gave my name to the police in the Ingram case. And I know she suspects more."

Teresa Johnson stood up abruptly. "I'm leaving," she cried. "This is craziness. Count me out. I won't be part of any attack on another woman, I don't care how much of a threat she might be."

The other three women also started to rise.

"You can't do that," Brinkman shouted.

"Watch me," Johnson replied, starting toward the door.

"Sit down, Teresa, the rest of you, too," Sarah said. "Let's talk this out."

The other women settled back into their chairs, but Johnson stood her ground by the door. "More talking won't do any good," she said. "I became part of this because I hated what happened to my daughter and to others who'd had the same horrible things happen to them. It hasn't been easy, but I've been able to live with it because we were saving other women from the pain and suffering my Ginny went through. This is different. This is all wrong. As far as I know, Meecham never hurt a woman, and this Jessica certainly hasn't. Being a righteous vigilante is one thing. A cold-blooded killer is something else."

With that, she stalked out the door.

Jessica could see Teresa Johnson emerge from their new position farther down Summit Avenue. The rain had eased, but a murky gloom had settled in.

"Looks like the meeting may be breaking up," she said.

Kendrick started the engine. They had already decided that if the women came out of the house singly, they would watch until each got to her car and then try to get license numbers.

Teresa was walking away from them, holding a small umbrella in one hand, a bag in the other, moving briskly toward Pascal Street. Kendrick waited until she had turned the corner before easing the van ahead, creeping at about the same pace as her walk. She covered a block and a half without looking back. As she was putting the key into the lock of a Buick Century, Kendrick sped ahead, and Jessica moved to the back of the van. He pulled up slightly behind the Buick and quickly got out before Teresa could close the car door.

"Excuse me," he said. "Happen to know where Cretin Avenue is?"

The woman shook her head. "Sorry. I'm from Minneapolis. I get lost over here myself."

"Thanks, anyway," he said, getting back into the van, watching as the Buick pulled away in front of them.

"Get it, Jess?"

"Got it," she said from behind him. "Five-one-three-FDM."

Another hour passed before the other women left the house. Sarah and Brinkman were the first, walking together, engrossed in conversation. Jessica's eyes fastened on the bag in Sarah's hand as the pair strode toward the red Honda. She could only hope the recorder was working.

"Want to follow them?" Kendrick asked.

Jessica was torn. Why were they leaving together? She would love to know where they were going, but she also needed to know who the other woman was. And she was still inside.

"Make up your mind," Kendrick said. "They're at the car."

Jessica's head pounded. "We'll stay here," she finally said. "We need the other license number."

"Your call," Kendrick muttered.

By now, dusk had settled fully into night. As Nancy Higgins left the house, it was fairly simple to follow her car for a few blocks, the van's headlights illuminating her license plate. Jessica knew it would be easy to trace the ownership of the cars and not much harder to discover who lived in the house. They also had four of the women on videotape and, hopefully, the conversation inside on audiotape.

Not a bad night's work, she decided proudly as they headed back for the station.

"When do you get the recorder back?" Kendrick asked.

"Tomorrow, I hope. Kim's supposed to call me."

"How long a tape did you use?"

"Four hours. It should work out fine."

"I hope Kim can turn it off before it beeps."

"What?" Jessica exclaimed.

"Don't those recorders beep when they run out of tape?"

"They do?"

"Some of them do, anyway," he said.

"Why didn't you say something before?"

"It just occurred to me now," he said lamely. "Besides, I assumed you'd thought of it."

"I didn't know," she mumbled. "I didn't think."

She quickly looked at her watch: 8:45 P.M. Kim must have turned the recorder on at five or so. That would give them until nine or shortly after. It was going to be close.

Kim heard the front door of the apartment open and close. The carpeting muffled any footsteps, but a sliver of light from the hallway suddenly appeared in the crack beneath the closed bedroom door. Sarah was home.

Kim turned over in the bed, facing away from the door, burying her head in the pillow. Waiting for the door to be flung open, for the overhead light to flash on. Waiting for a tape recorder to be thrust into her face. But there was nothing.

She could hear the muted sounds of the television set in the living room and, later, the splashing of the shower in the bathroom across the hall. Still nothing.

She stared into the darkness, feeling the pounding of her heart gradually slow, her breathing level off, her body relax. For the last three hours, she had imagined—expected—the worst. She had tried to prepare her story, to get her lies, her denials, in order. But she knew it would be useless, that in the face of Sarah's anger and accusations, she would be helpless. Face it, she told herself sadly, you've always been helpless.

The spray of the shower stopped. The light beneath her door went out. A deep quiet settled over the apartment. Kim wasn't sure when she slept, but when she did, it was a deep, relieved sleep.

THIRTY-EIGHT

Jessica was at her desk at eight in the morning, waiting, watching the clock. Would the phone never ring? It was now ten past ten and counting. While they had set no specific time, Jessica had expected Kim's call long before now. Had something gone wrong? She shuddered at the thought. Imaginary beeps had kept her awake half the night.

Twenty minutes later, the phone rang. It was Kim. "Everything okay?" Jessica asked. "I thought I'd hear from you before this."

"Sorry. Sarah hung around the apartment. I had to fake being sick again."

Jessica could hear the fear in her voice. Her words seemed strangled, struggling to get out.

"Where are you now?" she asked.

"Still at the apartment."

"Have you got the tape?"

"Yes. The tape and the recorder are in my purse."

Jessica took a deep breath. The recorder either didn't beep, or they hadn't heard it. She considered telling Kim of the close call but decided against it. She was frightened enough as it was.

"Did you listen to the tape?" Jessica asked.

"Heavens, no! I want you to take it. I want to be rid of it."

"Can I meet you somewhere?" Jessica asked.

"Sure, but I don't have a car."

"How about the Lake Harriet bandstand? It's only a few minutes' walk for you."

"When?" Kim asked.

"Half hour. By the concession booth."

"Jessica?"

"Yes."

"I don't like any of this. It scares me."

"Me, too, Kim."

With the heat of the morning, Jessica was surprised more people were not on the beach or around the pavilion. On the weekend it would have been packed, but now only a few old men fished from shore, and occasionally a runner or biker passed by on the path around the lake.

Kim was waiting alone, nervously licking a strawberry ice cream cone. She smiled weakly and fell into step beside Jessica.

As they walked, Kim struggled to retrieve the recorder from her purse without losing her grip on the cone. "It was right where we left it," she said. "In the bottom of the bag, and the bag was back in the closet."

"Good," Jessica said, taking the recorder from her. "Let's grab one of those," she suggested, pointing to a picnic table set well back from the path and partially hidden by lilac bushes.

Then she pushed a button and listened to the tape rewind. So far, so good, she thought.

"How did Sarah seem?" she asked.

Kim's brow furrowed. "Okay, I guess. Edgy, maybe. It was strange that she got off to work so late. It's not like her."

"Were you up when she got home last night?"

"No, but I was awake. And scared. I had convinced myself that she'd find the recorder."

The rewinding tape stopped, and Jessica pressed the PLAY button. "This could take a while," she said. "We won't get to the meeting part until later in the tape."

She was ready to hit the FAST FORWARD button when a voice, full volume, came through the small speaker. Sarah's voice.

"Hello, Kim. Is Jessica with you?"

Kim's mouth fell open, and the cone toppled from her hand, the ice cream making a gooey heap in her lap. "What?" she demanded.

"Surprised? I thought you would be." Sarah's taped voice went on, slowly and calmly. "What's going on, Kim? I thought we were best friends. Since when do we spy on one another, Kim? It's Jessica, isn't it? What'd she tell you, Kim? What kind of lies to get you to do this?"

Jessica could only stare at the recorder, transfixed. Sarah not only found the recorder and erased the tape but now was using it as a weapon to taunt and frighten them. One glance at Kim's stricken face told her she had already succeeded.

"I'm going to be gone for a couple of days, Kim," Sarah continued, "but when I get back, I want you out of the apartment. You violated a trust, and I don't want to see or talk to you again."

Kim could not disguise her pain. "My God, what have I done?"

"As for you, Jessica," the tape continued, "I can only urge you once more to drop this obsessive inquiry of yours. It will get you nowhere, and as I said once before, it could be dangerous for you. That's not a threat, Jessica, just friendly advice."

The tape went silent.

Kim's anguish suddenly turned to violent anger.

"How could this happen?" she shouted, rising to face

Jessica. "You said they'd never find the tape. You told me. You promised."

"Settle down, Kim. For Christ's sake, control yourself."

"You did. You promised."

"I didn't promise you anything," Jessica said, trying to control her own voice. "They got lucky, that's all."

"What do you mean?"

Jessica calmly explained about the beeper on the recorder. "That must be how they found it," she said. "I know I should have thought about it, but I didn't. It's history."

Kim shook her head slowly, anger dissipating, voice choking. "What am I going to do now?" she asked plaintively.

"I don't know, Kim. But I'd sure as hell stay away from Sarah and Brinkman for a while. It could be dangerous."

"Sarah would never try to hurt me," Kim cried.

"Maybe not, but you can't say the same for Brinkman. I think she's crazy."

Kim started to walk away, then stopped. "I'm not moving out," she said defiantly. "Sarah can't make me do that. Not this way!"

Jessica was startled. "You'd better think about that, Kim. This isn't over yet. I wouldn't push Sarah right now."

"Who's pushing who? I don't have to think about it. I'm not moving."

Jessica's surprise at the woman's spunk must have shown because it drew a quick response. "I know you don't think I have any backbone," Kim said. "Sarah doesn't, either. No one does, not anymore. But I'll only be pushed so far, Jessica. Sarah has no right to order me out."

Jessica found it hard to picture Kim that angry, but she didn't want to make an issue of it and moved on toward the car.

"When do I find out what's really going on?" Kim asked.

"When I'm sure myself," Jessica replied. "I think we're getting closer."

"Even without the tape?"

She nodded, trying to make the best of it. "By destroying

the tape, reacting as they did, they've at least told us something. Chances are, this Craft Club's involved somehow. If it wasn't, they wouldn't have panicked over the tape. We now know Brinkman's a part of the club, and we have leads to the other women. We also have Sarah's warning to me on tape. That's not bad."

"What about the warning?" Kim asked as they reached the car.

Jessica thought about Meecham's car tumbling over the cliff. "What can I say? I can't walk away from all of this, not now, not knowing what I know or think I know. I'll just have to be more cautious and hope they don't try anything foolish."

Brave words, Jess. In truth she was scared to death.

The binoculars had brought them so close that Sarah thought she could reach out and touch them.

"Need any more proof?" Brinkman asked, standing next to her, also gazing at Kim and Jessica through field glasses.

Sarah made no reply. She had studied Kim's face, seeing first the surprise, then the fear, the tears, and finally, the anger. She felt her own eyes well, blurring her vision. They were standing on a rise about a hundred yards from the picnic bench, hidden behind a large oak. As planned, they had followed Kim from the apartment and watched as Jessica joined her.

"I still don't understand," Sarah said. "Why would she do it?"

"Makes no difference now," Brinkman replied harshly. "I just wonder how much she knows, how much Jessica has told her."

"No foolish ideas, Freda. Not with Kim. She must be a dupe in all of this. She couldn't hide it from me."

"She sure as hell hid the tape recorder," Brinkman snarled.

When they heard the beep and found the recorder in the knitting bag the night before, it was instantly clear to both of them who must have planted it, the only person who knew where the bag would be, who would have had access to it. And now they'd confirmed who had put her up to it.

Brinkman had wanted Sarah to confront Kim, find out what she knew or suspected, what Jessica had told her. But Sarah had been adamant. Leave her alone. I'll get her out of the apartment, but that's all. No harm must come to Kim.

"Our problem is Jessica, not Kim," Sarah said again.

"And it's time to deal with her. She's not going to give this up. No way. If we needed any more proof, the tape was it. We were lucky this time. We may not be the next time."

"There's got to be something we can do short of—" Sarah couldn't finish the sentence.

"Don't kid yourself. This is a game to her, don't you see that? Cat and mouse. She's matching wits with us. Ten to one this little defeat will only make her more determined."

If Jessica's playing a game, Sarah thought, she's just changed the rules, first turning Kim against her, then arranging what she must know was an illegal recording of a private meeting. Still, this is another woman we're talking about. A woman who may be a danger to us but a woman nonetheless.

"You may be right," she said reluctantly, "but give it another day or two. Maybe she'll listen to the warning on the tape."

"Two days," Brinkman said. "But that's it."

THIRTY-NINE

"**M**ust be it," Jessica said, pulling the Impala to the curb.

"Looks like it," Nina French agreed.

The large fenced-in backyard enclosed a four-seat swing set, two slides, a jungle gym, a large plastic wading pool, and two sandboxes. Clambering over everything were at least a dozen kids, preschoolers, Jessica guessed, by the size of them.

Her car went unnoticed by the children but was watched with interest by the two women in the yard. A small sign, in red, blue, and yellow mock children's lettering, hung on the chain-link fence: Tot Care Day Care.

Bill Kendrick had driven past the house a couple of hours before, after tracing the license tabs of the first car they had spotted the night before. The Buick Century was listed to a Teresa Johnson on Queen Avenue North.

When he had told Jessica that the woman apparently ran a day-care center, Jessica had quickly enlisted Nina's help. "Just pretend you're a young mother looking for day care," she told her. "You've got a two-year-old son, Sean, and working part-time. Fake it, but find out as much as you can about the woman without causing any suspicion."

"You're not coming in?" Nina had asked.

"I'll stay in the car." Jessica knew the chances of being recognized were slim, but just in case, she wore sunglasses and a scarf tied tightly around her head.

From the car Nina studied the two women in the yard. "What if she asks my name and where I work?"

"Don't lie about your name, but avoid telling her where you work. Talk around it."

"Which one is Teresa?" Nina asked as she got out.

"In the shorts and halter," Jessica said, recalling the woman from the night before.

Nina walked through the gate and shook hands with Teresa, sitting with her and the other woman on the back step. If either of them noticed Jessica still in the car, she didn't show it. From what Jessica could see, the conversation seemed friendly and animated. And after about ten minutes, Nina and Teresa walked into the house, leaving the other woman outside with the children.

When they emerged, Teresa was pushing a wheelchair holding an older girl, maybe ten or twelve. Slack-jawed and skeleton-thin, her body was held upright by a support belt tied to the wheelchair. The other children paused in their play and gathered around, fawning over her. But she showed no reaction. She simply stared into space.

Sad, Jessica thought. Looks like cerebral palsy or MS. Jessica's eyes moved back to Nina, who was saying her good-byes. Moments later, she was back in the car.

"Neat lady," Nina said. "Runs a nice place. Clean, well kept, well staffed. If I really did have a kid, I'd take him there."

"What else?" Jessica asked as she pulled away from the curb.

"Not much. She's forty-something, divorced, earns her living running the day care. Has for ten or twelve years, since her own daughter was a baby."

"That's her daughter in the wheelchair?"

"Yeah. It's so tragic. Her name's Ginny. Can't seem to move or talk much. Just sits there, like she's in another world."

"What's wrong with her?"

"Got me. The mother was vague, something about an accident several years ago."

"An accident?"

"That's what she said. I didn't want to press her. Wouldn't have looked right, being too nosy."

"Can you dig a little deeper?" Jessica asked.

"For what?"

"For what happened to the girl. We know the names of both the mother and daughter. There must be records somewhere."

"Is it that important?" Nina asked.

"I don't know. It could be. I'm grasping for anything."

Kim was in her office, catching up on the morning mail, returning accumulated calls—going through her familiar, everyday motions. But her mind was floating, hovering somewhere above that picnic bench, reliving that unbelievable moment of discovery, of terror.

Life will never be the same, she knew. Her best friend was gone; an important part of her life was over. She'd be alone again, with all of the terrors that would bring. Like it or not, she'd have to begin again, here or elsewhere. The question was, Would she meekly retreat, as she always had, or stand her ground?

Sarah's words were branded in her brain. "You violated a trust . . ." Kim felt the anger rising again. Who had violated a trust? She picked up the phone and dialed her office.

"We should talk," Kim said when Sarah answered.

"There's nothing to talk about," she replied.

"Yes there is. I'm not leaving the apartment. You're not going to push me out."

There was a long pause, as if Sarah could not quite believe what she heard. "Fine," she said finally. "Then I'll leave."

"For God's sake, Sarah, what's going on? What have you gotten yourself into?"

"Ask your friend Jessica."

"I'm asking you," Kim said, pressing.

"Stay out of it, Kim. You'd never understand."

"Try me."

"Kim, listen. For your own good, forget it. I'm sorry it's ending like this, that you felt compelled to do what you did. You're in over your head, Kim. You'll get nothing but grief, believe me. Stay away from Jessica and stay away from me. I'll move out by the end of the week."

"Sarah, wait a minute . . ."

But the line was already dead.

When Jessica walked into Matt's hospital room, she found Deputy Chief Barton Oates already there, talking in a whisper.

Jessica stood for a moment, unnoticed, behind them. Then she coughed politely. "Sorry to interrupt," she said when Oates turned in his chair.

"Hi, Jessica," Matt said, his voice still gravelly. "Bart here wants to know what the hell happened to me, said you told him I was involved in some kind of investigation. That the accident was a setup. I told him I don't remember a thing."

Then he winked and smiled.

"He's fucking with me, as usual," Oates said angrily. "Says he's got amnesia, but I don't believe a goddamned word of it. He's always been a pain in the ass, but this is serious business."

"The doctor said he wouldn't remember anything for a while," Jessica reminded him.

"I'm talking about what happened before the accident. About this so-called investigation that involves other jurisdictions. I've got a right to know, for Christ's sake."

Looking past Oates, Jessica saw Meecham wiggle his eyebrows wickedly. She couldn't hide her smile.

"It's not funny, young lady," Oates said. "The chief's on my ass to get rid of Matt. He doesn't believe the setup business. Wants Matt out of Homicide, out of the department. Says he's an embarrassment."

Oates got up. "Maybe you can talk some sense into him. He's on medical leave right now, but that won't protect him forever. I need some answers soon."

As he was walking out the door, Jessica asked: "Who's running Homicide now, with Matt gone?"

"Lieutenant Brinkman. She's next in rank. Why do you ask?"

"Just wondering," Jessica said.

After Oates left, Jessica quickly brought Matt up-to-date on everything: Kim's cooperation, the Craft Club meeting, the botched tape recording, Sarah's warning, the identity of the other women in the club.

"You're telling me you're sure Brinkman's in the middle of all this?" Matt asked.

"No doubt in my mind," Jessica replied. "I think she's the one who did this to you. Or at least arranged it."

Meecham slowly shook his head. "I know she was acting strange, but Jesus . . ."

"It's the only thing that makes sense, Matt. She and Sarah and the others in this Craft Club."

Meecham strained to push himself up in his bed. "What do you hear from Jenkins and the other cops?"

"Not much," she said. "I'm supposed to meet with them, but there just hasn't been time."

"I'll try to get 'em here," he said weakly. "See if I can't goose them a bit."

"You can still barely talk," Jessica objected.

"The throat's getting better every day. I don't want to lay here doing nothing. I'm not dead. Maybe I can help."

"You ought to worry about getting well," she scolded as she got up to leave.

He reached for her hand, holding it awkwardly as he struggled to find words. "The nurses tell me you've been here more than anybody," he finally said. "I hope you know I appreciate that."

She sat back on the edge of his bed, smiling. "You'd have done the same for me. Friends have to stick together."

As she hurried across the hospital lobby, Jessica was lost in thought, oblivious to her surroundings. Only the sharp cry of a baby to her left caused her to glance over her shoulder. That's when she saw him. Sitting in one of the chrome-and-plastic-covered chairs, two away from the wailing child, a newspaper in his lap, watching her.

Lowell Ingram. Again.

She stopped in mid-stride as Ingram got up and walked slowly toward her. Aside from a stubble of beard and red-rimmed eyes, he again looked fairly well kept. His thinning hair was combed back neatly, his shirt was wrinkled but clean, and his pants even bore the trace of a crease.

"What brings you here?" she asked.

"Remember me telling you about the cop?" he said. "The one you said you didn't know?"

Jessica nodded, suddenly alert.

Ingram could not disguise the smirk. "I just thought you'd like to know that she's been following you. She's outside now, in a blue Pontiac." He grinned. "Strange that somebody you don't know would be following you, isn't it?"

"How would you know that?" Jessica demanded.

"Because I was following her," he replied smugly. "I trailed you both here from the station. It was like a parade."

Jessica looked toward the door. "You're sure of that?"

"Want her license number?" he asked.

Jessica nodded.

He handed her a slip of paper. "It's CV-one-nine-three. She's got a small antenna mounted on the trunk."

Jessica left him there, reversing her direction, her steps taking her through a maze of hallways, following signs that pointed toward the emergency room. She knew the entrance to the ER was around the block from the main hospital doors, allowing her to approach Brinkman's car from the rear, if it was still there.

It was. Parked where Ingram said it would be, at a meter five car lengths behind her own beat-up Impala. Jessica stayed to the far edge of the sidewalk, hoping to avoid being seen in the car's rearview mirror. When she was no more than ten feet away, she crossed quickly behind the car and walked up to the driver's side window.

An arm rested on the window ledge. Jessica tapped it. "Hello, Lieutenant," she said.

Freda Brinkman's head snapped back at an awkward angle, her vision partially blocked by the doorframe and by the glare of the sun behind Jessica's shoulder.

"What? Who's that?" Brinkman tried to shade her eyes while turning, but she was held tight by her seat belt.

Jessica moved a step ahead, into Brinkman's view. "Jessica Mitchell, Lieutenant. I understand you've been following me."

"What are you talking about?" Brinkman snapped.

By now she had removed her seat belt and pushed open the car door, shoving Jessica backward.

"Is that all you've got to do, follow reporters around?" Jessica said, standing her ground.

"You're full of shit," Brinkman said.

"Maybe you want to know how Matt is," Jessica offered sarcastically. "How thoughtful. He's fine. Getting more of his memory back every day. Shouldn't be too long before he recalls exactly what happened to him. That'll be nice, won't it?"

Jessica started to walk away but then stopped and turned. "Maybe I should just give you my schedule for each day. Save you a lot of time and trouble."

Brinkman followed her. "You're a real smart-ass, aren't you? A real hotshot reporter."

Jessica ignored her and began to walk away again. Brinkman lunged after her and spun her around. Two older women approaching them stopped a few feet away, watching the confrontation curiously.

"Move on, ladies," Brinkman ordered. "This is police business."

The two women quickly scurried across the street as Brinkman turned back to Jessica. But she was already striding defiantly toward her car. "Too bad, Lieutenant. I suppose that means you won't ask me to join your Craft Club."

Before Jessica reached the Impala, Brinkman shouted after her, "How's your kid sister?"

Jessica spun around. "What did you say?"

"Janie. Isn't that her name? Works at Dayton's, right? Better tell her to be careful," she continued. "Big cities can be dangerous places for young women."

Before Jessica could respond, the lieutenant got into her car and roared off.

FORTY

When Lowell Ingram saw Brinkman lunge after Jessica and spin her around on the sidewalk, he was more convinced than ever that this was the woman who had pistol-whipped him at the motel. There was the same quick, almost catlike movement. And he could again feel her rage, even from this distance.

While he couldn't hear most of their exchange, it was clear from their enraged expressions that the women knew—and hated—one another. Ingram wasn't sure what that meant except that Jessica had lied to him and was hiding something.

When Brinkman got into her car and pulled away, Ingram paused a moment, then followed.

Nina greeted Jessica as she walked into the newsroom, rushing over with a sheaf of papers in her hand. "I've been looking all over for you," she said.

"I've been at the hospital with Meecham," Jessica said, still shaken from the encounter with Brinkman. "What've you got?"

"The little girl, Ginny. Teresa Johnson's daughter. I've been on the phone for hours. Finally tracked her case down."

"Hang tight for a minute," Jessica said as she walked to her desk and picked up the phone. It took only a minute to reach her sister at work. "Listen to me, Janie. I'll explain things later."

"What are you talking about, Jess?"

"No questions, okay? You're working late tonight, right?"

"Yeah, till nine, but—"

"Wait for me to pick you up. Don't leave the store. No eating out, no walks on the mall. I'm meeting Jack after work, and we'll stop by for you at nine. Okay?"

"Did Charlie call again? Is that it?"

"No, I told you not to worry about that. Just stay put. I'll tell you more when I see you."

She quickly hung up to avoid further argument, then turned back to Nina. "Now, what's this about Ginny?"

"There was no accident," Nina said. "She was assaulted, years ago, when she was seven. Picked up at a playground a few blocks from her house. Brutally beaten, raped, and left for dead in a nature preserve a few miles away. Hikers found her, unconscious, in a bad way."

"You've got to be kidding."

"It's all in the police reports," Nina said, pushing the papers toward her. "Once I was able to find them."

"Did they find the guy who did it?" Jessica asked.

" 'Fraid not. The girl was brain-damaged. Lucky to be alive, I guess. Couldn't identify anyone. She's pretty much a vegetable, from what I can gather. Certainly looked that way today."

"I'll be damned," Jessica whispered. Her mind whirled. Another sexual assault. Another member of the Craft Club. It was becoming ever more clear.

Nina went on: "Kendrick traced the other license number. Listed to a Nancy Higgins. Don't know anything about her, though. And I'm still trying to find out who owns the house on Summit."

Jessica rifled through the police report but found little of importance beyond what Nina had already told her. There were no witnesses to the girl's abduction and no strange cars or people sighted in the neighborhood or in the remote area where the child was eventually found by the hikers. And the girl herself was of no help. Another in a long list of unsolved sexual assaults.

It was not until her second reading of the report that Jessica noticed the blurred signature of one of the investigating officers: Freda Brinkman.

Damn! She should have known. That's how they met. Brinkman investigates Teresa's daughter's abduction and assault. Teresa joins the Craft Club. Another link in the chain. But what about the other woman? Nancy Higgins? Jessica reached for the phone.

An hour later, after posing as an insurance investigator and using the station's cross-telephone directory, Jessica was able to speak to two of Nancy Higgins's neighbors. But she learned little. First of all, they were suspicious. Jessica could not blame them, but they also did not seem to know much. Higgins must lead a very private life, she decided.

She did discover that Higgins was an accountant who had owned her home for only a couple of years. She lived alone and according to one neighbor was a divorcée. Only after six more calls to major accounting firms did Jessica discover where Higgins worked, at Foster & Fine in suburban Hopkins. The trail ended there.

When Kim returned to the apartment from work late that afternoon, she found the door open and filled by two husky men on either end of a king-sized mattress, their T-shirts wet with sweat.

"Sorry, lady," one of them said as Kim stepped aside to allow them to pass.

"You just missed your friend," said his partner. "She left about a half hour ago."

Kim walked into the apartment. The only remaining pieces of furniture were those few items which Kim had brought with her the year before: an overstuffed chair, an end table, and an ornate china cabinet—a family heirloom—which had been Kim's college graduation gift from her parents in Kansas. Everything else in the living and dining room was gone.

She felt the tears begin but tried to hold them back as she walked slowly down the hall and into Sarah's bedroom. Nothing but the bare bedframe remained for the movers. Her closet was empty except for an old pair of pink sneakers which Sarah had borrowed from Kim months before.

In the kitchen, a few boxes filled with Sarah's dishes and pans stood by the door. A note was propped against the coffee-pot on the kitchen counter. Sarah's scrawl was unmistakable.

Kim: I'm taking only what's mine. We'll figure out what to do with the stuff we own together later. When all of this is over. If it ever is. Remember what I told you, Kim. For your own good. At least I won't have to drink your shit coffee anymore. Sarah.

Despite herself, Kim laughed. Leave the last word to Sarah. But as she picked up the note and read it again, there was no holding the tears back. She slumped onto one of the boxes, holding her head, weeping without stop.

"Excuse me, lady." It was one of the movers, hovering over her. "We need to get those boxes out. We're already running late."

"Sorry," Kim said, standing, reaching for a towel, trying to stem the flow of tears.

"It's none of my business," said the man, "but you girls need a fresh supply of tissues."

"What are you talking about?" she asked, stifling her sobs.

"The other lady. The one who's moving out. She was sniffling when she left, too. You must be good friends."

"We were," Kim said.

Then she went to retrieve her pink sneakers.

* * *

Ingram was confused. He followed Brinkman from the hospital to what he already knew was Sarah Andrews's apartment, only to find a moving van parked outside, with Sarah standing nearby supervising the movers. From a distance, he saw Brinkman park her Pontiac behind the van and join Sarah on the sidewalk, talking and gesturing with great animation. He could only guess Brinkman was describing her encounter with Jessica.

That was more than an hour ago, and now the movers were closing the big rear doors of the van. Sarah and Brinkman had left a half hour before, but Ingram had decided to wait, to follow the movers to whatever new location they might be heading.

Adding to his confusion was the recent arrival of a woman he knew only as Sarah's roommate. As far as he could tell, she was still inside the apartment. Was she moving, too? Were Sarah and Brinkman moving in together? Only one way to find out, he decided, as he put the car into gear and followed the van down the street.

Jack Tomlinson had parked his old convertible outside when Jessica emerged from the station late that afternoon. She slid into the car beside him, her face grim.

"What the hell's wrong?" Jack asked, alarmed.

"Just drive, okay," she said, leaning back and closing her eyes.

Jack pulled away from the curb and merged with the rush-hour traffic. "What is it, Jess?"

She opened her eyes and stared straight ahead, quickly relating the details of her confrontation with Brinkman outside the hospital. Then she turned to him, eyes wide. "She even knows about Janie. Knows where she works. She even threatened her, in a roundabout way."

"No shit," he muttered.

"I'm not sure I can keep going," Jessica said. "Not now,

not after this. It was scary enough for me, but now, with Janie . . ."

Jack pulled off the road and into a McDonald's parking lot, shutting off the engine. "That may be the best thing, but you should hear what I've got to tell you first."

"What?"

"You were right. Brinkman's fingerprints were on the brandy bottle in Meecham's car. The Fridley cops confirmed it. Now they want to know who the prints belong to."

"I knew it," Jessica whispered. "This definitely puts her in the car with him, doesn't it? She had to have set him up!"

"Not necessarily," he cautioned. "I've thought about it. She could have touched the bottle anytime, maybe even gave it to him. She could claim anything, and Matt probably won't remember."

Jessica sank back in the seat. "You don't really believe that, do you?"

"Of course not. I'm just telling you that it's no real proof. But it sure as hell shows you're on the right track."

"What about the Fridley cops?" Jessica asked.

"Like I said, they're on my ass. And I don't blame them. They did me a favor, and now I'm stonewalling them."

"You'll have to stall a while longer," she said, "at least until I can talk to Barclay and Laurie. And to Matt."

Jack grimaced. "Don't push it too far, Jessica. You've got me hanging out on a limb, and it's feeling a little shaky."

Janie was waiting at the side door of Dayton's when Jack and Jessica pulled up at the appointed time.

"Climb in," Jessica said, leaning forward so that Janie could slip into the backseat. Then she introduced her to Tomlinson.

Jack turned in his seat and shook Janie's hand. "Nice to finally meet you, Janie. Sorry it's taken so long."

"Me, too," she replied, studying him only briefly before turning her attention to Jessica. "Now what's going on, Jess? Why all the secrecy?"

"Let's get out of downtown first," she said. "Then I'll explain."

Top down, they drove slowly toward the lakes of south Minneapolis, their windblown conversation confined to get-acquainted small talk between Janie and Jack. The evening air was cool but not cold, even in the open car, but Jessica hugged her body tightly, as though she were freezing.

When they pulled into a parking area along Lake of the Isles, Jessica unwrapped herself and turned to Janie in the backseat. She took a deep breath and began to explain everything, ending with the confrontation with Freda Brinkman.

"How in the world does she know about me?" Janie asked.

"I'm not sure," Jessica said. "But if she's been following me, she probably saw us together at some time or other."

"What does she look like?" Janie asked, leaning forward.

Jessica described Brinkman in as much detail as possible. "She's an imposing woman, Janie."

There was silence in the backseat.

"I think I've met her," Janie finally said.

"What?"

"She was in the store a few days ago. Bought a skirt and jacket. Navy blue. A size fourteen, I think. Reason I remember is that she seemed so nice. But curious. Asked a lot of questions, but real casual-like. While I was ringing up the skirt and jacket. Said she had a niece about my age."

Jessica leaned across the backseat. "What kind of questions?"

"Oh, I don't know . . . where I grew up, if I was going to school, how I liked the job. That sort of thing. Just conversation."

Jessica and Jack exchanged glances. "She's a dangerous woman," Jessica said. "Fully capable of hurting you . . . or me."

"But you say she's a cop," Janie protested.

"Makes no difference. Trust me. The woman's a wacko."

"Why haven't you told me any of this before?"

"I didn't see the need," Jessica said. "I didn't want to get you involved or worried. You had enough on your mind as it was."

"So what do we do now?" Janie asked, a hint of fear now in her voice.

"I don't know," Jessica admitted. "I may give the whole thing up. I didn't bargain for all of this."

"Give it up because of me?" Janie demanded.

"In part, yes. It's not worth risking—"

Janie's eyes flashed. "Forget it, Jess. No way. You're not quitting because of me. I won't have it."

Jessica could see the defiance in her sister's eyes.

"You'll need to get out of that apartment," Jack said, speaking for the first time. "Brinkman must know where you live by now if she's seen the two of you together. Get into someplace more secure and then make sure you're not followed again."

"I can't afford another apartment," Jessica said. "I'm barely making it now."

"Maybe the station will help," Jack offered. "Or you can move in with me, temporarily. It'd be a squeeze, but I've got the room."

Jessica considered the options. "I just don't know," she finally said. "I've got to think about it."

"I wouldn't take too long," Jack said. "Who knows what that broad will try next."

FORTY-ONE

George Barclay studied her silently from across the desk, his gaze so penetrating that Jessica shifted self-consciously in her chair. Laurie Sanders, sitting by her side, seemed just as uncomfortable while both waited for Barclay to speak.

He had said nothing since Jessica began her story, listening intently, his eyes never leaving hers, never wavering. She had told them everything, including her bungled attempt to record the Craft Club meeting, the taped warning from Sarah, and, finally, about Brinkman's fingerprints and the confrontation with her at the hospital. As she spoke, Jessica had tried to read Barclay's reaction, but she found him impenetrable. She couldn't get beyond his eyes.

Laurie finally broke the long silence. "That's a hell of a story," she said. "Don't you think so, George?"

Barclay heaved himself out of his chair and walked to the window of his office, his back toward them, staring at the passersby outside. "I'd say it's a hell of a mess," he finally said, turning to face them. "I think we ought to get out of it."

"What?" Jessica was out of her chair. "You're not serious!"

"Sit down, Jessica," Barclay ordered.

She stubbornly remained standing, looking plaintively toward Laurie, searching for support. But Laurie's eyes were on Barclay.

"C'mon, Jess, sit down. Relax." Barclay's voice was more soothing.

"Tell me I didn't hear you right," Jessica demanded as she slowly settled to the edge of the chair.

"This has gotten out of hand. We're reporters, not cops. You've gone beyond investigative reporting. You're more interested in getting the killers than the story. There's a big difference."

Jessica was stunned. "Nothing's changed since the last time we talked," she protested. "And you didn't want to back out then."

"Who are you kidding? At that point, Jess, you hadn't been threatened, at least not directly. You hadn't been followed and confronted by some crazy cop. It was bad enough when Meecham got ambushed, but this is getting too close to home. Cops get paid to run these kind of risks; we don't. It could be a great story, but I'm not going to have one of my reporters end up dead in some goddamned alley. I'd never be able to live with myself."

"Why are you so worried?" Jessica demanded. "Because I'm a woman? Would you be saying the same thing if Jeff Hilliard or one of the other guys was sitting here?"

"That's bullshit," Barclay said angrily, "and you know it."

"Is it? You never ran risks in your news career, George?"

"Not like this, not when people could be killed."

Jessica knew she was treading dangerously close to insubordination, but she had come too far to turn her back on the story now.

Barclay had not finished. "You've gone off the deep end on this, Jess."

"What are you talking about?"

"You know damn well you shouldn't have secretly recorded that meeting. That's illegal, to say nothing of unethical.

You never talked to us about it; you just went on your merry way. And then you go ahead and pose as an insurance investigator."

"I didn't know how else to get the information," she argued.

"You took the easy way out," Barclay snapped. "Reporters don't lie to get information."

"Sometimes you have to lie to get the truth," she countered.

"Not in my shop, you don't," Barclay said. "I don't practice that kind of journalism."

"Can I get a word in here?" Laurie asked sharply.

In the heat of the exchange, Jessica and Barclay had almost forgotten about Sanders.

"I think you're both off-base," Laurie said, standing to face them. "Jessica may have made some mistakes, George, but give her a break, she's a freshman around here. Sounds like she showed more guts than good sense, but she's also on to a hell of a story."

Then she turned her attention to Jessica. "And you, get off this sexist stuff. George may be from the old school, but he'd be as worried about any of the guys out there as he is about you."

Back to Barclay: "I can't believe you're serious about giving up the story, George. I think it would be a mistake we'd all live to regret. We've just got to find a way to protect Jessica."

"How do we do that?" Barclay demanded.

Jessica cut in, repeating Jack Tomlinson's idea that she and Janie move into a new apartment. "It might not eliminate the risk, but it would probably reduce it. Keep 'em off guard, anyway. But I'd need some help financing it."

"That's not a problem," Barclay said, "but understand, I want to eliminate the risk, not reduce it."

"I'm not sure that's possible, George," Jessica said. "Not entirely."

"I have changed my mind about one thing," Laurie added.

"What's that?" Jessica asked.

"I think we should consider going with the story as soon as we can, even if it's incomplete. It'll take some of the heat off you and put more pressure on the cops."

"Meecham will go crazy," Jessica warned.

"Too bad. Maybe it will help flush the women out," Laurie argued. "The cops don't seem to be getting anywhere as it is."

"Let me think about all of this," Barclay said. "But while I do, Jessica, write a draft of the story based on what we know now. See if it makes sense to go with it."

"What should we do about Brinkman's fingerprints?" Jessica asked. "The Fridley P.D. is pressing to get a name."

"Keep stalling them," Barclay said. "I need to think about that, too."

As Jessica left Barclay's office, she spotted Nina French waiting impatiently by her desk.

"I found out who lives in that house on Summit," Nina said. "A woman by the name of Patricia Sample. She's an associate professor of history at Macalester."

"Anything else?" Jessica asked.

"Not much. She's tenured. Been on the faculty seven or eight years. Came from out east somewhere. She's owned the house about four years. I think she's single and lives alone, but I've got to do some more checking on that."

"Good," Jessica said, taking notes, "although I don't know what it means."

"I've got a friend who's a Mac student," Nina said. "Works on the college paper. I've asked her to nose around a little more for me. Discreetly, of course."

"I hope so," Jessica said.

As Jessica sat at her computer, trying to write an early draft of her story for Barclay, it quickly became clear to her how few real facts she had gathered, how tenuous the story remained. Of course, she had the facts from each of the killings, but even those were sketchy, since she had yet to see the missing police files. And the ties between the killings, which in her own mind seemed so clear and convincing, paled when she saw them in print on the computer screen.

Jessica tried to put herself in the place of a viewer at home, watching the story unfold on the news. Would she be convinced that a serial killer—or killers—was on the loose? Probably not, she had to admit. Obvious questions: Why weren't the police confirming it? What, or who, was her source beyond her own imagination?

She could report on the attempt to kill Meecham, but what proof was there that it wasn't an accident? Prints on a brandy bottle? C'mon. She could report the threats against her and the efforts to squash the investigation, but again, what proof could she offer? The taped warning from Sarah was vague at best.

And what about Lowell Ingram? She knew there was a connection between his abductors and the killers, but again, there was no hard evidence. And if she mentioned the Craft Club, she would be laughed out of town, but not before being buried in lawsuits.

Making matters even worse, there was precious little video to go along with the few facts she had. Nina had been able to dig back into the tape files and find a few scenes from each of the murders, but they were rudimentary and revealed no apparent links.

Jessica sat back in her chair. It was hopeless. There was no way she could go with the story now. It wouldn't stand up, and she knew it. So would Laurie and Barclay. But would Brinkman? Would Sarah? What if they *thought* the story was going to air? Would it flush them out? Would they make a mistake?

Jessica turned off the computer, staring into space.

Sarah was surprised to hear Nancy Higgins's voice when she picked up the phone.

"Something strange is going on," Higgins said. "It may be nothing, but I thought you'd want to know about it."

"What's that?" Sarah asked.

"Two of my neighbors called. I hardly know them, but they both told me they'd gotten calls from some insurance investigator, asking for information about me. They thought I'd be interested."

Sarah pressed the phone tighter to her ear.

"I'm not buying any insurance," Higgins said. "Haven't for years. I don't know why—"

"What kind of things did he ask about?" Sarah interrupted.

"It wasn't a he . . . it was a she," Higgins replied. "Personal stuff, they told me. Age, marital status, how long I'd lived here, where I worked, that kind of thing."

Sarah said nothing for a moment, allowing the information to sink in. It didn't take long to figure out who the "investigator" might be.

"Did she give a name?" she asked.

"She may have, but the neighbors don't remember it."

"It's probably nothing," Sarah said, trying to keep her voice steady. "May just be some salesman trying to get a line on you. But you should stay alert and keep an eye out."

"For what?"

"For anything out of the ordinary. Anybody doing more nosing around."

"You don't think it's that reporter, do you? The one you talked about?" There was an uneasy edge to Higgins's voice. "How could she know about me?"

"She couldn't," Sarah lied. "Just keep on your toes . . . and stay in touch."

"Hey, Jess! You awake?"

Jeff Hilliard snapped his fingers, then slid his chair across the aisle, catching her still staring, almost unconsciously, at the blank computer screen.

Jessica was startled. "What's the problem?"

"That's what I'm wondering," he said. "A lot of us are."

"What are you talking about?"

He brought himself closer to her, his words no more than a whisper. "C'mon, don't be cute. Something's going on. You're almost never around here. Haven't covered a story in weeks. People are wondering what the hell you're up to."

"I've been busy, believe me."

"Some people think you're just fucking off."

"That's bull, and you know it!"

But did he? Despite her anger, Jessica knew Hilliard could be right. She had not missed the curious, sometimes hostile, glances she would receive from other reporters. She had been hired to help cover the daily news, a rookie who should be carrying her share of the burden. Yet here she was, involved in something most of the grunts in the newsroom knew nothing about. Contributing nothing to the news programs, as far as they could see. No wonder some of them might think she was fucking off.

Hilliard kept prodding. "Are you really on to something?"

"C'mon, Jeff . . ."

"I'm serious. Maybe I can help."

"Someday, maybe, Jeff, but not now."

"Sure," he scoffed, and turned away, clearly frustrated.

Jessica hated the secrecy but knew she had no choice. The more people who knew what she was doing, even within her own newsroom, the better the chance of a leak.

When Jessica arrived at the hospital that evening, she found Matt in a bad mood, shuffling down the corridor with the aid of a four-legged cane. Grimacing with every step.

"They say I have to get my exercise," he grumbled as she walked up to him.

"Don't complain," she chided. "You're not exactly running a marathon."

"Easy for you to say," he growled, "but you're not the god-damned cripple."

Jessica walked slowly beside him until they reached a small lounge at the end of the hall. Then she helped him into a chair and poured each of them a cup of coffee.

"What's new?" he asked.

"First, you," she replied. "Your voice sounds better."

"Better every day. Hardly hurts anymore, although I can't say the same for the rest of me."

He told her he was getting two to three hours of physical

therapy a day and that despite the pain, his broken bones and bruised body seemed to be on the mend. "They say I may be out of here in another week or so."

"Really? Then what?"

"Stay at home for a while longer, maybe a month or two. Then, who knows? At least I'll be able to smoke a cigar again."

Jessica remembered Barton Oates's warning that Meecham might never return to the police department, and it was evident that Matt had not forgotten the threat, either.

"Enough about my troubles," he said. "What about you?"

"It's getting tense, Matt. Brinkman's been following me. She came after me outside the hospital. Threatened me and my sister. It was pretty frightening."

"It's still hard for me to believe that Freda—"

"Her fingerprints are all over the brandy bottle, Matt. She set you up . . . sent you down that hill. Tried to kill you, for God's sake."

"You're serious? Her prints? Have you told Oates?"

Jessica shook her head. "Not yet."

"Doesn't leave much doubt, does it?" Matt said. "Still, there's no real proof—"

"I know that. That's what makes it so maddening. It would help if you could remember something. Anything."

"Sorry," he said, shaking his head. "Nothing's come back."

"Have you heard from Jenkins?"

"Talked to him yesterday. He says they haven't gotten anywhere. The cops in Bloomington and Brooklyn Park have pretty much given it up. They can't find any more links among the murders."

"That doesn't surprise me," Jessica said, telling him of her own doubts when she tried to write a draft of the story.

"So what's next?" he asked.

"I wish I knew. I've got some ideas, but I haven't thought them through yet. I am going to get Janie and me out of my apartment, but beyond that I don't know."

Matt sipped his coffee in silence for a moment, then looked

squarely at her. "I don't have to tell you how dangerous this could be, do I? I'm a big boy—a big, bad cop—and look what happened to me."

"I know, Matt, and I'm frightened."

FORTY-TWO

Jessica and Janie waited until late the next night before hurriedly and secretly moving their belongings to a furnished apartment in a high rise on the edge of downtown. The building manager thought their timing was somewhat strange but seemed satisfied with their explanation that both worked late.

Although they took only their clothes and a few personal possessions, Jack Tomlinson was there to help, mainly to keep watch and to make sure they weren't followed. As far as he could tell, they weren't.

No question, the new place was more secure. It came complete with enclosed underground parking, lobby guards on duty twenty-four hours a day, and security cameras everywhere, including the elevators. Their new phone was unlisted, the number known only to their family and to key people at each of their jobs. What's more, the building was connected by skyways to the rest of downtown, which meant they never needed to venture outside to get to and from work.

When Jack brought up the last load from the garage, he

also carried with him a chilled bottle of champagne, which he promptly uncorked and poured into three plastic glasses. Everything else was still in boxes.

"Drink up," he said grimly, raising the glass. "To your new home. For however long it lasts."

"So what happens now?" Janie wanted to know.

Jessica got up and walked to the big window, staring down at the now-almost-deserted city streets. "Go on as before, I guess," she said, turning to face her, "only be terribly careful coming and going. Make sure nobody's following you, and don't tell anyone where you live. Stick with other people. Don't get caught alone."

Janie stretched and yawned, pulling herself out of the chair. "As nice as this place is," she said, glancing around, "I can see where it's going to feel like a prison before long. I hope you can get this whole business over with soon."

With that, she wished them a quick good-night and retreated to her new bedroom.

"I guess I should go," Jack said, glancing at his watch and moving to get up. "It's late."

Jessica gently pulled him back down on the couch and held him close. "Please," she whispered, "I need you." Then she reached across him and snapped off the table lamp, leaving the room in semi-darkness.

He felt the pressure of her breasts moving slowly back and forth against his chest, her nipples tantalizingly firm. One of her hands lay on the inside of his thigh, also moving slightly, edging closer.

"You sure this is a good idea?" he murmured, his eyes on the hallway Janie had taken.

"Yes," she replied. Her hand was now beneath his light cotton shirt, softly tracing the taut lines of his ribs, then moving up, her fingers running through his hair, tugging lightly at it, curling it. He could feel his breath quicken. Hers, too.

Her tongue was on his lips, warm and moist, flickering.

Then at his ear, licking, sucking. Back to his mouth, inside, probing, their breath mixing, the faint taste of champagne.

She held him wonderfully captive, arms pinned, hovering over him, straddling him. Her breasts, now bare, were warm against his skin. Her nipples made small circles, hovering, then touching his. Then she moved her hips forward, spreading over his stomach. Warmth. Wetness.

"My God," he whispered.

Jessica looked down at him, his body sunken into the soft cushions, his face half-hidden in the shadows. He felt his belt loosen. Then a button. And the zipper. He was free.

Her finger and thumb made a circle, tracing the length of him. Barely touching, up and down. Slowly at first, then faster. Then slower again. Agonizing.

"Be careful," he whispered, eyes still tightly closed.

"Not to worry," she said.

Then it was there. Where had she gotten it? The soft sheath rolled down over him, cool at first, but warmed by her hand. He felt her body raise, then settle back, enfolding him. It had never been sweeter.

Later, Jessica walked with Jack to the elevator, holding his hand tightly, wishing he could stay the night but knowing it was impossible with Janie in the next bedroom. As they stood waiting in the hall, she suddenly asked him, "Do you still see Sarah now and then?"

He seemed surprised by the question. "In staff meetings, sometimes, but that's about all. Why?"

"Just wondering," she said.

"C'mon. What are you thinking now, Jess?"

The elevator arrived, and she stepped in with him. "I don't know how you'd do it," she said thoughtfully, "but when you do see her, it'd be nice if you could let it slip out that I was about to go on the air with some kind of major investigative report."

"Jesus, Jess . . ."

"You'd have to do it casually and carefully. Like it was nothing of importance, just a little insider gossip."

"You really think she'd believe it?" he asked.

She shrugged. "Maybe, maybe not, but I'd like to keep them on edge, force them to try something foolish."

The elevator doors opened at the garage level, and Jessica walked with him toward his car.

"Look, Jess," he said, "I've tried to avoid giving you any advice in all of this, but you must see that you're putting yourself in a really precarious position. What did you say George Barclay told you? That you've gone off the deep end? What you're talking about doing is damned dangerous. Dumb, too, if you ask me."

"What would you suggest, Jack?" she asked angrily.

He raised his hands in mock self-defense. "Don't get pissed. I'm just telling you what I think. I don't want to see you take those kinds of chances. . . ."

"It's my story . . . my life!" she snapped.

"That's true," he replied. "But don't I have some kind of say? Or was that whole thing upstairs a few minutes ago just some sort of prurient exercise?"

"Of course it wasn't," she said, softening. "You know that."

Jack climbed into his car and started the motor. "I'll see what I can do, Jess," he said through the open window, "but think about what I said, okay?"

She leaned down and kissed him but made no promises.

When she got to the station in the morning, Jessica immediately reported on the move to George Barclay. "It's a great place," she told him. "I appreciate your help paying for it."

"No problem," he said. "But I don't think it's enough."

"What do you mean?"

"I think you should stay out of sight for a while. Keep your nose inside. If you have to go out, use one of the station vans and take someone with you. I'll have the desk intercept your phone calls and take messages."

"You really think that's necessary?"

"I wouldn't suggest it if I didn't," he said. "I've also written this memo to the staff."

He handed her a sheet of paper.

Be advised that Jessica Mitchell is pursuing a story that could prove to be significant, but which may also involve certain risks to her and others involved. Please refer all calls to Jessica to the desk, and please do not discuss her activities or her whereabouts with anyone outside of the station. Your cooperation is appreciated. Barclay.

Jessica read the memo twice. "Thanks," she said. "Maybe that'll stop some of the dirty looks I've been getting around here."

"Don't worry about that," he said. "But where does it go from here?"

She shook her head. "We're still trying to check out a couple of the women. And that may take some time. There's one more thing you could do, though."

"What's that?" Barclay asked.

Jessica picked up his memo again. "You know the TV columnists, right?"

"Of course."

"It'd be nice if you could leak a little of this," she said, pointing to the memo. "That we're on the verge of breaking a major story, something that will shake up the town. You'd have to be vague, and indefinite about the timetable, but still plant the seed."

He was aghast. "Are you serious? After asking the staff to keep it quiet?"

"You could be properly outraged when it appears," Jessica said with a grin. "And start a fake search for the leak."

"You're out of your mind," he grumbled.

"We've got to pressure them into doing something. I don't see how else we're going to break the story."

"Pressure them into what?"

Jessica shrugged. "Making a mistake of some kind. Rattle

'em. Make them think we're closer to airing the story than we really are."

Barclay settled back in his chair and stared at her.

That's the way she left him, staring at her empty chair.

FORTY-THREE

Freda Brinkman didn't know what to make of it. For two days she had divided her free time between Jessica's apartment and the television station, watching in vain for some sign of her. Taking elaborate precautions to avoid being seen herself, always keeping at a safe distance, even renting a car Jessica would not recognize.

But it was all for naught. At first, she thought Jessica was simply lucky in slipping past her private stakeout, but then she began to wonder. Her car wasn't in the ramp, and when she would call Jessica's apartment, at all hours, she would hear only her recorded voice on the answering machine. Then she tried phoning the station, only to be told Jessica was off on a special assignment. But where?

The newsroom operator wouldn't say, politely asking if she would like to leave a message. Brinkman declined.

Maybe she just went home for a few days. Then why the apparent secrecy? If she's actually gone into hiding, Brinkman decided, she must have taken their warnings seriously. Which meant she was either giving up on the story or pursuing it much more carefully. Which? Brickman had a good guess.

On the evening of the second day, in frustration, Freda returned to the second floor of Dayton's, wandering past the women's-wear section where she had met Jessica's sister the week before. If she's still there, Brinkman thought, she might lead her to Jessica. And it should be safe, she told herself, since Janie had no way of knowing who she was.

Janie was there, working behind the same counter, almost hidden by a heavyset woman customer. As Brinkman walked past, Janie happened to glance up, spotting her over the customer's shoulder. There was an instant double take. Her mouth fell open, and she stared, stricken.

Brinkman froze for a moment herself, then hurried away. She does know.

Jessica was still at the station when she got the frantic call from Janie. "She was here, Jess. That Brinkman woman. Watching me. No kidding, I almost peed in my pants."

"Take it easy, Janie. Tell me about it."

"There's nothing more to tell. I looked up, and there she was, standing across the aisle, staring at me. Then she took off."

"Are you off work soon?" Jessica asked.

"In about ten minutes."

"Okay. Come directly over here. Stick to the skyways. You'll be fine."

After she hung up, Jessica leaned back in her chair, thinking. Why would Brinkman return to the store? Was she getting nervous? Was Jessica's strategy actually working?

For two days, Jessica had followed Barclay's instructions, keeping a low profile, rarely venturing outside, using the skyways to and from the apartment, working the newsroom phones in search of more information. Waiting and growing increasingly impatient.

So far nothing had appeared in the newspapers, and Jack said he had seen nothing of Sarah Andrews. The investigation seemed to be at a standstill. Then why did Brinkman show tonight?

Sarah had finished shampooing her hair and was still toweling it dry when she heard the security buzzer. Who the hell's that? she wondered. The late news was long since over, and she was exhausted, minutes away from tumbling into bed. The buzzer sounded again, insistently, as she pulled on a robe and walked from the bathroom to the living room.

"Yes?" she said into the phone.

"It's Freda. Buzz me in."

"Freda?" Sarah's voice betrayed her surprise.

Moments later, she was at the door, pushing past Sarah without a word. She walked quickly to the kitchen and pulled a beer from the refrigerator.

Sarah trailed after her, still rubbing her hair dry. "What's going on? I was ready for bed."

"I don't know," Brinkman said, straddling a kitchen chair, her arms resting on the back. "That's why I'm here."

"What are you talking about?" Sarah demanded.

"She's disappeared," Brinkman said.

"Jessica?"

"I've been trying to spot her for two days. She's nowhere. Something's happening. I think they're hiding her." Brinkman went on to explain the fruitless surveillance, ending with her visual encounter with Jessica's sister. "The girl obviously knows who I am. She freaked out."

Sarah eyed her suspiciously. "What's her sister got to do with this? How would she know you?"

Brinkman brushed aside the question. "That's not important."

"Yes, it is," Sarah snapped. "What aren't you telling me?"

"I spoke to her, okay," Freda admitted. "Last week. At the store. She didn't know who I was. At least she didn't then. It was just idle conversation while I pretended to be shopping. I thought she might be useful."

"Useful? For what?"

"To put pressure on, a little leverage on our friend Jessica. But she must have told her about me, described me, because tonight I scared the shit out of her."

"Jesus, Freda, do you know what you're doing?"

"Trying to solve our problem, that's all."

"You're crazy!" Sarah said. "First it's Meecham, then Jessica. And now her sister? This is madness."

"You want to sit back and watch yourself and the others go to prison?" Brinkman demanded.

"Don't be ridiculous," Sarah said. "Nobody can prove anything. I've told you that. They may know about the murders, but so what? They may know about the Craft Club, but there's no proof, nothing to connect us to anything but a group of women who supposedly get together to stitch and knit."

"You're kidding yourself, Sarah. I'm a cop, I know how other cops think. If this thing ever gets out, they won't let go of it, not with somebody like Jessica and then the rest of the media egging them on. I can hear it now. 'Serial killers on the loose! Sexual predators biting the dust! Cops ignore a five-year trail of blood!' It'll be a fucking sensation, and you know it!"

"She has no story," Sarah insisted.

"Oh, yeah? You sure as hell remember that judge a couple of years ago. The one who was screwing kids. They crucified him on the air, for Christ's sake. And look at their story on Ingram. Caused a goddamned uproar. They don't give a shit what they do."

"You're seeing phantoms," Sarah said. "I want no part of it."

"You are part of it. You and the others."

"I've never touched anybody," Sarah said.

Brinkman scoffed. "Tell that to a judge. You know the law; you're as guilty as any of us."

"I didn't kill Edward Hill," Sarah shouted. "I wasn't even there."

"Who lured poor Eddie to us with the phone calls?" Brinkman demanded. "Who made him so angry with your taunts that he walked right into our arms? You might as well have put the knife in him, and you know it."

Sarah was desperate. "And you know that Jessica Mitchell is not Edward Hill," she cried.

"She can put us in jail as quick as any judge. And she will, if we let her."

Sensing that more argument was futile, Sarah said, "I don't want to know anything. Understand that? Nothing. I can't stop you from what you're going to do, but you're on your own."

"Too late, Sarah. If I go down, you're all going down with me."

When Jessica picked up the *Star-Tribune* the next morning, she again flipped to the entertainment section, looking for Sam Riley's television column. She found it at the bottom of the page and quickly skimmed it. Most of the article was devoted to David Letterman's preparations for his new late-night show on CBS, but at the end, under "Odds & Ends," was what she'd been waiting for.

Inside sources at Channel 7 tell us the station is preparing what could be a major investigative scoop. Everything is hush-hush, but the sources say the crime series could knock our socks off. Take that with a grain of salt, but I'm told there's genuine excitement, and concern, in the newsroom. The reporter doing the story is said to be in hiding, working secretly. No word on exactly when this blockbuster may hit the air. . . .

Thataway, George! she thought. Barclay had done the job. The tone was perfect. Enticing. Not too much information, but enough to stimulate the imagination and get people talking. And, she hoped, to make other people nervous.

* * *

It was not until later in the morning that Sarah saw the same newspaper item, and then only when she received an angry call from Freda Brinkman. "What did I tell you?" Brinkman said. "I knew they wouldn't give it up."

Sarah scanned the paragraph three times, trying to read between the lines. "I still can't believe it," she said. "What is she going to report? She has no facts."

"How can you be so sure?" Brinkman demanded. "Maybe she knows more than we think she knows. Maybe somebody in the Club is talking."

"What? That's ridiculous."

"Is it?" Brinkman asked. "One of them could be doing it anonymously. You've heard them. They don't like what I'm doing, either."

"You are insane, Freda. Forget it."

After she hung up, Sarah picked up the newspaper and set out in search of Jack Tomlinson. She finally found him in the law library, sitting alone, surrounded by a stack of thick legal books.

"Got a minute?" she asked as she sat down across from him.

"I guess so," he replied, putting a marker in the open volume in front of him.

Sarah pushed the paper toward him and pointed to the television column. "Have you seen this?"

He shook his head. "I've been stuck in here since six this morning."

He took the paper, his eyes following her pointed finger. "So?" he said after reading the paragraph, hiding his surprise.

"Know anything about it?" she asked.

He gave himself a moment to think. Careful, he thought. Play it coy. "Not really," he finally said. "Why?"

"Because if it's true, it could make the cops and this department look like assholes. They're talking about a major investigative report on crime, and I don't know what the hell they're talking about."

"Why are you asking me?" he said innocently.

"Don't be cute," she snickered.

"You mean Jessica? I've hardly seen her. She doesn't have the time, she says. I know she's wrapped up in something, and they're pressing her to get it on the air. But that's it."

"She hasn't told you anything about it? The details, I mean."

"I told you last time, we don't talk business. It's off-limits."

Sarah sat back in the chair, looking past him. Jack waited for a moment, then went back to his book.

To Jessica, it seemed that all eyes were fixed on her as she walked across the newsroom. There were furtive glances, the expressions a mixture of apology or sympathy, as though silently seeking her forgiveness for whichever asshole in the newsroom was responsible for the leak. She had trouble keeping a straight face.

Before she could sit down, Jeff Hilliard pushed his chair across the aisle. "It wasn't me, Jess, believe me."

"I know that, Jeff," she said.

"Barclay's already chewed our ass," he said. "Got up in front of the whole newsroom. Told us someone was not only jeopardizing the investigation but your safety. He was really pissed."

Good for George, she thought. He's following the script.

"Any idea who it could have been?" she asked, feigning a touch of anger in her voice.

Hilliard shook his head. "Anyone, I suppose. Barclay's memo was posted all over the newsroom."

Jessica sat down and pulled her files out of the desk drawer, but Hilliard didn't move. "I'm sorry about pulling your chain the other day," he said contritely. "You should have told me."

"I couldn't. I still can't."

"It goes back to that Hill murder, doesn't it?" he pressed.

"Jeff, please!"

"Okay," he said. "But remember, I'm here if you need me."

In the next ten minutes, Bill Kendrick and two or three others stopped by, each expressing anger at the leak and offering comfort and support. Jessica had begun to feel guilt over the success of the ruse but quickly decided if it worked that well in the newsroom, it might also have the desired effect with Brinkman and her friends.

A moment later, Jack Tomlinson called. "Sarah just left," he whispered. "She came looking for me, pumping me about the piece in the paper."

"What did you tell her?" Jessica asked.

Tomlinson repeated his conversation with Sarah. "I tried to be cool," he said, "but she caught me by surprise. I hope I did okay."

"Sounds like you did fine," Jessica said. "How did *she* seem?"

There was a pause at the other end of the line. "Worried, I guess, but certainly not desperate or panicked. Said a TV crime exposé could make the cops and the department look like assholes."

Jessica thanked him and then went in search of Barclay. She found him at the assignment desk with Laurie, and they all walked back to his office together, Barclay closing the door behind them.

"I just want you to know that I feel like shit," he said. "I don't like lying to the newspapers or to my own newsroom."

"Don't, George," Jessica protested. "It was perfect. And it's already working."

"What do you mean?" Laurie asked.

She told them of Sarah's visit with Jack Tomlinson. "You can bet that she and Brinkman have already talked. They're worried, and that's what we wanted."

Barclay sat down heavily in his chair. "What's next?" he asked.

"Keep the pressure on," Jessica said. "Keep them on edge."

"How?" Laurie asked.

"I've got a couple of ideas," Jessica said.

* * *

Nina French was waiting by her desk when Jessica returned from Barclay's office. "Sorry about the leak," she said. "I can't imagine anyone in the newsroom doing that. It's horrible."

"Don't worry about it," Jessica said. "It may actually help."

Nina gave her a puzzled look but then continued. "I heard from my friend at Macalester," she said. "The one who works on the college paper."

"I remember," Jessica replied.

"She's been poking around, like I asked her to. Trying to find out more about the professor, Patricia Sample."

"And?"

"She's actually doing a story on the woman, part of a faculty-profile series that the paper does every issue. Nice lady, my friend says. Good teacher, respected by the students and by the other faculty in her department. But stays to herself, doesn't mix much on campus, lives alone in that house on Summit."

Jessica tried to hide her impatience, but Nina noticed it immediately. "Easy, Jess. I'm coming to the interesting part."

"Sorry," Jessica said.

"She's single. Divorced long before she came to Mac. She raised a daughter, a teenager who died in New York a few years ago."

"Died?" Jessica moved to the edge of her chair.

"Drug overdose. Found her in a hotel, just off Times Square. She was a runaway, apparently had been hooking in New York. Wasn't even twenty when she died."

"Sample told your friend all of this?"

"Not Sample. Others did. They think that's why she's such a loner. Never has gotten over the shock of it."

Jessica sat back in her chair, suddenly recalling her lakeside conversation with Matt Meecham. What had he told her about one of the dead predators? That he ran a prostitution ring, recruiting and shipping young Minnesota runaways to New York to work the streets.

Of course. It had to be. Sample's daughter must have been one of them.

Nina was watching her carefully. "Does that mean anything?" she asked.

"More than you know," Jessica said. "Please give my thanks to your friend at the paper. She did a hell of a job."

"What's next?" Nina asked.

"I think it's time to turn up the heat a little more," she said, and reached for the phone.

FORTY-FOUR

Jessica's hand trembled slightly as she pushed the buttons on the phone.

"Tot Care Day Care." A woman's voice. A chorus of children in the background.

"Teresa Johnson, please," Jessica said.

"Speaking."

"Ms. Johnson, this is Jessica Mitchell. I'm a reporter at Channel Seven . . ."

The sharp gasp at the other end was clearly audible. Then a clank, as if the phone might have fallen.

"Ms. Johnson? Are you there?"

A long silence, except for the babble of the children. Then: "What do you want?"

"Ms. Johnson, I'm calling to ask you about a group called the Craft Club. I was wondering—"

The line went dead in her ear. Jessica slowly replaced the receiver. She was not surprised; she had expected that response. In fact, she wasn't sure what she would have said next if the woman hadn't hung up.

But she had achieved her goal. She quickly punched the next number, giving Teresa no time to alert the other women.

This time, a man answered. "Foster and Fine, Public Accountants," he said. "May I help you?"

"Nancy Higgins, please," Jessica said politely.

"Sorry, she's not here at the moment. May I take a message?"

Jessica hesitated, then decided. No need to speak to the woman in person. "My name is Jessica Mitchell. Would you tell Ms. Higgins that I'm calling about the Craft Club."

"The what?" the man asked.

"The Craft Club," Jessica repeated. "She'll understand."

Then she gave him her number and hung up.

Two down and one to go, she thought. But she decided against calling Patricia Sample. Coming so soon after Sample's college-newspaper interview, contacting the professor could cause trouble for Nina's friend. Besides, Sample would get the message from the others soon enough, anyway. If they didn't know before, they would know now that the Craft Club was no longer a secret haven.

Jessica kept her head low, hidden beneath the darkened windows of the van, as Kendrick pulled out of the station garage and headed toward the hospital.

"Just drop me off at the emergency-room entrance," she said, slowly raising her head to look over the seat and out the rear window. "I'll give you a call after I've seen Matt."

Kendrick nodded, his eyes on the rearview mirror. "You sure you know what you're doing?"

"No," she said, sighing. "I wish I did."

When Kendrick was sure they'd not been followed, he pulled the van into the hospital's ER driveway. "I'll just cruise around," he said. "Give me a call on the car phone when you want to be picked up."

Jessica nodded and jumped out, hurrying inside to one of the back elevators. She found Matt sitting on the edge of his bed, in street clothes, a small suitcase at his feet.

"What's going on?" she asked, standing in the doorway.

"I'm going home," he said. "As soon as the cab gets here."

"No kidding," she said. "You're sure you're ready?"

"They tell me I am, although my body doesn't necessarily agree. You know hospitals. If you're not going to die, they don't want you here."

Jessica walked into the room and sat next to him, quickly updating him on everything that had happened.

"I saw the paper," he said. "So did Jenkins and the other cops. They called me. They're wondering what's going on."

"I thought it might get their attention," Jessica said. "But I didn't know what else to do, Matt. Things were going nowhere."

"Call Jenkins," Meecham said. "Tell him what you've told me. You can't go alone on this, Jessica. He'll help; I know he will."

"What about you?" she asked. "You're hardly in shape to protect yourself."

"Don't worry about me," Meecham said. "I won't get caught twice, believe me."

A nurse appeared at the door with a wheelchair. "Time to go," she said. "Your cab's downstairs."

Meecham got up and shuffled toward the door. "I can walk, for Christ's sake."

"Afraid not," the nurse said. "You ride. Hospital policy."

As he got into the wheelchair, he looked back at Jessica. "Call Jenkins," he ordered. "And get me those goddamned cats back."

Then he started to unwrap a cigar, smiling as the nurse wheeled him down the hallway.

Sarah spent most of the afternoon in court, not returning to her office until late in the day. When she finally arrived, Molly, the receptionist, gave her a handful of messages.

"I don't know what's going on," Molly said, "but the same two women have been calling you all afternoon. They left their names. Didn't say why they had called. They seemed very excited. Upset, really."

Sarah took the stack of messages and thumbed through them, seeing the familiar Craft Club names. She retreated to her office and shut the door. What's happening? Could the item in the newspaper cause this kind of panic? Doubtful. What then?

She picked up the phone and called Teresa Johnson. "What's the problem?" she asked.

Teresa's words were so rushed that she had difficulty understanding them. But the name Jessica Mitchell came through loud and clear. "Hold on, Teresa. Slow down. Start from the beginning."

"She called, Sarah. Asked for me by name. Wanted to talk to me about the Craft Club. What's happening, Sarah? How would she know I have anything to do with the Craft Club? How does she even know about the Craft Club?"

Before Sarah could respond, Teresa rattled on. "And I wasn't the only one! She called Nancy, too. Left a message for her."

"Did you talk to her?"

"Of course not. I hung up."

"What about Pat Sample?" Sarah asked. "Did she get a call?"

"Not that I know of," Teresa said. "We can't get hold of her."

"That's strange, isn't it?" Sarah mused aloud, thinking back to Brinkman's suspicions that one of the group might be talking. "Have you or Nancy talked to Freda?"

"No way," Teresa said. "I want nothing to do with her."

Sarah desperately craved a few minutes to think, but Teresa pressed on. "How does this Jessica know about the Craft Club?"

Sarah made a quick decision. She would lie. She had neither the time nor the energy to explain how Jessica knew what she knew. If the explanation had to come, it would have to be later.

"I don't know, Teresa. She must have her ways. But don't

panic. She has no proof of anything, and she won't have if we keep our wits about us. Stay calm, and no matter what happens, don't say anything to anybody. You hear that? It's crucial. Say nothing to no one, ever. And get that word to the others."

"What about Freda?" Teresa asked. "Is *she* staying calm?"

"Don't worry about Freda," Sarah said. "I'll handle her."

As she spoke, the words sounded hollow, unconvincing, even to her.

Kim Hawkins felt miserable and utterly alone. The nearly bare apartment had become her solitary fortress. She rarely ventured outside except to go to work and to shop for necessary staples. Since Sarah had moved out, time passed ever so slowly, especially the nights and weekends, when she was without even the distractions of her job.

She had heard nothing further from Sarah and had made no effort to contact her. She was living in a void, with no real friends and only her fears for company. The nightmares and unanswered questions continued to haunt her, and her determination to break free, to make a new life, remained as empty as the rooms around her.

Each morning, she pledged that day would be different, that she would seek out new friendships, force herself to become active, put the past behind her. But every evening, she would return to wander the silent apartment, admitting failure.

She felt occasional flashes of anger at herself for her own helplessness, at Sarah for her duplicity, and at Jessica for abandoning her, but most of all she felt an overwhelming sense of lethargy from which she had neither the strength nor the will to emerge. She had been tempted to call Jessica, to find out what was happening, but even that small task seemed beyond her. Besides, she was afraid to know.

* * *

It took Matt several minutes to answer the door, and when he appeared, he wore the same robe he had used at the hospital. And he leaned on the same four-footed cane. Jessica and Jack waited on the step, each carrying one of Meecham's cats.

"C'mon in," Matt said, shuffling backward to give them room to get through the door.

Jessica quickly made introductions. "We can only stay a minute," she said. "But I wanted you to meet Jack and knew you would want these two back as soon as possible."

"You've probably spoiled the shit out of them," Meecham said as he put his cane aside and took one of the cats in his arm, snuggling it against his cheek. Then he put it down and did the same with the second. Both scampered off as soon as they hit the floor, in search of food or the litter box or both.

"I've only got coffee," he said, "or iced tea. But you're welcome to either."

They followed him through the house and into the kitchen. Jessica made him sit while she retrieved the iced tea from the refrigerator and poured three glasses.

"Jessica's told me about you," Meecham said to Jack. "I hope you're taking good care of her."

Jack laughed. "I'm trying, but she's not exactly a woman who likes to be taken care of."

Meecham grunted agreement.

"How does it feel to be home?" Jessica asked.

"Great," he said. "But I'm still trying to get used to it."

Matt got up and walked to the pantry door, opening it wide. "See that window," he said, pointing. "I always leave it partway open. Fresh air for the cats. It was closed when I got here."

Jessica looked over his shoulder. "Maybe the neighbor who had your key shut it," she said.

"The screen outside is slit. It wasn't that way before."

"They were waiting for you here?"

He nodded. "They must have been, although I still don't remember anything after the cribbage game."

"You're sure you're going to be okay now?" Jessica asked.

He walked slowly to the other end of the kitchen, pulling a

rifle from behind the door. "I've got this," he said, holding it up. "I plan to sleep with it, too."

He put the rifle back and returned to his chair. "I talked to the office to let them know I was back home. Guess what?"

"What?" Jessica asked.

"Freda Brinkman's taken a personal leave of absence. Said she doesn't know how long she'll be gone. Maybe a few days, maybe more. A sickness in the family, she told them."

Jessica closed her eyes and took a deep breath.

"Maybe you ought to be carrying a rifle, too," Meecham said.

FORTY-FIVE

Jack Tomlinson had no sooner walked into his office than Lionel Hamilton, the county attorney, was at his door.

"Got a minute, Jack?"

Tomlinson froze. Hamilton rarely spoke to him, and then only in staff meetings or some other group setting. Hamilton had made it clear that he had no time to spare for junior members of the department. And as far as Jack could remember, he had never set foot in his office before.

"Of course," Jack said, recovering but still fumbling with his briefcase.

"Come along," Hamilton said.

"Should I bring anything?" Jack asked.

"Just your body."

Jack followed him down the hallway, his mind whirling. What the hell was this about?

Hamilton's office was really more of a suite, occupying a full corner of the floor. Fully three times the size of any other office, it had floor-to-ceiling windows on two sides overlooking downtown and a huge teak desk at its center. Large pictures of Hamilton with George Bush, Ronald Reagan, and Richard Nixon, all smiling and shaking hands, dominated another wall. One of the chairs in front of the desk was already occupied by a man Jack had never seen before. A man in uniform.

"This is Deputy Chief Barton Oates," Hamilton said as the policeman stood and shook hands. "He has a problem, I'm afraid."

Jack remained standing until the other two sat down, then slipped into the chair next to Oates. He knew now, without asking, what the problem was. But he feigned ignorance. "So how can I help?" he said.

Hamilton leaned forward, his heavy glasses slipping down on his nose. "The chief here says you brought a set of fingerprints to the Fridley P.D., prints that happened to match some of those found on a brandy bottle in Matt Meecham's wrecked car. He'd like to know whose prints they are. So would the Fridley police."

Jack swallowed hard and swore to himself. His contact in Fridley had promised to keep a lid on things, but the lid had obviously popped off.

Goddamn it, Jessica! Now what do I do?

Both men stared at him as he struggled for a response. Talk about a rock and a hard place. Lie and risk being found out and fired. Tell the truth and face embarrassing questions about how he had gotten the prints and why he had taken them to Fridley. And, yes, probably be fired, too.

"I don't feel free to answer that question," he finally said.

"Really?" Hamilton replied. "Why is that?"

"I'd be breaking a confidence," Jack replied with more bravado than he felt.

"I'm not sure I understand," Hamilton said. "Breaking the confidence of someone in this office?"

"No."

"In the police department?"

"No."

The county attorney leaned back, perplexed. "You did take the prints to the Fridley P.D., didn't you?"

Jack nodded.

"Where did you get them?" Hamilton was now bearing down.

"From the files," Jack said.

"Which files?"

Tomlinson took a deep breath. "I'd rather not say."

Hamilton suddenly rose from behind the desk and whipped off his glasses. His face was filled with fury. "You damn well better say!" he said. "You work for me. I'm getting tired of this crap!"

Jack was staggered by the outburst but did not shrink back.

"Hold on, hold on," Oates said, raising his hands in a plea for calm. "Let's not get all excited here."

Hamilton sat back in his chair but kept his eyes on Jack.

"Let me ask you this, Jack," Oates said in a conciliatory tone. "Does this have anything to do with Matt's so-called secret investigation?"

Jack nodded.

"What investigation?" Hamilton demanded.

Oates quickly explained what little he knew about the case to the county attorney, then turned back to Tomlinson. "Let me guess. You got the prints for that reporter. Jessica whatever. Matt's friend. Am I right? Is it her confidence you'd be breaking?"

Jack shrugged, unable to lie but unwilling to speak.

"You're working with some reporter without my knowledge or permission?" Hamilton demanded.

Oates held up his hands again. "Whose prints were they, Jack? We'll find out sooner or later, and if this investigation of Matt's is so important, the sooner the better, I'd say."

Jack studied him, knowing he was probably right on both counts. "You won't like the answer," he finally said.

"Try me," Oates replied.

"The prints belong to your lieutenant Freda Brinkman."

The color drained from Oates's face, and he sank back into the chair. "You're shitting me."

"Afraid not. The prints came right out of her personnel file."

Before either man could respond, Tomlinson stood, pulling his body erect. "You've got your answer. I won't say anything more except this. I did take the prints as a favor for Jessica, but in a way, I was taking them for Matt Meecham. I have no real proof besides the prints, but I believe it was Brinkman who set up Matt's accident. For reasons I cannot and will not talk about."

Then he turned to face Hamilton directly. "I wouldn't have done what I did if I hadn't believed Jessica Mitchell was on to something important, something Matt Meecham also believed was important."

Then he leaned across the desk, his face only inches from Hamilton's. "Do what you want to me, but never, ever, talk to me like that again. I'll smash in your goddamn face."

With that he whirled and stalked out the door, slamming it behind him. Hamilton and Oates sat quietly, absorbing his anger and what they'd learned.

"What are you going to do now?" Hamilton finally asked the chief. "Sounds like you'd better talk to Brinkman."

"I'm not sure I can," Oates replied.

"Why's that?"

"She's gone, on personal leave. I don't know where she is."

"Son of a bitch," Hamilton muttered.

From her desk, Sarah had seen Hamilton and Tomlinson walk hurriedly past her office, and a few minutes later, she watched as Jack, red-faced and agitated, rushed back toward his own office. Curious, she waited a few minutes before wandering out into the reception area, in time to see Deputy Chief Oates walk out.

"What's going on?" she asked Molly, casually.

The receptionist shrugged. "Don't ask me. Some kind of

blowup in Hamilton's office. You could hear them from out here."

"With Jack and the chief?"

"I guess so. Sounded pretty intense for a while."

Sarah lingered at the reception desk until Molly was busy on the phone, then strode to Hamilton's office and stuck her head in the door. He was standing by the big window, staring out.

She rapped lightly on the doorjamb. "Got a minute, Lionel?"

He turned quickly, eyes narrowed, jaws clenched, relaxing slightly when he saw it was her. "What do you need, Sarah?"

"I just saw Jack Tomlinson tear down the hallway, looking upset and angry."

"He should be. I'm going to fire his ass!"

"What?" Sarah quickly stepped into the office and closed the door behind her. "What did he do?"

"He violated departmental policy," Hamilton replied vaguely.

"C'mon, Lionel. Jack and I are pretty good friends," she lied, "and I know a straight arrow when I see one. I can't picture him getting into that kind of trouble."

Hamilton only stared at her.

"Anything I can do to help?" she offered.

Hamilton shook his head. "Too late for that, I'm afraid."

Although Sarah and her boss were both strong personalities who often fought over issues within the department, like the case of Lowell Ingram, they had also developed a mutual respect.

"C'mon, Lionel," she said, pressing. "What'd he do?"

Hamilton slumped into his chair. "He took something from the police files that he had no right to take, then gave it to a reporter, all without my knowledge or authorization. It was a clear-cut violation of our rules, and he knows it!"

"The police files?" Sarah repeated, stepping up to his desk.

"I can't tell you any more," Hamilton said. "It's something I have to deal with."

He didn't need to say more; Sarah quickly realized whose police file it must be.

"Who was the reporter?" she asked.

When he hesitated, she said, "Let me guess. Jessica Mitchell."

Hamilton's head snapped up. "How'd you know that?"

"I know the woman. I suspect she may have taken advantage of Jack. I think he's hot for her."

"That's no excuse," he replied.

"Maybe not," she said. "But why don't you give it some time. Jack's a good lawyer, and we're not exactly overrun with those around here."

Hamilton made no response and swung his chair around, his back to her, facing the window. She knew it was time to go.

"Thanks for coming, Jerry," Jessica said as she led Jeremiah Jenkins into a small conference room off the newsroom. "Sorry to bring you all the way from St. Paul."

"No problem," he said, "but why all the secrecy? Getting in to see you is like getting into Fort Knox."

"Sorry about that, too," she said, laughing as they both sat down at a small table. "My boss insists on precautions."

He gave her a puzzled look but said nothing more.

"Matt basically ordered me to call you," she said. "He's home but still too lame. He says you'd be willing to help."

"In what way?"

She patiently explained everything that had happened since they had last spoken. It took a half hour, interrupted several times by Jenkins's questions.

"So basically," Jessica concluded, "we know who the women are and how they're organized. We know their backgrounds, except for one. We know who the victims are and what they did. But we still have no real proof, not enough to go on the air with."

"To say nothing of going into court," Jenkins said with a hint of exasperation. "Nothing's really changed, has it?"

"Except that I think we're making them nervous enough

that they may make a mistake. They may think we're closer than we really are, and that may force their hand in some way."

"You think they may come after you, is that it?"

"If they're desperate enough, they might. Especially Brinkman. I think she's truly crazy."

"Doesn't that worry you?"

"Of course, but we're not taking any chances," she said, explaining the safeguards they had arranged.

"So what do you want from me?" he asked.

"Two things, I guess. One, be available in case there's any kind of trouble. And two, try to get a handle on Nancy Higgins. She's the one member of the club we don't know much about."

Jessica quickly told him what they did know about Higgins, including where she lived and worked. "If she's like the others, she's had some kind of sexual trauma in her past. I'd like to know what it is or was."

Jenkins looked away, as though searching his memory. "For some reason," he said, "that name's familiar. I can't place it now, but I'll do some checking." Then he handed her a card. "This has all of my numbers on it. Work, home, car, beeper. If you need me in a hurry, you'll be able to get me at one of these."

Jenkins had no sooner left than Jessica was handed a message to call Jack Tomlinson. He answered on the first ring, and it was immediately clear to her that something was terribly wrong.

"Guess what, Jessica?" he snapped. "I think I'm about to get fired because of those fucking fingerprints."

Jessica was stunned by the anger in his voice. "What are you talking about?" she demanded.

"Hamilton just raked me over the coals real good. Made me tell him and that deputy chief, Oates, whose prints they were. I had no choice; they had me in a corner."

"God, I'm sorry," Jessica said.

"That doesn't help much now, does it," he replied. "I told you that you had me hanging out on a limb."

Jessica clung to the phone, unable to speak.

"Hamilton all but canned me on the spot," he continued. "I expect I'll get the official notice any minute. He was really pissed."

Jessica could picture Jack's legal career crumbling, lying in shambles at her feet. "Is there anything I can do?" she asked, her voice back but trembling.

"How about helping me update my resumé," he said, more calmly now.

Jessica took a deep breath, then asked, "How did they react when you told them the fingerprints were Brinkman's?"

"With shock, I'd say. At least Oates did. Hamilton didn't know anything—"

At that moment, he abruptly stopped speaking and covered the mouthpiece of the phone. She could hear him speaking to someone but could not make out the words.

Then his voice again, full volume: "I've got to go. I'll talk to you later."

"Wait, Jack! Who's there? Hamilton?"

"Guess again," he said.

Sarah was standing in the doorway as Jack put down the phone. A small smile played at the edge of her lips. "Talking to your sweety, were you?" she asked.

"What do you want, Sarah?" he replied tiredly.

She closed the door and leaned back against it. "You've not been totally honest with me, have you, Jack?"

"About what?"

"I think you know. I just left Hamilton's office."

Jack got up and walked to the door, trying to open it against the weight of her body. "Out, Sarah!"

Her smile broadened. "Come now, Jack. Treat me nice. I just tried to save your job."

"Why's that?" he asked, stepping back.

"Because I think you're an innocent pawn in all of this. I think Jessica's got you under some kind of spell."

Jack laughed. "Give me a break, Sarah. I'm a big boy. I know what I'm doing."

"Do you really?" she said. "Did you know she could get you fired?"

Refusing to answer, he again tried to force open the door, but she would not be moved. "This is ridiculous," he said, giving it up and returning to his desk.

"Whose files did you take? Freda Brinkman's?"

"I don't have time for this. Please leave."

Sarah stepped closer to the desk, leaning in. "Hamilton listens to me, Jack. Respects me. I could do you some good, maybe change his mind."

"At what price, Sarah?"

"A pittance. Just a little information, that's all."

Jack leaned back in his chair and put his feet on the desk. "Sarah, you're right. I may be looking for a new job. But from what I know and from what I expect the public will know shortly, you and your friends will have much bigger worries than that." He took a deep breath. "Now get the hell out of my office!"

For the first time since he had known her, Jack thought he saw a flicker of uncertainty in Sarah's eyes. Even a touch of fear.

FORTY-SIX

Kim Hawkins walked from her apartment to the bus, taking her time, knowing that she was early and that the bus would probably be late. It was the same every morning.

Still sluggish from another restless night, she took some comfort from the blessedly cool and fresh air. Rain during the night had washed away the heat and humidity from the atmosphere and the grime from the streets. The skies had cleared before daybreak, leaving a glistening morning that even the birds seemed to enjoy. Kim knew that the cardinal in a big elm overhead was singing especially for her.

She was still a half block from the bus stop when a blue Pontiac pulled alongside her, keeping pace. She stooped to see who was inside the car at the same time the right front window was lowered automatically.

Freda Brinkman leaned across the seat. "Morning, Kim," she said as the car slowed to a stop. "Give you a lift?"

Kim was at first startled to see her, then frightened, fighting an immediate instinct to flee. But she caught herself. Why worry? It was broad daylight on a public street.

"No, thanks," she said hesitantly, "I'll wait for the bus. It'll be along in a few minutes."

As she started to walk on, Brinkman called after her. "Sarah wants to talk to you, Kim. She asked me to pick you up and bring you along. She says it's important."

Kim paused as the Pontiac pulled alongside her again. "Then why didn't she call me?" she demanded.

Brinkman shrugged. "This just came up. She's in trial, and her car's in the garage, getting fixed. Brakes almost went out on her."

This woman must think I'm crazy or dumb or both, Kim thought, although in the back of her mind she had always hoped that Sarah might someday want to talk, to explain all of this away. But she was not about to put her trust in Freda Brinkman.

"I don't believe you," Kim said angrily, "not after everything that's happened. Leave me alone." Then she hurried away again.

"Suit yourself" was the last thing she heard Brinkman say as the Pontiac moved past her.

Twenty seconds later, another car passed Kim, unnoticed by her or by Freda Brinkman, whose car was now a block away, picking up speed. Lowell Ingram, hunched low in his run-down old Plymouth, gave Kim a quick glance as he sped by, trying to close the distance to Brinkman's car. He recognized her as Sarah's ex-roommate, the one he had seen at the apartment after Sarah moved out. And although he had been four car lengths back when Brinkman spoke to her, it was clear, even from that distance, that the exchange had not been friendly.

Ingram had been following Brinkman as often as he could since witnessing her angry confrontation with Jessica at the hospital. His surveillance since that day seemed to verify that something serious was going on between the two.

He had seen Brinkman stake out the station and Jessica's old apartment for hours on end, at all hours of the day and night, using what he discovered was a rental car. She had followed the station's vans in apparent hopes of spotting Jessica. But for the life of him, he couldn't figure out what the hell it was all about.

Ingram was proud that he had so far escaped Brinkman's notice. Following her had become a game to him, but one driven by an unrelenting desire for retribution. He would never forget what Brinkman and Sarah had done to him, and he continued to watch and wait for a chance to retaliate.

There had been opportunities in the past week, when he had been watching Brinkman, alone, late at night, on her stakeouts. But he'd held back, partially out of fear, he had to admit, but also because he'd become intrigued with her pursuit of Jessica and where it all might be leading.

With an unlisted number, the phone seldom rang at Jessica's new apartment. So when it did, just as she and Janie were finishing breakfast, they both jumped. After looking at one another, Janie finally answered, then motioned for Jessica.

It was Jerry Jenkins, who got quickly to the point of his call. "Now I know why the name Nancy Higgins sounded familiar," he said. "I should have remembered."

"What are you talking about?"

"I went back to Eduardo's file."

"Yes?"

"And there it was. Nancy Higgins was one of his victims."

"You've got to be kidding!"

"Not once but twice. He got caught the first time, sent up for two years but got out after one. A day later, he came back and raped her again. He would have killed her if a neighbor hadn't heard her screams and pounded on the door. He got away that time, slipped out a window and ran."

"You never found him?" Jessica asked.

"Sure. You know when. A year or so later, split apart on those railroad tracks."

"It's hard to believe," she said, "but it certainly makes sense. Did you question Higgins about the murder?"

"C'mon, Jessica, give us some credit. I didn't personally talk to her, which is why I didn't remember her name right off, but one of the other cops did. According to the notes in the file, she had an airtight alibi. Was at a resort up north with a couple of other women."

"What women?" she demanded.

"Those names aren't in this file," he said, "but I'll talk to Dick McGuire, the detective who did the interview. He should have them somewhere."

"Let me give you some names," Jessica said, listing off the other members of the Craft Club. "Ten to one they're her alibi."

"We'll see," he said. "I'll let you know."

In his office at the Government Center, Jack Tomlinson sat behind his closed door, staring at a memo he had just received from Lionel Hamilton. Cutting through all of the bureaucratic bullshit and official legalese, the bottom line was this: Tomlinson would be on a paid leave of absence pending a full investigation of his actions. And should the investigation substantiate the initial findings, his position in the department would be terminated.

Until the investigation is complete, the memo said, Jack should vacate his office, turn over all of his cases to other members of the county attorney's staff, and be prepared to answer more rigorous questions concerning his unauthorized appropriation of a police personnel file.

The final sentence read: "While your rights to a fair hearing and due process will be vigorously upheld, considering the potential consequences, you may choose to contact another attorney to represent your interests in this matter."

Jack had read the memo so many times, he had it memorized. It never got any better. His dream of becoming a top prosecutor, and someday, perhaps, a judge, was evaporating before his eyes. He would fight the firing, of course, but he knew his hopes were slim unless Jessica's investigation could somehow vindicate his actions. He knew he was too old to cry, but that didn't stop a few tears from getting through.

Down the hall, Sarah was also closeted in her office, still debating whether to call Freda Brinkman, to report that her police file probably had fallen into Jessica's hands, whatever that might portend.

But she knew calling Brinkman would mean getting further involved, which Sarah had sworn to herself—and to Brinkman—she would not do. However, to keep the information to herself would, in effect, help Jessica in her relentless efforts to bring them all down. In the end, she decided she had no choice. That's when she discovered Brinkman was on personal leave.

"Where'd she go?" she asked the secretary in the Homicide office.

"Got me," the woman said tiredly. "She was here one day, gone the next. Said something about a family illness. You're not the only one trying to find her."

"Really?"

"Bart Oates is searching high and low. You can try her at home, but I doubt that you'll get her. I haven't. She must have left town."

As Sarah hung up, she felt a touch of panic. Was she skipping out on them? No way, not Brinkman. What, then?

Sarah knew. She was preparing to attack.

FORTY-SEVEN

When Sarah finally left her office in the Government Center, it was early evening, and she was exhausted. Not only plagued by worries over Freda Brinkman but also bone-tired from almost a full day in the courtroom attending pretrial hearings for two accused rapists and an alleged wife beater. While the names and faces of these particular defendants were different, the mocking smiles, the swaggering walks, and the arrogant protestations of innocence were the same as she had seen a hundred times before. By the end of the day, she was ready to scream in anger and frustration.

Now, sliding into the elevator just as its doors were closing, she suddenly found herself face-to-face with Jack Tomlinson, a box of his belongings under one arm, another at his feet. Embarrassed, she tried but failed to step out before the doors closed. So she stood with her back to him, waiting as the elevator began its silent descent.

Ten floors passed before she finally spoke, still without facing him. "I'm sorry this happened, Jack. You're a good lawyer."

She heard a grunt from behind. "Save your sympathy, Sarah. It's not over yet."

Five more floors slipped by before she turned to him. His eyes were fixed on hers, his face expressionless. "What are you going to do now?" she asked.

"Fight it," he said simply.

The elevator slowed to a stop, and the doors opened. "Remember what I told you," she said, stepping out. "I could help."

As she turned, she felt a hand grip her arm. "And you remember this, Sarah," he said. "If anything happens to Jessica, I'm coming after you. That's a promise. Call off Brinkman."

She shook her arm free and walked off, whispering to herself, "If only I could."

Freda Brinkman had been inside the apartment for two hours, growing increasingly edgy as she watched the numbers flip past on the digital clock in the kitchen. She had already downed three beers and was beginning to feel them. Better watch it, she told herself. No time to have a buzz on.

A flash of her badge had gotten her past the security guard downstairs, and the lock on the door had proved to be no problem for her pick set. The minutes had crawled by since then, but she had managed to contain her concern. There was still time.

As she sat quietly watching the door, she thought back to that morning's unsuccessful effort to entice Kim Hawkins into her car. It had been worth a try, but Kim's refusal had not really surprised her. It had simply forced her to go to Plan B. Which was why she was sitting here now, waiting.

Twenty more minutes passed before she heard a key turn in the lock. The apartment was dim but not fully dark. Brinkman made no effort to hide but again touched the hard steel of the .38 Police Special tucked into the cushions of the chair. The door swung open, the light of the hallway backlighting the figure in the doorway. Brinkman said nothing until Sarah had closed the door.

"Welcome home."

Sarah leaped back, her body banging into the wall, her head swiveling in the direction of the voice. "Who's that?" she shouted. Then her eyes found Brinkman in the shadows. "Freda. What are you doing here?" There was both surprise and fear in her words.

"Relax," Brinkman said easily. "Just waiting for you."

"Jesus Christ!" Sarah said, stepping forward cautiously. "You scared the hell out of me. How'd you get in here? Why didn't you call?"

Brinkman's voice was calm and casual. "I didn't know if you'd see me, not after the way we left things the last time."

"I've been trying to call you," Sarah said, edging farther into the room. "They said you'd taken a leave, that no one knew where you were."

Brinkman chuckled. "They're not supposed to."

Sarah reached a lamp across the room and flicked it on. Her exhaustion had vanished, replaced by a flood of adrenaline. "What do you want?" she asked.

"Some help, that's all."

Sarah was wary. "For what? I told you I wanted no part—"

"Quiet!" Brinkman said. "Let's not go through that again. I don't have the time."

Brinkman continued. "I want you to call Kim. Tell her you need to talk, that you want to see her tonight at her place."

Sarah was aghast. "You're nuts. I won't do that."

"Yes, you will."

"Why?" Sarah demanded.

"Because you're the only way I can get to Kim, and Kim's the only way I can get to Jessica. It's that simple."

"Listen to me," Sarah said, pleading. "Give this up, Freda. It won't work. Too many people know what's going on. Even Jessica's boyfriend, Jack Tomlinson, the lawyer who works in our office, knows. He's been working with her. He stole your personnel file for her. Don't you see? Our only chance is to stay calm. They have no proof."

Brinkman grew more agitated. "Dream on. Jessica is at the

heart of it, Sarah. Don't you see that? If she's gone, our problems are gone. We should have done it long ago."

"I won't have you involve Kim," Sarah said defiantly. "I told you that before. I won't stand for it!"

"We don't have much choice, not now." Brinkman sighed, pointing to the phone. "Call her. Tell her you need to see her. Now. Tonight. To talk it out. Tell her you'll come there."

Sarah turned her back to the phone.

"Do it!" Brinkman shouted. "Don't fuck with me, Sarah."

Sarah didn't move.

Brinkman reached into the cushions and pulled out the pistol. She walked slowly to Sarah and raised the gun, holding it to the side of her nose. "Do it," she said more gently.

Sarah couldn't believe what was happening. "Put that away," she said. "For God's sake, Freda!"

Brinkman grabbed a fistful of her hair and gave it a violent yank, popping Sarah's head back with such force that she momentarily went black. "Make the call," Brinkman whispered into her ear.

When the knock came, Kim was waiting. She looked through the peephole in the door and saw Sarah standing alone in the hallway. She must have used her old key to get into the building, Kim thought. She hesitated, her hand on the doorknob. Am I doing the right thing? She had asked herself the question a hundred times in the twenty minutes since Sarah's phone call.

The call had not come as a complete surprise. Not after this morning's encounter with Freda Brinkman. Hadn't she said Sarah wanted to talk to her?

There was a second knock on the door, louder this time. What harm could come of it? Maybe Sarah was finally ready to explain everything, to put things right. To end the craziness. She had heard nothing more from Jessica. Maybe it was all a mistake. She turned the lock and opened the door.

"Hello, Kim." Sarah made no immediate move to enter,

glancing quickly to her left. She tried to smile, but her face was pained. Had she been crying? Was that fear in her eyes?

"Hi, Sarah," Kim replied, stepping back.

Sarah walked through the door, but before Kim could close it, the figure of Freda Brinkman slid into the opening, filling it. "Surprise, Kim," she said with a grin.

Kim stumbled back, almost falling. She felt faint.

Brinkman closed the door and snapped the lock. "You should have come with me this morning, Kim. Would have saved all this."

Kim looked angrily at Sarah. "What's this about?" she demanded.

Sarah looked away, unable or unwilling to meet her eyes.

"We need a favor," Brinkman said, putting a hand on each of them, pushing them farther into the room, away from the door.

Kim grabbed at Sarah. "What have you done? You said you wanted to talk. What's this about?"

"Calm down," Brinkman ordered. "This is my idea, not hers. But I'm afraid it doesn't make much difference."

She commanded them both to sit, then told Kim what she expected her to do. "I want Jessica to meet you someplace private. Alone. Tonight. You'll have to be persuasive. Act panicked, if you have to. I'll tell you what to say. But you'd better make it good, because I'll be listening in on the other phone."

Kim stared back belligerently. "I won't do it. You can't make me do it."

Sarah spoke for the first time. "She has a gun, Kim."

Kim's face paled even more. Then she stood, facing both of them, eyes wide open. "Jessica was right, wasn't she? About Edward Hill and those other men. Sarah, how could you?"

"Shut up and sit down," Brinkman ordered.

Kim dropped into the chair, her gaze moving from one to the other. "How could you?" she demanded again. "My God!"

Brinkman took the pistol from her purse. "Put a lid on it, sweetheart. We have work to do."

*　*　*

When Jessica arrived at the apartment, she was surprised to find Jack already there. He had let himself in and was now slouched on the sofa, glumly nursing a beer. One glance at him told her that he had not lost all of his earlier anger.

"I thought we ought to talk things out," he said as she walked over to him.

"Fine," she said, "but give me a minute."

She retreated to the bedroom to change into shorts and a T-shirt and then went to the kitchen to pour herself a glass of wine. Jack was up and pacing when she returned to the living room.

"Need another beer?" she asked.

He glanced down at his empty glass. "No, thanks. I've had enough."

She stood quietly, waiting for him to speak.

"I got the notice," he finally said. "I've already cleaned out my office."

Jessica felt her knees weaken, and she quickly sat down.

"Hamilton says I should probably get an attorney if I want to fight the firing."

"You will fight it, won't you?" Jessica asked.

"Of course. But it could take a long time and cost a lot of money. Money I don't have. And even then, I may never work again. It'll be a black mark even if I were to eventually win."

Jessica felt her eyes welling but fought to contain the tears. "I feel horrible," she said. "But I don't know what else to say or do. I'm sorry I got you into all of this, but you did realize there were risks."

"I know that," he said, "but I never thought it could lead to this. It's incredible."

He sat down next to her and leaned back. "Guess who wants to help me out?" he said. "Sarah Andrews."

He heard a small gasp from Jessica.

"She came to my office, and then I saw her again in the elevator. Said she'd help save my job in exchange for a little information about what you're up to."

"And what did you say?"

Jack laughed. "I think you know. But she's a strange

woman, Jess. There's this dark side of her. You can see it in her eyes sometimes. Hear it in her voice. The threat. But then there's another, more human side. I may be wrong, but I think she's genuinely concerned about me, that she actually feels badly about what's happened to me."

As Jessica was about to reply, the phone next to her rang. She picked up the receiver on the second ring. "Yes?"

She listened for a moment, then wrote something on a pad next to the phone. "Thanks," she said, and hung up.

Jack sat up, eyeing her quizzically.

"It was the newsroom. They say I have an urgent message from Kim Hawkins. Wants me to call her right away."

"What can that be about?" he asked.

Jessica shrugged. "Who knows? I haven't talked to her since the day with the tape. I'd better call."

She glanced at the number on the pad, then pushed the buttons.

When Kim answered, her voice was hushed, almost strangled, like the night she had phoned to tell Jessica of the Craft Club meeting. Again, Jessica had to strain to hear. "What is it, Kim? What's wrong?"

"I've got to see you, Jessica. Right away, tonight."

"Tonight? Kim, what's happened?"

Kim looked at Freda Brinkman, standing ten feet away, holding a phone tightly to her ear with one hand, the gun loosely in the other. Sarah was huddled in a chair by Kim's side, vacantly staring into space. They had rehearsed the possible conversation, Brinkman trying to anticipate what Jessica might say, coaching Kim's responses.

"Sarah came to me," Kim said, struggling to remember her instructions, "and told me everything. I've finally convinced her to tell you herself. But she's very afraid, Jessica."

"What did she tell you?" Jessica asked.

"I can't say, not on the phone. We have to meet with you. Alone. If not tonight, never, she says."

"Wait a minute, Kim." Jessica cupped the phone and

looked at Jack, repeating the essence of the conversation. He shook his head. "Not alone," he whispered.

"Kim?"

"Yes."

"I can meet you tonight, but not alone. I don't go anywhere alone these days."

There was a pause at the other end as Kim looked to Brinkman for instructions. The interruption was not lost on Jessica.

"Is Sarah with you now?" she demanded.

Brinkman nodded yes.

"Yes, yes, she is," Kim stammered. "But she won't talk to you, not on the phone."

Jessica could hear the tremor in her voice. "Are you okay?"

Brinkman raised the gun slightly.

"Of course," Kim said. "I just don't like being in the middle of this."

"I don't blame you," Jessica said. "Where shall we meet?"

"The same place we met before. By the picnic table at Lake Harriet. I can walk there from here."

Jessica cupped the phone again and conferred with Jack. "Okay, Kim, here's the deal. I'll meet you in an hour. But with a couple of conditions. That Sarah come with you, tonight, just the two of you. And remember, I won't be alone. I'll have someone with me. It has to be that way."

"Hold on," Kim said, looking toward Brinkman.

"Tell her that's okay," Brinkman whispered. "But no cops or Sarah will walk away and say nothing."

Kim repeated the words over the phone.

"An hour, then," Jessica said, and added: "Have you or Sarah seen Freda Brinkman?"

Brinkman shook her head violently. "No," Kim said quickly. "Sarah says she's on leave or something."

"You're being straight with me, aren't you, Kim?"

Kim wanted to shout a warning, but Brinkman's gun was now pointed directly at her heart.

"Of course. But I don't like any of this."

Jessica paused, and when there was nothing more, she said, "I'll see you in an hour, Kim."

FORTY-EIGHT

Ignoring the insistent buzz of the dial tone, Kim was unable to free her fingers from the phone or her eyes from the pistol in Brinkman's hand, even when she saw the hand relax and the barrel drop from her heart to the floor.

"Good work, Kim," Brinkman said as she walked across the room and wrested the phone from her grip. "Now, c'mon, we've got to get going."

Kim couldn't move. Her body seemed frozen in place.

"It'll never work," Sarah said tiredly from her chair. "They're not stupid. You're setting yourself up, Freda."

"No way," Brinkman replied. "It's a no-lose situation. If she brings any cops, they'll never see me, and you'll say nothing. You'll just walk away. If she doesn't, well . . ."

"For Christ's sake, Freda. She said she wouldn't come alone," Sarah argued.

"Let's see who she brings. Then I'll worry about it."

Sarah got up slowly and walked toward the kitchen. "I'm not going," she said flatly. "Gun or no gun. This is nonsense. Your mind is so muddled you've lost all sense of reality."

With a wave of the pistol, Brinkman motioned Kim into the chair Sarah had vacated. "Stay there," she said. Then she followed Sarah to the kitchen, stepping up close behind her. "I don't have time for this, Sarah. You'll go, or I swear I'll take your friend out there someplace where they'll never find her."

Without thought and with more speed and strength than she knew she possessed, Sarah swung around and lunged for her. "You bitch," she screamed.

Brinkman was caught by surprise, but it made no difference. Sarah simply bounced off her body and fell backward, desperately clutching for a chair to break her fall. Brinkman sprang, grabbing her arm and pulling her back, twisting her body until she held her throat in a viselike grip. And squeezed.

Sarah gasped for air, struggling to pull free, digging her fingernails into the flesh of Brinkman's arm. But there was no give to the skin. With little effort, Brinkman tightened her hold and dragged her back through the kitchen and into the living room, dumping her at the feet of Kim, who was still sitting, paralyzed, in the chair.

"Time's a wasting," Brinkman said.

Sarah, still choking and dazed, looked up at Kim. What she saw in her face was pure terror.

"Jess, I'm telling you, I wouldn't go," Jack said. "It's too out of left field."

Jessica listened but made no reply as she packed a small tape recorder into her purse, then looked around the room to see if she had forgotten anything.

Jack persisted. "What's Sarah going to do, confess?" he asked skeptically. "You know better than that. At best, she'll try more intimidation. At worst, well, anything could happen."

"But you're going to be there," she countered.

"I'm not a cop, Jessica. And I'm not exactly a tough guy. You could do better for a bodyguard."

They had been arguing since Jessica had hung up the phone. She agreed that the timing of Kim's call was strange and that there was at least the potential of danger. But the attraction was too strong. After all, hadn't she been waiting for this kind of a break? Isn't that what she'd been aiming at? To force them into some kind of a mistake or admission.

Besides, she told him, she couldn't let Kim hang out to dry. If Sarah was with her, Kim had to be confused, perhaps scared. She certainly sounded that way on the phone. If Jessica didn't owe it to herself and the station to show up, she certainly owed it to Kim.

Jack interrupted her again. "What if Brinkman's there? What if she's behind this whole thing?"

"That's a risk, I agree," she said.

"What are you going to do about it?"

"C'mon, Jack! I can't bring a goddamned army with me."

"Call Jenkins," he urged, recalling that the St. Paul detective had given Jessica his numbers in case of an emergency. "Let him know what's happening."

"I told you, Sarah won't talk if there's a cop around."

Jack threw up his arms. "He doesn't have to be there, for God's sake. He could be somewhere nearby. You know, protecting our rears."

Jessica turned on him angrily. "You don't have to come, you know." She immediately regretted her words, but he ignored them, anyway.

"Call Jenkins," he pressed. "Or let me."

She glanced at her watch. "We've only got thirty minutes. There's no time."

"Then use the car phone," he said, following her to the door. "Use your head."

Brinkman sat with Kim in the backseat as Sarah slowly drove from the apartment toward Lake Harriet. The gun rested comfortably in her lap. "Stop here," she ordered.

Sarah pulled to the curb. They were still a few blocks from the pavilion. Brinkman glanced at her watch. A half hour remained before the appointed meeting time.

"You walk from here," she said. "I'll take the car."

Sarah turned in the seat. "Don't do this, Freda," she pleaded. "Give it up now, while there's still time."

"Shut up and listen!" Brinkman said. "When you get there, forget about me. Just meet them like you said you would. Play it cool. Bullshit them. Take your time."

"Where will you be?" Sarah demanded.

"Around," Brinkman said. "Scoping things out. Don't look for me. Make whoever's with her move away, close to the path. Don't let him listen to what you're saying. If I don't show up within twenty minutes, it means I've decided something's screwy. Just break off the conversation and go home."

Kim huddled in her corner of the backseat, staring plaintively at Sarah.

"And don't play hero, either of you," Brinkman snapped. "You have no proof that any of this has happened. I'm a cop, and I'm on leave, remember? Out of town. And don't forget what I told you in the kitchen, Sarah. If you fuck this up, your friend here will pay the price. And you know I don't make idle threats."

When neither Sarah nor Kim made any move to get out of the car, Brinkman raised the gun slowly from her lap.

"Now," she barked. "Move."

As they walked away, Kim leaned heavily on Sarah, glancing nervously over her shoulder at the darkened car they had left behind. "We can't do this," she whispered. "We've got to run, get out of here."

"Keep walking," Sarah said grimly. "And stop looking back."

"What was she talking about in the car?" Kim persisted. "What did she mean, that I'd 'pay the price'?"

"You don't want to know. Just keep walking."

"Tell me, Sarah! I've got a right to know."

Sarah continued straight ahead, her stride unbroken until they rounded a corner, out of sight of Brinkman's car. Then she stopped and faced Kim, gripping her by the shoulders. "You really want to know? Okay. If I don't go through with this, she said she'd hurt you, Kim. Maybe more. And she's fully capable of doing it, believe me."

Kim gasped, but Sarah kept going. "I tried to keep you out of this, I really did. We wouldn't be here if you hadn't decided to go to Jessica—"

Kim cut her off angrily. "I only went to her because you wouldn't talk to me. You wouldn't tell me what was going on. I still can't believe that you'd—"

"Quiet," Sarah said. "What's done is done. You don't know anything."

"But those men," Kim protested. "Edward Hill and the others."

Sarah resumed walking, pulling Kim along. "I had nothing to do with most of them. But they were scum, Kim, all of them. They would still be out there tonight, somewhere, raping or killing. I don't want to hear any more about them."

They were approaching the lake. The pavilion where Kim had met Jessica weeks before was closed for the night, but streetlights illuminated the area around it. From this distance, they could see a few people, late-night strollers and joggers, along the path around the lake. And offshore the outlines of a dozen sailboats were etched against the moonlit water, the boats bobbing in the breeze, pulling against their moorings.

"There has to be another way out of this," Kim cried. "We can't do this to Jessica."

Sarah grunted. "Worry about yourself, not Jessica. She's had her chances. She's been warned over and over again."

Kim grabbed her arm. "Do you hear yourself? Do you know what you're saying? My God, what's happened to you?"

Sarah started to answer, but no words came out.

Brinkman waited until Sarah and Kim were out of sight, then quickly retrieved a canvas bag from the trunk. Slipping into the backseat, she struggled to pull on a black running suit over her blouse and slacks, the same running suit she had used the night she'd ambushed Matt Meecham. Then the black tennis shoes. She shoved a ski mask, two pairs of handcuffs, and other supplies into a fanny pack and hung the holstered pistol and nightstick from a belt inside her running suit.

Putting the bag back into the trunk, she quickly surveyed the street but saw no one. She was already sweating from the two layers of clothing, and the gun was heavy against her side. Nothing one could do about that, she told herself as she got behind the wheel and eased the car into the street.

Jack and Jessica drove past the Harriet pavilion twice, their eyes searching unsuccessfully for anyone lingering in the shadows near the area of the picnic bench.

"See anyone?" he asked.

Jessica shook her head. "It's too far and too dark."

"And you still want to be there?" he scoffed.

"It's not that dark," she argued, and then pointed to a jogger on the path. "Besides, there are still people around."

For the past twenty-five minutes, the time it had taken to drive there, Jack had continued to argue against the meeting. But Jessica was unmoved, repeating again and again that the potential rewards were worth the risk.

"If Sarah's ready to talk, I'm ready to listen," she said.

At his insistence, she tried to reach Jerry Jenkins with the car phone. She used all of the numbers on the card he had given her several times without success, until he finally answered his own car phone.

"Jessica?" It was no more than a whisper. "What's going on?"

After she explained where she was and what was about to happen, Jenkins had told her, "Hell, Jess, I'm on a stakeout on the east side of St. Paul. I won't be relieved for a half hour; I can't leave now."

"I understand," Jessica had said apologetically. "I'm sure there won't be any problems, but a friend who's with me insisted that I call."

"Who's that?" he'd asked.

"Jack Tomlinson. I've told you about him. The friend from the county attorney's office who's been helping me in this."

"And he's worried?"

"You could say that," Jessica had admitted.

"Then listen to him."

She ignored the warning. "I'll let you know what happens, Jerry, and thanks," she had said, ending the conversation.

After passing the pavilion a third time, Jack parked on a side street about a block from the lake. After locking the doors, he opened the trunk and grabbed a steel lug wrench from beside the spare tire.

They circled the pavilion and approached the picnic bench from the edge of the lighted area. They stayed to the path, and close together, as their eyes adjusted to the deepening darkness.

"This is ridiculous," Jack said, gripping the wrench more tightly.

Two joggers passed them, one from either direction, breathing hard, the sweat on their bodies glistening as they ran beneath the pavilion lights.

"I just remembered," Jessica whispered. "I forgot to leave a note for Janie. She'll be wondering what happened to me."

"No time now," he said.

That's when they heard the plane, an airliner making its final approach to the nearby Twin Cities International Airport. Jack had known this part of south Minneapolis was on the glide path, but he had never been here when one of the giant jetliners actually came in. The noise was overwhelming, ear-splitting, the 747 so low that its underbelly seemed almost close enough to touch.

Jessica stopped and pointed to the left. Jack peered in that direction, his eyes straining to see what she saw. Two figures, phantomlike, standing no more than thirty feet away but barely visible. Jessica waited for the noise of the jetliner to subside, then called out, "Kim? Sarah? Is that you?"

One of the figures came forward a few steps, a stray stitch of light crossing her forehead. "Yes," she said. "We're here."

FORTY-NINE

Jessica glanced at Jack, then cautiously took a few steps herself. "Are the two of you alone?" she asked.

"Yes," came the reply from one of them.

"Come out here, more into the light," Jessica demanded.

"No, thanks." It was Sarah's voice, muffled but recognizable. "Is that Jack with you?"

He stepped forward. "That's right, Sarah."

Jessica continued to move ahead despite the restraining pressure of Jack's hand on her arm. "Kim, are you all right?" she asked. "I can barely see you. Say something."

"I'm all right, Jessica." The tremor in Kim's voice, even from that distance, was unmistakable.

As the gap between them closed, Sarah, still disguised by the dark, asked, "You didn't bring a photographer, did you?"

"Of course not," she replied.

"How about a tape recorder?"

Jessica stopped. The recorder she carried in her purse was already running. If she lied and Sarah discovered it, it would be all over. Best not take a chance, she decided. "Yes," she said. "It's in my purse."

"I thought so. Give the purse to Jack and tell him to move back to the path. This conversation will be between us, and us alone."

"Wrong," Jack whispered, raising the wrench slightly. "I'm not leaving you."

Jessica handed him the purse. "It's okay," she said. "You won't be that far away."

With no more than twenty feet now separating her from the two women, Jessica made her approach slowly and tentatively, ready to bolt at the first sign of trouble. At each step, her eyes scanned the shadows, while her ears strained to detect any sound beyond the hushed movement of her own feet through the grass. From what she could tell, only the night surrounded her, and she silently scolded herself for her fear. When she finally reached them, Kim was standing slightly behind Sarah and off to one side, arms clutched to her chest, looking down, refusing to meet Jessica's eyes.

Sarah, on the other hand, stared straight at her, unblinking. "No other recorders on you, are there?" she asked.

"Want to search me?" Jessica asked.

Sarah hesitated. Then: "No, I'll take your word."

Jessica glanced over her shoulder, reassured by the sight of Jack still standing, poised and alert, by the path.

From fifty yards away, hidden behind a boat that had been pulled ashore for the night, Freda Brinkman watched the scene unfold. She had been there as Jessica and a man she decided must be Jack Tomlinson had circled the lighted pavilion and approached the picnic bench. She watched as they made contact with Sarah and Kim, and although she couldn't hear the exchange of words from this distance, she could see Jessica walk forward and Jack retreat to the path.

To her own surprise, it seemed to be going according to plan. Even the passing plane was an uncounted blessing. It was the second to have roared overhead since she had arrived, and she only hoped there would be more.

She had also been relieved to see several joggers pass by in the space of the past ten minutes. Jack, she saw, after watching the first couple of runners, seemed to take no further notice. His attention was fully focused on the women by the bench. Time for a test run, Brinkman decided.

Jessica and Sarah stood two feet apart, studying one another in the darkness, their bodies tense, each apparently waiting for the other to speak. There were no sounds now except for the distant drone of a bus and the chirping of the crickets hidden in the grass at their feet.

Jessica was the first to break the silence. "You asked for this meeting, Sarah," she said. "I'm here to listen."

It's not like I chose to be here, Sarah thought, glancing quickly at Kim cowering behind her. In fact, it's the last place in the world I want to be. But she knew she had to say something. Kill time, Brinkman had said.

"Was the newspaper right?" she finally asked. "That you plan to go ahead with this story of yours. This fantasy."

"It's no fantasy, Sarah, and I think you know it."

"Here's what I know. I understand that in your warped little mind you think there's some sort of vigilante group out there, a bunch of women, myself included, who are doing in perverts and predators, knocking them off one by one in the name of some kind of perverse justice."

"Am I wrong?"

"You're obsessed. You have no proof of anything."

"You didn't answer the question," Jessica said.

"I don't have to answer your questions," Sarah shot back.

"Then why did you ask me to come here?"

Because Freda Brinkman forced me to, Sarah thought. Because she's crazy, out there somewhere with a gun. Give it up, Jessica, she thought, while there's still time.

"To try to persuade you one last time—"

Jessica broke in. "Forget it. It won't do any good."

Sarah stood back. How much time had passed? She didn't dare glance at her watch. What had Freda said she needed? Twenty minutes. Then walk away, she had said.

Another jetliner passed overhead, this one seeming even closer and louder than the last. All three women watched, necks craned, saying nothing, knowing their words would never be heard. Then the plane was gone.

"Just for the fun of it," Sarah finally said, playing for time, "let's say you're right, that somebody's offing these predators. What do you know about them? The dead ones, I mean."

Jessica paused. "A fair amount, actually. Enough to know they were all despicable men. Filth, you'd probably call them."

"Tell me about them," Sarah pressed.

"I think you know about them," Jessica replied.

"Tell me, anyway."

Jessica went down the list name by name, and their records. Edward Hill. Eduardo Priaz. Ezra Scott. Michael Anthony.

"I see that kind of scum every day," Sarah said. "I know firsthand what they do to women."

"That doesn't mean they deserved to die," Jessica replied calmly.

Sarah laughed. "Such a pure little priss. You might think differently if one of them was standing here now, holding a knife or gun on you, his prick hanging out of his pants, panting, demanding that you strip, maybe give him a blow job for starters. . . ."

"C'mon, Sarah, I don't need this—"

"Then he'd slap you around. Maybe break your nose, knock out a couple of teeth, shove your face into the dirt. Maybe cut you. They like the sight of blood, you know. Makes 'em feel tough, powerful. Then he'd probably screw you, laughing the whole time."

"Stop it," Jessica said.

But Sarah refused to be deterred. "You may not want to hear it, but that's the way it happens, Jessica. That's reality. If you're lucky, you might survive. Then you can be like Kim here, who's alive but living in a hell you or I will hopefully never know. Who's hardly slept a night since her rape, who's literally afraid of her own shadow. Her life will never be the same again no matter how much therapy and support she might get."

As Jessica glanced at Kim, her thoughts flashed back to Janie, to the day she had found her on the steps, still in shock, dazed and frightened and ashamed. She knew Sarah was right, that despite the therapy and the support groups and regardless of the passage of time, Janie, like Kim, would never be the same woman she was before the attack.

Before she could speak, Sarah asked, "You think they would catch this make-believe rapist of yours? Not likely. They hardly ever do. And even if they did, he'd probably cop some kind of plea and be back on the streets in a year or so to do it all over again."

"This isn't getting us anywhere," Jessica protested.

"No? Let's keep pretending that you're right, that someone has been doing in these perverts. You've never heard of justifiable homicide?"

"C'mon, Sarah. You're the lawyer. This hardly fits the definition, and you know it."

"Tell that to most rape victims, Jessica. See what they say."

Freda Brinkman rose from behind the boat, her dark running suit merging with the shadows. She kept her body low until she reached the path, then started a slow lope in the direction of the bench. As she ran, she again looked in all directions, searching for anyone else that Jessica might have brought along. She could see no one.

Making no effort to be quiet, Brinkman listened to the slap of her tennis shoes against the asphalt of the path. She forced herself to breathe heavily, allowing the air to gush in and out of her mouth as though she had been running for miles.

As she approached Jack, she could see his head turn slightly in her direction, but his body signaled no apparent alarm. She was just another jogger on a summer's night. To her knowledge he had never seen her, but she took no chances, looking away toward the lake as she passed by him.

Ten yards farther on, she glanced over her shoulder. He had not moved, was not looking in her direction. After another forty yards, she stopped, ducking into some overgrown lilac bushes away from the path. Count to twenty, she told herself. Catch your breath.

Sarah, looking over Jessica's shoulder, saw the dark-suited figure run past Tomlinson. In this light, and from this distance, it was difficult to tell. But something about the size and gait of the runner registered. Could it be Freda?

Jessica followed her eyes and quickly turned. She saw only Jack, still standing in the same spot. "What's going on?" she asked.

"Nothing," Sarah said. "Just making sure Jack was staying put."

"Tell me about the Craft Club," Jessica said.

"What about it?" Sarah demanded.

"I know the women who are part of it," Jessica said. "At least some of them. I know what they've gone through. . . ."

"You know nothing," Sarah said.

Jessica persisted. "How did you get involved?"

"Is that so hard to figure out?" Sarah asked, turning to Kim. "I saw what happened to Kim, what the rape did to her. I lived with her, and with it, for months, only to see Edward Hill skip out of court, free as a bird, ready to do again what he'd already done to Kim and others. It was more than I could take."

"So you had him killed?" Jessica said.

Sarah laughed. "Back to your fantasy, right?"

"Once the story gets on the air," Jessica argued, "the cops won't give up. You know that. The public pressure will be too much."

"You may be right," Sarah admitted, "but the story's not on the air yet, and I suspect it never will be."

* * *

Brinkman removed the nightstick and the ski mask from her fanny pack, then moved the belted gun and holster from the inside to the outside of her running suit, tying the holster to her leg, gunslinger style, so it wouldn't flap as she ran. Her inside layer of clothing was wet with sweat, and she could feel the droplets run down her back and legs.

She stepped carefully from behind the lilac bush to the path, peering in each direction, satisfying herself that no other joggers or walkers were in sight. Were they still there by the bench? Or had Sarah given it up and left? Brinkman couldn't tell from where she stood, but she knew it would be close.

It had been at least ten minutes since the last plane had passed overhead, and she could only hope it wouldn't be much longer before the next one made its approach. She would give it three minutes, and if none had come by then, she would make her run, anyway. There wasn't time to wait longer.

She glanced at the luminous watch on her wrist, dividing her attention between it and continued surveillance of the path. One minute passed. Then another thirty seconds before she heard the distant whine of a descending airliner.

Ten more seconds, she told herself, then go. She pulled the mask over her head, quickly adjusting the eye and mouth openings, breathing deeply. The timing had to work. Fifty yards to run. Twenty seconds, give or take a few. By then the plane had to be directly above them.

As the roar of the jet engines closed, she launched herself down the path, clutching the nightstick like a relay baton, running half speed at first, trying to judge the plane's approach, then picking up the pace as she saw the plane's lights through a break in the trees. Coming fast, lower and lower. That's when she saw Jack, still standing by the path, no more than twenty yards away.

* * *

Jack stared at the giant airliner, landing lights blazing, gears locked down, swooping in over the trees, no more than a few hundred feet above him. In the time he had been standing there, it was the third or fourth plane to land, each one with an ear-shattering roar that must shake the windows of the nearby houses. No wonder people living around here are always complaining, he thought.

Jack turned his head away from the noise, as if that might protect his ears, in time to see another jogger approaching from his right. Dressed in a black running suit, head down, moving at a pace he could never match. Had the same one passed in the other direction earlier? He couldn't be sure.

It wasn't until the runner was only a few feet away that he saw the ski mask. It took another split second to register: Why the hell would somebody be wearing a ski mask in the middle of summer? By then it was too late.

Brinkman would never forget the changing expressions on his face, all within the two seconds it took for those final few steps. First there was curiosity, then confusion turning instantly to surprise, then shock. The blow from the nightstick landed before she could see fear.

Unlike Meecham, there was no chance this time for a carefully aimed blow, not while running at nearly full speed. She simply lashed out at his head, hoping for at least a glancing blow that would stun him, if not drop him. If she missed, she would simply keep on going, knowing there was little chance he would pursue and virtually no chance that he would catch her.

But bingo! She felt the nightstick connect, the force of the blow jarring her outstretched arm. With the noise of the plane, she heard no sound, but a quick backward glance saw him heave forward, toppling like a felled tree.

She skidded to a stop, her eyes shifting first to the picnic bench—Jessica's back was still toward her—then to the path. There was no one. The plane was now beyond them, but the backwash of its engines was still deafening.

Brinkman crept back and knelt beside Jack. There was no movement, and blood was dripping from his nose and oozing from his hairline, just above the left temple. She left him there and began to walk toward the picnic bench, the gun now firmly in her hand. She was no more than ten feet away when Jessica turned.

Brinkman ripped off the ski mask and smiled. "Hello, Jessica," she said.

FIFTY

The first thing Jessica saw was Brinkman's smile. Then the silver-plated gun, held tightly in her outstretched hand, pointing directly at Jessica's right eye. The nightstick was held loosely in the other hand.

"My God," she said.

Sarah and Kim were as stunned as Jessica. They had all been watching the plane pass overhead, eyes uplifted, paying no attention to one another or the path. Waiting for the roar to subside.

"Stay calm, girls," Brinkman ordered, closing the final few feet between them. "No silliness. No screams."

Despite the warning, Jessica moved quickly to one side, straining to see around Brinkman. "Jack. Where's Jack?" she demanded.

Brinkman turned slightly, allowing Jessica to see past her. That's when Jessica spotted the dark heap on the ground where Jack had stood only moments before. "What did you do to him?" she cried, starting to move forward. "Is he all right?"

Brinkman stopped her with the barrel of the gun at the tip

of her nose. "Know what this would do to that pretty face of yours?" she asked.

"We have a job to do," she went on. "I want the three of you to pull him back here, away from the path. He's not going to be much help, and neither am I. So get going."

For the first time, Jessica looked closely at the other two women. Kim was clinging to Sarah like a life preserver. Sarah struggled to hold her up, fear showing in her own face.

"You knew this was going to happen, didn't you?" Jessica said, challenging them. "You led me right to her."

Before either of them could reply, Brinkman said, "Cut the shit. We don't have the time."

With a wave of the gun, she herded them toward the path, moving ahead of them at the last moment to make sure that no one else was within view. When satisfied the path was clear, she motioned them forward.

Jessica dropped by Jack's side, leaning down, touching his face with her lips, listening for signs of life. That's when she saw the blood, drying now under his nose, matted in his hair. The purse he had been holding for her was next to his head.

"My God," she whispered, "what did she do to you?"

There was no response, but she could feel a pulse at the side of his neck, could hear shallow but labored breathing.

Brinkman pushed her aside with a shove of her foot. "Pick up the purse and get him the hell out of here," she ordered.

It was after ten o'clock before Janie arrived at the apartment. It would have been even later if her repeated phone calls to Jessica had not gone unanswered. Janie had been working extra hours at the store, to assist with inventory, but had been excused before the task was complete because of her concerns.

Now, as she walked through the front door, she knew the place was still empty. A few lights were on, but there was a stillness that bespoke no human presence. She called out, anyway, and was not surprised when there was no reply. She quickly checked all the predictable places for a note but found none. A half-empty glass of wine sat on an end table next to the sofa, and a suit coat she recognized as Jack's was thrown over one of the dining-room chairs.

They must have gone out for a drink or dinner, she thought, but found it strange—and troubling—that there was no message of any kind. She and Jessica had what Janie thought was an inviolable pact: If I don't know where you are, leave word.

After wandering the apartment for ten more minutes, growing ever more agitated, she picked up the phone and punched out a number from Jessica's book. George Barclay answered his home phone on the fourth ring.

Janie quickly identified herself and explained why she was calling. "I'm sorry to bother you this late," she said, "but I'm worried. Jessica and I always let each other know where we are."

Barclay asked a few questions, then told her to hang on. "I'll call the newsroom on my other line," he said. "See what they know."

He came back in less than a minute. "The desk said they gave Jess an urgent message from Kim Hawkins earlier tonight. Never heard back from her."

"Kim Hawkins?" Janie said. "What could she want?"

"Can't tell you that," Barclay replied. "But do you happen to have Jerry Jenkins's phone numbers there?"

"Let me look," Janie said, again thumbing through Jessica's phone book. "Yes, here they are." She recited the numbers to Barclay, then repeated them. "What should I do?" she asked.

"Sit tight," Barclay said. "I'll see if I can find out what's going on."

"You think she's okay?" Janie asked.

"I'm sure she is," Barclay said. "Relax until I check it out."

It was a struggle, but it took the three of them no more than five minutes to drag Jack's inert body from the path to the bench. Jessica tried to cradle his head as she pulled at his upper body, all the time whispering to him, willing him awake, just as she had with Matt Meecham in the hospital weeks before. But Jack, like Matt, showed no sign of consciousness.

"Drop him by that tree," Brinkman ordered, pointing to an oak a few steps from the bench. Two feet in circumference, the tree towered at least fifty feet in the air.

Jessica knelt beside him again, choking on her own fear and a deep sense of guilt. Jack wouldn't be here, like this, if she had not stubbornly ignored his warnings. And what about Kim? So utterly afraid and helpless. A victim again of more senseless violence, through none of her own doing. What would happen to her? What would happen to all of them?

Brinkman's harsh voice again cut into her thoughts. "I'll say this only once—so listen carefully. If any one of you utters a shout or scream or tries to run, I'll kill you . . . or whoever remains. That's a promise."

With that, she opened her fanny pack and pulled out two pairs of handcuffs, a handful of rags, and two rolls of duct tape.

"Here's what I want," she said. "Sarah, tape Jack's ankles and gag him. Put one of the cuffs on his right wrist, then tape the wrists together."

As Sarah hesitated, Jessica pleaded, "You can't leave him like that. He needs medical help, for Christ's sake."

"Quiet," Brinkman said.

When Sarah saw the barrel of the gun shift from Jessica to herself, she obediently followed the instructions. Jessica could see the tremor in her body and hands, knowing they were matched by her own.

When Sarah was finished, Brinkman told her, "Now, lie down on the other side of the tree."

"No," Sarah whimpered.

"Yes," Brinkman said. For emphasis, she pulled back the nightstick and shoved the butt of it into the pit of Kim's stomach, doubling her over with a cry of surprise and pain.

"Leave her alone," Sarah cried out.

"Do it!" Brinkman ordered.

Kim was on her knees, holding her midsection, retching. Sarah reached for her, but after another grunted warning, she gave it up and slowly lay down by the tree.

"Now, Jessica," Brinkman said, "do the same to Sarah as she did to Jack. Then cuff them together around the tree."

Sarah's eyes were wide with fear as Jessica knelt beside her, slowly taping her ankles and then her wrists. With every turn of the tape, Jessica would glance at Brinkman, then toward the path, desperately hoping that someone would pass by and look in their direction. But she knew the chances were slim. The lateness of the hour, the darkness, and the fear of involvement would work against them. No one except a cop would be eager to investigate a group of shadows lingering off the beaten track. Especially with no shout for help or other sign of trouble.

She thought again about Jerry Jenkins. Why had she brushed him off? Ignored his warning, as she had ignored Jack's? Foolish bravado, she told herself. Would he come, anyway? He said he'd be relieved in a half hour. But he was in east St. Paul, which was at least another half hour away.

Jessica completed the taping and pushed the gag into Sarah's mouth as gently as possible. Then she snapped the free ring of the handcuff onto Sarah's wrist, binding her to Jack and both of them to the giant oak.

"How do you expect to get away with this?" she asked, still kneeling.

Brinkman replied, "It's simple. Jack doesn't know who hit him, and Sarah sure as hell will never say. Will you, Sarah? Not unless you'd like to spend a lot of years behind bars. They were simply mugged and robbed by somebody who then made off with the two of you. You shouldn't have been out, not at this time of night, not around here. Worse things have happened in this town."

"Jack will never go along with that," Jessica argued.

"That's true, if he survives," Brinkman said. "But what can he prove? I'm videotaping every CBS prime-time program at home and will certainly have time to see and remember them before any of you is found. Who can argue that I spent the night there? Besides, as far as anyone knows, I have nothing to do with any of you. Why would I want to do you harm? I am a cop, after all."

Jessica knew it was crazy, but it was also clear that Brinkman had thought it all through. What was ominously left unsaid was Brinkman's plan for her and for Kim. She couldn't make herself think about it.

"Other people know about you," Jessica finally said. "People at the station. Other cops. You know I'm not alone in this."

"Big deal. Let 'em have their suspicions. There's no proof, and with you not pushing it, the whole thing will eventually fade away. It's too bizarre to believe, anyway. Except by you."

Brinkman then handed her the second set of handcuffs. "Hook yourself up to Kim. We're going to take a little trip."

With a muffled scream, Sarah's body bucked, her feet coming off the ground, aimed at Brinkman. But the kick fell far short.

"Sorry about that, Sarah, but Kim's the only other person outside the club who really knows anything about this. I just can't take the chance. Wish it didn't have to be, but there's really no other choice. Besides, remember the tape recorder? She tried to fuck you over, too."

Kim was still on the ground, clutching her stomach. Her head slowly came up, panicked eyes going first to Jessica, then to Brinkman. Disbelieving. Pleading. Jessica could see the scream rising in her throat and reached to cover her mouth. "Take it easy, Kim," she whispered.

Brinkman leaned over both Sarah and Jack, checking the gags and the tightness of the tape. Then she snapped off two low-hanging branches from a nearby maple and threw them over the pair.

"Time to go," she announced.

Jessica pulled Kim to her feet and held her close.

"We'll walk together," Brinkman said, holding the pistol loosely at her side. "Like we're out on a friendly stroll. Keep your cuffed hands to your sides and don't make a goddamned sound."

As they walked away, Jessica looked back over her shoulder and thought about something for the first time. She had never told Jack Tomlinson that she loved him.

FIFTY-ONE

Jerry Jenkins was in his unmarked squad car on the interstate between St. Paul and Minneapolis when the car phone buzzed.

"George Barclay here," said the voice at the other end. "From Channel Seven. You got a minute?"

"No problem," Jenkins replied. "I'm just heading for your town."

"Have you heard from Jessica?" Barclay asked.

"Yeah, an hour or so ago. That's where I'm going."

"Where?"

Jenkins quickly described the call he had received while on stakeout. "Said she and Jack Tomlinson were over by Lake Harriet. They were supposed to meet Sarah Andrews and Kim Hawkins . . . to talk."

"Shit," Barclay muttered, then told him that Jessica had not yet returned home and that her sister was worried. "So am I," he admitted. "Jessica doesn't always use the best judgment."

"Tell me about it," Jenkins said dryly. "I tried to warn her away, but she was having none of it."

There was a long silence at the other end of the line. "How far away are you?" Barclay finally asked.

"Fifteen or twenty minutes," Jenkins said. "But remember, I'm out of my jurisdiction. On my own. If something's happened over there, we're going to have to involve the Minneapolis cops."

"I'll call Meecham at home," Barclay said. "He'll know what to do."

"Make it quick. I don't like doing this alone."

Sarah tried to bury her head in her shoulder to escape the hordes of mosquitoes swarming around her. But it was of no use, and she eventually gave up the struggle. She did manage to push most of the branches off herself by using her bound legs and feet. But the leaves still covered Jack, who lay unmoving next to her, their wrists—and lives—linked by the handcuffs. She could hear his breathing, and now and then a soft groan, but that was all.

Once, a golden retriever, free of its master's leash, had bounded up to them, sniffing and whining, but a sharp command from the pathway had taken him away. Sarah had tried to cry out from behind the gag but knew the sound carried no more than a few feet.

She was not sure how much time had passed, perhaps twenty minutes, maybe less. Morning would almost certainly bring their release; someone was bound to spot them in the light of day, but what would she say then?

Freda was right. Sarah could not identify her as the attacker without beginning to unravel the entire twisted story of the Craft Club. She would have to protect herself and the other women. There was little choice. If Jack recovered, she would deny what certainly would be his contention that she had led them into a trap. He had no proof, and the fact that she was now as helpless as he, as much of a victim, should convince any investigator of her innocence.

But what about Jessica and Kim? She shuddered to think of them in Brinkman's hands but knew she could be of no help.

Not now. Freda was crazed, capable of anything, and, she was afraid, would show little mercy toward the two women. Most of all, Sarah's heart went out to Kim, whose innocent meddling might well cost her her life. She now deeply regretted ever opening her doors to her.

Jessica was different. While Sarah didn't want to see her harmed—she wouldn't wish that on any woman—she knew Jessica had become her own worst enemy, forging ahead despite all the warnings. Give her an A for courage, Sarah thought ruefully, but an F for common sense.

The cracking of a branch suddenly brought her back. Where? Behind her. She raised her head and twisted her body, staring into the darkness. Another dog? A squirrel? No, she could hear the footsteps. Then she saw the figure, moving cautiously through the trees. Was Freda back? She rolled her body and kicked her bound feet, making as much noise as possible, then tried to get up. But she was held down by the weight of Jack's body.

The figure was now only a few feet away. A man, his face still in the shadows. Sarah made a muffled cry for help as he leaned down next to her.

"Well, well," he said. "Who do we have here?"

The last person Sarah ever expected to see was now staring down at her. Lowell Ingram.

She was speechless. Uncomprehending. What was he—of all people—doing here? It must be a dream, she thought. For an instant, she decided that she, too, had gone crazy.

Ingram saw the confusion in her face and laughed. Then he pulled the gag away but clapped his hand over her mouth. "Surprised to see me, pussy?"

She tried to shake free of his grip.

"Is that Jessica's friend there?" he asked, nodding his head toward Jack's still figure while loosening the pressure of his hand on her mouth.

"Yes!" she gasped.

"Shhh," he cautioned.

She sucked in the air. "What are you doing here?" she whispered.

"I saw the whole thing," he said, "from back there, behind those trees. I tried to follow Brinkman and the others when they left, but I lost 'em. So I decided to come back for you."

Strangely, Sarah felt no fear. "How'd you know we'd be here? I don't understand any of this."

"Neither do I. I've been waiting and watching for a long time, following that cop Brinkman for days."

"You followed her tonight?"

"Sure. From your place to the old apartment and then here."

"You saw it all? Why didn't you help? Call the police?"

He chortled. "And spoil the fun? Did you really think you'd get away with what you did to me?"

Suddenly, the fear came back. "What are you going to do?"

"What'd I tell you I was going to do?" He glanced toward the lake. "Back in the courtroom. Remember?"

Before she could scream, the gag was back in her mouth.

Jenkins got the call on the car phone when he was only a few blocks from Lake Harriet. It was Matt Meecham. "Barclay called me. Told me what's going on. A couple of Minneapolis squads will meet you at the pavilion, help you look around."

"Do they know I'm from St. Paul?" Jenkins asked.

"Yeah, but not much more. These are buddies of mine, plainclothes guys. I just told them you might need some help."

"Thanks," Jenkins said as he doused his car lights and pulled in next to the pavilion.

One of the unmarked squads was already there, and the second arrived minutes later. Jenkins introduced himself to the two detectives and apologized for bringing them there. "This may be nothing," he said, "but a young reporter from Channel Seven is chasing a story and may have run into trouble."

"What kind of trouble?" one of the detectives asked.

Jenkins shrugged. "Don't know. She's a friend of Meecham's and mine. It could be a wild-goose chase."

The two Minneapolis cops exchanged glances but then picked up their high-powered flashlights and followed Jenkins up the path along the lake.

Ingram was struggling with the tape around Sarah's ankles, trying to free her legs to get her slacks off, when he heard the car doors slam. Down by the pavilion. Then he saw the glow of the flashlights. He quickly retaped her ankles and crept forward on his hands and knees, hoping for a better view.

Three flashlights, bobbing up the path, their beams being thrown in all directions. Ingram scurried back to Sarah. "Sorry I can't stay around for the rescue," he whispered.

He began to crawl away, then came back. "But trust me," he said, "I'll finish what I started someday. Count on it."

Then he disappeared, more quietly than he had come.

Jenkins had no idea where to begin. The only thing Jessica had told him was a picnic bench near the pavilion. There must be dozens of benches along this path, he thought.

"Why don't we spread out a little," he suggested.

The two detectives grunted and split apart, moving in a line into the grassy area between the path and the wooded area next to the boulevard. They continued to swing their flashlights in wide arcs, the beams poking in and among the trees.

They'd walked less than a hundred feet when the one to the far left stopped. "Look over here," he shouted.

There, in the middle of the shaft of light, was Sarah Andrews, fighting to raise herself up. The other two flashlights immediately swung in that direction, bathing the whole area in light. All three of the men unholstered their guns and walked slowly toward her, their lights now swinging wildly in all directions, searching the darkness for whomever might have done this.

Then Jenkins broke away and rushed ahead. "There's another one here, too," he said when he reached Sarah. He pulled the gag from her mouth and pushed aside the branches covering Jack. He leaned over him, shaking his shoulder gently. "This one's out cold," he shouted. "Better get an ambulance."

While one of the detectives reached for his walkie-talkie and made the call, the other began to untape Sarah's wrists and ankles. He stopped when he got a good look at her face. "Hell, I've seen you around the courthouse," he said. "Aren't you with the county attorney's office?"

Sarah nodded, whispering her name as she tried to catch her breath. Her mind was spinning wildly.

"Better get a bolt cutter," the detective said when he saw the handcuffs. "Or a chain saw to cut down the goddamned tree."

After Jenkins did what he could for Jack, wiping away the blood and putting his suit coat beneath his head, he returned to Sarah. "Is this Jack Tomlinson?" he asked. "Jessica's friend?"

"Yes," Sarah said. "We work together at the county attorney's office."

"Who did this to you?" he asked, his face only inches from hers. "Where's Jessica and the other woman, Kim?"

Sarah knew the importance of this moment. Tell the truth and there was a chance, however remote, that the police would find Brinkman before she could further harm Jessica and Kim. They might be saved, but at what price to herself and the other women in the Craft Club? Exposure. Prison.

She made a decision. Lie. Save yourself. If Jessica and Kim somehow survived Brinkman, the lie would surely be revealed. But what were the chances of their surviving? Not great. Play the odds, she told herself.

"I don't know," she whispered. "He took them."

"Who?" Jenkins demanded.

"I have no idea. He had a ski mask on. Hit Jack with some kind of a board. Made us drag him here, then tied us up."

Jenkins didn't know what to think. It was moving too quickly. "You have no idea who he was?" he pressed.

She shook her head and began to sob. "He came out of nowhere, along the path where Jack was standing. He had a black running suit on, black tennis shoes. He must have seen us walk back here earlier. It was horrible."

"Why'd he take them and leave you?" Jenkins asked.

"God, I wish I knew," Sarah said, clutching her body. "Maybe he thought three were more than he could handle. I just don't know."

Knowing what he knew—what Jessica had told him—Jenkins had little doubt that Sarah was lying. That the rogue cop, Freda Brinkman, was somehow involved in all of this. But where was the proof? More important, where the hell were Jessica and Kim? They could be anywhere, facing anything, and he didn't know what to do about it.

He quickly briefed the two Minneapolis detectives on the missing women, describing Jessica himself and asking Sarah to describe Kim. "I know this isn't my territory," he told them, "but they're obviously in danger. If you can get their descriptions out in Minneapolis, I'll take care of St. Paul. Maybe somebody will spot them."

By now, more squad cars had arrived. Uniformed officers were searching the area, which had been quickly cordoned off to protect it from the press and curious passersby. As they awaited the ambulance, Sarah was taken to a squad car. Jenkins followed her and stopped to speak to one of the detectives.

"I'll call Meecham," Jenkins said. "He'll go crazy. This Jessica is like a daughter to him."

"Good luck," one of the cops said. "The word's already out to all of our squads. We'll give it our best shot."

FIFTY-TWO

They had been driving for almost a half hour. Jessica was behind the wheel, Kim next to her, with Brinkman in the backseat, keeping watch and providing directions. Every few minutes she would lean forward and touch each of them behind the ear with the barrel of the gun. "I'm still here, remember," she had said the last time.

Although Brinkman acted as though she knew where she wanted to go, they seemed to be following an aimless course, first keeping to the boulevards around the lakes of south Minneapolis, then moving on to the freeway and into the downtown area. Was she killing time? Jessica wondered. Or having second thoughts? She grasped for hope.

The car was a Dodge of some kind, its interior spotless and still smelling new-car new. Probably a rental, Jessica decided, glancing at the low mileage on the odometer. She was driving one-handed. The other hand was still cuffed to Kim, whose body was slumped against her, her head buried in her arm.

Jessica tried to control her fear, to keep it inside. No way did she want Brinkman to have the satisfaction of knowing just how frightened she was. Not only for Kim and herself but for Jack, who could be dead or dying in the park without medical attention. Stay calm, she kept telling herself. Look for a way out.

Early on, she had considered the possibility of ramming the car into a post or another car, anything, to bring this trip to a halt. But Brinkman had seemed to read her mind. "Keep it slow," she'd said. "If I even sense you're thinking of having a little accident, I'll blow off the back of Kim's head."

More conversation was impossible because of the interruptions from a portable police scanner that sat on the ledge behind the backseat. Jessica listened as the dispatcher's monotone voice spit out a routine string of calls and assignments. A domestic dispute on East Sixth Street, a loud party on Queen Avenue, a burglary in progress in the warehouse district.

During one break in the transmissions, she turned in the seat. "Where are you taking us?" she asked.

"You don't want to know," Brinkman replied. "Keep driving."

Jessica tried to put herself into Brinkman's head. If she and Kim ended up dead, who could prove that Brinkman was responsible? Only Sarah, and in her own self-interest she would never reveal the truth. Why should she? To save Kim? Don't count on it. Others who were aware of what Jessica was up to—Jack, Matt, Barclay, Jenkins—would certainly suspect Brinkman, but they would be hardpressed to prove it. Especially if she could hold to the alibi she had so elaborately concocted.

They were on Washington Avenue, at the edge of downtown, approaching Third Avenue. "Take a right," Brinkman ordered. And, two blocks later: "Another right."

A narrow and rough cobblestone street took them behind two old, abandoned warehouses parallel to the Mississippi River. Near one of the river's locks, Jessica remembered.

"Swing in here," Brinkman said, pointing to a darkened parking lot between the warehouses. "Park next to that Grand Am."

Jessica did as she was told.

"Hand me the keys and get out," Brinkman said, then followed them to the Grand Am, carrying the scanner in one hand, the gun in the other. "Get in," she said. "The keys are on the floor. Same routine. You drive, I watch."

"Why another car?" Jessica asked.

"None of your business," Brinkman said.

As they were heading out of the parking lot, the scanner came back on. The dispatcher's first transmission carried a sense of urgency they had not detected before. "Cars 302, 303, and 304, report to the south side of Lake Harriet. An assault and possible kidnapping. An ambulance is en route."

"Son of a bitch!" Brinkman shouted.

They'd found them. Either some passerby had stumbled onto them, or Jerry Jenkins had come back from his stakeout to investigate. Jessica's first thoughts went to Jack, who—thank God—must now be getting some kind of help; they said an ambulance was en route. Then to Sarah. What would she do? What would she say?

Kim's head popped up, and she stared at Jessica with a mixture of hope and confusion. "What's happening?" she whispered.

Before she could respond, Brinkman ordered, "Quiet." In the confusion, Jessica had slowed the car but then felt the barrel of the gun in her ear.

"Give it up, Freda," she pleaded. "It's all over, and you know it. It's too late."

"Nothing's changed," Brinkman said. "We just have to move more quickly, that's all."

At Lake Harriet, the television crews arrived at the same time as the ambulance. But a quickly organized police line held the photographers at bay until the stretcher bearing the still-unconscious Jack Tomlinson was loaded into the ambulance and whistled away. Jerry Jenkins was preparing to follow, but as he stepped up to his car, he felt a hand on his arm. It was Matt Meecham, leaning on a cane.

"What the hell are you doing here?" Jenkins demanded. "I was going to call you."

"It ain't easy, but I can still drive," Meecham replied testily. "I left the house right after I talked to you on the car phone. Thought I should be here, too."

Jenkins quickly explained what they had found and what Sarah had told him.

"That's bullshit," Meecham said. "If they're gone, it was Brinkman. Has to be."

Jenkins shrugged. "You may be right. I'm just telling you what she told me."

"Where is she?" Meecham demanded.

Jenkins pointed to a squad car, sitting to one side. "In the backseat, waiting to go downtown."

Meecham strode over, nodded to the uniformed cop standing by, and opened the back door. "Hello, Sarah," he said. "You okay?"

Even in the darkness, her surprise was apparent. But she quickly recovered. "Matt? I thought you were out of commission."

"Not entirely," he said, bending over and sliding in next to her. "Tell me what happened here?"

"I've already told the other cops," she replied, but then agreed to repeat her hurriedly prepared story. "It was terrible! He took Kim and Jessica. Have they found them yet?"

"You're sure it was a 'he'?" Meecham asked.

She paused. Protect yourself, she thought. "I'm almost sure, but I never saw his face. He had a ski mask on. He was big. I just assumed it was a man."

"He never spoke?" Meecham pressed.

"I don't think so," she murmured, "but it happened so fast and was so confusing. I'm just not sure."

Like Jenkins, Meecham knew she was lying. But he could hardly accuse her. Not now. "I'll talk to you later," he finally said. "Down at headquarters."

As he left the squad car, Meecham saw the ranking detective on the scene, a sergeant named Henry Carson, holding forth with the reporters and cameras.

"We don't know much," Carson told them. "Looks like an assault and kidnapping. Two of the victims were found here. One of them, a man, was injured and is unconscious. The other, a woman, was badly frightened and is in shock. Two other women may have been abducted, we're not sure. I can't give you any names or any more details because we don't know anything more."

The reporters shouted questions at him, but he turned his back and returned to the safety of the police lines.

Meecham was back with Jenkins. "How bad is Tomlinson?"

Jenkins shrugged again. "Hard to tell. The paramedics seem to think he'll make it, but as you sure as hell know, head injuries can be tricky. I was going to the hospital to check on him now."

"I'll go with you," Meecham said. "We'll pick up Janie on the way. She's got to know what's happening."

Jessica had no idea where they were. Maybe if she had grown up in the Twin Cities or had lived here longer, she would. But right now it was a blank. She could have been in Cleveland or St. Louis for all she recognized of the area. And Kim was of no help; she continued to stare blankly through the side window, saying nothing. Even her quiet sobs had ceased.

In the time it had taken them to get here, wherever they were, the police scanner had continued to buzz with urgent information. Jessica and Kim listened as their names and descriptions were broadcast to all of the cruising squad cars. But there was no mention of the identity of their abductor. In fact, it was obvious from the transmissions that the cops believed Brinkman was a man. Their descriptions of "him" were vague at best.

No surprise, Jessica thought. Sarah had lied.

Brinkman must have come to the same conclusion, because after her original outburst, she had shown no signs of panic. In fact, she seemed quite secure, sitting quietly in the back, listening to the messages on the scanner, occasionally giving Jessica curt directions.

"Right at the next corner," she now ordered.

Jessica slowed the car and signaled the turn. The road was more like a trail, narrow and bumpy, moving downward at a fairly sharp angle. Jessica tried to dodge the potholes, but there were too many. The car lurched and shook as the wheels fell into one gaping hole after another.

"Take it easy," Brinkman warned. "You'll break an axle."

The car crawled along for what must have been a quarter mile before Brinkman ordered Jessica to pull into a driveway surrounded by a thick growth of trees. It was pitch-black and absolutely quiet as she switched off the engine and lights.

Brinkman stepped out of the car and then ordered them out. Standing, still manacled, their eyes were immediately blinded by the glare of a flashlight. "Put this gag in Kim's mouth," she ordered Jessica, "and then tape it."

Jessica hesitated. "Don't even think about trying anything," Brinkman warned, flashing the gun in the beam of light. "There isn't a soul around who'd hear this gun."

As Jessica put the gag into Kim's mouth, she whispered, "Keep cool, Kim. Don't panic. Show some of that backbone you once told me you had." She thought she saw a barely perceptible nod of her head before Kim was ordered to repeat the gagging process on Jessica.

"Now lay down on the ground, face first," Brinkman said. "And don't move."

The earth against their faces felt gravelly, dry and rough. And hard. No grass here, Jessica thought. She could hear the trunk of the car open and then the rustling of clothing. She tried to move her head slightly, to bring Brinkman within view, but the light still played on them, and she could see nothing beyond its circle. The trunk slammed, and an instant later Brinkman was standing beside her. Her feet and legs were bare.

FIFTY-THREE

"Get up," Brinkman snapped.

They rose to their knees, then slowly pulled themselves fully to their feet, the light again filling their eyes. Jessica tilted her head slightly, trying to see around the beam. She caught only a glimpse, but it was enough. Brinkman was in a swimming suit. One-piece, black; that's all she could make out.

"Turn around and start walking," Brinkman ordered. "But watch your step, it's steep."

She played the light ahead of them, down a path that fell away at almost forty-five degrees, bordered on both sides by thick underbrush. A rudimentary railing ran alongside it, but it was rotting away and provided precious little stability.

Kim stumbled twice and without the handcuffs would have fallen, taking Jessica with her. But Jessica was able to steady her, both managing to keep their feet until they finally reached the bottom of the hill.

They found themselves on a small dock, its narrow planks

spongy, as rotten as the railing. Tied to the dock, front and back, was a small wooden boat, an inch of water from recent rains sloshing in its bottom. In the spillover from the light, Jessica could see the current rippling past the boat. This is no lake, she suddenly realized. We're on the river.

"Get in," Brinkman told them. "Both of you in the bow."

Jessica held Kim back and turned on Brinkman. Was this the time to take a stand? While they were still on dry land? For an instant, she was tempted to lunge. But the cuffs held her captive.

Again, Brinkman seemed to read her thoughts. "It won't work, Jessica. Just get in."

Once they were all in the boat, Brinkman doused the light and threw off the mooring lines. "In case you're wondering," she said softly, "I own this little piece of property and this boat. But only a few people, a few select friends, know that they're mine." Jessica thought she knew who the few friends were.

"See that anchor rope at your feet," Brinkman said. "Wrap it around your ankles. Tight. It'll make sure you stay in the boat."

Jessica and Kim were squeezed together on a small seat at least ten feet from Brinkman. Jessica reached down and grabbed the rope, which was attached to a heavy, round steel anchor. She slowly intertwined the rope between her ankles and Kim's, trying to keep it loose.

Brinkman was not fooled. "Tighter!" she demanded.

Jessica complied, feeling the pinch of the rough rope against the skin of her ankles. And she heard Kim's muffled gasp of pain. Brinkman turned in her seat and yanked the rope on the old Evinrude motor. It caught on the first pull, settling quickly into a quiet purr. She backed out into the current, handling the motor with practiced ease as she slowly came about and pointed the bow downriver.

They had been on the water for ten minutes before Brinkman spoke again, in a hushed voice only slightly louder than the throbbing of the motor. She knew how clearly words could carry across water.

"You're probably wondering why I'm going to all of this trouble," she said. "The truth is, I don't particularly relish the idea of killing women. It's really contrary to everything I believe. But you two have given me no choice."

Jessica glanced at Kim but found her leaning over the side of the boat, staring into the darkened depths of the river. She seemed to hear nothing, feel nothing. It was as though she were in a trance.

"Couldn't really stomach the idea of shooting you if I didn't have to," Brinkman continued. "It would have been, I don't know, too messy. But I can't set you free, either. No way could I take prison. I'd go crazy after the first day, if I managed to last that long. There are some mean mothers inside there who wouldn't take kindly to a cop in their midst."

Jessica could do nothing but listen, as fascinated as she was frightened by the rambling monologue.

"We didn't really do anything wrong, you know. Not really. Those assholes didn't deserve to live. They were the scum of the earth, the entrails of society. They were mourned by no one except maybe their mothers, and if the truth be known, I doubt that even they truly gave a shit that their sons were dead."

Jessica thought of Gladys Hill. Brinkman wasn't that far from the truth.

Another ten minutes passed. The boat was moving into more populated areas, carving a watery path in the center of the river, underneath the Camden bridge, then the Lowry bridge. The towers of downtown Minneapolis were ahead, to the right of the river, the lights of many of them still blazing despite the late hour.

Brinkman began again, seeming to talk as much to herself as to them. "When they find you, they'll know it wasn't an accident, I suppose. But they'll sure as hell wonder how you got there. By then I'll be long gone, back to my VCR."

They cruised under the Broadway bridge, then Plymouth Avenue. Jessica desperately searched the shorelines and the overpasses for someone who might help them. A few cars passed over the bridges, but she saw no one on foot. And even if there were, what would they see? Three dark figures in a boat out for a midnight ride.

The current started to pick up as the river narrowed, pushing the boat faster. Jessica knew the first lock and dam was maybe a mile or so ahead. Suddenly she understood Brinkman's plan. Why she was wearing the swimming suit, why she had the extra car near the locks.

Brinkman crawled to the middle seat, holding out something in her hand. "Here," she said. "Take the key and uncuff yourselves. You can take the gags off, too. But if you make a sound, you're dead." Then she returned to the motor.

Jessica took the key with her free hand and, trying to hold it steady, finally managed to free the handcuffs from their wrists. Then each of them removed the gags, breathing deeply, filling their lungs.

"Wouldn't look too good if they found you cuffed and gagged, would it?" Brinkman laughed.

"What's she talking about?" Kim whispered, as if awakening from a long sleep. "What is she going to do?"

"She's going to send us over the dam," Jessica replied as calmly as her pounding heart allowed. "Isn't that right, Freda?"

"She can't," Kim shouted. "My God!"

"Easy, Kim," Jessica said. "Remember what I told you."

The water seemed to be moving faster now, the shoreline slipping by ever more quickly. The previously placid current rippled around them, and Jessica heard the motor throttle up, pushing them ahead even faster.

"When I tell you, you can unwrap the anchor rope from your legs," Brinkman said. "But not until then."

They passed beneath the Hennepin Avenue bridge, and from here, in the stillness of the night, Jessica could detect the distant roar of the water over the dam. Brinkman reached down, and as the two women watched, she quickly slipped black rubber flippers on her bare feet. The river was now beginning to boil around them, splashing their backs, spilling into the boat. They were rocking from side to side, Brinkman working the motor to keep the boat straight and in the center of the river.

"Okay," she shouted, her eyes wide with excitement. "Unwrap the anchor rope. Now!"

Jessica reached for the rope, but Kim pushed her hand aside. "No, let me," she whispered. Jessica could hear her gasping breath and caught a glimpse of anger and defiance on her face.

The arc lights illuminating the locks were off to the right, a quarter mile away, maybe less. The dam spillway was to the left of the lock, the water rushing over it like a wild canyon gorge. Brinkman killed the engine and stood up, peering over them, trying to measure the distance with her eyes.

Kim had completed unwrapping the rope, freeing their legs, but she remained bent over. When Jessica glanced down, she saw her hand gripping the steel anchor at the end of the rope.

My God, not Kim, she thought. Not gentle, shy Kim.

Brinkman's eyes dropped at the same time, saw what Jessica saw, but she, too, must have been disbelieving. For it took her an instant to react, and by then, Kim was on her feet, lunging toward the back of the boat, grasping the anchor in both of her hands. Her scream was piercing, like a small animal caught in the jaws of a predator.

As Jessica sat paralyzed, Kim, in one motion, leaped to the middle seat and flung the anchor at Brinkman. The anchor was heavy, but the distance was small. Brinkman raised her arms to protect herself, but the anchor slammed into her chest. There was a sharp grunt as she went backward over the motor, her flippers flying in the air. Her gun was nowhere to be seen, in the water or the bottom of the boat.

Kim didn't pause, stumbling the final few feet, throwing herself on Brinkman's outstretched body. As Brinkman struggled to pull herself up, clinging to the transom with one hand, fighting off Kim with the other, Kim grabbed the anchor rope and wrapped it around one of Brinkman's legs.

* * *

Her wild screams of anger were matched by Brinkman's panicked obscenities.

The boat was now sideways to the river. Jessica was on her feet, struggling to keep her balance, grasping the gunwales for support as she fought to reach the two in back. Before she could get there, she saw Kim put her shoulder under Brinkman's legs and, with great effort, rise up and pitch her over the back of the boat, the anchor rope uncoiling behind her. Then the anchor itself went overboard. They could feel the jerk on the boat as Brinkman's submerged body pulled the tether taut. Kim's face was wet and flushed, showing both fear and triumph.

Jessica glanced over her shoulder. The dam was no more than a hundred yards away and closing. No time to take a chance on the motor. The current was pushing them too fast.

"We're going to have to swim for it," she shouted. "There's no time."

Kim shook her head. "Sorry, Jessica," she said. "I can't swim. I'll never make it."

"For Christ's sake, you've got to try. I'll help you."

"And drown yourself?" Kim shouted. "Don't be stupid. I'll take my chances with the boat."

"There is no chance," she screamed. "C'mon. Please."

Jessica crawled back to her, grabbed her shoulders, and tried to pull her over the side. But her clothes were wet and slippery.

Kim wrestled free. "No, I told you."

Jessica took one more look at the dam. She could see the white foam, could feel the pull against the boat. She turned back to Kim, who was staring at her, sadly but defiantly. Jessica made one more lunge for her, but Kim sidestepped and caught her beneath the arm and shoved. Jessica felt herself tumbling backward, then the water closing over her.

* * *

Underwater, her first instinct was to get her shoes off, to rid herself of their weight. But she quickly realized there wouldn't be time. Not with the current. It was like she was in a watery gale. The force was that strong.

With the shallow dive, she quickly regained the surface, her arms flailing in fear, desperately trying to pull herself away from the dam and toward the shore. She felt the muscles in her arms tighten immediately, then the first twinge of a cramp in her calf.

Calm down, she said to herself. Relax! Swim!

In high school, she had been a strong swimmer, even serving one summer as a lifeguard at a beach near Madelia. But that was long ago. In the years since, she had spent more time on the beach sunning than she'd spent in the water swimming. But she had not forgotten the fundamentals, the first of which was: Don't panic! Remember: even breaths, strong, even strokes and kicks. Conserve your strength, control your fear.

Luckily, the water was warm, a far cry from the iciness of Lake Superior and the streams of the North Shore. There she would be dead by now. But while the water was warm, it felt gritty on her skin and in her mouth, smelling of dead fish and who knew what else. She tried not to swallow.

She didn't look back at the boat. She couldn't. But even with the roar of the river around her, she was sure she heard one final, terrifying scream. Kim's scream.

The lights of the lock seemed far away, but no farther now than they were a minute before. She wasn't losing ground. But her arms were growing weary, her legs heavy. Her breaths came more quickly, and her lungs were crying out.

Keep going! Pray for a second wind.

For several strokes, she kept her head above water, blinking the drops away, clearing her vision, judging the distance. Twenty yards, maybe less. The water seemed calmer here, the pull against her body less intense.

Dig! she told herself. Kick! Fifteen yards. Then ten. The concrete wall of the lock loomed just ahead. Her legs stopped working. They would kick no more.

She cupped her fingers and pulled, clutching the water as

she would rocks on a steep climb. Three more strokes and she felt the rough concrete against her fingertips, sliding past her. Desperately, she grasped for anything that would stop her drift. Her body would no longer do it for her.

That's when she saw the steel rungs embedded in the concrete. A ladder leading down the side of the lock. She lunged for it, and held on. For how long she didn't know. Finally, when the numbness in her arms disappeared, she reached for the rung above her, then the next, pulling herself slowly up the ladder, never looking down into the swirling water below. At each step, she paused to gather strength, willing herself to make just one more effort.

With three rungs to go, she heard the shouts from above. And, in the distance, the wailing of the sirens.

EPILOGUE

They found the bodies the next morning.

The boat had split apart when it hit the concrete base of the dam. Parts of it floated away, but divers retrieved the rear half, weighted down by the motor, at the bottom of the river just beyond the spillway. A piece of the bow was discovered farther downstream, hung up on a piling. The anchor rope was still attached, stretched tight by the weight of the anchor and Freda Brinkman's body.

A later autopsy would reveal that Brinkman had not drowned but died of a massive head injury, probably from the same concrete that had crushed the boat.

Kim had apparently been thrown free in the fall but had not survived the swift currents. Her body, without a mark on it, had washed ashore just beyond the dam.

Jessica was there, waiting, when they found them. She had been released from the hospital in the early-morning hours, exhausted but otherwise unhurt, and had insisted on being at the river when the search began at dawn. Watching as two more bodies were pulled from the same river where she had seen her first.

Meecham, Jenkins, and Janie were with her, standing on the observation deck of the lock, silently staring down as the police and fireboats moved up and down the river and as the divers clambered in and out of the boats. Two uniformed officers stood behind them, at Meecham's orders, keeping the television crews away until the vigil was over.

Jessica had promised to hold a news conference that afternoon, to tell the story of the abduction to all of the media. George Barclay, who had been at the hospital with her, reluctantly had given his okay, resigned to the fact that there was no way he could keep this story exclusive.

And she already knew what she would say to the media. That Kim Hawkins was the real heroine. That without her courage, Jessica would be dead, too, and Brinkman would be alive. And free.

She would not go into the details of what had brought them to the lake in the first place. She would simply say that she was pursuing a story, revealing nothing of the Craft Club or the serial murders of predators. That would remain her exclusive story, if she ever had the chance—and the facts—to tell it.

She knew the other reporters would not be satisfied with her explanations, that they would badger and pester her to get more. But for now she was determined to give them nothing beyond the gripping details of the abduction itself.

The police, for their part, were treating Brinkman as a rogue cop gone crazy. Her motives for the assault and abduction, they said, were a mystery and still under investigation. But they did admit there was evidence that she'd also been responsible for the assault on Capt. Matt Meecham weeks before.

Sarah Andrews, Meecham told Jessica, was in seclusion, refusing to speak to anyone but the police. She maintained that she had been forced to lie to the police about the identity of the abductor because of Brinkman's threats against Kim and her promise to come back after her.

"She's lying!" Jessica said. "I didn't hear any of those threats."

"She claims they were made to her and Kim before you got there," Meecham replied. "And since neither Kim nor Freda is around to refute her, they're going to be damned hard to disprove."

"So she goes free?" Jessica demanded. "She bears no blame for what happened to Kim?"

"Not legally," Matt said. "Not at this point, anyway."

They walked back toward Meecham's car, Jessica matching his slow gait, stopping now and then to allow him to rest. Matt had already been offered his old job back by Bart Oates, once he was fully recovered, but Meecham had told him he wanted to think about it. Maybe it was time to retire, he said.

"Where to?" Meecham asked when they reached his car.

"The hospital," Jessica said.

Aside from her time with the police and Barclay, she had spent the hours between her own release from the hospital and the river search in Jack's room, sitting quietly by his side. He had regained full consciousness and his senses but was under sedation and slept the entire time she was there. A nurse had told her he had a fairly serious concussion and a nasty bruise but was expected to recover.

Once in Meecham's car, Jessica turned to Jerry Jenkins. "I'm sorry I haven't had a chance to say a formal thanks. If you hadn't come to the park, Jack could still be lying out there."

Jenkins shrugged. "Just part of the job," he said, then paused. "But speaking of things unspoken, I haven't had the chance to tell you that you were stupid to be out there in the first place."

Jessica ignored the remark. "What about the other women? The others in the Craft Club?"

"Who knows? I suspect Sarah has talked to all of them by now. We'd be hard-pressed to get anything from them. They would probably deny even knowing Brinkman."

"I've got them on tape," Jessica protested. "Going into the same house as Sarah and Brinkman."

"Okay," he said, "so they met her. But what does that prove?"

Jessica knew he was right, that nothing had really changed. "Have you talked to them? Asked them where they were the night Hill was killed?"

"On what basis?" he asked. "If we approach them now, they would run to an attorney so fast it would make all of our heads spin."

Jessica quietly fumed. "What about Nancy Higgins? Did you check the names of the women who gave her the alibi the night Eduardo was killed?"

"Sure. You were right. They were the same names you gave me. The other Craft Club members."

"Well?"

"The woman at the resort swears they were all there that night. She even has the records and charge slips to prove it."

"Did you check her out?" Jessica asked.

"Way ahead of you, Jess. She and her husband bought the resort five years ago, after she was roughed up and raped in Minneapolis."

Jessica shook her head. "I should have known. So the club's bigger than we thought."

"Looks that way," he admitted.

"So what are you going to do?"

"Keep poking and probing around, I guess. And wait to see if another slimeball turns up dead."

When the car pulled up in front of the hospital, Janie asked Jessica if she could come along to visit Jack.

"Sure," Jessica said. "But if he's awake, I need a few minutes alone with him. I want to tell him something I should have told him long ago."

The next week, Jessica took two days off to fly to Kansas for Kim's funeral. She met privately with her parents before the service, then stayed in the background as Kim's family and friends said their final goodbyes. Jessica was back on the plane an hour after the casket was lowered into the ground.

Freda Brinkman was buried the same day, only in Minneapolis. Dozens of cops were there, but none of the ranking officers. Also missing was any of the traditional ceremonial pomp that normally attends a police officer's funeral.

Sarah Andrews attended neither service.

When she returned to her office from a week of personal leave, Sarah was not surprised to learn that Jack Tomlinson had been given his job back the day after Brinkman's attack. Lionel Hamilton had acted after just one phone call from Bart Oates. Jack was now out of the hospital and home but was not expected to be back to work for at least another month.

Despite intensive questioning by Matt Meecham and others, Sarah had clung to her story, denying Jessica's version of events and claiming she was as much Brinkman's victim as were Kim and Jessica. She had simply been lucky, she maintained, that Brinkman had chosen to take the other two and leave her behind. In the end, it was her word against Jessica's, and try as he might, Meecham could not shake the truth free.

Sarah kept to herself. She still had not spoken publicly about the night in the park and had no plans to do so. She deflected any questions about it with the claim that the experience was simply too painful to discuss.

By night, she walked the apartment, unable to sleep despite the pills, haunted by images of Kim which would not fade. The last image, always, was dark, hard to make out. Kim in the water, swept along, tumbling in the current, struggling to stay afloat, calling out for help. Calling her.

By day Sarah buried herself in her work, going to court virtually every day to face the same long line of predators. To many in the courthouse, she seemed to have lost her drive, her zeal to convict.

* * *

Three nights after her return to work, Sarah walked into her apartment, prepared for yet another sleepless night. But she knew immediately that she was not alone. She could sense it. Smell it. Smell him. She lurched for the door but was stopped by one guttural word.

"Don't!"

Lowell Ingram was sitting in the same chair where Freda Brinkman had waited. Holding a gun only slightly smaller than Brinkman's.

"I told you I'd be back," he said calmly. "C'mon in."

She refused to believe her eyes. In the confusion of the past days, she had almost forgotten him and his threats.

"Too bad about your friend Brinkman," he said, rising from the chair and walking to her.

"You won't get away with this," she said. "If you touch me, I'll see that you're put away for the rest of your life!"

Ingram held up his hands. "Relax, please. I've changed my mind." He smiled. "I don't want to fuck you, not now, anyway."

The confusion showed on her face momentarily. "Then what do you want?" she cried. "Get out, now!"

"Take off your clothes," he ordered.

"What?"

"Strip. Everything off. I want to see your bare ass."

"You said you wouldn't touch me," she whispered plaintively, hanging back, looking for escape. "This building has tons of security, you must know that. You'll never get away."

"I got in, didn't I?" he replied smugly. Then, more impatiently. "Now, are you going to take the clothes off, or do you want me to do it for you?"

He pulled up a chair as she unbuttoned her blouse, slowly.

"Make it quick!" he ordered.

The blouse was off; then the skirt fell.

"Why are you doing this?" she pleaded.

"Just so you know what it feels like," he said. "It's too bad there's not a store window handy, but I knew that, for you, standing naked in front of me would be almost the same."

Sarah stared at the gun, then reached behind her back to unhook the bra. Then slipped the panties off. When she was naked, she cowered in a corner, her back to him.

"I didn't deserve what you did to me," he said, almost in a murmur. "No way. I played your game. I pleaded guilty. I was going to pay the price. But it wasn't enough for you, was it?"

She said nothing, trying to still her trembling body. Ingram got up, took one final look, then put the gun away and walked to the door.

"One more thing you should know," he said with a satisfied smile. "You'll never be rid of me. I'll always be around. You won't always see me, but I'll be there. Waiting. Know that. One day, maybe next week, or next month. Hell, maybe even next year, I'll be back. The thing is, you'll never know when. Sweet dreams, pussy."

With that, he turned the lock on the door and walked out.

Two nights later, on the ten o'clock news, Jessica Mitchell broke the story of the serial killings of four sexual predators over the past four years in the Twin Cities and suburbs. Jerry Jenkins and Matt Meecham confirmed the murders and the possible links among them. There were suspects, Jessica reported, but unfortunately they had not been officially identified or arrested. The investigation, she said, would continue.

Sarah Andrews did not see Jessica's report. She had walked into Lionel Hamilton's office the day before to submit her resignation, effective immediately. She said she had decided to accept a long-standing offer from the prosecutor's office in a city she would not name.